HOTSHOT

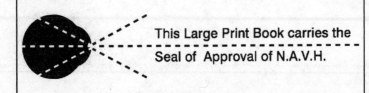

HOTSHOT

JULIE GARWOOD

THORNDIKE PRESS
A part of Gale, Cengage Learning

GALE
CENGAGE Learning®

Detroit • New York • San Francisco • New Haven, Conn • Waterville, Maine • London

GALE
CENGAGE Learning®

Copyright © 2013 by Julie Garwood.
Thorndike Press, a part of Gale, Cengage Learning.

Thorndike Press® Large Print Core.
The text of this Large Print edition is unabridged.
Other aspects of the book may vary from the original edition.
Set in 16 pt. Plantin.

LIBRARY OF CONGRESS CATALOGING-IN-PUBLICATION DATA

Garwood, Julie.
  Hotshot / by Julie Garwood.
    pages cm. — (Thorndike Press Large Print Core)
    ISBN 978-1-4104-5976-3 (hardcover) — ISBN 1-4104-5976-4 (hardcover)
  1. Olympic athletes—Fiction. 2. Love stories. 3. Large type books. I. Title.
  PS3557.A8427H68 2013b   2013024767

Published in 2013 by arrangement with Dutton, a division of Penguin Group (USA)

Printed in the United States of America
1 2 3 4 5 6 7 17 16 15 14 13

For Elizabeth, Bryan, and Gerry.

My hotshots!

PROLOGUE

On the night of May 11 at precisely eight forty-five in the evening, Finn MacBain stopped being a colossal pain in the ass and grew up. He also became a hero.

Until that Saturday evening, he and his twin brothers, Beck and Tristan, had caused all sorts of mischief. They were daredevils and loved to play pranks.

Neighbors cringed when they saw them coming. The brothers weren't bad boys. They were just idiots . . . according to their father, anyway. Smart as whips, but still idiots. Over the years they had built up quite a repertoire of stunts, like the time they strung a zip line from the roof of their house to a huge walnut tree in the wooded area behind the backyard. There was just enough of a downward slope to send them flying. Unfortunately, they didn't anticipate the impact of reaching the tree at the bottom, and they were lucky they didn't break any bones. And then there was the time they tried to build a trampoline. Their parents couldn't even think about that one without shuddering. That was the day they got rid of their chain saw.

The boys especially enjoyed playing jokes on one another. Setting alarm clocks to sound off in the middle of the night, making all sorts of ridiculous things fall when their victim opened his closet door, or wrapping their prey in his bed with Saran Wrap while he slept — their imaginations worked overtime.

The boys didn't limit their tricks just to the family. They had fun with the neighbors as well. When their neighbors the Hillmans returned from their week-long vacation, they found yellow crime-scene tape circling their house and a chalk outline of a body — compliments of Beck — drawn on their sidewalk. The Hillmans weren't amused.

The MacBain brothers were also shockingly ungraceful. It was a fact that the three of them couldn't seem to walk through a room without tripping over their own feet and crashing into a wall or a table. They were growing so fast, it simply wasn't possible to be agile. They were rambunctious, loud, and loved to laugh. Even though they were constantly told to "take it outside," they still got into push-and-shove fights inside the house. Heads and shoulders went through drywall too many times to count, and their home was in a perpetual state of repair. Their parents, Devin and Laura MacBain, put the contractor's phone number on speed dial.

The boys were handsome devils, all approaching six feet, though barely in their teens. Finn, the oldest of the siblings and the ringleader in most of their schemes, was fourteen and still hadn't shown the least inclination to stop growing. Like his brothers, he attended an all-boys Jesuit high school and was an honor student. He aced every test thrown at him, had a phenomenal memory, and according to his frustrated teachers, wasn't living up to his potential. He breezed through advanced classes and didn't challenge himself because he didn't have to. He was lazy in that respect. He was also easily bored, and there were times when he actually fell asleep in American History class. Finn didn't have much passion for anything but girls, swimming, football, and having a good time. A school counselor told his parents that their son was too smart for his own good, which didn't make a lick of sense to them. How could anyone be too smart? Several teachers called Finn arrogant, which Finn's father decided was code for smart-ass.

Everything about Finn was a contradiction. His IQ was in the genius range, and on paper he was the perfect 4.0 student, but he also had been in more fights than Muhammad Ali. He couldn't seem to walk from one end of the block to the other without punching one or more of the Benson boys.

Finn had a rascal's grin and a sparkle in his eyes. He also had a powerful fist and a right hook that was lightning quick. Though he really didn't have much of a temper — it took a lot to get him riled — he couldn't abide a bully, and each of the seven Benson boys was exactly that. They preyed on the younger boys and girls in the neighborhood and got a real kick out of making them cry. All the kids knew they could go to Finn for help if they were being tormented. He wasn't afraid to stand up to the bullies, no matter how many of them there were.

When Devin saw his son's latest black eye, he remarked to his wife that Finn had many fine qualities, but he was lacking in common sense. How else could he explain why his son would take on seven Bensons at the same time?

Fortunately, Finn had never been arrested

— none of the boys had — and Devin determined that the only way to save his sons from getting into real trouble was to keep them busy from early morning until late at night, especially now that school would soon be over for the summer.

During the school year, his sons stayed occupied with part-time jobs and sports. They played football, lacrosse, basketball, and soccer. Those were seasonal sports, however. Swimming, on the other hand, could be an all-year sport. This was a revelation that came to him when he heard from a neighbor that there was a brand-new fifty-meter pool only a few miles away at the just-opened Lee Center, where it was believed Olympic hopefuls would start training. He also found out that tryouts for a competitive team were in one week.

That night in bed Devin discussed his plan with his wife. He told her about the Lee Center and the Olympic-size pool. "I want the boys to try out for the team. I think Finn has a good chance of making it."

"Who does this team compete against?" Laura asked.

"I don't know and I don't care. If Finn makes the team, he'll have to be at the center by four forty-five. He'll swim from five until six thirty. Practice is every day but

11

Sunday," he added, grinning. "It's year-round, too. Even if Beck and Tristan don't make the team, they can do laps with Finn. That ought to wear them out."

Laura didn't see any harm in letting the boys try out. She agreed that they needed to channel their energy into something wholesome and exhausting, and swimming laps at the crack of dawn just might be the answer.

Her husband was just drifting off to sleep when a thought struck her. She poked him in his shoulder and said, "Wait a minute. Who's going to be driving them to practice every morning?"

His snore was her answer.

Without mentioning his plan to his sons, Devin filled out the forms, paid the fee for a family membership, and signed up all three boys for time trials. That evening he broached the subject at dinner. He sat at the head of the table and watched his sons inhale their food. They were good-looking boys, he thought. Their hair was thick and dark, like his used to be before he had children. It was streaked with gray now. Beck and Tristan were identical twins. The only way Devin had been able to tell them apart when they were babies was by a small birthmark on the side of Beck's neck. They were exactly eleven months younger than Finn, and for a few weeks each year, all three were the same age. Their personalities were different, though. Beck lived to have fun and had recently become quite the ladies' man. He was just now beginning to show signs of having a little sense. Of the three brothers, he was the sweetest and most compassionate, and he definitely didn't hide what he was thinking. Tristan, on the other hand, was the analytical one. He reasoned through everything, no matter how insignificant, and yet he still let Finn talk him into doing the most outrageous stunts. He was generous by nature and would always put his brothers first, but he also took things to heart, and Devin worried he would end up with ulcers if he didn't learn to relax. As idiotic as they sometimes acted, Devin loved the fact that all three boys protected one another. Their loyalty was absolute.

Finn was pushing away from the table and asking to be excused when his mother nodded to her husband and said, "Didn't you want to speak to the boys about . . ."

"Yes, that's right. Now, boys . . ."

"Sir?" his sons responded in unison.

"Did you know there's an Olympic-size pool over at the new Lee Center? Boys and girls will be training there every day."

Before he could continue his explanation, Beck asked, "Girls? How many girls?"

Devin held his patience. "I don't know how many girls."

Tristan frowned as he asked, "What are they training for?" He slouched in his chair, and his hair hung down over his eyes.

"Sit up straight," his father ordered before answering. "The team. They're training to be on the team."

"What does the team do?" Beck asked.

"Compete against other teams," Finn said. "Fastest swimmers end up competing to be on the Olympic team. Right, Dad?"

"Yes, that sounds about right. I'm not sure how it works or how many levels there are."

"You boys love to swim," their mother reminded.

"I like to swim," Beck said. "I don't know that I love it the way Finn does."

"Finn, you practically lived in the pool next door last summer," Tristan said.

"Yes, I did swim a lot when Justin lived there. We did laps all the time. Then his father got transferred. It's a great pool," he added enthusiastically. "Twenty-five meters, I'll bet. Biggest backyard pool I've ever seen."

"It's not twenty-five meters," Tristan

argued. "It's not even close."

"You're fast, Finn. Real fast," Beck said. He decided he wasn't quite finished eating and reached for the bowl of mashed potatoes.

"Did you ever get timed to find out how fast you are?" Tristan asked.

"No. Why would I?" Finn asked.

"We sure can't swim next door anymore," Tristan said.

"Yeah, and it's your fault, Finn," Beck said, waving his fork at him.

"You were told not to play baseball in the street," their mother snapped. Thinking about the incident still made her angry. "Breaking a window isn't a great way to meet the new neighbors. They'd only just moved in," she added. "John Lockhart was quite irritated."

"They were eating dinner," Devin said. "The baseball landed in the middle of the table in the salad bowl."

Beck nudged Tristan. "I'll bet lettuce went flying everywhere."

"This isn't funny," Laura scolded. "One of the parents or one of the girls could have gotten hit in the head."

All three boys leaned forward. "The Lockharts have daughters?" Tristan asked.

15

"Why didn't you tell us, Finn?" Beck asked.

"I didn't know. Mr. Lockhart stormed out of the house, and I apologized and promised to pay for a new window. He's the only one I saw. Mom and Dad went over later to talk to him."

"Did you see the daughters?" Beck wanted to know. "How many are there?"

"Three," Devin answered.

"What do they look like?"

"That's a shallow question," his father said.

"I'm thirteen, Dad. I'm supposed to be shallow," Beck told him cheerfully.

Devin decided to have a little fun with his sons. "As a matter of fact, I did see the daughters. They're beautiful. Aren't they, Laura?" he asked his wife.

"Oh my, yes. They certainly are."

Tristan was suspicious. "Beautiful on the inside or the outside?"

"Both," Laura answered.

What their parents failed to mention was the age of the daughters.

"May I be excused?" Finn asked again.

"No, you may not," his father said, his voice a bit sharper than he'd intended. "I want to talk to you about this competitive swimming."

"Okay," Finn agreed, dropping down into the chair again. "What about it?"

"I'd like you to try out for the team."

"Sir, I'd rather not. I won't have time. I've got plans for the summer."

His father rubbed his temples. He could feel a headache coming on. "And what might those plans be?"

"I'm going to work at the Iron Horse Country Club."

"Oh? Doing what?" Devin asked.

"Lifeguarding. I've already done the Red Cross safety thing, and I'm certified in CPR."

"We're all certified in CPR," Beck reminded. "Dad made us take the course."

"You can't be a lifeguard until you're fifteen or sixteen," Tristan said.

"I'll bet they'll make an exception," Finn said.

Devin closed his eyes and prayed for patience.

"I'll bet they won't," Tristan countered. He reached for another chicken breast with his fork and put it on his plate. Beck took another one, too.

Laura looked at all the empty bowls. There hadn't been any leftovers since Finn had started eating solid food.

"They need lifeguards, and I'm qualified,

except for my age, so I'll already be in a pool every day," Finn explained.

"Have they hired you?" Devin asked.

"Not yet. I was going to take my application over, but then I got grounded for fighting."

"Finn, you're not going to work at the country club," Devin said. "Maybe next year," he added to soften the disappointment. "And since you're not going to lifeguard, you might as well try out for the team at the center. Aren't you curious to know if you could make it?"

Finn shrugged. "I guess."

"I'll try out for the swim team if you will," Beck said. "It's a great way to build muscle, and girls like muscles."

"Girls? Is that all you think about?" his mother asked, exasperated.

"Pretty much," Beck admitted.

His brother nodded. "Yeah, we all do, pretty much all the time," Finn said. He turned to his father. "I'm grounded for another week, remember? How can I go to the Lee Center —"

"I'll lift your grounding Sunday. You're home until then."

"If I try out."

"Yes, that's right."

Finn didn't have to think about it. "Okay,

sure. I'll do it."

"Do you think the Lockharts will ever let us swim in their pool?" Tristan asked.

"No." Laura was appalled. "Absolutely not. They think you're all delinquents."

"What did *we* do?" Beck asked. "Tristan and I weren't even home when Finn broke their window."

"You're related to him," she explained. "Delinquents by association."

"That's not fair," Beck complained.

"Life isn't fair. Get used to it," his father said.

"Whose turn is it to do dishes?" their mother asked.

An argument among the brothers ensued — a nightly ritual, it seemed — and they ended it by playing rock, paper, scissors three times until Beck conceded defeat.

As the boys began to clear the table, Devin issued an order. "I want all of you to stay away from the Lockharts. Especially you, Finn. I don't want you to even make eye contact. You hear me? And stay out of their pool, for God's sake. Give me your word right this minute."

Finn wanted to roll his eyes but didn't dare because it would be disrespectful, and he was really sick and tired of being grounded. "Okay," he answered resignedly.

■ ■ ■ ■

Exactly one hour later, Finn had to break his promise.

His brothers had gone with their parents to Burton's appliance store to buy a new television, and Finn had gone up to his bedroom, which was on the third floor in the back of the house. He was looking out the window at the Lockhart pool, remembering how much fun he and his brothers had had swimming laps last summer. It really was a great pool. The Lockharts' huge deck was about ten, maybe twelve, feet off the ground with a thick wood railing surrounding it. It overlooked a concrete patio and the pool beyond. When Justin's parents weren't around, he and Finn would jump up on the railing and, soaring out over the lounge chairs on the patio below, dive into the deep end of the pool and race each other to the steps. Finn always won.

The pool looked especially inviting today. It was really hot, and his T-shirt stuck to his back. The central air wasn't equipped to cool the attic bedroom, so he turned on the fan he'd dragged up from the basement and opened the window.

Laughter from below caught his attention,

and he looked to see where it was coming from. The Lockharts were having a big party. Finn then remembered his mom calling it a housewarming. Cars lined Concord Street. From what he could hear, there were quite a few guests, and all seemed to be enjoying themselves. A couple of people stepped out on the deck, drinks in hand, then strolled back inside, no doubt because of the heat and humidity.

He really wanted to get in that pool. The clear blue water sparkled and beckoned. He loved swimming. He forgot his worries, and his mind seemed to clear of all thoughts as he sliced through the water with long, smooth strokes. The faster he swam, the more relaxed he became. His body took over. One of his friends told him he turned into a dolphin in the water. While he was swimming, he felt completely at peace, and at the same time he felt energized. It didn't make sense, he knew, yet that's how he felt. The more he relaxed, the faster he swam.

He sure couldn't swim tonight, though. He'd given his word to his father, and he wasn't about to break it. Besides, he figured Mr. Lockhart would call the police and have him hauled away for trespassing if he tried to sneak over the fence. No sense tormenting himself by looking at that beautiful pool, he decided.

He shut the window and was just starting to turn away when he noticed her. Man, she was little. She couldn't be more than five or six, he guessed — way too young to be out by the pool without supervision. Maybe one of the Lockhart daughters was babysitting the little girl, but if that were the case, where was she?

Finn was getting a real bad feeling in the pit of his stomach. The child slowly walked to the side of the pool, but she kept looking over her shoulder. Was she waiting for someone, or was she checking to make sure she wouldn't get into trouble? Maybe she knew how to swim, he reasoned. Still, she shouldn't be out there alone.

The child sat down, scooted to the edge of the pool, and put her feet in the water. Finn kept waiting for someone to grab her, but no one came forward. She splashed her feet for a minute or two, inching closer and closer until the water covered her knees. She stayed that way for another minute, then tilted forward and began to splash the water with her hands, smiling as she created waves that lapped over the lip of the pool. When she leaned over farther to dip her hands deeper, she lost her balance and plunged headfirst into the water. She was gone without making a sound.

Thirty seconds. That's all the time he had, he thought, to get to her. He shouted to his father as he raced down the stairs. "Call nine-one-one."

No one answered him, and he remembered they'd all gone to Burton's.

He ran out the front door, nearly tearing it off its hinges, crossed his and the Lockharts' yards at a dead run, then sprinted up the steps to their front porch. Mr. Lockhart was standing in the doorway greeting a couple, blocking the entrance. No time to explain, Finn decided. He shoved the big man out of his way, and while Mr. Lockhart was bellowing his outrage, Finn shouted, "Call nine-one-one," though he doubted anyone heard him over Mr. Lockhart's roar.

Finn pushed people aside, knocked over a cheese tray and a dining room chair, then slammed through the barely open French doors. He leaped up on the railing and, using it as a springboard, made a clean dive into the pool.

He had the child in his arms less than five seconds later. She was limp and lifeless, and he knew she had water in her lungs. God, he was scared. He had to get her breathing again, and fast. Her lips were already turning blue. He held her against his chest as he

23

got out of the pool, then gently placed her on the ground and began CPR.

Finn could hear the CPR instructor in his mind telling him how much pressure to exert. Airway free . . . don't forget to count . . .

He could hear screaming in the background, but he ignored it. Suddenly John Lockhart was dropping to his knees next to his daughter. He tried to pick her up. Finn knocked him back.

"Do you know what you're doing?" the desperate father panted.

Finn nodded. His full attention was on the little girl. He kept up his compressions, silently counting as he worked on her.

A woman let out a bloodcurdling scream. "Peyton," she called. "What's happened to her? Peyton . . ."

Mrs. Lockhart knelt beside her husband. Sobbing, she whispered, "Take a breath, baby . . . come on. Please, breathe . . ."

"They're coming. The ambulance is on the way," a woman shouted from the deck.

Suddenly, Peyton opened her eyes and began throwing up a fair amount of water. Finn turned her and held her head until she was able to take a deep breath. She was back with them.

Finn had yet to say a word. Adrenaline

24

was coursing through his veins. Peyton tried to sit up and reached for him. He stood, cradling her in his arms, and only then noticed the crowd surrounding him, all silently watching. Several women had their hands over their mouths. They looked frightened, but as soon as Peyton lifted her head and they saw that she was going to be all right, everyone began to talk at once.

Peyton's mother held out her arms for her little girl, and Finn gently handed her over. Holding the little girl tightly, she whispered, "You're all right now. You're all right," as the tears streamed down her cheeks.

All of a sudden, Peyton's father grabbed Finn. He hugged him and pounded his back. "Thank God for you," he said, his voice quivering with emotion.

Finn thought the man was going to cry, too. When he finally let go of him and stepped back, Mr. Lockhart's light blue shirt was soaked.

"How did you know . . ."

"I saw her go under," he explained. "Sir, your daughter needs to learn how to swim. . . . and right away."

"Yes, of course," he said. "Peyton was supposed to be upstairs with the babysitter . . . I don't know how she got outside . . . I don't understand how this could have happened." He sounded bewildered as he added, "All these people here, and none of us saw her go outside."

Peyton reached for her father, and he immediately took her into his arms. She put her head down on his shoulder, but she was staring at Finn.

Peyton's mother dabbed at her eyes with a wrinkled tissue as she rushed over to Finn and hugged him.

He was trying to back away so he could go home, but the crowd was squeezing in on him now. They patted and pounded his back, and several women kissed him on his cheek. He was mortified by all the attention. Getting away quietly was out of the question. They were holding on to him, making escape impossible.

The paramedics arrived and quickly checked Peyton. "This child is lucky someone saw her in the water," one of them remarked.

"Finn . . . our neighbor, Finn, saw her, thank God. He dove off the deck to get to her, and then he did CPR. He knew CPR."

They asked Finn several questions, wanting to know how long Peyton had been in the water and how long it had taken him to revive her. Everyone was quiet and hung on Finn's every word, but as soon as the paramedics left, they all started talking, and Finn once again was grabbed, patted, petted, and kissed. Mr. Lockhart finally noticed how uncomfortable Finn looked and let him go home. He couldn't get out of there fast enough.

After changing his clothes, he made himself a couple of sandwiches — it had been almost two hours since he'd finished dinner — grabbed a bag of chips and a root beer, and headed into the den. He turned the television on, sat back, and tried to watch a movie. Only one half of the screen had a picture, and it no longer was in color, just a blurry black and white. It didn't really matter, though, because he wasn't paying any attention. His mind kept replaying what had happened. He had been so scared that Peyton wouldn't come back, and he thought about that moment when she began coughing. Holding her lifeless body in his arms and helping her breathe again . . . it seemed a miracle to him. The feeling was overwhelming. What if he hadn't seen her? From his window he couldn't see the bottom of the pool. What if he'd been too late to bring her back?

Finn buried his head in his hands while he thought about how close to death she'd been. It had happened so fast. Going under without even a splash or a scream, her short life could have been over in a matter of minutes. What a piece of luck that he had noticed her.

He reached for the sandwiches, saw the empty plate, and only then realized he'd already eaten them. He heard the garage doors open. Shaking himself out of his thoughts, he went into the kitchen and found Beck and Tristan carrying in a huge box with the new television.

"Wait until you see it, Finn," Beck said. "The screen's twice the size of our old one, and the color is awesome."

"I can't watch television until Sunday," Finn reminded. "I'm grounded, remember?"

His father pulled the door closed. "Help your brothers, Finn. I don't want the television dropped. Put it on the table in the den. Tristan, you figure out the cable hookup for the VCR. Put the old television in the garage."

"Listen, Dad, something happened," Finn began.

"Oh, before I forget, I ordered an air conditioner for your bedroom," Devin said. "It will be in next week."

"Thanks," Finn said. "But listen, while you were gone —" he began again.

The doorbell rang, interrupting. "Let me get the door," his father called over his shoulder. "Then you can tell me."

The Lockharts were waiting on the porch. Their daughter Peyton was standing between them, holding her mother's hand. Mrs. Lockhart had tears in her eyes.

Devin's shoulders slumped. "What'd he do?" he asked, his voice deflating as he opened the door wider and beckoned them inside. Before either of the Lockharts could explain, Devin turned and shouted, "Finn, get in here."

Laura saw who was in the foyer and whispered, "Finn, did you leave this house while we were gone? You didn't, did you?"

Not waiting for his answer, she hurried to greet the distraught neighbors.

"Did you?" Beck asked.

"Yes," he answered. He couldn't resist adding, "I dove into the Lockharts' pool."

Beck burst into laughter. "You did not. Did you? Oh, man, you're going to be grounded the rest of your life."

"While they were having a party?" Tristan sounded incredulous. "You went swimming while they were having a party?"

"Yes."

Tristan smiled and shook his head. "Why'd you do such a dumb thing? You only had until Sunday."

"You better get in there," Beck said when he heard his father shout Finn's name again.

Laura was trying to soothe the Lockharts. She insisted they come into the living room and sit, hoping they would remain calm while they discussed Finn's latest infraction.

"It's certainly warm tonight, isn't it? Would you like some lemonade?" she asked nervously. She prayed Finn hadn't broken anything valuable.

She noticed Peyton watching her. She was such a pretty little girl, with big blue eyes that didn't seem to miss a thing. Laura couldn't help but appreciate how quietly she sat between her parents, looking so serene. None of Laura's boys had ever been able to sit for more than a minute without squirming. When they were little, they were always in motion. Now, as teenagers, they still were.

"I assure you that Finn will pay for any damage," Laura began.

Finn laughed. That didn't sit well with his parents. His father glared at him.

"Yes, he most certainly will," Devin assured the Lockharts.

"Your son saved our daughter's life tonight," Mr. Lockhart announced.

"He . . . what did you say?" Devin asked.

Mr. Lockhart explained, and by the time he was finished, Mrs. Lockhart was hugging her daughter and crying again.

While Beck and Tristan were elbowing their brother and smiling, their parents sat motionless, looking dumbfounded.

"Over forty people in our house while she was drowning," Mrs. Lockhart told them. "She wasn't breathing . . . Finn did CPR . . . got the water out of her lungs . . ."

They talked about how terrifying it had been and how blessed they were that Finn had seen Peyton go under the water. As they were giving their account of how heroic Finn had been, he stood looking at the floor. He wasn't used to such praise.

When there was a pause in their flattering testimonial, Finn spoke up. "Mr. Lockhart, aren't you having a party?" he reminded.

"Yes," he answered and turned to his wife. "We should get Peyton to bed."

Mrs. Lockhart headed to Finn. He braced himself, knowing she was going to grab him again.

As the neighbors were leaving, Laura and Devin followed them out onto the front porch. Beck and Tristan followed.

"Mr. Lockhart, how old are your other daughters?" Beck asked.

"Lucy is seven and Ivy is going to turn four soon."

Beck shot a quick accusing glance at his parents, who were trying to hide their grins. While his mother continued to chat with the Lockharts, Beck moved close to his father's side. "You knew they were little, didn't you?"

"Yep," he answered with a chuckle.

"Not funny, Dad."

His father's laughter indicated he disagreed.

Finn stayed behind in the living room while the two families were saying goodbye. He was about to go upstairs when the door opened and Peyton came running back inside. She stopped a foot away from him, cranked her head back, and stared at him for a long minute.

"I was scared," she whispered.

He barely heard her. He squatted down until they were eye to eye. "I was scared, too."

She smiled. Her mother called to her, but she didn't leave. She stared at Finn another minute while she made up her mind. Then she leaned close and whispered, "Thank you." Spinning around, she ran back to her parents.

Finn watched from the window as the

parents took Peyton's hands and walked toward their house. He didn't think he would ever forget that moment when he lifted her out of the water. What made him turn back and look down at the pool again?

Maybe something bigger was at play here. Maybe Peyton Lockhart was supposed to do something important with her life.

ONE

Every year on January 4, the very first thing Peyton Lockhart did as soon as she opened her eyes and rolled out of bed was to go to her laptop and e-mail her guardian angel to say thank you for saving her life. Today was January 4. It was her birthday, and if it weren't for Finn MacBain, she wouldn't be celebrating it.

Her mother had started the tradition of sending a thank-you card to Finn on Peyton's birthday, but once Peyton learned how to print, she took over the task. In high school she started e-mailing Finn instead of sending a card, much to her mother's disapproval. Sometimes Peyton heard back from Finn; most times she didn't.

She understood. Finn was busy accomplishing the most incredible feats. Even before graduating from Oakhurst High School, he was competing in the Olympics. She watched on television as he won three gold medals in swimming: one for the 200-meter freestyle, one for the 400-meter freestyle, and one for the 4 × 100-meter freestyle relay. In the process of winning all those medals he set new records.

Peyton was in the third grade at the time. While Finn was swimming his heart out for all the world to see, she was learning how to keep her hands to herself. She had shoved Ashton Lymon because he was making fun of her friend Hillary. Their summer school teacher, Sister Victoria Marie, made Peyton sit in the "thinking" chair a good long while. Come to think of it, she remembered spending an awful lot of time in the chair that summer.

Peyton didn't believe in comparing people's lives, but when it came to Finn Mac-Bain it was simply too hard not to. After his incredible performance at the Olympics, he enrolled at Stanford — on a full scholarship, of course. Four years later, after graduating at the top of his class, he had his pick of law schools. He chose to remain at Stanford because it allowed him to stay involved in the fitness competitions he loved. After winning several triathlons, he helped develop an athletic program for at-risk youth. Peyton knew all about this because the program was so successful it was featured on *60 Minutes*. That's when she started addressing her e-mails to "Hotshot," which, Finn immediately let her know, he didn't like at all. He was recruited into the FBI after law school and was now a special agent on the West Coast. He was too well-known to do undercover work, and she wondered how often he was recognized for winning the gold. Though his current accomplishments weren't publicized, Peyton had no doubts that even in the FBI he had made his mark. He'd probably saved dozens of lives already. She speculated that, by the time she would be earning more than minimum wage, Finn would be president of the United States, or at least director of the FBI.

Peyton finished writing her e-mail to Finn and reached for her cell phone. The second tradition she followed on her birthday was to call her uncle Leonard and give him her good wishes because they shared the same birth date. The call went to voice mail. She left a message and then got into the shower. She wouldn't be blowing out any candles today. There wasn't time. Her car was packed and she would soon be heading out to her new job in Dalton, Minnesota. She calculated the trip from Texas would take two full days.

It's funny how things happen, she thought. Her life had definitely taken a turn in an unexpected direction. In college she'd majored in journalism with a minor in English lit, and for all four years she had supplemented her living expenses by working in restaurant kitchens. In the summers she worked at Bishop's Cove, her uncle Len's resort in Florida. Each summer she rotated between two restaurants within the resort. She did everything from scrubbing pots to helping the sous-chef, and none of these duties were drudgery for her. In fact, she discovered she actually enjoyed them all. Soon she was given more responsibility and was allowed to develop a couple of dishes on her own. She loved experimenting with spices and herbs, creating new flavors. It had taken her a while to figure out what she wanted to do with her life, but by her senior year she recognized that cooking was her passion. She might even want to own her own restaurant one day.

With that goal in mind, and being nearly penniless, she applied for a grant to study at Institut Le Jardin in Lyon, France. She thought she had a better chance of being chased by lions than being accepted into the prestigious school, but that didn't stop her, and miracle of miracles, she was awarded the grant. For four glorious months she studied and cooked and learned from the renowned chef, Jon Giles, the master of sauces. It was the most amazing experience, and she would have been content to stay for another year or two, but unfortunately, reality intruded and she had to return home to face her future.

Once back in Brentwood she moved in with her sister Lucy — a temporary arrangement, she promised — and got down to the business of finding a job. She updated her résumé and applied for every position in every restaurant in town. She knew there were people, especially Uncle Len, who could pull some strings for her, but she was determined to make it on her own. She expanded her search and scoured through every culinary magazine she could get her hands on. While perusing one of the trade publications, she came across an article that mentioned a dream-come-true opportunity. Swift Publications, publisher of several national magazines, was looking for another food critic for their flagship magazine, *The Bountiful Table.* They had four critics already, and now, because they were expanding, wanted five. The lush magazine with well over two million subscribers was considered the bible for food sophisticates and health fanatics alike. Peyton read it from cover to cover every month.

She had absolutely no experience, wasn't even sure she wanted to be a food critic, but it was *The Bountiful Table,* for Pete's sake. She simply had to apply. She knew she had a better chance of being hit by lightning while being chased by lions than getting the job, yet she felt compelled to give it a try. She sent her résumé with a lovely I'd-be-perfect-for-the-job cover letter, then put it out of her mind.

Even though she had been back in Texas less than a month, her mother was already calling to nag her into getting a real job. As opposed to a pretend job, Peyton supposed. Then, just as she was beginning her second month of unemployment and still dodging calls from her mother, a woman named Bridget from Swift Publications called. After a surprisingly brief interview on the phone, she offered Peyton the position.

Peyton was in shock. Her initial reaction was to say, "You're kidding," but fortunately she didn't utter the thought aloud. Stunned, she silently listened as Bridget told her about the job. The more she heard, the more excited Peyton became. Not only were the hours decent and the salary generous, there would also be enough time off for her to work on her own projects developing recipes.

One of the conditions for the job was that she relocate to the company's home base in Dalton, Minnesota, a small town northwest of Minneapolis, too far to commute from the cosmopolitan city. The magazine was produced there in a brand-new facility and employed most of the town. Peyton would be under the tutelage of Drew Albertson, the managing editor and the son-in-law of the owner of the company. While she was learning all the facets of the magazine, she was expected to also be one of Drew's personal assistants. Bridget explained that Peyton's first year would be spent learning about each department, and Peyton wanted to ask why the training would take an entire year but thought that would be overstepping. They obviously had their reasons. After that first year, Bridget told her, she would be given assignments to travel to different locales and write articles for the magazine.

Peyton rarely did anything impulsive. She always weighed the positives against the negatives before she felt comfortable making a decision, and sometimes that took a while. She hated to be rushed, a trait that drove her sisters, Lucy and Ivy, crazy. She didn't have to think about the job offer, though, nor did she need to take time to weigh the pros and cons. Working on *The Bountiful Table* for the Swift organization was a tremendous opportunity, and she wasn't going to let it slip through her fingers.

And so she was going to drive her third-hand, reconditioned Toyota Camry with 85,000 miles logged on the odometer from the lovely, warm climate of southern Texas to the blistering cold of northern Minnesota. In January no less.

Was she out of her mind? Apparently so.

Dressed in comfortable clothes, jeans and a T-shirt, she pulled onto Interstate 35 and headed north. It was seventy-four degrees when she left Brentwood; the sun was out, and there wasn't all that much traffic. The drive was really quite pleasant. She listened to music she'd downloaded on her iPhone as she crossed the state line into Oklahoma. She was especially proud of herself when she drove past two outlet malls and didn't stop at either one. It nearly killed her, especially when she saw a sign for Sur La Table and another for La Cuisine.

She made good time the first day and spent a luxurious night at the Hyatt in Kansas City because she had a Groupon for two-thirds off a single room. After a long hot shower, she fell into bed. She was reaching for the television remote when her uncle Len called.

"Happy birthday, Peyton," he said in his slow southern drawl.

"Happy birthday to you, too," she replied, smiling.

She dearly loved her uncle and was a bit in awe of him. Her father's older brother was a confirmed bachelor and quite the businessman. He owned several resorts, but his favorites were King's Landing in northern California and Bishop's Cove in southern Florida. He traveled the world buying and selling properties, so Peyton and her sisters didn't get to see him all that often, but they could always reach him on his cell phone. No matter where he was or what he was doing, he would stop to chat with them.

He swore he didn't have a favorite niece, but it was obvious that he felt closest to Peyton because he talked to her the most. He loved hearing about her adventures in dating. They were always so entertaining. He'd be sympathetic on the phone, but as soon as he disconnected the call, he'd have a good, long laugh.

She told her uncle about her new job and he seemed genuinely excited for her. Before ending the conversation, he asked, "Had any interesting dates lately?"

She could hear the amusement in his voice. "Sorry, no," she said. "But don't worry. I'm sure there's an ex-con in Dalton just waiting to ask me out."

"You sure know how to pick 'em, darlin'," he told her.

He was right. When it came to men and relationships, Peyton had the most god-awful luck. She either turned them into priests or felons. There didn't seem to be any in-between. Not one but two of her high school crushes "got the call" to go into the seminary. One wanted to become a Jesuit and eventually did; the other, a Dominican. Granted, she attended a Catholic high school, but still, what were the odds of that happening to anyone else? By the time she graduated, she felt she had majored in unrequited love.

While in college she developed a propensity for dating only misfits. Allen Maxwell made the top five. She met him her first year and liked him immediately, which really should have been a warning. She still hadn't learned the lesson that, if she liked someone, there had to be something wrong with him. He wasn't a Catholic, so the odds were in her favor he wouldn't become a priest. It wasn't a sure bet, but it was close. She had two dates with Allen before he was arrested and later convicted of selling drugs out of his dorm room. Apparently she was the only student in the entire university who didn't know about his illegal activity.

And then there was Brendan Park, the graduate student extraordinaire, who became a millionaire overnight. He, too, made her top five. He blushed whenever he spoke to her and followed her around campus like a lost puppy. Although he was terribly shy, he was persistent, wearing her down until she finally agreed to go out with him. Brendan was a socially awkward computer genius. He certainly wasn't awkward about hacking into Goldman Sachs and helping himself to a large chunk of stock, though. He was arrested after their one and only date.

There were others. Josh Triggs came to mind. He wanted to cook dinner for her, but before she accepted, he needed to know if she was allergic to cats. Turned out he had seven of them living with him in his tiny studio apartment. The smell nearly knocked her over as soon as he opened the door. Needless to say, she passed on the dinner.

Since she was reminiscing, she mustn't

forget Greg Middleson, who could only talk to her using football terms. He once told her how he felt about her by saying, "Sometimes I feel like a quarterback who's forced into a bootleg without a lead blocker and I have to lateral to a wingman." She didn't have a clue what he was talking about, and she didn't think he did, either.

It seemed that all the men she dated were dysfunctional in some way. Troy Calloway was her most recent nightmare. Peyton had just graduated from college when he asked her out. She had only one date with him, but in his gin-soaked mind that meant they were a couple. It was a horrible evening. She shivered thinking about it. He took her to a lovely restaurant with white linens and soft candlelight, but after several cocktails and a bottle of wine, Troy began to slur his words. As the dinner progressed he talked louder and louder. The man was a raging alcoholic, and, yes, apparently she and her mother, who introduced her to Troy and encouraged her to go out with him because he was such a nice churchgoing gentleman, were the only two people in Brentwood who didn't know he was a drunk. A mean drunk at that.

Troy was as relentless as an Amway salesman in his pursuit. The phone calls would start around five in the evening and go on through the night. By two in the morning, he would be screaming into her voice mail threatening all sorts of vile things. Some made sense; others didn't. The following afternoon he would call and apologize, and when she didn't respond, the cycle would start all over again. She blocked his number, but that didn't help. He simply called her from another phone. Fortunately, the grant to study in France came through, and the timing couldn't have been better. She spent those glorious months in Lyon, and when she returned home and didn't hear from Troy again, she assumed he had forgotten all about her and had moved on . . . hopefully into rehab.

Her dating life really was laughable, she thought. It was a good thing she wasn't looking for love. Her last thought before she fell asleep was that she would be just fine without it.

Because of the weather it took more than two days to get to Dalton. The last day was harrowing. About forty miles from her destination she drove into a blizzard. The weatherman on the radio insisted there would be a few light flurries stirred up by high winds. The man obviously hadn't bothered to look out the window.

She had driven in snow but never like this. It was thick and heavy and stuck to her windshield in between swipes of her wipers. She decided she would take the next exit and find a place to wait out the storm. Visibility near zero, she could barely keep the car on the road. She had a death grip on the steering wheel and, when she hit a patch of ice and went into a spin, she tried to remember what her father had told her. Slamming on the brakes, though an automatic response, was definitely not the thing to do. She spun around and around so many times she lost count, narrowly missing a steep drop into a deep ravine before miraculously ending up back in her own lane — facing the wrong way but still in her lane. Thankfully, she was the only car on the isolated stretch of highway.

As it turned out, the next exit that offered any promise was the one to Dalton, and by then the snow and the wind had died down. She reached Dalton around four in the afternoon. She drove through a neighborhood and was surprised by how flat the area was. Street after street of tract housing, each home painted a pastel color. Everything around them looked clean and white, but then the snow blanketed the town. She didn't think it would look so pretty when it thawed. There weren't any trees. The terrain was barren, as though someone had bull-dozed the land before slapping up one prefab house after another. They were all ranches, too. There wasn't any individuality and it was a little depressing. Maybe the other side of town was more interesting, she thought. Curious to find out, she continued to drive down the main street until she re-alized there wasn't any other side of town. All the restaurants, gas stations, grocery stores — there were two — were clustered together with the fast-food drive-throughs and three small apartment buildings. It wouldn't take Peyton any time at all to know where everything was.

She stopped and picked up a hamburger for dinner before checking in to the Dalton Motel. Her room was small but clean and warm. After unpacking, she got ready for bed in flannel pajamas and socks. She was sitting in the middle of the bed texting her parents and her sisters to let them all know she'd arrived safely when her uncle Len called.

"Did you have any trouble on the road?" he asked. "I watched the Weather Channel, and it showed a blizzard up there in no-man's-land."

"I didn't have any trouble at all," she said, deciding not to mention the spinout that nearly gave her whiplash. Telling him the truth would only make him worry. "Where are you calling from?" she asked, deliberately changing the subject so she wouldn't have to lie again.

"I'm back in Bishop's Cove," he said, "sitting on my glider on the deck with a gin and tonic. Know what I'm looking at?"

"The ocean," she said, smiling.

"That's right, the ocean. The moon's bright tonight. The water sparkles. No worries here about blizzards or power outages. You love Bishop's Cove, don't you?"

"Yes, I do." Since she'd spent every summer working there while she was in school, she felt as though it was her home away from home. It was a beautiful resort. A little worn, but still charming. There were a dozen bungalows, a small hotel, and a two-story apartment building.

"Your cousin Debi feels the same way about King's Landing in California," he remarked. "It's worth a lot more money," he pointed out, "and yet you prefer Bishop's Cove."

Of course Debi preferred the more expensive resort. She was all about how much things cost with no real appreciation for tradition or character or charm. If it cost a lot, she liked it. Debi's father was just as superficial. He was the youngest of the three Lockhart brothers, and maybe because he was the baby, he was spoiled. That's what Peyton's father thought, anyway.

Debi was married now, and Peyton wondered if she'd changed at all and perhaps done a little growing up. She was the only woman Peyton knew who could still throw a tantrum like a child.

"You know I love Bishop's Cove. What are you thinking?" she asked, wondering why he had brought up the resorts.

"I'm going to be making some changes," he explained. "After I've thought it through, I'll tell you about it."

It? What *it?* Was he thinking about selling the properties? She hoped not.

"Are you ready to come home?" he asked then. "I'll give you a job. You can be the new sous-chef at Leonard's."

She politely declined the offer. While it was sweet of her uncle to make it, she wanted to prove herself on her own. Besides, she'd heard that the new head chef at the resort's five-star restaurant was a real piece of work and a nightmare to work for. He was a screamer and kept his staff in a state of perpetual hysteria. Rumor had it he made

Chef Gordon Ramsay look like a Buddhist monk in comparison.

"Come on down to Florida and let me put you to work," Uncle Len persisted.

Peyton thanked him for his concern but assured him she was making the right choice. "I just got to Dalton, and I can't wait to start the job. I know I'm going to love it."

TWO

She lasted four whole weeks and was lucky to get out alive.

Peyton's poor record with men hadn't improved. It had even spilled over into her budding career. She'd already met more than her share of felons, weirdos, and degenerates. Could it get any worse? As a matter of fact, it could.

Looking back she realized that Allen Maxwell, Brendan Park, Josh Triggs, Greg Middleson, Troy Calloway, and the countless other misfits she'd encountered had all had a hand in preparing her for Drew Albertson, the biggest degenerate of them all.

She wished that she could say that this was the first time she had ever lost a job, but the truth was, losing this one made it three . . . unless she counted Millie's Ice Cream Shop. Then it was four. Peyton didn't think Millie's should be included in the tally because she had worked there only one hour before the manager found out she was just thirteen years old and made her go home.

None of those jobs mattered, though. They all happened before she found her true calling to the culinary world, and they were simply a means to an end. In high school the part-time jobs kept her in Mary Lynn apple-flavored lip gloss, tattered jeans, and oversize sunglasses. In college they paid for her laptop and all the other extras not covered by her scholarship. But this job did matter because, in her mind, it was going to be the start of a stellar career. Too late, she realized she should have been more skeptical. From the very beginning, the job seemed too good to be true, and after a few days at the magazine, she discovered it definitely was. The boss, or rather, the pervert from hell, was responsible for her misery.

Her first day could only be described as bizarre. She had been told she would have a parking spot assigned to her inside a heated garage, which was attached to the main building. Since she wouldn't have to trample through the snow to get to the door, she decided to wear a dress and heels. She settled on a wool fitted pale-pink dress with a high V-neck and a straight skirt.

54

It was five below zero when she left her motel room, and getting to her car in the parking lot was painful. God only knew what the wind chill was. Within a minute her skin was burning. She slipped the key in the ignition while she whispered, "Please start, please start." She added a Hail Mary, and on the third try the motor came to life. She'd had a new battery installed before she left Texas, yet with this cold it was amazing that anything with moving parts would work. Her lips were blue before the heater started blowing warm air.

Peyton didn't need directions to the *Bountiful Table* headquarters because it was the tallest building in Dalton. According to Bridget, Peyton would be able to see it from anywhere in town. She was right about that. It was a giant monolith, extremely contemporary, with gleaming silver letters on top spelling *Swift Publications.* You couldn't miss it.

As she drove toward it, she tried to figure out what the structure was supposed to be. It was round and cylindrical. The closer she got to it, the more it looked like a silo, but it appeared to be black. By the time she reached the winding drive leading to the garage, she realized the surface of the building was made of dark reflective glass. Any windows were obscured. She surmised that the structure wouldn't win any awards from *Architectural Digest* unless they gave one for what-were-you-thinking. Like a giant statue of the bogeyman in the middle of Disneyland, it didn't belong.

Bridget was waiting for her in the lobby. She wasn't friendly. Thin and gaunt, she frowned as she gave Peyton the once-over.

"I'm pleased you're wearing a dress," she said. "We don't have an official dress code here and most of the women wear slacks, and the men wear whatever they want, but Drew — Mr. Albertson — prefers his assistants and trainees to wear dresses or skirts. You'll be working on the eighth floor. Come along and I'll get you settled. Mr. Albertson is out of town, but he'll be back in the office tomorrow or the day after. You'll meet him then."

At five feet five inches, Peyton wasn't all that tall, but she felt like a giant next to the petite, skin-and-bones woman as she walked by her side to the bank of elevators. Bridget's expression was so rigid, Peyton thought her face might crack if she smiled . . . assuming she knew how.

They passed two women in the hall. Both were smiling until they spotted Peyton. Then they frowned and, like Bridget, gave her the once-over. Feeling terribly self-conscious, Peyton looked down at her shoes to make sure they matched.

The elevator ride was strange, too. Most people in elevators stare straight ahead at the doors or up at the numbers above the doors until they reach their floor, but not the crowd in the elevator she and Bridget stepped into. Peyton stared straight ahead while everyone else, including Bridget, stared at her. It was unnerving.

The executive offices were nicely appointed, though the colors were a bit bland. Everything had been done in light and dark gray — the walls, the furniture, and the fixtures. It was as though the decorator wanted the furnishings to match the computers. They did, exactly.

Reception was in front of a wall of glass. A stunning redhead sat behind a sleek white counter, speaking to someone in her headset. She smiled at Bridget, but when she turned her attention to Peyton, the smile stiffened and appeared to be forced. The reactions Peyton was getting were becoming comical, and she worried she'd start laughing. What was wrong with these women? Why were they so hostile toward her?

Bridget led the way to the inner sanctum. Several cubicles separated by low four-foot walls were clustered in the middle of a large room. Beyond was Drew Albertson's office. His name was printed on the door along with his title, Managing Editor. Directly in front of Peyton, a large open cubicle held two desks facing each other.

An older woman with delicate features and big brown eyes walked up to greet them, and Peyton was relieved to see that, unlike the others, the woman was smiling at her with genuine warmth.

Bridget's sour expression lessened. "Mimi, this is the new trainee, Peyton Lockhart. Will you take over with her? You know, go through the manual and show her around? I've got to get back to my office."

Before Mimi could agree, Bridget took off.

"Welcome, I'm Mimi Cosgrove," the woman said, extending her hand. "Let's put your coat away. The closet's down the hall. Your desk is here." She pointed to the one on the right in the large cubicle. "You have lots of space." She nodded toward the desk on the left. "That's where Lars Bjorkman sits. He's an assistant editor . . . still learning the ropes," she explained.

"Where is your work station?" Peyton asked.

"Right in front of Drew's office. I'm one of his personal assistants."

"Have you worked here long?" she asked as she followed Mimi down a hallway.

"Over seven years," Mimi answered. "I used to work on five, but I was transferred to Drew's office about eight months ago." She added, "It's a change."

Mimi didn't volunteer any other information about her transfer, and Peyton felt it would be intrusive to ask. The woman was being very sweet to her. She didn't want to grill her with questions right away.

"Did you know we have a professional kitchen here?" Mimi asked. "One entire floor. Any recipe that's printed in our magazine has to be tested several times and then voted on. Would you like to see it?"

"Oh yes, please," Peyton answered eagerly.

"Come on then. We'll take the stairs. I'll give you the grand tour. Then I'll show you the manual. You'll have a lot of reading to do the next couple of days."

They spent the morning together going from floor to floor, meeting employees. The test kitchens with their state-of-the-art appliances and gleaming countertops were definitely the highlight for Peyton. When they returned to the eighth floor and stepped out of the elevator, Mimi turned to her right and pointed to large double doors made of highly polished mahogany.

"That's Randolph Swift's domain. It's a gorgeous office. You won't meet our CEO right away. I was told he's gone to visit relatives, but I don't really know where he is. I haven't seen him in quite some time. None of us have. Ever since his wife died, he's become somewhat of a recluse and doesn't come to his office much. When he was here all the time, he used to address the employees on the intercom, catching us up on the latest happenings because he thought of us as his family." She glanced at her watch. "I'm starving, and no wonder. Look at the time. It's already after noon. Let's go down to the cafeteria. The food's quite good, but then it should be, right?"

The morning had flown by. As they took their trays and made their way to a table in front of the windows, Peyton noticed heads turning and conversations becoming more hushed.

She set her bowl of vegetable soup and cup of hot tea on the table. Mimi commented that she'd forgotten utensils for her salad, but before she could get up, Peyton handed her a fork and an extra napkin.

"Thanks," Mimi said. She studied Peyton for a long minute and then said, "You know, if you don't like working for Drew, or if you decide you don't want to be a food critic, there are a couple of other positions available. Bridget could help you . . . if you decide . . ."

"I'm not so sure Bridget would help me. She doesn't seem to like me. Neither do any of the other women here. Have you noticed, Mimi? Look around the cafeteria. Most of the women are glaring at me."

Mimi laughed. "The last trainee left a sour taste in their mouths, I guess. Don't let it bother you. They'll get used to you. I notice the men are all smiling at you."

Peyton looked around the room. Mimi was right. Several men were smiling at her. "That's kind of creepy, too," she whispered.

"Don't pay attention to them," Mimi suggested. "Tell me about yourself. Any sisters or brothers? What's Texas like? I've never been south of Minneapolis. I always wanted to see the world, but my husband, Don — my ex-husband — didn't want to travel."

It soon became apparent that Peyton was proud of her state. She bragged about all it had to offer. "I could go on and on. Texas really does have everything you could ever want."

"What about your family?"

"I have two sisters," Peyton told her. "Lucy is two years older. She's an interior designer and really creative. She would like

61

to start her own business, but in this economy it's tough. Ivy is the youngest. She's a senior at the University of Texas. She's doing her student teaching now and wants to teach kindergarten. She loves children, and of the three of us, she's the most patient."

"Are your parents still alive?"

"Yes, and still living in the house they bought over twenty-some years ago. Okay, now it's my turn, Mimi. Tell me about your family."

"Not much to tell," she said as she stabbed a leaf of spinach. "I have two younger brothers. They're both married and living in Minneapolis. No nieces or nephews, sorry to say. After college I married the only man I ever dated. We lasted almost twenty-five years."

"Twenty-five years," Peyton repeated. "That's a long time. You don't look old enough to have been married that long."

Mimi smiled at the compliment. "I'm old enough to be your mother." Her expression changed and she looked out the window. Peyton noticed a hint of sadness in Mimi's eyes as she shrugged her shoulders and said, "Don and I never had any children."

They continued to talk about their backgrounds while they ate, and after lunch

Mimi walked Peyton back to her desk and handed her the company manual. She opened the two-hundred-page volume and began reading all about *The Bountiful Table*. The material wasn't what she would call riveting, and Peyton did a fair amount of yawning and daydreaming.

Occasionally, Mimi would check on her. Once, on her way back from the printer, she stopped at Peyton's desk and in a low whisper said, "You don't have to do anything you don't want to do. You know that, don't you?"

"Yes," she answered, perplexed by the odd question. "Why —"

Bridget interrupted when she called Mimi's name from across the room. "I'll explain later," Mimi said, patting Peyton's shoulder and then hurrying off.

Peyton didn't have the opportunity to talk to her new friend again until the end of the day when they were walking to the garage together. Mimi was turning to go up the stairs to the top level when Peyton stopped her.

"Mimi, what did you mean when you said I don't have to do anything I don't want?"

Mimi halted on the step and thought for a second before saying, "Don't be in a hurry to sign a lease. Take your time and talk to me before you commit. Okay?"

"Okay, but I don't understand why —"
Peyton began.

Before she could finish her sentence,
Mimi said, "Don't worry. You'll be fine,"
and then she turned to continue up the
stairs.

As Peyton made her way to her car, she
reflected on her first day at her new job.
Very peculiar, she thought. It wasn't at all
what she had expected, but then, she reasoned, one couldn't expect to feel completely comfortable from day one.

On Tuesday she met the man who would
share the cubicle with her, Assistant Editor
Lars Bjorkman. He was already at his desk
furiously typing on his keyboard when she
walked over to introduce herself. He was
young, in his twenties, and handsome. He
wore one of his signature ski sweaters. According to Mimi, he owned one for every
day of the month. Lars was from Stock-
holm, and he had the most wonderful accent. He told her his goal was to become a
chef, and he'd taken the job at the magazine
as a first step, explaining it would provide
exposure to some of the finest restaurants
in the country. She liked him. She noticed
how kind he was to everyone, no matter

how rude or impatient they were when demanding his attention.

Peyton took up where she left off in the manual, but it was a much more pleasant task with Lars's help. He was generous with his advice, telling her which procedures she would need to learn now and which ones she could postpone to a later date. Whenever she had a question, he would stop what he was doing and answer her.

All in all, Tuesday was a much better day. Wednesday her nightmare began.

THREE

Drew Albertson looked like a Scandinavian movie star with his blond wavy hair, gray-blue eyes, and long eyelashes. He was tall and thin but quite muscular. His custom-made shirts were fitted a tad too tight, giving the impression that he was so buff his muscles were about to bulge through.

For Peyton's first few days on the job, he was very warm and welcoming, expressing his desire that she feel at home and enjoy her work at *The Bountiful Table* and assuring her that if she had any questions or concerns he was there to help her.

Drew was married to Eileen, the daughter of Randolph Swift, the patriarch of the company. Peyton met Eileen briefly when she swept through the office one morning to drop something off at Drew's office. She was a big-boned woman with shoulders a linebacker would envy, but she wore beautiful clothes. Her cashmere coat was definitely black label, and her boots cost well over a thousand dollars. Peyton recognized them from a Neiman Marcus ad she'd seen in a magazine. After two minutes with the woman, Peyton decided the clothes were the only beautiful thing about her.

Eileen stopped at her desk and looked Peyton up and down as though she were scrutinizing a specimen in a jar. "So, you're the new girl," she said, not hiding her disdainful smile.

Peyton put on her most pleasant face and extended her hand. "Yes, I'm —"

"I know who you are," Eileen snapped. "Peyton . . . something."

"Lockhart," Peyton offered.

"Yes . . . whatever," Eileen said with a dismissive wave of her hand. "Just do your job, and you'll get along here. My husband has high standards . . . very high standards," she repeated. "If you want to make it in this company, you'll see that he gets what he needs."

Peyton bit her lip to keep from snapping back at the rude woman. She managed a faint smile before saying, "I'll do my best."

"See that you do," Eileen said and then turned and walked away.

Peyton didn't think she'd ever met a more abrasive woman in her life. If this was her normal way of communicating with people, it was a wonder anyone would speak to her, let alone get close to her. The one thing she had going for her was money. Most likely that was what had attracted Drew. She came from money and was due to get lots more. Peyton had learned from Lars that Eileen and her younger brother, Erik, would inherit the publishing company and a fortune in stocks and bonds just as soon as their father retired as CEO. Even more money would come to whoever took over and ran the business after Randolph was gone. Since Erik had been away at school for several years, it was fully expected that Drew would step into his father-in-law's shoes.

Peyton thought Eileen was the most repulsive person she had ever met. That is, until she got to know Drew Albertson.

One wouldn't expect such a handsome man with the sweetest smile and the softest voice to be a sexual predator — at least Peyton didn't expect it, which was why she was slow to react. But a sexual predator was exactly what Drew was, and in hindsight, she realized she had been foolishly naive.

His creepy seduction began almost immediately. On her fourth day at work his hand brushed against the side of her left breast . . . and lingered. It happened while she was sitting at her desk and he was leaning over her to point to a graph on her computer screen. She was mortified, but because he didn't say anything or apologize, she thought he hadn't realized what he had done. She assumed it was an accident.

The seventh day on the job he followed her into the file room, shut the door, and trapped her as she was trying to get past him. Pretending to get out of her way, he pinned her against the wall, his pelvis against hers, and said, "You must be used to men telling you how beautiful and sexy you are. I'll bet they make fools of themselves fawning all over you."

She shook her head. "No," she said. "Please move away from me. You're making me terribly uncomfortable."

He acted as though he hadn't heard her and brushed a strand of her hair over her shoulder. "So silky," he crooned.

She pushed his hand away, squeezed around him, and without a word, left the room. She resisted the urge to slam the door in his face.

That evening she spent a long while researching sexual harassment on the Internet, gathering information to take to Human Resources. She had a strong feeling that Drew wasn't going to let up, and she needed to know what she legally could do about it.

A few days later he trapped her at her desk. He snuck up behind her, put his hands on her shoulders to keep her from bolting, then leaned down until his lips were next to her ear and whispered, "I look at you and all I can think about is touching you. I dream about you and me."

She dreamed about Tasing him. She twisted in her chair, forcing him to let go of her. Anger radiated in her voice when she said, "Mr. Albertson, it isn't appropriate for you —"

"Call me Drew, honey. I can tell, you and I are going to be real close."

That thought was so repulsive she cringed. He didn't seem to notice. He raised up and crossed his arms, assuming the posture of an authoritative boss. In his professional voice, he said, "I'll give you a couple of weeks to find a place and get settled here in Dalton, but then you and I are going to Hartford. There's a restaurant there I want to review. From there we'll fly down to Miami and do an interview with the owner of a new Cuban restaurant I've been hearing raves about." He leaned closer and lowered his voice. Minty fresh breath blew in her face when he added, "Our schedule will be tight, but there will be a little time for relaxation. Be sure to pack your bikini."

Right. Bikini. Like that was going to happen. The only way she would go anywhere with the letch was if she could take a cattle prod, a Taser, a couple of pepper sprays, and maybe a pair of handcuffs. She doubted, however, that any airline would let her carry these weapons on board, so that left a three-hundred-pound bodyguard. Where could she find one of those in Dalton?

He smiled his most seductive smile, and with his voice still low said, "I'm sure you'll warm up before then." Finished with his sexual harassment for the afternoon, he went back to his office to get his coat and strolled out the door.

Peyton was so angry her hands shook. She took a deep breath and tried to calm down, but it didn't work. She still wanted to scream. There had been a moment when his lips were actually touching her ear and his hands were pushing down on her shoulders that she had felt trapped and helpless. The feeling was so foreign it almost overwhelmed her. Almost. And only for a few seconds. Now, outrage was taking over.

Armed with the information she had gathered from the Internet on sexual harassment Peyton went to Human Resources to lodge a complaint. The office of the director, Annette Finch, was usually guarded by Bridget, and, thankfully, she had already left for the day. The director's door was open. Peyton knocked to get her attention.

"May I have a moment of your time?" she asked.

The heavyset woman with a severely short haircut pointedly looked at her watch before giving a nod. "Make it quick," she said, her tone brisk. "What do you need?"

"I would like the necessary forms to fill out to file a complaint against my immediate supervisor, Drew Albertson." Peyton could have sworn she saw a hint of a sneer on Annette's face.

"What kind of complaint?"

"Sexual harassment."

Tapping her lips with one finger, she said, "Hmmm."

"Excuse me?" When the woman continued to stare at her without saying anything, Peyton asked, "Would you like me to tell you what happened, or should I write it down and —"

"No, absolutely not," she snapped. "Do not tell me what happened."

Her reaction was so hostile Peyton wasn't sure how to proceed. "May I have the forms, please?" she asked.

"No."

Annette was drumming her fingers on the desk now as she stared at Peyton. Her lips were pinched together, and her eyes had narrowed. For some reason the request had infuriated her.

"It's your job to —" Peyton began, flabbergasted by the woman's behavior.

"Don't tell me what my job is," she said. She forced a smile then, and it was creepier than her scowl. "You took me by surprise. No one has ever wanted to complain about Drew, you see. That surprised me. You've only been here a couple of weeks, right?"

"Yes."

"It's a policy that you can't file a complaint until you've been here three months. If you still want the forms then, I'll give them to you." As a dismissive gesture, she stood and reached for her coat.

"That's it?" Peyton struggled to keep her temper controlled. "Come back in three months?"

"That's our policy," Annette insisted. "You're new here, and once you've settled in you'll calm down." She turned her back to Peyton as she put on her coat and began to clear the credenza behind her desk.

Now what? Peyton wondered, astounded that the head of HR refused to let her file a complaint. She didn't know what else she could do to stop Drew's lecherous behavior. He was such a vile person. She came up with a couple of sadistic ways to do him in, but unfortunately none of them were legal. She justified her bloodthirsty attitude by telling herself she was protecting future women who came to work for the magazine. She had never had murderous thoughts about anyone before — not even when Troy, the drunk, was slobbering all over her hand as he tried to stop her from giving his car keys to the restaurant manager — but she was certainly having those thoughts about Drew now. She could just see the sisters of Saint Michael's shaking their heads. Peyton knew what they'd say, too: "Murderous thoughts? You're on the highway to hell, young lady."

Thank heaven she'd listened to Mimi and hadn't rushed to sign a lease. The thought popped into her head and helped her get rid of some of her anger. That was a positive. There was another positive, as well. She hadn't given in to the urge to punch him when he was panting all over her, so she didn't have to worry she'd be dragged off to jail for battery. There was no question she was going to quit; however, she found it galling that the reason for her departure wouldn't be noted in her file or Drew's. She wished there was a way to prove he was a predator.

At least Drew was consistent. He stopped by her desk that afternoon to whisper, "I hope you're thinking about our trip."

Peyton didn't look up from her work.

She was sitting there contemplating her options when Mimi walked toward her cubicle. Unlike Drew, Mimi could never sneak up on anyone. She was partial to J'adore perfume and doused herself with it at least twice a day. The fragrance announced her approach.

"So the jackass is already at it again," Mimi remarked. She was shaking her head and had both hands on her hips. "He just never learns. I should have warned you. I started to a couple of times, but I thought, since you were different, he might go easy on you."

"You heard him?" Peyton asked.

"I was in the hallway just now and saw him come up behind you," Mimi explained. "I couldn't hear what he said, but I can guess. Your face looked like it was on fire. I wish I could tell you that it's going to get better and that he'll eventually give up and leave you alone, but I don't think that's going to happen. He was promoted to this job about a year ago, and he's already gone through two other trainees. I had a long talk with Sandy this morning. She's an assistant in Human Resources, and she was in an unusual mood to chat about Drew. Come to find out, like most of the employees she doesn't much care for him, either," she added. "Anyway, I found out how you were chosen for the job."

Before Peyton could respond, Mimi said, "According to Sandy, you fit all of his requirements and then some. Your photo gave you the edge over the others."

Peyton shook her head. "I didn't send a photo."

"Oh, he got hold of one," Mimi said. "Sandy told me that Drew had a stack of applications. He made her search the Internet for any photos or personal information she could find. All he wanted to look at were the photos of the women. She had to sort through the pile for him. He didn't want anyone over the age of thirty, and she had to be single. He didn't even glance at the applications from men. He told Sandy that, since the other food critics were male, he felt it was only fair to hire a female."

Mimi glanced around the cavernous office to make sure they were still alone, lowered her voice, and said, "You were the prettiest applicant, and that's why you were hired. I don't want to hurt your feelings, but think about it. You weren't hired for your experience. You just graduated from college and then did some postgraduate work cooking in France for a while. Didn't you wonder . . ."

"I was told it was a training program, and I thought working for this magazine would be invaluable." She didn't go on. She felt so foolish. "I just jumped at the opportunity." She thought about the long drive to Dalton and how excited she'd been to get started on her career. Now she felt crushing disappointment. "It's so unfair."

Mimi nodded her agreement, and then as though her own frustration couldn't be held in any longer, the floodgates opened and she blurted, "You want to talk unfair?" she asked. "I've got you beat there. I'm an accountant, a damned good one, too. I've been with this company for over seven years, and up until Drew came along, I've been happy here. Drew married Eileen three years ago. He was in charge of production then. I didn't really know him, but I had heard talk that he was a real letch. Apparently, there was trouble with one of the girls working under him. Rumor had it, he blatantly pursued her. I heard he gave her a ride home one night, and she didn't come back to work for a week afterward. When she finally returned, he treated her so bad, she was forced to quit. I don't know what happened, but the stories were flying. Eileen made sure everything was hushed up. And then he was promoted." She added with a nod toward Drew's office, "He didn't have the skills for the job, but I guess that wasn't important to Eileen. She's the one who pulled the strings to get him in.

"I was going through a divorce back then. My ex had a girlfriend on the side and thought I should be okay with it. I wasn't. Anyway," she continued, sounding as though it was exhausting to talk about it, "since we didn't have any children and he made more money than I did — even though he did the same job — neither one of us asked for anything from the other. It should have been a quick and easy divorce, right? But he worked here in accounting, too, and he was bitter —"

"Wait. How could he be bitter? He's the one who cheated," she pointed out.

"Yes, and he still has the girlfriend, but he didn't want his life to change. He liked my cooking, and he was used to being pampered. Did I mention that he and Drew had become friends? I guess cheaters bond with other cheaters."

"What happened?"

"Don, my ex, told me I was going to get fired. I swear he had a gleam in his eyes, the bastard. God only knows what reasons he and Drew came up with, but I was called into HR and they were both there. I said that was fine, go ahead and fire me — I was going to ask the judge for spousal support. I told Don he was going to support me financially for the rest of my life. I hadn't signed the divorce papers yet."

Peyton laughed. "He must have loved hearing that."

"I'll just say the gleam disappeared from his eyes." She reached up and patted her short curls. "So I wasn't fired. I was demoted to an assistant's position, and my paycheck was cut more than half. Now I fetch coffee for the jackass and keep his calendar for him. I just turned fifty; I'm thirty pounds overweight, and around here accountants are a dime a dozen. No one's going to look twice at my résumé." She sighed. "Ready to concede?"

"Okay, you win," Peyton said.

"What did you win, Mimi?" Lars asked as he walked into the cubicle and dropped a stack of files on his desk.

"My life is more unfair than Peyton's,"

Mimi answered. She looked at her watch. "It's already after five, and it's taco night at the Cactus. How come you're not there?"

Lars sat down and began to sort the files into piles. "Everyone from the company goes there. It's difficult to get away from all of them. I don't feel like I can speak freely. You know?"

"I know," Mimi agreed. Turning back to Peyton, she added, "Don't worry. No matter what you say, Lars and I will hold your confidence. I can't say the same for anyone else in this office. They'll all go to HR to tattletale."

"When you were demoted, why didn't you go to Human Resources and lodge a complaint? At the very least, it would have gone on the record."

"I did complain, but nothing ever came of it. I've been sending my résumé out and so has Lars. Until I can get away from this town, I have to work here. There aren't any other jobs. Trust me. I've looked. And even if there were — like I said — who's going to consider me?"

"What about applying for other positions in the company?"

"No, I'm being punished. The hope is that, if Drew makes my life miserable enough, I'll quit. I'm stuck."

Lars looked up from his task and nodded. "Since Drew took over, it's been stressful."

Peyton leaned back in her chair and crossed one leg over the other. "Did Drew bother the other trainees? Is that why they left?" Even though she knew the answer, she still asked the question.

"Of course he did. They were young and pretty, but you put them to shame."

Mimi's compliment, given so matter-of-factly, embarrassed Peyton. Her looks shouldn't have anything to do with her job performance.

Lars turned in his swivel chair and said, "You're a stunner. That's what Mimi means by putting the others to shame."

Mimi laughed. "Look at her, Lars. She's blushing."

"Tell her about the last two trainees," Lars urged.

Mimi pushed some papers aside and sat on the edge of Peyton's desk. "I was just getting ready to." She crossed her arms and began. "The first one was much older than you. Her name was Kayla, and she lasted a good six months."

"Eight months," Lars corrected.

"I didn't like her," Mimi admitted.

"No one liked her," Lars interjected.

"She was full of herself. She didn't seem

to have a problem sleeping with the boss, did she, Lars?"

"No, she didn't."

"She didn't try to keep the affair secret. She flaunted it. She was rude and obnoxious to other employees. I think she believed that having sex with Drew made her more important in the company."

"Did it?" Peyton asked.

"Not really."

"Why did she leave?"

"She wanted more," Mimi said. "There was a rumor that she actually fell in love with the jackass. Can you imagine?"

The disgust in her voice made Peyton laugh. "No, I can't imagine."

"Kayla wanted him to leave his wife and marry her, and of course, he would never do that."

Lars explained why. "Drew didn't have any money when he married Eileen, and if he were to divorce her, he wouldn't get a dime."

"It's common knowledge he signed a prenup," Mimi said. "I heard that when Drew told Kayla he wasn't going to leave his wife, she threw a fit."

"That's not all she threw. I was here. I saw it," Lars said. "She picked up a computer monitor and threw it into the wall next to Drew's office door. I think she was aiming for his head. I swear she threw it like it was a baseball."

"I wish I had seen it," Mimi said. "Eileen heard about it and that's when she got involved."

Peyton's eyes widened. "His wife knew about Kayla?"

"Of course she did," Mimi said. "She cleans up all of Drew's messes. Kayla was given a nice go-away package. I don't know how much it was, but I do know she had to sign a release of some kind before she got the check."

"I'll bet she had to promise not to talk about what happened," Lars said. "And promise not to sue."

"You're telling me Eileen is okay with his philandering?" Peyton was flabbergasted.

"She must be okay with it or she would have kicked him to the curb by now."

"What a sick marriage," Peyton said.

"You've got that right," Lars agreed.

"Want to know what happened to the second trainee?" Mimi asked.

Feeling completely disheartened, she replied, "Sure, why not."

"That would be April."

"I liked her," Lars said.

"Of course you did. She was especially

friendly to all the men here," Mimi said. "I've never met a more outrageous flirt, but I think underneath it all she was a nice girl. She put her purse in her desk drawer and — wham bam — Drew was hot on her tail. And I do mean tail. With her tight clothes and big boobs, she was exactly what he'd been looking for. I don't think she had any idea what she was getting into because after a couple of weeks her attitude changed, and she was running from him. I think she got far more than she'd bargained for. All of a sudden she was hiding from him and doing everything she could think of not to be alone with him. I tried to talk to her once . . . you know . . . just to see if she was okay, but she was tight-lipped and wouldn't say a word about Drew. The only thing I got out of her was how much she needed this job. I think she was scared."

Lars agreed. "That's the truth of it. I once saw her walking down the hall as he was coming toward her. She did a one-eighty and ducked in the first office she could find. And I noticed she never went into the file room if he was in there. It's dark and there aren't any windows. She'd always wait until he left."

"Drew ended up firing her," Mimi said. "She tried to make trouble, didn't she,

Lars?" She apparently didn't expect an answer because she continued right along. "April went to HR to complain. She accused Drew of sexual harassment, but she was wasting her time," she added with a nod. "Drew's wife is best friends with Annette, the head of HR. April's complaint didn't go anywhere but the shredder."

"No wonder," Peyton said.

"Sorry?"

"I went to HR to file a complaint. Annette wouldn't let me. She said I had to wait at least three months before I could file any complaints."

"That's nonsense," Mimi said.

"Didn't April intend to sue?" Lars asked.

"Eileen nipped that in the bud. I don't know what she threatened, but she and Drew have a guy who will do their dirty work for them when they need it. April packed up and left town in a real hurry."

"This is crazy," Peyton said. "In this day and age Drew shouldn't be able to get away with his obscene behavior, and neither should his wife. By helping him, Eileen is just as culpable."

"We agree with you," Lars said. "But most of the town depends on this company for their income, and they'll protect it any way they can. No one wants bad publicity or —

God forbid — a lawsuit. Randolph wants a big happy family."

"Eileen especially doesn't want any trouble. She's on thin ice with her father as it is, and if anyone were to sue Randolph Swift's beloved magazine because of something his daughter or her randy husband did, Randolph would be mighty upset."

"What do you think he would do?" Peyton asked. She picked up a pencil and began to twirl it between her fingers.

"It's hard to tell. He hasn't come to the office for ages, but I'd like to think he'd stay on as CEO until his son, Erik, is ready. I imagine Randolph would show him the ropes and let him run the company. Erik's smart. He'd do a good job. I'm guessing Randolph would cut Eileen out altogether," Lars suggested. "Randolph lost his wife a little over a year ago. He was devastated, and that's when everyone thought he would retire."

Mimi nodded. "Miriam was sick a long time, and he was always at her side. I think the worry wore him out. Both he and his son were very close to her. Erik took a semester off from college to be with his mother in those final weeks, but Eileen . . . well, she didn't have much use for her mother once she took ill. Eileen is what you would call . . ."

"A very self-involved woman," Lars supplied.

"I was going to say bitch," Mimi said. "She's a real bitch."

Peyton laughed. Lars looked shocked.

"How do you know so much about the family?" Peyton asked.

Mimi shrugged. "I listen. Being an assistant gives me a lot of time to do nothing but listen. I'm sort of invisible now. People gossip and they don't seem to notice I'm standing right next to them. When you've been demoted the way I have, I guess they figure I'm nobody. I certainly can't do them any damage. Who would listen to me? Working as an accountant, I never had time to gossip. These days I'm ashamed to admit gossip is the highlight of my days. That and chocolate." She shook her head. "I really have to get out of here." Turning to Lars, she said, "That job at the Quickie Market is looking better and better, except I can't live on minimum wage. No one can." She scooted off the desk. "Come on, both of you. I'll make tacos at my place."

Peyton hated going outside, especially in the evening. No matter how many layers she wore, she still froze. The temperature had already dropped well below zero, and the wind chill was so brutal it made her bones feel brittle. The heater in her car didn't start blowing warm air until she was pulling up to Mimi's apartment building. Peyton felt as though her toes needed to be defrosted. She didn't think she was ever going to get used to this kind of arctic cold.

An hour later she and Lars and Mimi were sitting around a small coffee table in the tiny one-bedroom apartment, coming up with one outrageous plan after another to take Drew down a notch. Mimi and Lars drank beer, but Peyton, still chilled, sipped hot tea.

"I can't stay here," Peyton said. "I'm going to quit, but I wish there was a way to let Randolph Swift and his son know what Drew has been doing. Tell me more about Randolph."

"He's a good man," Mimi said. "And he's kind. He built this community. I know the area looks bleak and dreary now, but when it thaws, it's a pretty place to live. Randolph cares about his employees."

Mimi took a drink of her beer and tilted the bottle toward Peyton. "If he ever comes back, you wouldn't be able to get to him. There's no way you'll get past that gargoyle, Eileen."

Lars choked on his drink. "Gargoyle? I've never heard that one before."

"Eventually Randolph will find out what Drew's doing," Peyton said. "Someone will tell him. It's only a matter of time."

"I agree, and I'm sure Eileen realizes it, too. But if Randolph retires, and Drew takes charge, it will be easier to handle the women who try to make trouble. Drew might be able to get away with his sick behavior for several more years."

"Someone needs to stop him," Peyton countered.

And get proof to take to Randolph Swift, she thought. But how?

She had time to think about it because Drew was traveling with Eileen on what he called a buying trip and was going to be away from the office for ten days. Surely, in that time Peyton could think of something brilliant to do that would trap the letch. And if it didn't work out, at least she'd know she had tried.

It became routine to go to Mimi's apartment after work with Lars. The three of them would take turns bringing in carryout or buying groceries to cook dinner. Mimi and Lars had become her confidants and her good friends. She was going to miss them when she left. She knew they were miserable and wished they could go with her, but what was the good in that? Then all three of them would be unemployed.

The office was quiet during the days Drew was gone, but they went by quickly. He was due back the following Monday.

Thursday night while Peyton was getting ready for bed, she came up with a plan of action. It was riddled with flaws, but she still thought she could pull it off. She had Friday to discuss it with Mimi and Lars, and the entire weekend to work out the details while she packed for her trip back to Texas. Monday, after meeting with Drew, she would get out of Dalton as fast as she could. Once she was finished wrecking his life, she doubted he would want her to give two weeks' notice.

Drew surprised her by coming home early. He was back Friday morning. He was in a foul mood and stayed sequestered in his office most of the day. He didn't want interruptions and, more important to Peyton, he left her alone. She was just closing up to go home when she heard him through the door snarling at someone over the phone. His anger was palpable. She could hear his heavy breathing as he berated whomever he was talking to, and then she heard a loud

90

noise, as though he had just thrown something into the wall. Peyton looked around the office. It was empty. Everyone had just left and she was the only one there. Fear raced down her spine, and her instincts told her to get out of there as soon as possible. If anything happened, no one would hear her.

She had her coat on and was digging through her purse for her keys when he shouted her name. Trying to be as quiet as possible, she bolted out of the office and ran down the hall. She had just turned the corner when she heard him shout her name again. She didn't respond and rushed up a flight of stairs to the garage entrance. Afraid that he might be coming after her, she didn't go directly to her car but ran to the floor above, reasoning that if he didn't see her, he would assume she was still inside working.

Was her fear unreasonable? A door opened, then slammed shut. She ducked down between two cars and waited. She felt foolish and told herself she was overreacting, but panic was edging in on her, and she couldn't seem to control it.

Drew was a man who was used to getting whatever he wanted, but was he really capable of violence? How far would he go to get his way?

Later that night, she found out just how dangerous he was.

It was well past midnight. She was huddled under the covers and just drifting off to sleep when she heard a car zoom past, then screech to a stop and back up. She didn't know what possessed her to get out of bed and peek out the window, but she thanked God she did, for there, backing into a parking spot, was Drew's big SUV. The back tires were on the curb and the vehicle sat diagonally across the lines, taking up two parking spaces. She watched Drew get out, slam the door, and stagger across the lot. The harsh light from the lamppost cast an eerie glow on his scowl. He looked angry and determined, and he terrified her. She ran to drag a heavy chair over to the door and shoved it under the doorknob, then checked to make certain she had locked the deadbolt.

Suddenly he started beating on her door with his fists. Then, ramming his shoulder against it, he tried to break the lock. The door shook and she knew it was only a matter of seconds before he forced his way in. She raced to the phone to call the front desk.

"There's a drunk man trying to break into my room," she cried out. "Please call the police."

The older teenager manning the desk said, "I'll come help you."

She didn't know if he would also call the police, so she decided she'd better do it, but she was so rattled she dropped the phone and had to dive under the bed to get it.

"Let me in, Peyton. I'm going to make you feel real good, baby. Come on now. You know you want it. I'll make you want it."

Over and over he promised to make her feel good, but his voice was getting louder and angrier. Peyton frantically searched the room for something to use as a weapon. It was the old man in the room next to hers who inadvertently saved her. He opened his door and shouted a litany of curses, ending with the threat that he would call the police if Drew didn't stop making a racket and leave.

"Go on, get out of here. I'll call the cops on you. Go on before they arrest you."

The pounding on the door stopped, and she heard Drew threaten the old man. Then she heard the young clerk asking if everything was all right. Drew started muttering, but she couldn't make out what he was saying. A minute later, she heard his car motor racing as he peeled out of the parking lot.

"He's gone. He's gone. He's gone." She must have whispered those words a hundred times while she sat on the floor in the tiny bathroom. Her back was pressed against the bathtub, and her feet were pushing against the door so that no one could come inside. He was gone, and she was safe now. The enormity of what had almost happened hit, and she folded her knees under her chin and wrapped her arms around them, rocking back and forth as she began to sob.

She didn't sleep at all that night. She stayed locked in the bathroom until the sun came up, then she packed a bag and drove to Mimi's. Her friend liked to sleep in on weekends, and it wasn't even eight o'clock when Peyton knocked on her door. Mimi didn't complain. She took one look at Peyton and knew something terrible had happened.

After Peyton told her everything, Mimi was horrified. "If he had gotten in . . ." She squeezed her eyes shut, took a breath, and said, "He would have raped you. My God, I knew he was a womanizer, but this . . . You should go to the police. I'll get dressed and go with you. You should file a report."

"And what do I tell them? That a man I'm afraid of banged on my door late at night and wanted to come inside. He didn't break any laws. He made a lot of noise; he was told to go away, and he left."

"It's not right. It's just not right." Mimi sounded as though she was going to cry. She put her arm around Peyton and led her to the bedroom. "Come on. You need to sleep. When you're clearheaded we'll figure out what to do."

"It's okay," Peyton said. "I'm going to stop him. I know what to do."

Afraid that Drew might come back to the motel, she stayed with Mimi all weekend, and on Sunday night she returned to pack up her things. By Monday morning, her car was loaded and ready to go. And so was she.

Drew didn't come into the office until eleven, and Peyton grew more and more anxious, wondering what his demeanor would be when he saw her. Would he show any remorse for what he had done? Or would he ignore it? She was just checking the time on her watch when she heard the elevator doors open. She looked up and saw him head to the receptionist and greet her with a wide grin. After a few friendly words with her, he walked over to Peyton's cubicle and cheerfully said good morning, then proceeded to his office. Peyton wasn't really shocked by his behavior. In fact, she rather suspected Drew would be his usual smarmy self, and she was glad he was exactly that because it played into her plan.

With all the sweetness she could muster, she got up from her desk, knocked on his door, and asked him if she could have a moment of his time. Responding to her smile, he quickly agreed. He even pulled out a chair facing his massive desk for her.

She waited until he had taken his seat, then leaned forward and placed a digital recorder in the center of his desk.

"Do you mind if I record our conversation?"

He raised an eyebrow. Then he laughed. "Sure, go ahead."

He leaned over the desk, pulled the recorder closer to him, and said, "I'll even turn it on for you." He pushed a button, sat back, and casually asked, "Have you decided to warm up yet?"

Instead of answering the question, she asked, "Aren't you curious to know why I'm recording this conversation?"

"Not really," he replied. "Now answer me. Are you going to warm up? Don't you feel the electricity flowing between us? You want me as much as I want you."

The man was certifiable.

"No, I don't feel any electricity. What I

want is for you to leave me alone."

"That's not going to happen," he told her, smiling.

"We are not going to have a physical relationship, and as far as traveling with you, that's out of the question. I don't feel safe with you."

He shrugged. "I'm your boss. If I say you go with me, then you go with me."

"Haven't you ever heard of sexual harassment?"

"That doesn't mean anything here. And you will travel with me."

"No." She didn't expound.

"No?" The smile was gone.

"That's right, no," she repeated calmly.

"You have a choice, Peyton. Either play ball with me or get fired. Don't even think about asking for a transfer. I won't let that happen, and I'm the one with all the power, not you."

"What exactly does play ball with you mean?" She wanted to get it on the record.

"You know. Spread your legs for me. Whenever I want and as often as I want."

She wanted to gag. She tried not to react.

Despite her efforts, her disgust must have shown because Drew looked displeased with her response. He leaned forward, frowning, and said, "Don't look so shocked. I'll make

you like it. If I have to force you, I will. I always get my way."

"Doesn't your wife —"

He interrupted. "Is that it?" His voice softened and his frown eased. He looked earnest now. "You're worried about my wife finding out? Eileen knows I like a little action on the side. She understands. It spices up our sex life, so she helps me get what I want, what I need. It's a win-win."

"What about Randolph Swift?"

"My father-in-law? What about him? He can get his own action," he said with a chuckle. "The way he mopes around since his wife died is pretty pathetic. I doubt he can even get it up anymore." He settled back in his big leather swivel chair and began to rock side to side, looking very smug. "Why he'd mourn after that old bat, I'll never know. She was nothing but a bag of bones the last couple of years. You'd think he'd be glad to be rid of her."

She didn't want him to see how sickened she was, but it was becoming increasingly difficult to keep her emotions inside. He was such a slimeball. "I was told the reputation of the company is very important to him. If he were to find out what you were doing . . . if there were a lawsuit . . ."

"He won't find out," he said confidently.

"Eileen manages him."

"I don't understand. How does she manage him?"

"She makes sure he doesn't hear anything negative about me. Eileen and I are progressive in our thinking, but Randolph is stuck in the past. He needs to go. So does that loser son of his. Once I get hold of this place, things will be different."

Peyton had heard enough, and she couldn't stand being near the degenerate another minute. She reached for the recorder, but Drew was quicker. He grabbed it. Squinting at the tiny buttons, he figured out which one he needed to push to erase the conversation. That done, he tossed the recorder at her.

"Don't look so disheartened," he said, laughing. "I let you record me."

Peyton dejectedly picked up the recorder and stood to leave.

"You're young still, but you'll learn," he said, as though consoling her. "If you want to make it in this business, you'll come around. And, Peyton, the next time I come to your motel room, you'd better let me in."

She reached for the doorknob.

"Have you found an apartment yet?" he asked, stopping her.

"I've narrowed it down to two possibilities." It was a lie, but she thought she told it convincingly.

"Hurry up and make up your mind."

She nodded and, without another word, pulled the door closed behind her. She wanted to smile but didn't dare. She was becoming so paranoid she worried that someone could be watching her. She wouldn't put it past Eileen to hide surveillance cameras around the office. Peyton had met the woman only once, but once was enough to see that she was every bit as vile as her husband. From what Peyton had learned, Eileen would go to any length to keep her husband happy and her father clueless. A fortune was riding on it.

Five minutes passed, and another five. Then Peyton reached into the little pocket hidden in the folds of her skirt and stopped the recording app on her smartphone.

Lars was down in the art department for the day, so Peyton sat alone in their cubicle trying to look busy. A half hour later, Drew walked past her announcing he was on his way to the cafeteria. As soon as the elevator doors closed, Peyton hurried to the file room. She pulled the phone from her pocket and sent the recording to her e-mail, as well as a copy to her sister Lucy. The message read: "Keep this safe for me." Once that task was completed, she headed to the coat closet for her things.

Mimi looked up from her book when Peyton passed her desk. "What's in the tote bag?"

"A change of clothes," Peyton answered.

Mimi's shoulders slumped. She knew what this meant. She followed Peyton down the hall to the ladies' room, and once she was sure they were the only ones there, she said, "I'm going to miss you."

"I'll miss you, too. I'll call you later and tell you everything, and I'm sending you a little present. You'll get a good laugh. Don't let anyone but Lars hear it."

While Peyton slipped into a pair of jeans and tennis shoes, Mimi acted as her valet, carefully folding her skirt and tucking it into the bag with her heels.

She gave Peyton a hug. "You keep in touch, you hear? I want to know how you're doing. Promise me."

"I promise."

Peyton hated good-byes. She had become close to Mimi. In the short time she'd been in Dalton, the dear woman had become a very good friend.

"Tell Lars I'll call him," Peyton said as she rushed out the door.

She didn't bother to go to HR to resign

and get a paycheck because she knew they would insist that she sign a release, and she wasn't about to do that. She took the stairs to the garage, and while her car was warming up, she sent the recording to Mimi.

Her anxiety didn't lessen until she was on the highway. It was beginning to snow again, and the visibility was diminishing. The weatherman was calling for blizzard conditions. She almost laughed. Why not? she thought. She had come to Dalton in a blizzard, and she was leaving in a blizzard. It seemed fitting. The impending storm was not going to stop her. No matter what, she was getting away from Dalton. A few miles out of town the tension eased from her shoulders, and her stomach stopped hurting. The farther she drove, the happier she became.

FOUR

Mimi was thrilled with Peyton's gift. She held the phone tightly against her ear so that no one else could hear, and she burst into laughter several times while she listened to the recording. Lars heard the sounds coming from Mimi's desk and came around the corner to see what she found so amusing. She had to play the recording for him, of course. Drew had gone to lunch, so Mimi took Lars into Drew's office and shut the door for privacy, and since she wanted to hear it again, she played it on speaker. Mimi sat in a chair facing Drew's desk and Lars leaned against the wall. Neither saw or heard Bridget open the door. She stood listening, and as soon as she realized what she was hearing, she whirled around and ran lickety-split to the cafeteria to tell. She would do anything to get Drew to pay attention to her, even if it meant losing Mimi's friendship.

Drew didn't take the news well. He stormed out of the cafeteria and back to his office to find out for himself if what Bridget had told him was true. He'd erased the recording, damn it. Did he hit the wrong button? No, he'd been careful. Or did Peyton have another device? He would find out when he confronted her.

Lars had gone back downstairs, and Mimi was all alone. She jumped when the door slammed against the wall and was just turning around when Drew grabbed her arm.

"Is there a recording? Bridget told me Peyton recorded a private conversation. Did she?"

Mimi pulled away. "Yes, she did. Would you like to hear it?"

He grabbed the phone from her desk and scrolled to find the message. He listened for only a few seconds before deleting the entire thing.

"Where is she?" he demanded. He was so angry his eyes bulged.

"On her way back to Texas."

He roared a blasphemy as he dug into his pocket for his cell phone. The second his wife answered, he started yelling at her, telling her what had happened, and ending with, "Get her back here. I want her back here today!"

He disconnected the call and turned his wrath on Mimi. "Who else has heard it?"

Realizing that Bridget hadn't told him about Lars, she answered, "No one."

Drew stormed into his office, slammed the door, and called his wife again. Because he was still shouting, Mimi heard every word.

"Get her back here and make her sign a confidentiality agreement. I don't care how you do it. I don't want that recording going anywhere. And get into your father's computer to make sure she didn't send the recording to him. We're toast if he hears it." Silence, and then he shouted, "No, I don't want to talk about what's on it."

Mimi decided now was a good time to go to lunch. She would eat her peanut butter sandwich in her car and call Peyton to warn her. She knew she was on the highway by now. Mimi disapproved of talking on the phone while driving, but this was an emergency. Peyton needed to be warned.

She trudged through the snow to get to her car because her parking spot was on the roof — another incentive from Drew and her ex to get her to quit. She sat freezing while she waited for the heater to come on. Her teeth were chattering as she dialed Peyton's cell phone.

On the third ring, Peyton answered, and before she could finish saying hello, Mimi spoke. "They know," she blurted. "Drew and Eileen know you recorded the conversation. Drew told Eileen to get you back here. I think she'll send Parsons after you. Be on the lookout."

"Who is Parsons?"

"Rick Parsons is the guy that does all their dirty work, and trust me, he's bad news. They want you to come back and sign a release of some kind."

Peyton tried to remain calm. "They were bound to find out sooner or later," she replied. "Later would have been better. How did they find out so fast?"

"I'm so sorry, Peyton. I was playing the recording for Lars and I didn't think anyone was around to hear it, but Bridget evidently did, and she ran to tell Drew. Did you hear me say that Parsons might be coming after you?"

"I heard you. I can't do anything about it now. I'm in the middle of a snowstorm, and all I can concentrate on is staying on the road."

"Are you close to Minneapolis? You could hide there for a while."

"Yes, I'll do that. Mimi, I thought I had time to figure out a way to get it to Randolph Swift, but now that Drew and Eileen know about it, maybe I'll just stick it on the Internet. Everyone will see what kind of man Drew is, and I'll be done with it."

"Oh dear God, don't do that," Mimi warned. "Once you put it out there, you lose all control and any leverage you'd have. You never know what some sick person might do with it. There was a case just last year in a town about fifty miles east of here. A mother was fed up with her son being bullied at school, so she recorded the bully going after her kid and put it on the Internet thinking that would put an end to it. What happened instead was that she was made out to be the villain, going after this poor innocent kid. She was even accused of doctoring the recording. And to make matters worse the bully's family went after the mom and sued her. As I recall, they ended up settling out of court, but that was after months of trying to prove the truth and thousands of dollars in legal fees. It was a real mess. Trust me. If Drew can turn this around on you, he will. He'll say you manufactured the recording or he'll make a joke, and before you know it, it will blow over and you won't have accomplished a thing." Peyton's silence told Mimi she was becoming disheartened by what she was hearing.

"I know it's tempting and you want to expose Drew, but you don't want this to backfire on you."

"You're right," Peyton admitted.

"Besides," Mimi continued, "Randolph Swift is a decent man who spent a lifetime building his company, and he doesn't deserve to have it destroyed because of his pervert son-in-law. If the horrible things that were being said about his wife went out for public ridicule, it would crush him."

"Okay, I'll hold on to it." She looked in the rearview mirror. There wasn't a car in sight. "What kind of car does this Parsons drive?"

"It's a new pickup, a really big one. I don't know the make or model. The color's white," she added, "which won't help much in the snow, will it? You won't see him coming. You've never met Parsons, have you?"

"No."

"He's average-looking, I suppose. Dark brown hair, squinty eyes. He wears really ugly suits and ties."

"Okay, then. I'll be on the lookout for a white pickup, and if the driver has bad taste, I'll know it's Parsons."

"Don't be cavalier about this. He's dangerous. I want you to be careful, and please, call me when you stop for the night."

Peyton thought Mimi was overreacting, but she promised she'd be on guard. She wasn't worried about anyone catching up with her. She had a good forty-five-minute head start, she estimated. How far would someone chase her in a snowstorm before giving up? And what would he do if he caught up with her? Honk until she pulled over? No, she wasn't worried. Besides, her little Camry got good mileage, and she bet a huge pickup didn't. The big ones had bigger tanks, but they were gas-guzzlers. She had a full tank and could go for a long time before having to stop.

A semi pulled onto the highway in front of her. She stayed behind him, using his taillights as her beacon. The snow decreased, but the wind picked up, howling and whining. The eerie noise reminded her of a ghost movie and the sound that came before the terror.

Her sister Lucy called a few minutes later. Peyton put her phone on speaker and laid it on her lap so she could keep both hands on the wheel.

Lucy's greeting said it all. "Oh my God," she shouted.

"I'm guessing you listened to the recording."

"Oh, I listened, all right. I couldn't believe

what I was hearing. He threatened to rape you. At first, I thought it was a joke. Then I realized he was serious. That creep. You're getting a lawyer and going after him, right?"

Before she could answer, Lucy made the decision for her. Peyton's older sister was a problem solver. She felt she knew what was best for everyone. Sometimes that worked out, and sometimes it didn't. "Of course you are. You're going to smash him. You quit, didn't you? After you reported him to Human Resources, did you —"

Peyton interrupted. "It's a long story, and I'll tell you everything later."

"The way he sounded, so arrogantly sure of himself — you have to get away from him. Just get in your car and come home."

"I'm on my way home now. Listen, please don't tell Mom or Dad. I don't want to deal with them just yet. May I stay with you until I figure out what to do?"

"Yes, of course."

Peyton smiled. Lucy was so dependable. Even when she was bossing everyone around, you could count on her.

"I've got to start job hunting again, don't I? This is all so demoralizing."

"You didn't do anything wrong. Remember that."

"Let's not talk about this anymore. Anything going on there?"

"Tristan MacBain is getting married. Did you know that already? Your invitation has been here for three weeks now. I kept meaning to tell you about it," she added.

Hotshot's brother was getting married. Peyton remembered Tristan. He'd always been such a serious boy. She wondered if he still was.

"The wedding's here in Brentwood at Saint Michael's. That's something to look forward to, isn't it?"

"Weddings remind Mom that she has three daughters she hasn't married off yet."

Lucy laughed. "She's a throwback to the fifties, isn't she?"

The semi was slowing for an exit, and her beacon would soon be gone. Should she follow him and find a spot to wait out the storm? The snow was coming down hard again.

"What's that noise?" Lucy asked. "That whistling sound."

"The wind," Peyton answered. "It's rocking the car. I've got to go," she said, ending the call and dropping her phone into the console.

She didn't hear the honking until he was almost on top of her. The driver was flashing his lights. Was it Parsons? Her back window was so fogged up she couldn't see the color of the vehicle.

Whoever was driving was a maniac. When she didn't immediately pull over, he gunned his engine and came up beside her, all the while continuing to honk and flash his lights. He nearly veered into her front bumper, but she kept right on driving. Obviously unhappy with her response to his demands, he zoomed ahead, cut over into her lane, and began to tap his brakes. He was trying to force her to stop, and had there been any other cars on the road, there would have been a collision. She should have been frightened, but she was too furious to feel any other emotion. She moved into the other lane and continued on.

He slowed down, let her pass, and got behind her. She thought he might ram her from behind and braced herself. The wind gusts were howling and making it difficult for her to keep the car steady. He stopped honking and slowed even more.

Peyton reached into her console to get her phone to call for help. How long would it take for someone to find her? If she were close to Minneapolis, there would be more cars on the highway, even in horrible conditions like these.

She glanced in her rearview mirror. No

sign of him. Had he given up? His headlights were no longer visible. She laid the phone back down. She needed to concentrate and keep both hands on the wheel. The road curved sharply to the east up ahead. She saw the warning sign and remembered the curve. It was closer to Dalton than to Minneapolis. What did she expect? Going forty miles per hour, it would take forever to get to civilization. She was lamenting that fact when she saw headlights again behind her, getting closer and closer. He hadn't given up after all.

The wind was howling again. She heard a noise that sounded like metal hitting metal. The car skidded. Had he hit her?

She was so angry she wanted to scream. And then she did. Certain he was going to hit her again as she was going into the curve, she hit the brakes. Before she could do anything about it, she was spinning out of control and flying toward his car head on. To get out of her path, he swerved, lost control, and flew through a barbed-wire fence into the field beyond.

God was merciful to her again. She didn't know how it happened, but she stopped on the right side of the road. She pulled over and, shaking from head to toe, rolled down the window. She could see the wheels on the pickup truck spinning and hear his motor gunning. He was good and stuck and wasn't going anywhere. Was he hurt? She had her answer a second later. She watched him climb out of the truck and pound his fist on the hood. She was too far away to see his face. His vehicle had landed in a gigantic pillow of snow. She'd let him call for a tow.

Resisting the urge to honk and wave, she pulled onto the highway again and never looked back.

FIVE

Peyton was back at square one.

Now that she was in Texas again, she had time to think. She knew she would have to begin looking for another job right away, but she also would have to decide what she was going to do about Drew and Eileen. She couldn't just go about her business and forget them. She had been lucky to get away from them and their lackey, Parsons, without any harm, but if she didn't do something, the next person might not be so fortunate. She realized she didn't have enough evidence to go to the police; however, she did believe she had enough to stop the Albertsons from endangering someone else.

What she needed was legal advice, but that required money. Attorneys wanted to be paid for their services, and she was flat broke. The trip to Dalton had been expensive and had eaten up all of her reserves.

She was also worried about Mimi. Her friend was in a no-win situation, trapped in a job she hated, working for a boss she abhorred. She was the only person at the company Peyton had sent the recording to, so that immediately put her in danger. Peyton knew what Drew was capable of and decided to check on her.

She was relieved when she heard Mimi's voice on the phone.

"Are you all right?" Peyton asked. "I was worried that Drew might do something to you after he found out that you had the recording."

"I'm fine," Mimi assured her. "Drew didn't say another word to me about it. I think he was afraid of what I might do with the information. In fact, Drew hasn't talked to anyone. The day after you left, he and Eileen dragged her father off to Europe, obviously shielding him from the bad news. They talked him into taking his beloved wife's ashes to Naples, the city she so loved because they were married there. I heard from Bridget — who, by the way, thinks it is all so touching and romantic — that they plan to take Randolph to all the places in Europe he and his wife had visited. God only knows when they'll be back. I imagine the longer they go without hearing from the legal department, the more time Eileen will have to get on her father's good side again, and she'll be able to discredit you if he ever hears the recording."

According to Mimi, the magazine was running just fine without them. It was a shame, she said, that Erik Swift wasn't ready to take over the helm. "He's the only normal one in the whole bunch," she insisted. "Have you decided yet what you're going to do with the recording?"

"Not yet," Peyton answered. "I need some legal advice."

"Whatever you do, be careful," Mimi warned.

"I will," Peyton promised.

Six

Finn MacBain was standing outside the entrance to Saint Michael's Catholic Church waiting for his brothers to arrive. He walked to the side of the building so that he wouldn't have to greet all the guests pouring into the church. More than three hundred people had been invited. The bride's father was a four-star general; the groom was an officer in the Navy JAG Corps; and the majority of guests were military.

Time was slipping away and Tristan was going to miss his own wedding if he didn't get moving. Finn adjusted the collar of his tux and rebuttoned his jacket to make sure his gun and badge were hidden from view. He hadn't intended to wear his weapon to his brother's wedding, but it wasn't his choice. Although the general had his own security detail, Finn's superior in the FBI, Special Agent Corben Henderson, suggested rather strongly that Finn carry his weapon. Henderson felt there should be an FBI presence just in case of trouble, which was why Finn's new partner, Ronan Conrad, was also attending and was also armed. Henderson claimed he didn't care how many military officers were there to protect the general, it would be up to the FBI to save the day.

Finn liked being prepared for just about anything, and he had been trained to be cautious to a fault. Though he was relaxed, he still watched every man and woman who got out of a car and walked up the brick path. He was always looking for trouble. He'd learned to be watchful when he started at the Bureau, and he'd been an agent long enough now that the habit had become second nature to him.

Ronan had volunteered to go to the MacBain house to find out what was taking so long. The family home was only five blocks from the church, and it wouldn't take him any time at all to get there.

Finn's cell phone rang.

"We have a little problem," Ronan began.

"What is it?"

"He's doing the math." Ronan had a thick Boston accent, but Finn heard the amusement in his tone.

"He's what?"

"Doing the math. That's what he keeps telling Beck and me. Counting the reasons he isn't good enough for her. He's not being real rational," he added in a whisper.

Finn thought that, if anyone could get through to Tristan, his twin brother could. "What's Beck doing?"

"Eating a sub and watching Tristan pace. He looks like he's gonna pass out. No color at all in his face."

"Beck or Tristan?"

"Tristan," he answered, clearly exasperated. "The groom, for God's sake. Why would Beck pass out?"

The conversation was getting away from him. "The wedding's supposed to start in twenty minutes."

"Yeah, I know," Ronan said. "But he's still doing the math."

"Nerves, huh?"

"That's about right."

"Put him on the phone."

Tristan must have paced his way over to Ronan because he answered a scant second later.

"Finn, I'm just not sure I'm right for her. She deserves —"

"Tristan," he interrupted. "Does Brooke love you?"

"Yes, she does, but —"

"Do you love her?"

"Of course I do. It's just that —"

"Do you trust her?"

"What kind of question is that? Yes, I trust her . . . with my life . . . but I —"

"Put Ronan back on the phone."

"Yes?" Ronan said.

"You're gonna have to knock him out and toss him in the car. Clip his jaw . . . you know how . . . but stay away from his nose. You don't want to get blood all over his dress whites. And don't let him see it coming. He's got a mean right hook."

Ronan wasn't sure if Finn was serious or not. "You really want me to slug him?" he asked in a whisper.

"Do you know how many people are waiting in the church, including a frickin' four-star general? Do whatever it takes to get him here, and tell Beck to put the damn sandwich down and help you."

"Yeah, okay."

Finn ended the call and put the phone back in his pocket. He began to laugh. Tristan was doing the math. How like his brother with his overly analytical mind. If left on his own, he'd figure it all out, but it would probably take him a couple of days to come around to the realization that he was good enough for his bride. The guests weren't going to wait that long, though.

Finn was sure that Beck, with his warped sense of humor, probably helped get Tristan all worked up. The twins were so much alike and yet so different. Beck was the action guy, and Tristan was the thinker. Like his brother, Beck was in the Navy, but while Tristan had chosen to enlist in the JAG Corps after attending law school, Beck had taken the more direct route through Annapolis and was now with the SEALs. Finn knew that Beck had seen terrible things while on active duty, and he was glad that he had been able to retain his sense of humor. He hadn't become nearly as jaded or as cynical as Finn.

Less than five minutes later, with plenty of time to spare, the groom arrived. He was rubbing his jaw and frowning at Ronan as he stepped out of the car. Then he saw Finn and, with revenge in his eyes, started toward him, but Beck grabbed his arm and pulled him into the sacristy entrance.

Ronan walked up the hill from the parking lot to where Finn waited.

"You really hit him?" Finn asked.

"Yes, I hit him. That's what you told me to do."

"Yeah, I did, but I didn't think you'd do it."

While Finn was having a good laugh, Ronan explained, "Tristan had gone beyond panic, and he wasn't making a lot of sense. Beck kept trying to reason with him, but it wasn't helping. He was just getting him more worked up."

"So you coldcocked him?"

"No," he said. "I swear I hit him hard, and he should have gone right down. Beck was behind him, and I figured he'd catch him. Tristan took the blow and just . . . flinched. Yeah, he flinched," he said, nodding. "Then he looked at me like he thought I'd lost my mind. I know how to put someone down," he added. "You've seen me do it, right?" He sounded bewildered.

Finn nodded. "Yes, I've seen you." He remembered the crazed football player high on PCP. He would have ripped Finn from limb to limb if Ronan hadn't come up behind him and knocked him out. He'd saved Finn's ass that day. A couple of days later, Finn returned the favor.

"Maybe your heart wasn't in it. Maybe you really didn't want to knock Tristan out."

"Yeah, maybe."

"So how did you get him here?"

"I must have jarred something loose in his

head when I hit him because all of a sudden he didn't want to do any more math. He just wanted to get to the church to punch you. Oh, wait . . . did I mention I blamed it all on you?"

"Hey, you got him here. That's all that counts."

"I think I'll go on inside," Ronan said. "I found a great spot where I can watch both the entrance and the side door during the wedding. Some of the general's soldiers are there now. I'll push a couple of them out of my way and take over. I know we don't expect trouble, but better to be prepared. I'll see you after."

Finn wasn't ready to go inside yet. Beck would come and get him when it was time. It was warm today. The sun was shining, and it was at least seventy degrees, he guessed, maybe seventy-five. He and Ronan had spent a week working in Chicago where it had been around ten degrees every single day with crazy below-zero wind chills. The heat felt good on his face. He liked being outside, cold or hot, and he liked being home, too. It had been such a long time.

His cell phone rang, reminding him that he needed to turn it off before the ceremony. He saw who was calling and felt a wave of exhaustion. On-again off-again Danielle was trying to reconnect with him. He wasn't about to get into that drama. He'd had enough, and he simply didn't have the stamina for any more of her games. He declined the call and turned off the phone. He should go in, he decided, and was about to do just that when he saw her. The vision in blue. He watched her cross the parking lot and start up the walkway, her high heels clicking against the brick. He noticed her body first, of course. It was damn near perfect. The short, fitted dress showed off her curves and her long, gorgeous legs. Her stride was every bit as sexy as her body. The way she moved was sensual and seductive. She was absolutely beautiful. Her long dark hair, the color of midnight, fell in soft curls just below her slender shoulders.

She must have felt him watching her, for she suddenly turned and looked up the hill. When she saw him, she stepped off the path and started walking toward him. He wanted to swallow, but he couldn't seem to remember how. He had never reacted to any woman this fiercely, this quickly. What had happened to his self-control? He excused his bizarre behavior by reasoning that she was no ordinary woman. He didn't want to stare, but the closer she came, the better she looked. Beneath her thick dark eyelashes were the most beautiful, crystalline blue eyes he had ever seen, and her rosy lips were full and inviting.

She stepped directly in front of him and gave him a heart-stopping smile. The dimple in her cheek was sexy as hell. So was her scent, which was light and feminine.

Her eyes sparkled with laughter when she stretched up, kissed him on his cheek, and said, "Hello, Hotshot."

He was speechless. Peyton Lockhart? He couldn't believe it. She was all grown-up. She had gone from a skinny little girl to this beautiful woman with a devastating smile. When did this happen? The transformation seemed to have taken place overnight, but then Finn realized he hadn't been around while she was growing up. He'd gone to California to do his undergraduate work at Stanford and had stayed there for law school. During that time his parents had downsized to a smaller, more energy-efficient home about a mile from their old house in Brentwood. Whenever Finn was home on break, he never had enough time to go back to the old neighborhood.

Finn overcame his surprise enough to speak. "Don't call me Hotshot."

"You didn't know who I was, did you,

Finn?" she asked, saying his name to placate him.

"I didn't have a clue," he admitted. He was still trying to get past his initial reaction and stop acting as though he had never seen a beautiful woman before. This was Peyton, the little girl who would sit on the front steps and wait for him to come home from high school so she could tell him about her day. She was a nuisance back then, and now a temptress.

"Are your sisters here? I won't recognize them, either, will I?"

"Yes, they're here already. I'm running late."

Beck whistled from the doorway to get Finn's attention.

"Aren't you in the wedding?" she asked.

He nodded. "Yeah, I should go in. It's good to see you again."

Peyton didn't want to miss the bride walking down the aisle. "It's good to see you, too."

It had suddenly become awkward, and she didn't understand why. He wasn't leaving. Beck whistled again, but Finn didn't move.

"Are you going to the reception?" he asked.

"No, I'm afraid I can't."

"Maybe I'll see you after the wedding, then."

Peyton continued on, but when she glanced back, she thought it strange that Finn was still standing in the same spot.

The church was packed. She was able to squeeze into the back row just in time to watch Beck and Tristan escort their mother down the aisle. Finn walked behind with his father.

The MacBains were all good-looking men, but Peyton thought there was a little something extra with Finn. Charisma, she decided. He was definitely charismatic. The camera sure loved him. The last time she'd seen him being interviewed on television, which was quite a while ago, she thought he looked so handsome and sophisticated. There was a weariness about him now, though. She didn't know what kind of work he did for the FBI, but she had the feeling it was taking its toll.

The priest walked up to the altar, signaling for the ceremony to commence. It was a perfect wedding without a single misstep. Even Father John, who was known to ramble on and on during his sermons, kept his remarks short and interesting. He spoke of love and marriage and the blessings that would come from them. Peyton wondered if true love really did exist anymore. Was there such a thing as happily-ever-after? She hoped so. She didn't want to become a cynic. She saw the way Tristan looked at his bride, and she wanted to believe in love, even though she had never experienced it herself.

She was one of the last to leave the church because she kept running into people she hadn't seen in years. Most of them wanted to know what she was doing now. She answered with half-truths. While she didn't come right out and lie, she made it sound as though she had just returned from France where she had been cooking up a storm. There wasn't any need to go into the details of her employment fiasco.

Finn stood outside with Beck, watching the guests file out of the church. He spotted Peyton as she emerged. She was immediately surrounded by Navy men in white, all vying for her attention.

"Beck, see that woman over there?" Finn asked, nodding to the group. "Do you know who she is?"

"No, but I'm gonna find out. She's gorgeous, isn't she? Have you met her yet?"

"Yes, and so have you. That's Peyton Lockhart."

Beck didn't believe him. "That scrawny

little kid? *That* Peyton Lockhart?"

Finn didn't bother to answer because Beck was already pushing his friends out of his way to get to her. He watched his brother lift her off her feet and hug her, and her smile indicated she didn't mind.

The guests mingled outside the church, waiting to offer their good wishes to the bride and groom, and Finn was smack in the middle of them. Ronan stood off to the side, having a conversation with Father John. Finn joined him, and while they listened to the priest, they watched the crowd.

By the time Peyton congratulated the happy couple, it was getting late. She noticed what time it was and headed toward her car. The reception wouldn't begin until seven, and she was going to miss the celebration because she had to report to work. She had taken a temporary job as a sous-chef at Harlow's restaurant. This definitely was not her dream job, but she hated being poor, and it was a way to make ends meet while she looked for something else. The owner had given her enough time off to attend the wedding, but only after she promised to be back for the Saturday dinner crowd. She had promised to be there by six.

She couldn't find her sisters, but she saw

her parents talking to some friends near the church steps. She waved to them as she made her way through the crowd.

Finn had walked down to the parking lot to get away from the noise. He was listening to phone messages and turned just as Peyton was approaching. He offered to walk her to her car.

"How come you aren't coming to the reception?" he asked.

"I have to work," she answered. She dug the keys out of her little clutch and hit the unlock button. Standing beside her car, she said, "It really was good to see you."

"I'm sorry we didn't get to —" He stopped. "When did you get this car?" he asked, staring past her and frowning.

"About a year ago. Why?"

Finn moved closer and squatted down behind the rear bumper. "These are bullet holes."

"Yes, they are," she agreed. She didn't seem the least fazed. "I've got to get going or I'll be late for work."

He wasn't about to let her leave. "They haven't been here long."

"The bullet holes?"

"Yes, the bullet holes," he said.

"It happened a while ago." Peyton wasn't going to explain the Dalton nightmare now.

It would take hours. She remembered how shocked she'd been when she first noticed the holes below her bumper. If she hadn't dropped her keys behind the car, she probably never would have seen them, and when she realized they were from bullets, she nearly had heart failure.

"Look at the paint around the holes. It wasn't that long ago. Do you know when it happened? You do, don't you? Did you park it and when you came back . . . you weren't in the car, were you? One of the holes is damned close to the gas tank. Tell me you weren't in the car."

He was asking questions so rapidly he wasn't giving her time to answer.

"Yes, I was in the car. I was on the highway when it happened. He wanted me to stop. I didn't know he shot at me until I was back in Texas. The holes are so low, I didn't see them until a few days later. In fact, you're the only other person who's noticed them."

"You couldn't hear gunshots?" His voice was brisk, no nonsense. He was all FBI now.

Her hand went to her hip. "I was in the middle of a blizzard at the time. All I could hear was the howling wind."

"Where exactly were you?"

"Northwest of Minneapolis. Finn, I've got to leave."

She wasn't going anywhere until she gave him a few more details.

"Who did you report it to?"

Peyton knew he wasn't going to like her answer. "I didn't report it."

"Because you didn't realize he was shooting at you."

"Exactly."

"But when you did see the bullet holes —"

She cut him off. "I didn't report it."

"Why the hell not?" Frustration made his voice sharp. "He could be out there now trolling for his next victim, and maybe this time he'll hit the gas tank or, worse, the driver."

She shook her head. "No, he won't."

"Did you get the make or model?"

"I have to leave."

"No, you have to answer me."

"You know what, Finn. You're just as bossy and stubborn as you were when I was a little girl."

"And you're just as aggravating. Now answer me."

She gave in. "It was a big white truck, and I know for a fact that he isn't out on the highway looking for other victims." *Unless someone gets on Drew Albertson's bad side,* she silently added. She took a step closer.

"And I'm not a victim. I took control of the situation and forced him to stop chasing me."

"How?" he asked, trying to concentrate on what she was saying and not how sexy she was or how good she smelled.

"I sent him into a field. Actually, I sent him through a fence into a field."

"How did you do that?"

"Some . . . intricate driving moves." Slamming on the brakes and going into a spin that she was helpless to control could be considered an intricate move, couldn't it?

"Intricate driving moves, huh?" he repeated, smiling.

"Yes," she said. "He didn't get hurt," she hastened to add. "His car sank into the snow, and he was stuck. I pulled over to make sure he didn't need an ambulance. I watched him get out and start pounding his fists on the truck."

"You saw the shooter?"

Uh-oh. Too late, she realized she shouldn't have mentioned that fact because now he was going to ask her another hundred questions. She decided to stop him before he got started.

"I didn't get a close look at him, but I've got a good idea who he is."

He seemed to take the news in stride.

"Okay. Who is he?"

"His name is Rick Parsons, and he works for the company that hired me."

He nodded calmly, but she noticed his jaw was clenched. "Since you never reported the incident to the police, he wasn't arrested."

"That's right."

"Why was he chasing you?"

"Because I left," she said, evading the details. "They really hate it when you leave the company" — she shrugged — "so they shoot at you."

Peyton thought he would think her answer funny, but apparently he wasn't amused. She was sure he would have kept her there with his questions for the rest of the evening, or until he had the entire story, if a groomsman hadn't appeared and told him he had to return to the church for photos.

Finn answered that he would be right there, then opened the car door for Peyton. Before he started back up the hill toward the church, he turned to Peyton and said, "We aren't finished with this."

SEVEN

Peyton dragged herself out of bed early Sunday morning, dutifully went to Mass, then changed into her workout clothes and ran four miles. She stopped for a convenience store Danish on her way back. There were power bars and granola cereal at home, and Lucy would try to push both on her. Her older sister had recently gotten into calorie counting and being responsible about the food she ate. She would be horrified to know that Peyton, with all of her gourmet training, actually liked junk food. Peyton didn't live on it, but occasionally a bag of salty chips hit the spot. So did Taco Bell.

She loved her sisters, but both of them had their quirks. Maybe it was all part of being the oldest that Lucy thought she knew what was best for everyone. Her life would be so much happier if only Peyton and Ivy would do what she told them to do. That was never going to happen, of course, and after several weeks of living in such close quarters and being "suggested" to death — Lucy's way of giving orders — Peyton was ready to pull her hair out.

Despite being bossy, Lucy was a kind and loving sister who would do anything for her and Ivy. She couldn't commit the crime, but she'd help bury the body. She was generous to a fault, refusing to take any money to help with the rent or groceries, even though she was struggling financially. Her education was in interior design, and she'd taken a job in a furniture store to support herself until a career opportunity came along. Peyton was going to help pay this month's rent as soon as she got her paycheck, which meant getting into a major argument. Her sister would carry on something fierce, but Peyton was determined to get her way and do her share until she could find a decent job and move into her own place. She was pretty sure her own quirks were driving Lucy crazy, too.

All three sisters knew that, in desperate times, they could go home to their parents. They would always be welcomed. Their father would do anything in the world for his girls, and so would their mother. It wouldn't be a peaceful homecoming, though, for the sisters would be constantly subjected to talks about finding the right man and settling down. Their mother simply couldn't help herself. In this day and age their mother's archaic views were almost embarrassing.

Ivy was the least bothered by their mother's nagging. The youngest sister could get along with just about anyone. She loved to have a good time. She had been quite the party girl until her grades began to slip and her father laid down the law. Then she got serious about her future. Of the three she was the most uncomplicated and the sweetest. She had an abundance of patience. Peyton wondered if she would change once she was out of college and in the real world.

When Peyton came through the back door from her run, Lucy was sitting at the kitchen table drinking coffee. She was dressed but still looked half asleep. Her light brown hair hung over her eyes.

"How much did you have to drink last night?" Peyton asked.

Lucy pushed her hair away from her face before answering. "Not much at all. I danced a lot, though. Those Navy guys are crazy." She opened the carton that was sitting on the table and poured some milk into her coffee. "Did you know Beck is a Navy

SEAL?"

Peyton leaned against the kitchen sink and drank a glass of tepid water. "Yes, I did know."

"He's wild," she said. "Works hard, plays hard, I guess. Tristan looked happy," she added. "I talked to Brooke. She seems nice."

"What about Finn?" Peyton asked. She turned on the faucet and filled her glass again. "Did you talk to him?"

"He came over to the table to say hi," she said. "God, he's good-looking. And sexy," she added. "The women wouldn't leave him alone."

Peyton felt a burst of irritation and thought her reaction didn't make any sense at all. Why did she care who was with him? She hadn't seen the man in years. "I spoke to Finn before the wedding outside the church. He didn't recognize me."

"When you were little, you used to think he belonged to you and only you. Do you remember?"

She smiled. "I do remember. Did Ivy have a good time? I wish I could have been there."

"Ivy always has a good time. She danced all night. I think Beck was kind of sweet on her. He was by her side a lot. I was supposed to drive her to the airport —"

"She can't stay an extra day?"

"She's student teaching, remember? She has to get back."

"I haven't seen her at all this weekend. I'll take her to the airport."

Lucy shook her head. "I was trying to tell you that Uncle Len is taking her. He's —"

"Uncle Len's in town?"

"Peyton, will you stop interrupting me?"

"Sorry."

"He wants to talk to all of us together —" she began, and when Peyton started to ask another question, Lucy raised her hand. "He and Ivy will be here in about an hour. And, no, he wouldn't say what he wanted to talk about. He sounded serious, though. You should have breakfast. Do you want some granola?"

"Later," she said to placate her sister.

Peyton took a shower, washed her hair, and after she blew it dry, put on a pair of leggings and a long cotton sweater. All the while she was getting dressed, she worried about her uncle. Was it bad news? Was he ill? Whatever he wanted to tell them had to be serious because he asked all of them to hear it together. Was he dying? Please, God, don't let him die. He was such a good man, and she needed him in her life.

She had to admit she might be overreacting. When Ivy and her uncle finally arrived, Peyton took a good long look at him. He appeared to be as fit as ever. His face was tanned from being in the sun. Len was in his early sixties but looked much younger, even though his hair was more silver than brown.

She hugged him, kissed his cheek, and told him how happy she was to see him. When she turned to Ivy to say hello, she laughed. Her sister looked exhausted. She wore a faded college sweatshirt over her gray sweatpants, and her hair was pulled back into a haphazard ponytail. With no makeup her complexion looked pale.

"I hear you had fun last night."

"Too much fun," Ivy admitted.

Len didn't waste time. He asked the girls to sit on the sofa, and he pulled a chair up to the coffee table to face them.

"I know you're all wondering why I want to talk to you," he began.

"Are you okay?" Peyton asked.

"Yes, I'm fine," he answered with a wave of his hand to eliminate any worries about his health. "I'm making some changes," he continued, "and I have a proposition for you."

Lucy looked at him skeptically. "What sort of proposition?"

"King's Landing and Bishop's Cove are no longer making a profit. It's the economy," he explained. "People are more frugal and don't have the extra money for resorts. And both properties have been a bit neglected."

"You're selling both properties?" Ivy asked.

"I'd prefer not to, but that's up to you," he said, smiling.

"How is it up to us?" Lucy asked.

"I'll give Bishop's Cove to the three of you to run for one year. If, at the end of that period, the resort shows a twenty percent profit, then it's all yours to keep or to sell."

The sisters looked dumbfounded. Len laughed in response. "I've made you speechless, haven't I?"

"Uncle Len, Bishop's Cove is worth millions," Lucy reminded.

"Yes," he agreed. "And if you three don't want to work together and run the resort, I'll sell it now. I'd make a good profit," he added, "but I'd rather see the property stay in the family. If you do decide to take it on and you succeed, you'll be millionaires. But I'll warn you, it's going to take a lot of hard work to turn it around."

"What happens if we don't turn it

around?" Peyton asked.

"Then I'll get rid of it," he answered. "And you can move on with your lives."

He looked at their faces and laughed again. "I've run this by your father, and he looked as shocked as you three do." He continued, "There is what I would call a consolation prize."

"A prize for what?"

"Losing Bishop's Cove. If you decide against taking me up on my offer and I sell it now, I'll give each of you a gift of five hundred thousand dollars."

Peyton shook her head. "No, you shouldn't give us your money."

"Why not?" he asked. "I have plenty, and I know you can use it. Lucy, you could open your design studio, and Peyton, you could buy a small restaurant if that's what you want." Turning to Ivy, he said, "You could pay off your student loans and have enough left over to supplement your pitiful teaching salary."

"Uncle, why are you doing this now?" Peyton asked.

"I buy and I sell. You know that. I don't hold on to things if they aren't showing a profit. I want to concentrate on other assets. I guess you could say I'm trying to simplify my life."

"Are you selling King's Landing?"

"I made the same proposition to your cousin. I told Debi that, if she ran that resort for a year and showed a profit, it would be hers. I also gave her the option of taking the five hundred thousand now. Can you guess what she decided?"

"She took the money, didn't she?" Peyton said, and both Lucy and Ivy nodded their agreement.

"That's a no-brainer," Ivy said.

"Yes, she took the money," Len said. "Debi talked it over with her husband and decided on the cash. She wasn't willing to make the effort even though she could end up with much more money at the end if she took the resort." He stood. "I'll let you girls talk it over while I make a fresh pot of coffee."

"I'll do it," Lucy offered.

"No, let me. I like the way I make it, and you three can talk about what you're going to do."

He turned the corner to the kitchen and Ivy called out, "Uncle, I'm committed to student teaching right now, and I won't be finished with school until June. How could I do this?"

He answered, "Your sisters can start the project and you can join them just as soon as you graduate."

"What happens if after . . . oh, say, six months . . . we decide we can't do it?" Peyton asked.

"I'll sell the resort. I'll compensate you for your time, but I want you to have some skin in the game. Your choice is simple. Do you want to take the five hundred thousand now, or do you want to be adventurous and create something that could be worth so much more?"

While their uncle was busy in the kitchen making coffee, the sisters whispered among themselves. Ivy was concerned that none of them would know what they were doing. Peyton agreed but argued they could learn and bring in help if they needed. She was so excited about all the possibilities, she could barely hold a thought. Lucy's mind raced with design ideas for each of the bungalows. "I could leave right away," she said. "The lease on my apartment is up in two weeks. Peyton, when do you finish your job?"

"I've got one more week before the chef I'm helping out comes back," she said.

Their uncle returned to the living room carrying a tray with four cups. He handed one to each of the girls. "There's one other detail you should know," he said. "Since

Bishop's Cove needs renovation, I'll fund the work. You won't have to worry about paying for any of that."

He could see that his nieces' heads were spinning as they bombarded him with questions. After he answered the last one, he stood to go. "I'll let you think about it, but I'll need your answer in a couple of days."

After he and Ivy left a short time later, Peyton and Lucy remained on the sofa talking.

"Think what this could mean," Lucy said. "We could build something wonderful and we wouldn't have to worry about money anymore. I could use my design training, and you could create the restaurant you always wanted."

The more Peyton thought about it, the more excited she became. Uncle Len was giving them the opportunity of a lifetime. How could they refuse? This offer would allow her to make all of her dreams come true.

One other benefit popped into her head, too. If they left right away, her salary wouldn't have to go to next month's rent. She could use it for something else. And she knew exactly what that something else would be. She would get a lawyer.

When Ivy returned to the apartment an

hour later, Peyton and Lucy were still talking about their uncle's offer.

Knowing they didn't have much time to discuss Len's proposition before giving him an answer, the three sisters immediately began debating. It seemed obvious to Peyton that they would all agree to run Bishop's Cove. They loved the resort, though she was more emotionally tied to it than Lucy and Ivy.

She wanted to accept it, yet she couldn't help but voice her reservations. "We don't have any idea how much work it will take to turn it around. Can we work together for a year and not drive one another crazy? And who makes all the decisions? Do we all vote? Is it majority rules? Two could always side against one. That's not good."

"Do you realize what each of us could do with half a million dollars?" Ivy asked. "To give that much money up for the possibility of making a profit running a resort when none of us has any experience . . . that's crazy."

"Are you saying you want to take the money?" Lucy asked.

"I'm saying we should consider what we're giving up," Ivy argued. "I would like to take the money," she admitted, "but I know you and Peyton want Bishop's Cove."

"We have to decide together," Lucy said. "We all have to agree to take the money or run the resort."

"And if we don't show a profit after a year, we lose it and the money," Ivy reminded. "So it's probably best if we all took the money. Let's vote."

It was unanimous. They were taking Bishop's Cove.

EIGHT

After the decision was made and Ivy had gone home, Lucy left to run errands and then meet a friend for dinner. Peyton was happy to have the apartment to herself. She took out a pad and a pen and began to jot down all the questions she needed to ask an attorney. If she was going to stop Drew and Eileen Albertson, she wanted to do it right.

Once she'd finished her list, she went to the Internet to research legalities. There were a lot of contradictory articles. She took notes on what she learned and then closed the lid on her laptop. Now, all she needed to do was find the right lawyer. A knock on the door interrupted her thoughts and she went to answer it. Finn MacBain was standing on her doorstep, and she nearly burst into laughter when she saw him.

"What's so funny?" he asked.

"You're an attorney!"

"I am," he answered, puzzled by her

peculiar greeting.

"I was just thinking that I needed an attorney, and here you are," she explained cheerfully.

When she saw the perplexed look in his eyes, she realized he had no idea what she was talking about. She opened the door wide for him to enter. She didn't need to ask why he was here. He wanted to hear the story behind the bullet holes in her car.

He was just as handsome in casual clothes as he had been in his tuxedo. He wore jeans and a worn-out T-shirt. His gun and badge were at his side. When he looked directly into her eyes, her heart skipped a beat. He really was something else. Just staring at him made her breathless.

He certainly wasn't feeling the same sensation. He was frowning and all business when he strode inside. "Are you alone?"

"Yes."

He nodded. "Do your sisters know about the bullet holes?"

Ah, so that was why he'd asked if she was alone. He was actually respecting her privacy.

"No, they don't know," she answered. "No one but you noticed them." He towered over her when he stood so close, but he wasn't intimidating. "I'm happy to see you, Finn.

150

Very happy."

Finn didn't respond. For some reason, he couldn't move. Her smile was messing with his concentration. It was the dimple, he thought. And her beautiful eyes . . . and her sexy mouth . . . and her body. My God, did she have a great body. Even in that loose sweater, she looked sexy. He'd been with a lot of beautiful women, but she was different. Her scent drove him wild, aroused him like no other, made him want to take her into his arms. No, he wanted to do a whole lot more than that.

He was standing too close to her, and that was why he was having such an intense reaction, he reasoned. Yeah, right. Ever since he had seen her at the church, he couldn't stop thinking about her.

Peyton picked up her cell phone and went to the sofa and sat with her feet tucked under her. "Have a seat. Please," she said sweetly. "Thank you for helping me."

Finn blocked all the crazy thoughts racing through his mind and followed, sitting at the other end of the sofa, facing her. "I didn't say I would."

"But you will. It's what you do."

He nodded. "Because I'm an agent."

She looked surprised. "No, because you're Finn."

He didn't know what to say to that. "I want to hear the story behind the bullet holes. From start to finish," he insisted. "Then we'll talk about why you need an attorney."

"I didn't break the law."

A hint of a smile softened his expression. "I didn't say you did."

"I'd like to play a recording for you first. Okay? I think you'll enjoy it. It's a conversation between my former employer and me."

"Go ahead. Play it."

Finn listened to the recording without showing a hint of emotion. He rubbed his jaw once, but other than that he didn't move. It was only after it was over that he reacted.

"How is that son of a bitch still walking around?"

"He's protected."

"Not anymore. Did he touch you?" He couldn't hide the anger that was building inside him.

"No."

"Hand me your phone. I want to send the recording to my cell, and I'll put my number in your contacts. If you need me, that's the number to call." The task completed, he sat back and said, "Now tell me what happened."

It didn't take as long as she thought it would to tell the entire story.

"I knew he was a letch, but I didn't realize just how dangerous he was until one night he tried to break into my motel room."

She told him some of the vile things Drew had shouted through the door, about how she would love what he was going to do to her.

"That bastard," Finn muttered. "Why in God's name didn't you call the police?"

Tears came into her eyes. "I should have. I was so scared I hid in the bathroom the rest of the night. I don't think I stopped shaking until morning. It took all I had not to get in the car and drive back to Texas. I wanted to get away from there as soon as possible, but I had come up with this plan to record him . . . I know that was stupid, too," she said. "I just wanted to find a way to stop him from going after other women." She took a breath and said, "I did try to file a complaint with HR, and I was told I hadn't been there long enough."

"Long enough to be sexually harassed?" he asked, shaking his head.

"I was told no one ever complained about Drew and that I should come back in three months if I wanted to complain."

"That's one hell of a company you worked

for," he said. "This isn't my area of expertise. Did you file a complaint with the EEOC?" Thinking she might not know what the letters stood for, he said, "Equal Employment Opportunity Commission."

"No, I haven't filed a formal complaint yet. I still have time to do that, don't I?" He nodded, and she continued, "I wish there was a way to go after the guy who shot at me, but I couldn't identify him."

"Let me worry about him."

"I had hoped that one of his bullets had lodged somewhere in my car, but they went through. I was thinking the bullets would lead back to him."

"I'm going to have a tech go over your car. Bullets can spin out and land in the oddest places."

"How long will you be in Brentwood?" she asked.

"Ronan and I are leaving in the morning, but I'll be back the following afternoon."

"Who's Ronan?"

"Agent Ronan Conrad," he said. "My partner, temporarily anyway. We have a meeting in Dallas, and then he's taking a week to see his girlfriend, Collins."

She stood when he did. She didn't want him to go, but she couldn't think of a reason to get him to stay.

"I'm going to do a little research and talk to an attorney who specializes in harassment cases. Be patient a little longer."

He was heading to the door, and she had the insane urge to throw herself in front of it to keep him from leaving.

"Would you like to stay for dinner? I'll cook for you."

He reached for the doorknob. "I can't tonight."

"Thank you for helping me."

She thought only to kiss his cheek, but he turned suddenly, and she ended up kissing his mouth. It was quickly done, and she should have stepped back, but she didn't. She kissed him again, and this time she lingered.

Finn didn't respond. He just stood there, looking astonished. She was mortified. What had she been thinking? He opened the door, and she thought he was going to leave without saying a word and pretend that the kiss never happened, but he didn't. He shut the door, pulled her into his arms, and kissed her back. And, oh, could he kiss. His mouth was hot as it covered hers. Passion flared as he pulled her tight against him. It was a long, intense kiss that held nothing back, and she never wanted it to end.

He came to his senses before she did, and

he gently pulled her arms away from his shoulders. Then he walked out the door and quietly pulled it closed behind him.

Peyton couldn't catch her breath. Her hands trembled as she pushed her hair back over her shoulder. What had just happened to her? One kiss and her insides turned to mush. She'd been kissed before but never like this. Kissing Finn was different. Why had she done it?

It was crazy, this connection she felt to him. She hadn't seen him in years, only wrote to him once a year on her birthday, and he rarely wrote back. She knew next to nothing about him, where he lived, what he did for the FBI. Her only link to him had been the bits and pieces her mother had passed on to her after talking to his mother. She had heard all about his triumphs; it was difficult not to. He had accomplished the most exceptional things.

She supposed, when she was a little girl, she felt a special bond with him, and in her child's mind he somehow belonged to her. But that was long ago. She doubted Finn knew anything about her life. Why would he? She hadn't done anything exceptional.

The truth stung. She wasn't a child any longer, and she wasn't part of his world.

NINE

The nightmare always began the same way. Finn was sitting at a desk looking at an empty file folder. He closed it, carefully placed it in the center drawer, then stood and slowly put on his suit jacket. The office was crowded with agents, and he could see them talking, but he couldn't hear anything, not a word or a sound.

He walked through a long, narrow tunnel to the interrogation room and adjusted his tie before he opened the door and stepped inside. Everything was gunmetal gray: the walls, the ceiling, the floor. He could smell death in the room.

His trainer and assigned partner, Special Agent John Caulfield, was sitting at a square metal desk, facing the suspect. His back was to the door, and Finn couldn't see his face. The suspect was chained to the table. He saw Finn and grinned up at him. Yellow teeth, one front tooth crossed half over the other, small beady eyes. His skin and clothes were mottled with dirt and ash from the fire.

Finn could feel the evil radiating from the man. It sickened him. The suspect averted his eyes as if he knew Finn could see through his shell to the filth beneath.

Caulfield opened a folder. Finn stood behind him and watched him place a photo of a young woman on the table. The back of the agent's hand was black, the skin gone. He presented four more photos — the woman's children — two boys and two girls, all under the age of ten.

The suspect looked down at the pictures, struggled to form a serious expression, and said, "I didn't have anything to do with that fire. I swear it."

Caulfield pointed to the mother's picture. "Lisa Packart's husband, Louis, must have gotten tired of her and their children. He didn't want a family any longer, did he? He paid you to set that fire, didn't he?"

"No, no, you're wrong."

The suspect continued to proclaim his innocence over and over, then changed his story. It had all been a terrible accident, and that was the truth of it. He just happened to be walking past the house and saw the flames shooting out the windows.

"I ran inside to help get the family out. That's why I'm covered in soot."

Caulfield told him, no, it hadn't been an accident, and he had the proof right there in his charred hands.

And once again the suspect changed his story. "Yes, Packart paid me, but I was told only his wife would be home. I didn't know the children would be there." His eyes darted to the left, and he snickered as he added, "I would have charged more."

Caulfield slammed his fist on the table and began to scream. The nightmare ended with the tortured sound jarring Finn awake.

Nearly every night now the same nightmare. He wished to God he could figure out a way to stop it. And why did the nightmare center on the Packart investigation? There had been others as horrific.

Usually the remnant of the nightmare would linger, but tonight was different. He awoke, and instead of focusing on the dream, he thought about Peyton. An image of her face replaced the dark images. From dark to light. He thought about her, and his mind stopped racing and became calm. And the kiss. He thought about the kiss, too. Her lips were even softer than he'd imagined they would be, and the taste of her was also better. He could linger on that memory all day, but it was time to get up. He pushed the thought aside and got out of bed. There was work to be done.

Early Monday morning a gentleman from the Bureau, showing proper identification, asked for Peyton's car keys and promised to have the vehicle back by the end of the day.

Though barely awake, Lucy heard the request. She waited until the man had left to question her sister. "Why does that officer want your car keys?"

"He's not an officer," Peyton said. "He's with the FBI and he's taking my car in to look it over."

"What's he looking for?" she asked on her way to the kitchen.

"Bullets."

That stopped Lucy in her tracks. "Did you say *bullets*?"

Peyton followed her into the kitchen and turned on the flame under the teakettle. She wanted a cup of hot tea. What she didn't want was to go into a lengthy explanation now. It was too early.

"Yes, I did. Finn noticed bullet holes in the back of my Camry."

Her sister opened her mouth to speak but was so dumbstruck she couldn't talk, which was a rarity. The silence didn't last long.

"It happened in Dalton, right?"

"On the way home from Dalton. I can't prove it, though. I didn't hear gunshots."

"I thought you told me everything about what happened with that creep. Jeez, Peyton. Bullet holes? Thank God you're out of there. Was it that degenerate, Drew?"

"No. I think he sent a man named Parsons after me. I can't prove that either because there was no one around to witness it."

"Bullets," Lucy whispered, shaking her head.

"I look at it as a little going-away gift from the Swift family."

"This is serious," she chided.

"I know it is. It's also frustrating. Finn's going to help me. Harassment isn't his specialty," she added, "but he's talking to some experts, doing some research. Isn't that sweet?" She filled the teakettle and put it on the stove. "I don't want to talk about bullets or anything else to do with Dalton."

Lucy didn't insist. She took two bowls from the cupboard and placed them on the table, then reached for the cereal. "Today's going to be my last day at the furniture store. I'll offer two weeks' notice, but business is so slow. They'll let me go right away. I won't be leaving them in the lurch."

They sat at the table eating their cereal in

silence. In between bites, Lucy made a list of everything she needed to get done before she left for Bishop's Cove.

"Are you still worried about what we're taking on?" she asked.

Peyton nodded. "Yes, but I'm not going to change my mind. I was thinking about the employees. I wonder how they'll react to all the changes."

"Uncle Len said there's just a skeleton crew there now. I know one thing. They can't have three women telling them what to do. We'll have to divide duties. Only one of us should be in charge of the staff. Don't you agree?"

"I want to hire an accountant."

"What about the accounting firm in Port James Len has been using?"

"They can continue on. I just think we should bring in our own."

"That's not a bad idea. Do you have someone in mind?"

She nodded. "I might also bring in a chef in training. What do you think about that?"

Lucy shrugged. "Depends on salaries, I guess. Oh God, there's so much to learn . . . so much to do."

"Uncle Len has great faith in the new manager, though he's only been in charge three or four months," Peyton told her.

"Len thinks he's good and insists we keep him on. He told Ivy we could learn from him." She propped her elbow on the table and rested her head in her hand. "There's a lot to think about," she said, trying very hard not to panic over the colossal job they were taking on. If they were successful, Bishop's Cove would stay in the family. That was something positive to aim for, wasn't it? Think of it as a wonderful adventure, she told herself.

Peyton didn't have to work today because the restaurant was closed on Mondays, so she spent the morning going through her recipe notes and organizing them. There were two new entrées she wanted to try, both including grits. Since she didn't have all of the ingredients, they would have to wait.

She spent a lazy afternoon going through her closet sorting clothes. Her bedroom looked like a cyclone had hit, but by five it was all picked up and organized again. A stack of clothes that she was going to donate had been neatly folded and placed in a large box by the door.

Her car was returned at six by a different young man, who couldn't, or wouldn't, tell her whether anything had been found.

Weary and hungry, she showered and put on clean clothes, pulled her hair back into a ponytail, and searched her room for her purse. She found it under a pillow and sat down to count her money. It didn't take long. She had exactly eleven dollars . . . and next to nothing to eat in the refrigerator. No wonder. She couldn't afford to shop, and Lucy, who would go to great lengths to avoid the grocery store because she absolutely hated to cook, went out every night. Thank goodness payday was tomorrow.

She needed boxes and her suitcases, which were stored in her parents' attic. She decided to get them now and eat dinner at their house. Her mother always wanted to feed her daughters. Peyton figured she could handle another one of her mother's lectures if she was eating.

Thunder rumbled in the distance, so she grabbed her khaki raincoat from the hall closet. As she was crossing the lot to her car, Finn pulled in and parked next to her.

He got out and asked, "Where are you going?"

"I thought you were in Dallas."

"I was. I'm back now."

They stared at each other for several seconds. Peyton felt uneasy with the awkward silence, but what could she expect, considering the way they had parted when they'd last been together.

She spoke up and broke the tension. "I'm hungry."

"Okay."

Okay? What did that mean? She wasn't asking him to take her to dinner. Yet, she also didn't want to go to her parents' house any longer now that Finn was here.

"I was going out to eat," she said. "I'd invite you along, but I've only got eleven dollars, and you look like you'd eat a lot more than that."

He smiled and walked around his car to open the passenger door for her. "Eleven dollars, huh?"

"I could probably buy you a soft drink, but that's it," she offered.

"Get in."

She slid into the seat and put on her seat belt. Finn seemed bigger to her in the confines of the rental car. He started the engine and asked her where she wanted to go.

"Nowhere fancy," she said. "How about Nelson's? They have the best fish and chips in town."

"Yeah, I remember," he said. As he pulled out of the lot, he asked, "What did you do today?"

"Today was quiet," she answered, "which was great, because I had some thinking to do."

"Oh, about what?" he asked.

"Do you remember my uncle Len?" she asked. "He used to come to the house every now and then when you lived next door."

"I do remember him. What about him?"

She told him all about Bishop's Cove and Len's proposition. As she described the crystal white sand that surrounded the resort, her enthusiasm made him smile. Finn could feel the tension ease from his shoulders and his mood lighten.

"You drive over the bridge, and there you are. It's really beautiful. You should come see it."

He promised to visit someday.

"Someday? That means you'll probably never get around to it."

He didn't argue with her, knowing there was a good possibility that she was right. They went into the restaurant and found an empty booth near the back. It was more of a dive than a restaurant, and Peyton made sure there wasn't any grease on the seat before she sat down. She realized how hungry she was when the food was placed in front of her. She ate every bit of the fish and most of the fries.

"Where do you live now?" she asked.

"San Francisco."

"That's a long way away." She said the thought out loud.

"A long way from where?"

"Here . . . home."

"I haven't lived here in a long time, Peyton."

"It's still your home. You were born in Texas. Your roots are here."

"Ah, roots," he said, smiling. "Then you'll be happy to know there's a good chance I'll be moving to Dallas next month. I fly out on a lot of assignments, and getting in and out of San Francisco is difficult on the best of days. Dallas will probably be as bad, but at least it's more centrally located."

"What do you do for the FBI?" she asked.

A long minute passed and she didn't think he was going to answer her.

He took a drink, put the glass down, and quietly said, "I get people to talk."

She waited a minute and then said, "And . . . ?"

"And what?"

Embellish, for Pete's sake, she wanted to say. He apparently wasn't going to tell her anything more, and she decided not to press. He looked so solemn all of a sudden, and she felt as though he was closing up on her.

"Want to change the subject?" she asked.

"Yeah, I do," he said. "Is there anyone special in your life?"

"I haven't had much luck dating, so I've given it up."

The look he gave her told her he thought she was joking. She decided to prove that she wasn't.

"Do you like cats?"

The question caught him off guard. "I don't know. I guess so. I've never thought about it."

"One of the boys I went out with asked me if I liked cats. Turned out he had seven."

Finn was in the process of taking a drink when she said the number, and he nearly spit it out. She handed him a napkin.

"What about ferrets?" she asked.

He set his glass down. "What about them?" A hint of a smile creased the corners of his eyes.

"I went out with a boy who had —"

"Let me guess. Seven?"

She laughed. "No, just one. Before I agreed to meet him for dinner, I asked him if he had any cats, but I didn't think to ask him about ferrets. My mistake," she added. "He kept it in his coat pocket. We were at dinner when it poked its head out and looked around. I saw it and screamed, and, FYI, ferrets don't like loud noises. At least this one didn't."

Finn couldn't stop laughing. He kept picturing Peyton's reaction. "In his pocket?"

"Turned out he never left home without it."

Peyton loved watching Finn laugh. He'd been so serious, and it was nice to see him let go and relax. "What about you?" she asked.

"You've got me beat."

"No stories to share about the women you've dated?"

Several hilarious stories popped into his head, but he couldn't share them because they all had to do with getting naked and having hot, steamy sex.

He shook his head. "None that I can tell."

"I heard you were thinking about getting married a couple of years ago."

"Who did you hear that from?"

"Your mother told my mother who told everyone."

"It was three years ago, and I was going to ask the woman I was dating to marry me, but I changed my mind and broke it off."

"Why?"

He didn't see any reason not to tell her.

"The drama. I got tired of it. My job can get . . . tense, and I didn't want to come home to that every night."

The waitress put the bill on the table, and Finn reached for his wallet as he said, "I used to think I wanted marriage and kids, but not anymore."

Frowning, she said, "You want peace when you come home, right? You have to deal with serious issues, and when you finally get home you want peace and quiet."

He was pleased she understood. "Yes, that's exactly what I want."

She rolled her eyes. "Boring, Finn. You want boring. What you need is excitement and fun. Love and laughter. You need to balance the bad with the good."

"Yeah? And what do you need?"

Her answer was immediate. "Normal. I need normal. Did you find any bullets in my car?"

"No," he answered. "Come on. Let's get out of here before the rain starts. The clouds are black. We'll talk in the car."

She offered her eleven dollars to help with the check and laughed at his exasperated expression. They just made it to the car before the skies opened and the rain poured down.

"I didn't think you'd find anything," she

170

said. "I've thought about what happened, and I've decided I made all the wrong choices. When the guy was chasing me, I should have called nine-one-one, and after he drove into the field, I should have waited by the side of the highway for the police or highway patrol to come. I guess I was afraid it would take forever for anyone to get to me. I never got a good look at his face, but if I'd stayed, the police would have searched his car and found his gun."

"You also didn't know that he had a gun and was shooting at you," he reminded. "You know what I think? You should have gotten the hell out of there, and that's exactly what you did."

He was making her feel better about her decisions. "I was so angry when I left, I thought about sending the recording to the Internet and being done with it," she admitted. "Mimi talked me out of it."

"I'm glad she did," he said. "Once you put it out there, it becomes as much about you as it is about Drew Albertson. You don't want that. What is it you do want to accomplish?"

"To look Randolph Swift in the eye while he listens to the recording and to hear what he will do about Drew. If he doesn't get rid of him, I'll sue. You're right," she added.

"The recording is leverage."

"Albertson and his wife should be pretty complacent by now."

"I'm sure Eileen has been checking her father's e-mail while they're in Europe, and I'll bet she has someone checking his phone while they're away. They've also had plenty of time to fill his head with stories about me, don't you think?"

"It won't matter," he assured her. He turned on the engine, then reached into his pocket and pulled out a folded piece of paper. He handed it to her and said, "If you decide to sue, this is the attorney you want."

"I hate the idea of suing. There will be mudslinging, and the publicity will be terrible. It's more complicated now because of Bishop's Cove," she added. "Swift Publications has never been sued, and their attorneys will come out swinging. They'll try to destroy my credibility and maybe go after the restaurants in the Cove. Anything is possible." She stared out her window, reflecting on the ramifications if she retaliated against the Albertsons. Taking a deep breath, she said, "It doesn't matter. I'll do what I have to do to stop him."

He nodded. He watched Peyton for several seconds without saying a word. Who was this amazing woman? She was breathtakingly gorgeous. That was obvious to anyone who looked at her — he'd barely been able to take his eyes off her luscious mouth all through dinner — and she was also funny and smart and caring. He was used to game players, but Peyton wasn't coy or pretentious. She was refreshingly honest, and maybe that was why he liked being with her so much. No, he decided, it wasn't just her honesty. He liked everything about Peyton Lockhart.

"I have to get back," he said as he put the key in the ignition and backed the car out of the parking space.

Finn was quiet on the drive to the apartment. At first Peyton felt comfortable with the silence, but after several minutes, she looked over at him. He seemed lost in thought and she wondered what he could be thinking that would make him so pensive. Maybe he was thinking about a case he was working on, she surmised, or maybe he was mulling over her dilemma with the Albertsons. Oh God, she thought, maybe he was thinking about saying good-bye to her. That was it. He was trying to figure out a way to say good-bye without her throwing herself at him again. How humiliating! She'd have to think of a way to let him know she didn't expect anything from him, to let him leave without making it awkward.

By the time he pulled up to her apartment building, the rain was coming down in torrents. Finn ran around the car and opened her door, and they made a mad dash up the steps. Standing in the small recess at her front door, they were barely inches apart and soaking wet.

"Finn . . . ," she began. She looked up into his eyes and lost her train of thought.

"Yes?" he said.

"About the kiss the other day," she blurted. "I'm really sorry . . . I don't know what came over me . . . I guess I was just glad to see you after all these years . . . I don't want you to think I do that all the time . . . I don't blame you at all . . . it was all my fault . . . I —"

Her rant stopped when his mouth covered hers. Pulling her to him, he kissed her like she'd never been kissed before, a long, hot, ravenous kiss, and then he turned and hurried out into the rain leaving her weak-kneed and dazed.

TEN

Finn decided he was out of his mind. He had to be, he reasoned, because there he stood outside Peyton's door. It had been several days since he'd left her, and flying back to Brentwood for the sole purpose of seeing her again was crazy. He knew it was, yet he still did it.

He was leaving for Philadelphia tomorrow afternoon. He could have taken a direct flight from San Francisco, but he left a day earlier so that he could stop in Texas. For her. He wanted to see her one more time before she left for Bishop's Cove and he moved on with his own carefully structured life. No, that wasn't quite right. He didn't want to see her; he needed to. He couldn't stop thinking about her, and, yes, that was one of the reasons he was sure he'd lost his mind.

She would be surprised to see him, and if she asked him why he was here, he didn't know what he would say. That he was drawn to her? That he felt the same peace and joy with her that he did when he was in the water? Or maybe he'd give her a little more of the truth. That every nerve in his body wanted her. Craved her. He wondered how she would react to that chunk of honesty. When he'd scheduled that flight, had he planned to have sex with her? He told himself no, yet he'd put a condom in his pocket.

It was a little after seven. He knocked on her door and waited. Maybe she still worked at that restaurant. No, she'd told him she had one more week to go and then she was finished. And the week was up.

She opened the door just as he was about to knock again. His intention was to ask her if she would like to go out to dinner with him, and if she told him she had other plans, he would try to figure out a way to talk her into changing them. It wasn't a great strategy, and he was feeling a little nervous about it, but as soon as he saw her, he relaxed. She wasn't dressed to go anywhere. Her hair was wet, and she was wearing a baggy, long sweatshirt over a pair of leggings. Her face was scrubbed clean. Her cheeks were rosy, and so were her lips. She smelled wonderful, too.

She smiled, letting him know she was happy to see him, but she also looked surprised. "I didn't expect to see you so soon. Is everything all right? Why are you back in Brentwood?"

"I wanted to check on you." Yeah, right. That was as believable as "I was in the neighborhood." What would she think if he told her the truth, that he had made the detour because he couldn't stay away.

"You're just in time. Come in," she said.

"In time for what?" he asked. He shut the door and locked it. He saw all the boxes against the wall and asked, "Do you want me to help you pack?"

"Oh no, I've got that covered. You're just in time to eat," she explained. "I've been cooking . . . experimenting on three new dishes. Two have shrimp in them. Do you like shrimp?" she asked as she moved a stack of folded laundry from the sofa. "The third dish is chicken. Will you try them?"

Peyton thought she'd done an adequate job of acting casual about his sudden appearance, considering her heartbeat was going wild. She'd been so shocked and happy to see him, it took all of her control not to throw herself into his arms.

"Come into the kitchen," she said. She nervously threaded her fingers through her hair to separate the strands. God, it must look like hell. "What would you like to drink?"

Finn took off his jacket and draped it over a chair. "What have you got?" he asked.

"Water."

Smiling, he said, "I'll have water."

Her recipe book with notes sticking out every which way was spread open on the table. She moved it to one side and got two bottles of water out of the refrigerator. Finn found the utensils and napkins while she prepared the first entrée.

"It's still nice and hot," she said. She placed the plate in front of him and sat down across from him." Does it look appealing? You won't hurt my feelings if you say it doesn't, but does it? What do you see when you look at it?" She picked up her pen and waited for his answer.

He laughed. "Food, Peyton. I see food."

Finn didn't particularly like grits — he would never order them in a restaurant — but he took a bite of Peyton's and changed his mind. The dish was delicious. It was spicy, yet not overly so, and there was just the right amount of heat.

"It's really good," he praised.

She was pleased. "I thought it was, but everyone's taste buds are different. I'm glad you like it."

The second entrée wasn't quite as good, but he still ate all of it. She asked a few questions about the flavor, found the recipe she'd written, and crossed it off. Then she served the chicken. He told her it was okay. She thought it was bland and marked that recipe off her list as well.

"I don't eat a lot of rich food," he said. He picked up his plate and took it to the sink. "When I competed, food was fuel. I got used to bland, I guess."

Peyton picked up a round tin container from the shelf and put it on the table.

"Food doesn't have to be drenched in rich sauce to be good."

He rolled his sleeves up and rinsed his plate. Then he tried to find the dishwasher.

"There isn't one," she said. "Leave the dishes. I'll wash them later."

"Let's do them now, and you can tell me about France. Did you like it there?"

"How did you know I went to France? Surely not my mother."

He was bent over the sink scrubbing a pan, splashing water everywhere. "Ivy told me. Why not your mother?"

"Cooking isn't something she can brag about. I majored in English lit and journalism, and she can't understand why I turned my back on all that education to cook instead. I'm a disappointment," she ended with a dramatic sigh.

He rinsed the pan and handed it to her to dry. She patted the front of his shirt with a towel first. "You're getting water everywhere," she said. "I loved France. It's a beautiful country."

She talked about the culinary institute and Chef Jon and told him a few amusing stories about some of the students. The kitchen was cleaned up in little time. Finn grabbed another bottle of water and went to get his phone from his coat pocket so he could show her some photos from the wedding reception. She picked up the tin and followed him to the living room. He sat beside her on the sofa, scrolled through the camera roll on his phone, and handed it to her. The first photo was of a grinning Beck holding Ivy in his arms.

"He looks like he's bench-pressing her," she remarked.

All the photos showed happy couples celebrating with Tristan and Brooke.

"I wish I'd been there," she said. She was handing the phone back to him when it rang. She saw who was calling and so did he. When he declined the call, she asked, "Who's Danielle?"

He didn't immediately answer. She nudged him.

"She's a woman I used to date. That's all."

"The one you almost married?"

He nodded.

His relationship with Danielle was none of her business, but it still bothered her. "Why is she calling?"

"She wants to reconnect. I don't," he said, and before she could think of another question, he asked, "What's in the tin?"

She wanted to talk about Danielle. What did she look like? What did she do for a living? Had he loved her? She didn't ask any of those questions, though. She discussed cookies instead.

"Inside are chocolate cookies for dessert if you'd like. I make them for the restaurant. People say they're addictive. They're always asking to buy extra to take home."

"I don't usually eat dessert, but I'll try one."

She removed the lid and let him take one. "Be careful. They come with a warning," she teased.

"That they're addictive?"

"No, that there's a slip of paper inside with a little note. It wouldn't kill you if you ate it, but it's best not to."

"Like a fortune cookie?"

"No, those are clever sayings. Some of my cookies have notes; some don't. The diner chooses."

"Who writes the notes?"

"I do," she answered. "They're my words of wisdom," she added with a smile. "Lessons I've already learned. Don't laugh at me. I've learned a lot in the past five years."

"Give me an example."

"Turn the cookie over, and if there's a note, you'll see the end of the paper."

There wasn't a note. That was a shame because at the moment she couldn't think of a single word she'd written. It was his fault. Sitting so close to him, looking into his eyes, made it difficult to hold a thought. She kept getting distracted.

She loved his smile, and she loved how protective he was. When she was a little girl, she knew he would watch out for her, and when she was in high school and at the university, she knew that if she ever really got into trouble, all she had to do was call him, and he would help her. Yes, he was FBI, and he was trained to catch the bad guys and keep the good ones safe, but it was more than that. He was Finn, and in her heart he was still that hero. She hoped one day he'd realize she would always be there for him, too.

"Peyton?"

"Yes, the notes," she remembered. "Let's see. Don't trust a man who comes to dinner with a ferret in his pocket. That's one."

Finn's phone buzzed, indicating he had a text. He put the cookie back in the tin and quickly read the message.

She wanted to ask if the text came from Danielle.

"Mark wants to talk to you. You haven't called him yet, have you?"

"Who's Mark?"

"Mark Campbell, the attorney. I wrote his name and phone number —"

"Oh yes, the attorney." She closed the tin and put it on the table. "How much does he charge for a consult?"

"It's free advice. He has some suggestions for you."

She didn't want to talk about the attorney now. She wanted him to kiss her. How could he resist? She was such a seductress with her baggy clothes, her limp hair, and no makeup. How could he keep his hands off her?

"Mimi called today," she said. She sat back against the cushions. "They're all back home. Randolph and Drew and Eileen, the big happy family. It will be mighty interesting to see what happens tomorrow when

Drew returns to work. I worry that he will hire my replacement. She could be in the same predicament I was, and what if she doesn't have a way out? What if she can't leave? She would be trapped with him."

"I'm glad you're going to stop him," he said as he stood.

She thought he was planning to leave, and she wanted him to stay. "I was wondering," she began hesitantly.

"Yes?"

"If I comb my hair, will you kiss me?"

He didn't say a word. He stared into her eyes for several seconds, and then his gaze moved to her mouth. Slowly he pulled her to her feet and wrapped her in his arms. He didn't kiss her right away but held her against him. His hands stroked her back, sliding under her thick sweatshirt.

Finn loved the softness of her warm skin. His hands moved up, and when he realized she wasn't wearing a bra, he groaned and wanted to pull the shirt off and cover her with his body. She kissed the pulse at the base of his neck, then kissed his chin. "This is crazy," he said, his voice a rough whisper.

The day's growth of whiskers tickled Peyton's lips. She rubbed her cheek against his, inhaling his masculine scent, and sighed, "If you don't want to —"

"Oh, I want to," he said. Taking her face in his hands, he covered her mouth with his. His tongue sank inside, coaxing a response. She was soon trembling and wanting more.

She loved the taste of him, loved the way his mouth felt sealing hers. When at last he ended the kiss and lifted his head, the intensity in his expression thrilled her. He wanted her.

And she wanted him.

So this was what desire felt like. Real desire. Every part of her body reacted to him, and she had trouble catching her breath. Her skin tingled for more of his touch; her breasts ached, and a warm feeling invaded her limbs as the heat pooled inside her.

She began to unbutton his shirt, and he put his hand on top of hers. "Are you sure?"

She wrapped her arms around his neck and kissed him passionately, letting him know how much she ached for him.

Lifting her into his arms, he carried her to her bedroom. When he reached for the doorknob, she said, "No, I'm across the hall."

Amazed that she could speak a coherent word, she put her head on his shoulder. Her heart was beating like a drum, and she could hear the pulsing sound in her ears. Was he having the same reaction to her? Did he crave her the way she craved him?

He put her down beside the bed, and she watched him remove his gun and badge and lay both on the table next to the headboard. He turned to her while he undressed. He was magnificent. She caught the thought before she spoke it out loud. He had a swimmer's body, all muscle. She stepped closer and put her hand on his chest directly over his heart, feeling it pound under her fingertips. The muscles across his chest and upper arms were like steel, but warm.

Finn couldn't wait a second longer. The ache to be inside her intensified. He began to undress her, and she tried to help but she kept kissing him as she struggled to get out of her clothes. Her sweatshirt was like a heavy blanket, and he helped her tug it over her head. When he finally succeeded, he dropped her clothes on the floor and looked down at her full breasts and narrow waist. He was in awe.

He followed her down on the bed and covered her, gently nudging her legs apart. He settled himself between her thighs, his arousal pressed intimately against her pelvis. Burying his face in the side of her neck, he groaned with sheer bliss. "You feel so good, so soft."

Peyton was overwhelmed. Finn, naked, wrapped around her, holding her, warming her with his hot hard body. Never had she experienced anything as wonderful as this. Never. Should she tell him? Would he stop if she did? She didn't want to disappoint him.

She began to caress his shoulders, loving the feel of his strength. Her touch was light as she stroked him, moving lower to the base of his spine. He was nuzzling her neck, causing shivers to cascade all the way to her toes. It was heavenly.

"I know you've been with other women . . . of course you have . . . and I —"

His kiss stopped her confession — a long drugging kiss that let her know how much he wanted her. He lifted up on his elbows, saw the desire in her eyes, and said, "I don't care about your past, or the men you've taken to your bed. Forget them. You're with me now."

Forget them? He had no idea how easy that was going to be. She tried one last time. "But I —"

His mouth firmly settled on hers again, and the kiss became so consuming she stopped trying to talk. He made love to her with his mouth, his tongue moving in and out, teasing, tormenting. His chest hair tickled her breasts as he kissed her neck, then moved lower, his open mouth hot against the valley between her breasts. She arched against him when he ran his tongue across the sensitive nipple. She clung to him, her nails digging into his shoulders, demanding more. He was driving her wild, and she felt a profound need to make him feel the same.

"Finn . . . let me . . ." She lost the thought as she fought the sensations coursing through her. His hand had moved down between her thighs and his fingers were stroking her, making her burn.

Finn loved the way she moaned, the way she moved restlessly against him. Her response was so uninhibited. He kissed her navel and continued on, nudging her thighs farther apart, making her more demanding now, more out of control.

Peyton nearly screamed when he began to stroke her with his tongue. She thought she would die from the pleasure, but losing control scared her.

"Finn, no . . . no more," she cried out. Her hands tore at the sheets, and even as she was telling him to stop, her hips were moving against him begging for more.

"It's okay. Let it happen," he urged. "Ah, Peyton, you taste so good."

Suddenly he rose up and cupped the sides of her face, kissing her almost savagely.

Their passion erupted like a raging wildfire, uncontrollable and fierce. She was desperate to know all of him. "I want to touch you, to take you into my mouth, to know what you taste like," she panted. "Let me, Finn . . ."

She was shaking from head to toe, wanting to please him the way he pleased her, yet unsure how. He rolled onto his back and let her have her way. She started with his stomach, placing wet kisses around his navel, then moved lower to kiss and caress him.

His reaction was so intense, he couldn't let her continue for long, knowing it would be all over for him before he satisfied her. He roughly lifted her, pushed her onto her back, and reached for the packet he had placed on the nightstand. When he was ready, he braced himself on top of her and pushed her thighs apart. He thought to enter her slowly so that both of them could savor the incredible feeling of coming together, becoming one.

"You're mine, Peyton," he whispered, his voice raspy with his need.

"Yes," she said on a moan. "Please . . . I want you . . . now, Finn."

Her need overrode his desire to go slowly. He was desperate to have her. He wrapped her in his arms and thrust into her. He felt the resistance and heard her gasp, but it was too late. He was fully embedded inside her. He stayed perfectly still, and it nearly killed him. She was so tight, so perfect. She squeezed him, and all he wanted to do was plunge into her again and again until they both found release. Beads of perspiration covered his brow, and his jaw was clenched tight.

"Are you okay? Do you want me to . . . Did I . . ."

She wound her fingers through his hair and pulled him to her. Kissing him, she pushed against him with her hips. She'd felt a sharp pain when he'd entered her, but it was quickly gone, and now the feel of him inside her made her want more.

He began to move, slower now, more careful. Each thrust a little deeper, a little more out of control. He stroked the need inside her until she was writhing beneath him and pleading for more and more of the exquisite sensation. Her moans urged him on, excited him. He was more forceful now, delving deeper with each thrust, the pace growing

190

faster. She drew her knees up and met each thrust with equal passion. All restraint was gone. She cried out and held on to him as her orgasm consumed her.

Finn felt the first tremors and knew she was going to climax. When she tightened around him, he found his own release. It was staggering.

They stayed entwined for long minutes. He buried his head in the pillow, letting the sweet scent of her hair fill his nostrils, his breathing still harsh and his heartbeat still racing.

He was reeling from the revelation. She was a virgin. He knew he needed to talk to her about it. He kissed her neck and finally found the strength to move. Lifting up on his elbows, he looked down at her. God, she was beautiful. Her eyes were closed and she was still trying to catch her breath. For some reason that made him arrogantly proud. He'd made her lose control, and once that had happened, damn, she was wild. Her lips were swollen and rosy. He gently kissed them, then rolled to his side and stared up at the ceiling while he thought about what he would say to her. Needing a few more minutes to clear his head, he got out of bed and walked into the bathroom.

The second his warm body left her, Peyton

began to shiver. She was still trying to recover from what had just happened to her. It was the most amazing thing she'd ever experienced. When they had started making love, she'd thought it was rather pleasant. Afterward, that analysis was laughable. She now understood the true definition of ecstasy: mind-blowing. Yes, definitely mind-blowing.

She knew she had pleased him and that he'd been satisfied, but it would have been nice if he'd told her so. She was feeling a bit vulnerable. Was that all part of the aftermath? she wondered. She thought she heard him muttering but she wasn't sure. She got out of bed and put on her pink robe. The fabric pushed against her breasts and she realized they were sore. She kept glancing at the bathroom door while she tied the belt at her waist.

Frustrated now, she sat on the bed, her back against the headboard with one ankle crossed over the other, and waited for him. It had been only a minute or two since he'd shut the door, but every second felt like a minute. When he returned from the bathroom, he was dressed in his jeans. He reached for his shirt and put it on. Was he planning to leave without saying a word? It was a good thing she wasn't sensitive, she told herself, because he was frowning at her. He couldn't be disappointed . . . could he?

Finn didn't button his shirt. He threaded his fingers through his hair, took a deep breath, and sat down on the side of the bed. She moved to sit beside him.

"Did I hurt you?" His voice was soft and caring.

"No, you didn't."

Finn stared at her for a long minute. "Okay," he said, nodding. He didn't believe her, but he wasn't going to argue. "Why didn't you tell me you were a virgin?" His voice wasn't quite so caring now. There was a tinge of anger.

"I did try while we were . . ."

"It was a little late then, wasn't it? Why the hell didn't you tell me before I took your clothes off?"

Peyton was confused. Was he angry or feeling guilty? Neither reaction made sense. She stood and glared at him. "My mistake. I should have put it on my résumé. Of course, if I had, I'd have to revise it now, wouldn't I?"

He ignored her sarcasm. "There were plenty of times —"

"No, you're right. When I saw you at the church, I should have told you then. I should have said, 'Finn, it's so good to see you again. I'm still a virgin. Are you in the wedding?' Or how about while we were having dinner. I could have told you then. I could have said, 'Are you enjoying the shrimp? I'm a virgin. Would you like dessert?' "

She tried to leave the room, but he grabbed her hips and pulled her down on his lap. She didn't fight, but put her arms around his neck instead. The tenderness in his eyes was almost her undoing.

"I don't understand why you're so angry," she said.

"I'm not angry."

"You were."

She was gently rubbing the back of Finn's neck, driving him to distraction. She looked so intent on their conversation, he didn't think she was aware of what she was doing.

"No," he assured. "I wasn't angry. I was surprised." He almost laughed. *Surprised* didn't quite describe how he had felt. "I just didn't expect . . ."

He'd been so rough with her, so forceful when he'd entered her. That thought led to another and he remembered how tight and hot she had been . . . how perfect.

Peyton waited for an explanation. When he didn't continue, she said, "Okay, you're feeling guilty."

He slowly shook his head. "No."

"If I had told you, if you had known, would you have made love to me?"

He had to think about his answer. His immediate thought was no, he wouldn't have. They both had been carried away by the moment. Her first time should be with someone special. It should matter. He tried to convince himself that he would have kept his distance, that he wouldn't have let things go so far, but he finally decided to be honest with himself. Hell yes, he would have taken her. Being with Peyton had mattered to him. The first time he kissed her he'd known he would have her, and now the thought of any other man touching her angered him. It was crazy and illogical. But there it was all the same.

"Answer me," she demanded. "If you had known, would you have —"

"Yes." He was emphatic. "But I would have taken it much slower, and I wouldn't have been so rough with you. I would have made it easier for you . . . made it better."

Talking about it, thinking about how good it had been, was making him hard again. Her robe was partially open, exposing one beautiful leg. The temptation was too great to resist, and he began to stroke her silky skin from her knee to the top of her thigh and back.

"What are you doing?"

His hand moved up to her hip. "I like touching you."

She liked it, too. He was making her hot, and yet she was shivering.

He gave her a slow, wet kiss. She put her hand on top of his. "It couldn't be any better." She looked down and watched him untie her belt. She could stop him, but she didn't want to.

"Sure it could," he promised, and then he set about proving it.

ELEVEN

Finn left her bed a little after two in the morning. She lost count of the number of times he'd asked her if she was all right. Did he expect her to become hysterical when he walked out the door, or at the very least break down and cry?

All she wanted was sleep. There would be plenty of time to miss him tomorrow and all the days after.

No one would know how she felt. She was determined to keep her feelings bottled up inside her. No whining to anyone, no matter how much her heart ached. In high school, when her hormones were playing havoc with her emotions, she sometimes felt in need of a padded cell. Everything was so much more intense and dramatic back then, but she found a way to deal with a broken heart. Each time she suffered rejection — and God only knew there were plenty of those — she would get in the car and go for a drive. She'd play every bad love song she could find and sing along, wailing loud enough to crack glass. Other drivers who pulled up beside her at red lights and saw her hunched over the steering wheel crying and singing her heart out would look so appalled.

Those days were behind her now. Her hormones were under control, and she didn't carry on like that anymore. She couldn't remember the last time she had had a good, long cry. Her way of handling sorrow or misery these days was to keep busy and try not to dwell on things that couldn't be changed. Eventually the painful feelings would lessen and fade away.

She didn't want her feelings for Finn to fade away, and she didn't want to forget what they had shared. It had been so beautiful, so perfect. But now he was gone, and she had a hundred things to do before she left for Bishop's Cove. There simply wasn't time to think about him.

And yet she did. She stood in the shower a long while, letting the hot water pour over her shoulders and soothe her muscles. She was sore everywhere from their vigorous lovemaking. Her breasts and her inner thighs felt bruised, remembrances of how demanding both of them had been.

The day was half gone before she started packing. Lucy had hired movers to take her one good piece of furniture, a sofa, to her parents' house to store. Everything else was being donated and would be picked up tomorrow morning. Peyton planned to spend tomorrow night in her old bedroom at home and leave for Florida the following day. Lucy was already on her way.

Mimi's phone call late that evening changed Peyton's plans. Her friend was so upset, her voice shook. "He's looking for a new girl."

The news made Peyton sick to her stomach. "You're sure?"

"Oh yes, I'm sure. He came in late this morning as cheerful as could be. The jackass was whistling. I didn't find out what he was up to until I was leaving work," she explained. "I passed Bridget in the hall, and she mentioned she had just placed another ad."

"For my replacement."

"That's right. Drew and Eileen must think you've decided not to make trouble. Ever since they got back from Europe, they've acted like they don't have a care in the world."

"Then they're in for a surprise."

Several seconds passed in silence, and

199

then Mimi said, "Maybe you should forget about all of this."

"You know I'm not going to do that."

"Peyton, I'm worried about you. Drew's got a terrible temper. If he loses everything, he'll come after you."

"We've been over this. I know he can be dangerous."

"He's got Parsons, who will do anything Drew tells him to do."

Peyton thought about the bullet holes in the back of her car and the chilling expression on Drew's face the night he'd tried to break into her room. She knew exactly what he was capable of. "I can't let Drew do this again. I have to try to stop him."

"I know. I just worry," she said. "Holy smokes, I nearly forgot." Her thick Minnesota accent grew stronger. "There's going to be a memorial for Miriam Swift, and get this. According to motormouth Bridget, it was all Drew's idea. He's going overboard to get on Randolph's good side, and it's working. She said Randolph was very pleased. They're having it here at the company on a weekend and making everyone come in for it."

"Have you given your notice yet?"

"We agreed that you would get settled at the resort, and after you've been there a while, then decide if you need another accountant. I don't want a pity job."

Peyton laughed. "It isn't a pity job. I need you to help turn Bishop's Cove around. I explained my uncle Len's terms. We have to show a profit or we'll lose it."

"Yes, but how do you know I'm qualified for the job?"

Being married to that unfaithful so-and-so and then working for a degenerate who treated her abominably for the last eight months had beaten Mimi down and made her insecure, Peyton thought.

"I did my homework," she answered. "I know when you were transferred to Drew, the head of the accounting department had to hire two people to replace you. I also know you should have been promoted years ago, but your husband squelched it."

Mimi's indrawn breath told Peyton she hadn't known.

"He didn't want you to outshine him," she said.

"How do you know that?" Mimi asked. "And don't tell me Bridget. She'd never talk to you."

"No, Lars found out. He's made friends with Sandy in HR. She's not a fan of either Annette or Bridget, and she doesn't mind sharing. He even got me a copy of your résumé. You're very qualified for the job I have in mind. But there's something else just as important. I trust you."

She heard sniffling and thought Mimi might be tearing up.

"Holy smokes," she uttered.

"Isn't it time for you to travel south of Minneapolis?"

"Yes, I believe it is. Are you still hiring Lars?"

"Yes, of course."

"How about he and I give you a couple of weeks to get settled. Then we'll quit and be on our way. Drew won't want me to stick around. I'm not sure about Lars, though. I'll talk to him. When do you leave for Florida?"

"I thought the day after tomorrow, but I've decided to talk to an attorney here. He comes highly recommended. I'm hoping he'll work me in."

"Holy smokes, you're thinking about suing?"

"I'm going to discuss options."

Peyton ended the call a few minutes later and made a cup of tea while she thought about what questions to ask the attorney. She would call Mark Campbell first thing in the morning. He was probably booked for weeks, but she couldn't wait around.

She needed to get to Bishop's Cove. If he couldn't see her in person, they could schedule a phone conference, she supposed.

It took a long while for her to relax and fall asleep that night because she couldn't stop thinking about Finn. The last time she'd been in this bed, he was holding her, kissing her, making love to her. The memories made her groan. What was he doing now? Had he given her a thought since he'd left her? She hadn't expected a call, yet during the day she'd kept checking her phone for texts or messages.

Had last night simply been a hookup? She didn't know how her friends could do it: go to a bar, find a guy they wanted to be with, and take him home — each of them going their separate ways the next day. Was that what she had with Finn, a one-night stand? There were absolutely no expectations. No promises were made, no talk of seeing each other again. She knew all this. Why then did her heart ache for him?

She called the attorney at nine in the morning and was told he could see her at four that afternoon. Mark Campbell's smile was almost as appealing as Finn's. His office was large and smelled of leather. The receptionist opened the door for her, and as she walked in, Mark crossed the room to shake her hand. He was built like Finn, too, she thought. She realized the comparisons she was making and told herself to knock it off.

"Thank you so much for working me in today," she said.

"It's my pleasure," he replied. "I hoped you would call. Finn filled me in on what happened to you." He pulled out a chair for her, rounded his desk, and sat down as he reached for his notebook. "Tell me what you want to accomplish," he began.

She briefly told him what she had experienced from the time she was hired until the time she returned home. Her voice trembled while she related how Drew had tried to break into her motel room. Mark put her at ease right away, but she was still embarrassed when he asked to listen to the recording.

"He's crude," she warned.

She placed her phone in front of him and touched the arrow to begin the recording. Mark listened intently and didn't show any reaction until Drew threatened to make Peyton's decision for her. He raised an eyebrow then but didn't comment.

Peyton did react. Hearing Drew's voice gave her chills.

After it was over, Mark leaned back in his

chair and said, "Oh yes, we can go after him. Finn's right. We can't let him get away with this."

"I made a lot of mistakes," she said. "I tried to report him but when I didn't get anywhere with that, I didn't document what was happening. I left. It's nearly impossible to win a sexual harassment suit if you've left the job, isn't it?"

"If you're in danger, you leave, and you were in danger." After explaining what a lawsuit could entail, he asked, "What sort of settlement were you expecting?"

"Oh, I don't want any money," she answered. "I just want Drew Albertson gone from that company, and if he tries to get a job where he can prey on women again, I want the new employer to see his record. Randolph Swift, the owner of the company, hasn't heard this recording, but I would love to play it for him and look in his eyes when he listens to it," she said, imagining the fury that would ensue. "If he refuses to do anything about Drew, then I want you to go after them."

Mark gave her several options on how they could proceed, and she promised to consider all of them before making up her mind.

"Finn would like to be kept apprised of what's happening. Is that okay with you?"

Mark asked. "If you wish to keep this confidential, then that's what I'll do."

"No, that's fine. I welcome his input."

"All right then. I'm your attorney now. Think about your options and get back to me."

"I'm not sure I can afford you just now. What is your hourly rate?"

"There isn't going to be any charge. I'm repaying a favor for a friend. But I'll tell you the truth. After listening to the recording, I wouldn't charge you anyway. I really want to get this guy."

"Thank you," she said. "I realize you're doing this for Finn, but I insist on paying. It might take a while."

"Whatever you want to do."

"How do you know Finn?" she asked, curious.

She expected him to tell her they had been frat brothers or that they had gone to the same Jesuit high school, but he didn't.

"We were on the same swim team," he answered. Remembering made him smile. "I'm three years older than Finn, and I was the youngest on the team. There were five of us that swam the same events. We already had our team all set in our heads when the coach held tryouts. I think he had to as part of a deal that allowed us to use the Olympic-size pool at the community center.

"The first time I saw Finn I figured he wasn't going to come near our time record. He wasn't going to be any competition." He admitted, "We were pretty cocky back then."

She was hanging on his every word.

"Imagine us, if you will. The five of us with our buzz cuts and sleek caps, our Speedos and goggles, the works, and in walks this guy with long hair wearing swim trunks that come down to his knees. I remember what they looked like — bright yellow with green palm trees." He laughed. "Those trunks alone would add at least ten, maybe fifteen seconds to his time, and his long hair would drag him down. We didn't laugh, but we did a lot of elbowing one another.

"The coach had four of us on the blocks waiting for Finn. He jumps in the pool to get wet, then gets out, rolls his shoulders once, and he's ready. He gets on the block in the lane next to me."

"What happened?" she asked, loving the picture he was painting.

"He flew. That's what happened. His start off the blocks alone put him way ahead of all of us, and then I swear he turned into a fish. A dolphin maybe," he added, grinning. "We were told to swim two lengths. I had just made what I thought was a perfect turn when I looked over and didn't see Finn in his lane. By the time I got to the finish, Finn was walking toward the bench where his brothers waited for their turns. I thought maybe he'd quit in the middle of the try-out . . . until I looked at coach's face." He shook his head as though the memory still amazed him.

"All I can say is that Finn taught me a little bit about humility that day." He added, "And we've been friends ever since."

TWELVE

No one was going to get in Drew's way on his path to happiness, and happiness for him was money. Randolph Swift's money to be exact.

It wouldn't be long before the reins were handed to him, and the only person who could ruin his future was Peyton Lockhart. If she didn't keep her mouth shut and go away peacefully, he would make sure she went away permanently. He'd worked too hard for this life to let her snatch it from him. A long time ago he had figured out what he wanted. In his mind it was a simple equation. Money equaled power, and power garnered respect. He wanted it all — the wealth, the prestige, the women — and Eileen was helping him. She would go to any lengths to get him what he needed, any lengths at all.

Drew knew he had it in him to be a killer. During his junior year in high school he almost killed his father, and to this day he regretted that he hadn't. He remembered what had happened with such clarity, even though it had been years. He had come home from school and discovered that dear old Dad had found the hiding place where Drew kept his money. He had been saving for over a year, taking every degrading job he could find to earn a dollar here and there. He was saving to run away, but his father took every bit of the cash to play the numbers and get drunk. Furious, Drew's temper exploded, and he beat his father until his own knuckles were bleeding and his father was unconscious. Drew got scared that his old man would die in the apartment and he'd be tried for murder, and so he dumped him in front of the hospital. When his father regained his senses and was questioned by the police, he couldn't tell them anything because he'd been too drunk to remember.

Those rough days were behind Drew now. If Peyton tried to make trouble, Drew wouldn't have to worry about the method or the place or the mess of silencing her because he had people who would take care of it for him. His knuckles would stay clean.

It had been over a month since Peyton made the recording, and not a peep out of her. Mimi hadn't said a word, either, but then he'd made it worth her while. The substantial raise he'd given her assured her silence. There was no other company she could go to that would give her the money or the job security she now had at the magazine. With each passing day, Drew became more relaxed, believing that Peyton had forgotten about him and moved on.

Eileen was more cautious. She wasn't ready to assume the matter had been dropped.

One way to find out, she suggested, was to monitor Mimi's communications. Since Mimi was Peyton's friend, the two may have remained in contact.

The e-mail was easy to check. All it took was an adjustment to the company's computer network so that every time Mimi received a message or sent one Drew saw it. The cell phone presented a problem. Eileen couldn't figure out how to monitor Mimi's conversations or her texts, but Drew came up with an easy solution. He knew that Mimi's cell phone was in the outer pocket of her purse, and her purse was in the bottom drawer of her desk. All he needed to do was get Mimi away from her desk, so he concocted dozens of errands for her to run, especially during the times when no one else was around. He managed to get a peek two or three times a day. He discovered records of a few calls between her and Peyton, but they appeared to be short, and for the most part, Mimi's texts were boring.

Drew finally convinced Eileen that the danger had passed. He was becoming more and more complacent as the days moved on. He was even ready to train another assistant and had ordered Bridget to place the advertisement.

His smug complacency ended on a Tuesday afternoon, however, when he read Mimi's latest text to Peyton: When is your attorney going to file suit?

THIRTEEN

Peyton read Mimi's text but didn't have time to call her until that evening.

"Why did you send me that text? If Drew saw it, he would go ballistic."

"I know," Mimi said apologetically. "I sent the text from home just before I got in the shower, and I was in a rush. The minute I saw it I got rid of it. Drew was in and out of the office all morning, so I don't think he could have seen it."

Peyton told her all about her meeting with Mark Campbell and again insisted that she didn't want to sue the magazine unless it was absolutely necessary. The attorney had made several alternative suggestions for her to consider, but she wasn't going to do anything about Swift Publications until she got settled in Bishop's Cove.

There was so much to finish up before she left Brentwood, yet despite all the chaos of the move, she still had time to think about Finn. She hadn't heard from him since he left her bed, and that, she told herself, was the way it should be. For one amazing night she had connected with the man she cared about, but now she was moving on. If she happened to see him again, that would be fine, and if she didn't run into him, that would be fine, too.

Yes, fine. She almost talked herself into believing that nonsense. It might have been casual sex for him, but it had been much more than that for her. She missed him, simple as that. She wished she could be more sophisticated about it all, and maybe in time she could. Right now she felt foolish and naive about her vulnerability.

It was a sunny Thursday afternoon when Peyton drove over Elizabeth Bridge to Dove Island. There was little humidity; the wind was calm, and the temperature was in the low eighties. A perfect day to play at the beach, providing one had plenty of sunscreen.

About two-thirds of the beachfront property on the island had been developed by Scott Cassady, and now sleek high-rise condominiums covered the area, all facing the beach. The other one-third of the island belonged to Bishop's Cove. There was only one way in or out of the ultra-secluded estate, through an iron gate. A security team manned the gatehouse and monitored every car coming or going.

Peyton recognized the guard on duty, who welcomed her back with a big smile. He pushed the button to open the tall, ornate gates, and she drove into the tropical paradise. On either side were manicured shrubs, which served as backdrops to the lush flowers in full bloom. Giant palm trees lined the long drive that led up to the entrance of a stately four-story hotel. Several streets branched off the main drive. They curved into green foliage and disappeared. One of them led to the two-story condominium building where Peyton would be staying. Another street wound toward the twelve bungalows, each set far enough apart to provide absolute privacy. Though there was room for at least twenty more, Uncle Len hadn't been in a hurry to build additional units. He liked the Cove the way it was, a peaceful oasis.

As was her ritual after passing through the gates of Bishop's Cove, she drove straight to the beach. She parked the car and sat there listening to the seagulls complain and the surf lap against the sand. Rolling down the windows, she let the gentle wind brush across her face. She inhaled the wonderful scents of the island, and the tension melted away. Forgotten was the long, tedious drive. She took a deep, cleansing breath and smiled. It was amazing what a change of scenery, temperature, and pace could do. No longer weary, she was in a wonderful mood.

Then Finn called and ruined it. His greeting wasn't filled with affection. "You are not going back to Dalton, Minnesota. Got that?"

Ignoring the anger in his voice, she wanted to respond that it was about damned time he called her and that it wasn't his job to dictate what she could and couldn't do. Instead, she said, "How lovely to hear from you."

"Peyton, I'm serious. I talked to Mark, and he told me you were considering going to Dalton."

"I was simply saying that I would love to see Drew and his wife get the boot. I guess that's vindictive, isn't it? I'm not actually going to go."

"Damn right." It was taking Finn time to get past his worry, and his voice was still harsh.

Although she had no intention of ever returning to Dalton, she didn't like Finn telling her she couldn't. She tried not to be annoyed. He was concerned about her, and that was sweet. Unnecessary, but still sweet. "Is that the only reason you called? To yell at me?"

"I wasn't yelling," he said, his voice calmer now. "After I spoke to Mark, I started to think that maybe you had lost your mind, and if that were the case, I was going to suggest that you look at the bullet holes in your car to bring you back to reality."

So much for the gentle breeze and the soothing sounds of the lapping surf. Both irritated her now. "I was in a peaceful mood until you called."

"Promise me you won't go near Dalton."

"I promise. Happy now?"

"Yes, I'm happy now. Okay, then," he said, his tone brisk. "I've got to go. I'm late for a meeting."

"Where are you?"

"D.C."

"Finn?"

"Yeah?" He sounded impatient.

"Thanks for worrying about me."

She disconnected the call before he could argue with her. Her good mood restored, she drove back to the hotel and parked near the entrance to the business office. She gathered her purse and her phone, and was about to head into the hotel when she looked up and saw her cousin, Debi, walking out the door.

What was she doing in Bishop's Cove? Peyton didn't open her car door or call out to her cousin. She could barely be civil to the woman, and she was determined to hold on to her peaceful, everything-is-wonderful mood. She watched her get in a blue sedan. Peyton thought Debi was alone, but as her cousin backed out of the parking space, she saw the top of a man's head. His seat was tilted way back. It had to be Debi's husband, Sean. Was he sleeping? Peyton wouldn't be surprised if he was, for Sean was one of the laziest people she'd ever met.

Debi had been smiling. That wasn't good. The only time her cousin was happy was when she had gotten away with something vile. Maybe this was different, Peyton thought, trying to stay optimistic. She took a breath and talked herself into her calm, peaceful mood again. Everything was fine.

Then she walked into the business office, and her Zen mood flew out the window. Everything wasn't fine; it was in chaos. Lucy was standing in the doorway of an office at the back of the room barking orders to six employees. She clutched a Pearson Furniture catalog against her chest as she shouted. She looked a fright. Her bangs were sticking up on end; her horn-rimmed reading glasses were tilted precariously on the tip of her nose, and her cheeks were bloodred. Her sweet — most of the time — problem-solving, level-headed sister had turned into a raving maniac.

Peyton was mortified. She quickly said hello to the employees she knew and introduced herself to the rest, then suggested they take off for the evening, promising them it would be much better tomorrow. From the look on Lucy's face, it couldn't get worse.

She tackled Lucy next, all but shoving her into the office before shutting the door.

"What is wrong with you? You don't shout at your staff. That's horribly disrespectful. You treat them the way you want to be treated."

Lucy wasn't in the mood for a lecture. "This place is a mess. I've done nothing but put out fires since I got here." She dropped the book on the desk and folded her arms across her chest. "What took you so long? I expected you days ago."

"I was busy packing your stuff and putting it in storage. What's with the attitude, Lucy?"

Her sister closed her eyes for a few seconds. "I'm tired," she admitted.

"What about the general manager? Christopher . . ."

"Ellison," Lucy supplied. "He doesn't take suggestions well. I can't work with him."

"Uncle Len thinks highly of him."

Lucy shrugged. That reminder obviously wasn't important to her. "I won't fire him, not yet anyway. He needs to know I'm in charge."

That comment jarred Peyton. "You're what?"

"I've already made some changes . . . necessary changes," she said. "I'm just so weary of everyone fighting me on every little thing."

"You need to calm down."

"You have no idea the pressure I'm under."

She didn't want to get into an argument with her sister, so she didn't call her a drama queen. Instead she asked, "What was Debi doing here? I saw her leaving the office."

"She wants in on Bishop's Cove. She said she made a mistake taking the money instead of King's Landing. You're not going to believe how much it sold for," she added.

Peyton recalled that Debi had been smiling when she left the office. She started to get a bad feeling. "What did she do when you told her no?"

Lucy braced herself. "I didn't tell her no. In fact, I agreed to let her in. The four of us will run Bishop's Cove." She put her hand up before Peyton could protest and said, "She's trying to save her marriage. She told me Sean wanted to run King's Landing, but she was against it. She wanted the money. She's sorry about her choice now. They've already spent quite a lot of it."

"No," Peyton said emphatically. "Debi is not going to be part of this. She's lying. Sean would never want to run a resort. That would mean he'd have to work."

Lucy rounded the desk and dropped onto a chair. "It's done. I've made the decision, and you're going to have to live with it."

Lucy expected her sister to put up a fight. She was unprepared for her laughter.

"Did Dad call and ask you to let Debi get her way?"

"Yes. You know the drill. Debi will win. She always does. Whatever she wants, she gets by siccing her father, our dear uncle Brian, and our father on us. I gave in to save time."

"You know it would be a nightmare. She wouldn't lift a finger; she'd fight over every decision, and Sean is completely useless.

221

You didn't really believe he wanted to run King's Landing, did you? No, it's out of the question."

Lucy's lips were pursed. "I already told Dad I'll let Debi be part of this."

"When did you talk to him?"

"Just a few minutes ago while Debi was here. She listened in."

Peyton pulled out her cell phone, hit speed dial, and waited for her father to answer.

"Hi, Dad. Love you," she began. "I called to let you know that Debi isn't going to be joining us at Bishop's Cove. Lucy was having a little nervous breakdown when she agreed. She forgot that it would take all three of us to decide to let Debi in, and neither Ivy nor I would ever do that. Do you want me to call Uncle Brian or will you?"

She was relieved to hear that her father would call his brother and give him the decision but warned Peyton she had better be ready for a fight.

The second she ended the call, Lucy said, "You know this isn't over. Debi will make all sorts of trouble."

"She can try," she said. "Give me her cell phone number."

A minute later Sean answered. She asked to speak to Debi, but Sean, who had the personality of a three-toed sloth, explained that his wife was too busy to talk.

"That's okay," Peyton said in a gratingly cheerful voice. "Just give her a message from me. Tell her she is never going to be part of Bishop's Cove. We don't want her . . . or you . . . to have anything to do with this resort. You had your chance to run King's Landing, and you turned it down for the money. Live with it, Sean. You aren't touching ours. Bye now."

Sean was shouting, "Wait . . . wait . . ." as Peyton disconnected the call.

Lucy had stopped frowning and was slowly regaining her sense of humor. "I'll bet they're in the car. Debi told me they were staying at a motel off the main highway. She thinks the two of them will move into this hotel . . . free of charge, of course. She's probably turning around right now. Hope you're up for the screaming match that's coming."

"I'm not going to scream," Peyton said. "And I'm not in the mood to see them tonight." She found the resort directory and made one more phone call to the gatehouse, informing the security guard that Debi and Sean Payne were not allowed in, no matter what reason they gave.

"That's not going to deter them," Lucy

scoffed. "They'll park at one of Cassady's high-rises and walk the beach to get to us."

"It's a very long walk, and it will slow them down. Let's go get something to eat. I'm starving."

Their two phones rang at the same time.

Lucy picked hers up and looked at the screen. "Sean's calling me."

"Debi's calling me," Peyton said.

Both sisters turned off their phones as they walked out the door.

FOURTEEN

Finn had just finished a grueling interrogation. Both he and Ronan couldn't have been nicer to the suspect, Jory Tyson, and his inept attorney. It was a real stretch for Ronan, who much preferred terrifying the suspect to befriending him to get what he wanted, but in this instance that wouldn't have worked. Charm ruled the day. Ronan went to get a cola for Tyson while Finn sat across from him and chatted about everything from the weather to Billy Kearns's batting average.

It didn't take Finn long to figure out how the suspect's twisted mind worked. Tyson wanted to prove how smart he was, and all Finn had to do was guide him in that direction, three hours of back-and-forth until Tyson was so relaxed and comfortable he stopped fencing and began to do some real boasting. It was obvious he was proud of his accomplishments. Tyson knew they had him cold for two murders and understood he would be going away. In the hope of becoming a celebrity in prison — a possibility Finn had suggested — he told them about two other women he'd killed. He even gave them directions to the park where he had buried them.

Finn ended up spending the entire day with Tyson, and by the time he got home, all he wanted was a shower and a beer . . . and Peyton. It was funny how she would pop into his thoughts and he'd find himself smiling. He wanted to call her, but he didn't. They were wrong for each other. She was eight years younger than he was, and she certainly didn't have his warped ideas about marriage. She probably wanted a family. He didn't. They were going in opposite directions. He'd told her he was moving to Dallas, but now there was talk that he'd be transferred to D.C. She was going to live at Bishop's Cove for at least a year, probably longer.

He shouldn't have taken her to bed. He had let the situation get out of hand. Yet, he wasn't sorry for any of it. Their night together was incredible . . . but it was just one night. He knew that if he saw her again, the same thing would happen. And so he didn't call her.

While he was debating all the reasons he should leave Peyton alone, Mark Campbell phoned.

"About Peyton," Mark began and then hesitated.

"Yeah? What do you think?"

"I'd marry her in a heartbeat," he said. "That's what I think. I'm still mad you didn't mention how frickin' pretty she is. Nearly bowled me over when she walked in."

"Yeah, yeah, she's pretty," Finn agreed, letting his irritation show. "You already mentioned that fact last phone call, and we both agreed she's frickin' pretty. Now let it go."

"Do you think she'd go out with me?"

"Depends. Do you have any cats? She loves cats. The more you have, the better your chances."

Mark laughed. "I guess I'll have to get some."

"She lives in Florida now. You live in Brentwood. It'd be a hell of a commute. Tell me why you called."

Serious now, Mark said, "I know a guy who knows a guy, and he did a little investigating for me. I'm telling you, Finn, Albertson is dangerous," he added. "But I figure you already know that. What I found out is that he goes ice fishing and hunting with a buddy who's a real badass. Name's Rick Parsons."

"Yeah, I know about him."

"He's got a record a mile long. He's been hauled in on assault charges a couple of times, did a short stint in prison a while back for drug trafficking, and his most recent prison stay was for armed robbery. Doesn't look like he can stay out of trouble. He now works for Albertson at the magazine and also does other odd jobs for him. These aren't nice people, and I hate to think about Peyton going up against them."

"I don't like it, either. Let me think about this and get back to you."

He had only just disconnected the call when the phone rang again. Peyton was on the line. He was surprised by how relieved he was to hear her voice.

"I hate to bother you," she said. "I've just got one quick question. When you were looking at my car, did you happen to notice any bullet holes in the roof?"

"No, I . . . bullet holes?" He tried to sound calm. "No, there weren't any bullet holes in the roof."

She muttered something he couldn't hear,

and then said, "Finn, someone shot at me again."

He didn't hesitate. "I'm on my way."

FIFTEEN

There was a screaming match going on inside the lobby of Bishop's Cove, and Finn walked right into the middle of it. The hotel was undergoing a renovation, so no guests were present to witness the battle that was raging among the small group gathered by the front desk.

Peyton's full attention was on the spectacle. Debi was throwing a rather theatrical tantrum complete with tears and torn tissues. Everything about the woman was excessive. From her overly bleached hair to her tarantula eyelashes to her surgically amplified chest — it was apparent that moderation was definitely not her strong suit. Her husband, Sean, a large man with a receding hairline and a potbelly that suggested an aversion to physical activity, was trying his best to keep up with her. He actually stomped his foot once or twice to make his point.

Lucy stood in the thick of the fight. Her responses to the pair bounced back and forth between shouting and cringing. She hated drama unless, of course, she was the one causing it and there was a principle at stake.

When first confronted by the angry couple, Lucy had been quite calm and reasonable as she told them that all three sisters had to agree to let Debi join them in this venture. She then informed them that Peyton had refused. If they had a problem, they should take it up with her. For the first few minutes, Lucy had been relatively composed, but when Debi started making threats, she lost it.

"I'll ruin this place," Debi shouted. "I can do it, too. You're not pushing me out of this."

"You were never in it," Lucy reminded.

Christopher Ellison, the general manager, a tall and tanned man with laugh lines around his eyes, stood next to Peyton, waiting for the storm to be over. He was an impartial observer and seemed to be taking it all in stride.

"This is mortifying," Peyton whispered. Dear God, she was actually related to these people.

Christopher heard her comment and, in

an attempt to offer sympathy and support, put his arm around her shoulder and patted her. "Maybe I should come back later," he said. "This seems to be a family issue."

Finn walked over and stood behind Peyton. He could have politely asked the guy next to her to remove his arm from her shoulder, but he chose to shove the arm away instead. He didn't even try to reason why he was acting so territorial. He simply didn't like another man touching her, and so he stopped it.

Peyton was still focused on the argument and didn't notice Finn. Debi's voice had risen to a teeth-grinding level, and her wrath was now turned on Peyton.

"You better agree to let me in on this, or you'll be sorry. I'll burn this place to the ground if I have to. If I can't make any money, neither can you," Debi shrieked.

"It's time for you and Sean to leave," Peyton said.

Debi tried another tack. "I'm trying to save my marriage," she cried. "And you're ruining it."

When she paused to take a breath, Peyton said, "Maybe you'll do better with your next one."

Neither Debi nor Sean liked hearing that. Sean nudged his wife out of his way so he could get in Peyton's face. He pointed a long, chubby finger at her and said, "You could save yourself some time. We both know that Debi's father will force you to do the right thing. You can't say no to him."

Peyton folded her arms across her chest defiantly. "I already did say no to him. I'm through talking about this. Now please leave."

Sean took another threatening step toward her, but she refused to back down. If he pushed, she planned to push back. She was a little disappointed it wasn't necessary. Finn was suddenly standing next to her, putting his arm around her and pulling her into his side. Sean's gaze immediately went to the gun at Finn's waist.

Peyton was so happy to see him, she wanted to throw her arms around him. He'd gotten to Bishop's Cove in less than twenty-four hours, texting her at least ten times throughout the day, making sure she stayed inside and out of harm's way.

"Are you a cop?" Sean sounded angry over the possibility.

Peyton answered. "No, he's an FBI agent, and I believe he heard your wife threaten to burn this place down." Looking up at Finn, she innocently asked, "Isn't arson against the law?"

He kept his attention on Sean as he slowly nodded.

In a huff, Debi grabbed her purse, paused to glare at Lucy who was leaning against the front desk, then pointed at Peyton and said, "I'm not through with you. I won't let you ruin our plans. Come on, Sean. Daddy will fix this."

The couple marched to the double glass doors at the entrance. Each took one of the long brass handles, yanked the doors open, and stormed outside. Peyton hurried to flip the deadbolt so they couldn't come back in.

"Who are they?" Finn asked.

"Debi's our cousin," Lucy answered. "And the oaf with her is her husband." She crossed the lobby to hug Finn. "I didn't know you were coming. I'm so pleased to see you, but I'm sorry you had to witness that little scene."

Christopher had been waiting patiently to find out who Finn was and if he was related. Peyton introduced them.

Finn scanned his surroundings. He knew this was a luxury resort, but it certainly didn't look like one.

"The hotel will be reopened in two weeks," Lucy explained. She looked around the lobby and laughed. There were drop cloths everywhere; the reception desk was draped in bubble wrap; the beautiful new marble floor was covered to protect it from paint splatters, and aside from a few folding chairs, the large rectangular space was empty. The new crystal waterfall that ran down the length of one wall hadn't been turned on yet. The two-story windows were bare, waiting to be draped.

"It will be at least a month before we can reopen," Christopher corrected.

Lucy frowned. "We're waiting for the painters to finish up in the lobby —"

"They haven't started yet," he said.

Her frown intensified, but she continued to look at Finn while she spoke. "The new furniture will be delivered this week."

"Probably not for another two weeks," Christopher interjected.

Lucy turned to him, her irritation obvious. "Do you have to be so negative about everything?"

"I'm being realistic, Lucy. I have realistic expectations, whereas you . . ."

Here we go again, Peyton thought. Lucy and Christopher couldn't seem to get along or agree on anything. She hurried to interrupt the budding hostility. "Uncle Len had already started the renovation before he decided to let us take over," she told Finn. "Everything for the hotel had been ordered and paid for, so we went ahead with his plans."

"All the rooms have been renovated," Lucy added enthusiastically. "They're quite beautiful, aren't they, Peyton? You'll have your pick, Finn."

"Where are you staying?" Finn asked Peyton.

"In one of the condos behind the hotel."

"Then that's where I'll stay."

Lucy glanced from Peyton to Finn and back to her sister again. "With her?"

"Yes, with her."

"There are two bedrooms in the condo," Peyton said.

"You didn't tell Lucy why I was coming here?" Finn asked.

"I thought I mentioned it —"

"Then she doesn't know —"

Peyton nudged him. "I didn't think Lucy needed any more worries. You can see she's on tilt now."

"Hey," Lucy muttered. "I'm tense, that's all."

What the hell? Finn thought. Someone taking shots at Peyton was just a worry? Was that how she described it?

"I want a word with you." He took her hand and pulled her along, following the exit sign to the back door. He could hear

Lucy and Christopher at it again, arguing over something or other.

"Those two shouldn't work together. They're complete opposites," Peyton said.

"He wants her." He made the statement as he pushed the door open. "And she wants him."

"You can't possibly know that."

"Yes, I can."

"Not everything is about sex."

He flashed a smile. She sounded so incensed. "Yes, it is."

Finn had already scoped out the resort. He was pleased with the setup for safety concerns. There was only one way in and out for a vehicle. Just as important, the resort wasn't open for business, which meant there wouldn't be a horde of strangers milling around. Workers would be coming and going, but they would have to show identification and be vouched for by the others in the crew. There were a lot of places to hide on Dove Island, Finn knew, but protecting Peyton was still going to be easier than if she were in the city.

"Where's your car?" he asked.

"Across the parking lot," she answered. She tried to pull her hand away so that she could walk ahead of him, but he wouldn't let go. "Thank you for coming down here to

237

help me."

She waited for him to say something, and when he didn't, she asked, "Was it difficult for you to leave your job so suddenly?"

"No."

It dawned on her that Finn wasn't paying any attention to her. He was busy scanning the area, looking for possible threats.

"It's pretty much deserted here this time of day," she remarked.

Her Camry was unlocked. He opened the driver's door and told her to sit. The bullet hole was on the curve of the roof, just above the window frame. There was no exit hole, and he suspected that the bullet might be lodged in the ceiling.

One arm draped over the door, he leaned in and said, "You didn't hear this one either? Someone shot at you and you didn't hear —"

"Yes, I did hear something. It sounded like a spitting sound and a ping. I know where it happened, too," she added. "I was parked in front of Van's Pharmacy in Port James. I stopped to get aspirin. When I came out, there was a bunch of teenagers on skateboards making quite a lot of noise. I opened my car door, and that's when I heard it."

"What did you do?"

"I didn't know what it was so I looked around. I even checked my tires. I thought maybe I had a flat and that spitting sound was air leaking."

"How could you not know . . ." He stopped when he realized he had raised his voice. "And you walked around your car . . ."

"That's right." She nodded. "And then I drove home."

Finn was in a mood. Great, Peyton thought. She'd had to put up with Debi and Sean, Lucy and Christopher, and now Finn. Enough already. She wanted to snap at him, but then she remembered he had dropped everything to come to her. She guessed he was entitled to be irritated. Swinging her legs out, she stood. Finn didn't move back, so she put her palms on his chest and pushed against him. It took all her willpower not to slide her hands up his powerful shoulders, wrap her fingers behind his neck, and kiss him. From the moment she saw him, she'd wanted to move into his arms and rest her head on his shoulder.

She stepped around him and said, "I'll show you where you'll be staying."

She led the way up a short incline to a pink stucco building. There were only two units ready for occupancy. The other two on the backside of the building were being used for storage and wouldn't be renovated until next year. Lucy had moved into the larger unit on the first floor because there were three spacious bedrooms, and she thought all the sisters should stay together. She insisted it was going to be fun.

Peyton insisted it was a homicide waiting to happen. They would probably kill one another within the first month if they had to work together and live together. All of them needed a little space and a little privacy, she argued. Ignoring Lucy's protests — her sister thought they should rent the second floor for more income — Peyton moved into the condominium upstairs. It had only two bedrooms, but they were large with king-size beds. Like the one below, it had been updated recently with new tile floors, new beds, mattresses and bedding, and a dream kitchen with all the latest gadgets that Peyton couldn't wait to use.

The furniture in the living room was comfortable. A large white sofa with down-filled cushions and colorful throw pillows, two matching chairs, and a coffee table formed the sitting area. Across the room was a bleached pine console with a large flat-screen television on the wall above it.

Finn walked in, spotted the television, and

nodded approval. "Nice," he said.

"Wait until you see the kitchen," she said enthusiastically. "It's got a big granite island."

"I'll bet the kitchen was the first room you checked out."

"Of course it was. I think Uncle Len knew he was going to make the offer to my sisters and me months ago, and he had these units redone for our comfort. He's such a sweet, loving man," she added. "Unless he's negotiating a deal. Then he's pretty tough."

Peyton headed to the kitchen while Finn unpacked. He didn't have to ask her which bedroom was his. The first bedroom was hers. Her black silk nightgown laid out on the cream coverlet was a beacon, and he couldn't stop staring at it while his mind conjured up all sorts of ways he would take it off her. He remembered how good it had been, her body pressed against his as he made love to her.

He was jarred back to reality when she called out to him, asking him if he wanted something to eat or drink. No, he wanted her. That was the answer that came to mind. He settled on a cola instead.

Placing his cell phone next to hers on the island, he pulled out a stool and sat. The refrigerator door was open, and Peyton had all but disappeared inside. Only her back-side was visible, and it was one great back-side.

Peyton was trying to decide what to cook for their dinner. She didn't want to go out. It had been a long, fruitless day full of arguments and constant changes in plans, and she was weary from the struggle. On the outside, she put up an optimistic front, but on the inside she was worried that she and her sisters wouldn't be able to do it. Turning the resort into a successful business was, after all, a mammoth undertaking.

"Chicken or scallops?" she asked as she closed the refrigerator.

"Scallops."

"Then chicken it is." She pulled out a stool facing him and sat. "I don't have any scallops."

"Then why did you offer them?"

"I wanted to give you a choice. We should probably talk about finding out who keeps shooting at me, don't you suppose?"

"Yes," he agreed. He told her about his conversation with Mark and what he'd learned about Parsons and Albertson. He pulled up a photo on his cell phone and handed it to her. "That's Parsons."

"I didn't see him while I worked at the magazine. Of course, I wasn't there long," she reminded. "Where did you get this?" She immediately realized what a foolish question that was, and smiling, she said, "Never mind. You're FBI. You can get whatever you want."

"Not always."

"Do you think it was Parsons who shot at me again? We already know he's capable of it, but would he come all the way to Florida?" she wondered.

"We'll find out where he is," Finn assured her.

"I can help," she said eagerly. "I have an inside source." Reaching for her phone, she quickly texted Mimi. "Now we wait until she can get to a phone that isn't monitored."

Finn watched as her thumbs tapped out the message on her phone. He couldn't take his eyes off her. Everything about her appealed to him: her smile, her sexy voice, her incredible body, her feminine scent. God, he loved the way she smelled. His senses went crazy when he was around her. Yet, at the same time, he was able to breathe, to relax, when she was near. It was an odd contradiction he couldn't explain.

"You think all the phones at the magazine are monitored?" he asked.

"Mimi and I have become a little paranoid. We aren't taking any chances."

"Read the text to me."

"Just bought a gorgeous blue silk blouse at half price." The dimple in her cheek appeared when she smiled at him. Her sudden enthusiasm made him feel like laughing.

"It's code," she explained.

"Uh-huh," he drawled.

"I told you about Mimi," she said. "But did I mention that about eight months ago she was demoted and her salary was cut by more than half."

While giving a lengthy explanation as to why Mimi had been demoted, she went back to the refrigerator to get the relish dish she'd prepared earlier. She put it on the island between them. There were celery and carrot sticks, red and yellow pepper slices, and in the center compartment was a spicy salsa she'd made the night before.

"Did I tell you this already?" she asked. She didn't give him time to answer but continued on. "Anyway, Mimi had been sending her résumé out, and Drew would have loved it if she'd quit, but then something strange happened."

She opened a cabinet and pulled out a bag of pita chips as she talked. Tossing the bag to Finn, she reached for a blue bowl and put it next to the tray. Finn poured the chips in the bowl, and she stopped talking for a second, watching him, suddenly struck by the reality that he was actually here with her.

"You were saying something strange happened?" he prodded.

"Oh yes," she said and continued. "When Drew and Eileen came back from Europe, he called Mimi into his office and gave her a huge raise, and I mean huge. It was twice what she made as an accountant."

"To keep her from talking about the recording. He's buying her silence."

"Yes," she agreed. "But Drew also knows that Mimi and I are friends and that we stay in contact. The raise would keep her at the magazine, and he would have access to her e-mails as long as she stayed."

"And texts?"

"We think so. That's why we're careful. If I text her about food or clothes, she knows I need to talk to her. She told me she also erases all her texts every night."

Finn picked up her phone and scanned through the texts she had sent and received from Mimi. One stood out.

"She asked when you were going to file suit. Don't you think it's possible that Drew read that one?"

"I was concerned about it, but she assured me she erased it." She thought about it a

245

minute. "You're right. It's possible. She shouldn't have written it in the first place."

"How would he react if he believed you planned to sue?"

Her answer was immediate. "He'd try to stop me." Chills ran down her arms. "He'd be frantic," she guessed. "Once Randolph retires and Drew is named CEO, he wouldn't care what I did, but now he's vulnerable. There's so much money . . . and power . . . at stake. He won't let anyone take that from him."

"You're going to take it from him," he said emphatically.

The enormity of her situation was suddenly hitting Peyton. She could feel the panic building inside her, and she thought this might be the appropriate time to become hysterical. She wasn't quite sure how to go about it, though. Besides, she couldn't give in to the urge anyway. She needed to stay focused and in control. Falling apart would have to wait until later.

The color had left her face and Finn could see the fear in her eyes. He reached across the island and took hold of her hand.

"You're not going to faint on me, are you?"

"No, of course not. It's just that . . . you know . . . I dragged my feet on this. Maybe if I had tried harder, I could have found a way to reach Randolph."

"It doesn't matter. This is where you are now. What are you prepared to do?"

"Mark wants me to send an attorney to Erik and Randolph with the recording. He wants to keep me out of it."

"Okay, that's what Mark wants. What do you want?"

"To make sure."

She realized she was holding his hand now and pulled away. "Both of them could tell the attorneys that they would fire Drew, but how do I know they'd really do it? Mimi says they're good people, but I've never met either one of them, and I don't know how they would react. There's also the fact that once Drew becomes CEO, it's too late. He'll have complete control over anyone who works for him. Randolph won't be able to do anything about it once he's retired and hands the reins over."

"You haven't answered my question. What do you want?"

"Drew out, of course."

"That's a given."

"But a promise that he won't be back isn't enough. If possible, I'd like to get it in writing. I doubt they'll sign anything, though." She shrugged. "I can't do any more than that. Right? Oh, and I also want people to stop shooting at me. My car can't take much more."

"I'll work on that," he promised. He took a pita chip, dipped it in the salsa, and popped it into his mouth. Seconds later his eyes filled with tears. He grabbed his Diet Coke and guzzled it, trying to get rid of the heat.

"I should have warned you it has a kick," she said as she offered him a bottle of water.

"It's okay. I'm fine," he gasped.

She laughed. "Your voice is hoarse."

He stopped trying to be polite. "That stuff is lethal. I think it burned my vocal cords."

Ronan called then. "Is something wrong?" he asked. "You sound funny."

"I'm good. What do you have?"

Ronan gave him the information he had, and when the conversation ended, Finn summarized the details for Peyton. "Ronan is sending a tech over to get your car. He's also making some calls. That's all for now. If I need his help, he'll come."

He went into the bedroom to get his laptop to check his e-mails, explaining that he had sent out a couple of queries and hoped he had answers. While he sat on her sofa reading his messages, Peyton put the food away and dumped the salsa in the disposal. She stood at the sink watching him. How could it be possible for him to be even more handsome than before? He was one gorgeous man, and for one night he had belonged to her. He had been so loving then, but he seemed distant to her now. Did he regret the night they'd shared?

The fact was, she had asked for his help and he had come. Would she have heard from him if there hadn't been a problem? Would he have wanted to see her again? That, she decided, was the million-dollar question, and if she could summon up the nerve, she was going to ask him.

Lucy called twice while Peyton was thinking about her situation. She ignored both calls because she wasn't in the mood to deal with another emergency.

The third time Lucy called, Finn asked, "Aren't you going to get that?"

"It's Lucy. I'll talk to her later."

The technician arrived to pick up her car. Finn went down to the lot with him, but when he returned, he wasn't alone. Lucy and Christopher followed him inside. Finn looked resigned; Lucy looked angry; and Christopher looked like he wanted to throttle her.

"What happened?" Peyton asked warily.

"You want to tell her?" Christopher

snapped at Lucy.

"I didn't have a choice," she muttered.

Peyton's shoulders slumped and she felt as though she was deflating. "What did you do?"

Christopher crossed the room and leaned against the island. Folding his arms across his chest, he glared at Lucy. "She fired Chef Damien."

The announcement rendered Peyton speechless. Lucy was vehemently shaking her head. "No, I did not fire him. He was shouting at me to get out of his kitchen, and I suggested that he might be happier working somewhere else."

Peyton took a deep breath in an attempt to control her temper. "What were you doing in Chef Damien's kitchen?"

"It's not his kitchen," she argued. "The restaurant belongs to us."

"No, the kitchen belongs to Chef Damien." Had she been alone with her sister, she would have been screaming at her now.

"I went into the kitchen to tell Damien that there was a wine distributor waiting in the restaurant to speak to him," Lucy explained.

"No, he wanted to speak to Peyton," Christopher reminded her.

"Damien must have given him your

name," she told her sister. "Why is it okay for any of them to talk to you and not me?"

"You're upset because a distributor asked for me and not you? Could it be that I'm a chef and you're not, and that's why he wanted to talk to me?"

Lucy didn't answer. "Damien was in a real snit. And rude. He's terribly rude. I told him I would be doing the ordering from now on."

No longer able to control her temper, Peyton snapped, "No, you will not."

"I know wines."

"Good for you. You're still not going to be ordering any wines or anything else for the kitchen."

"But I have a responsibility —"

"Lucy, do you know how crazy you are?"

Her sister surprised them all when she dropped down on the sofa. "Yes, I do." She looked at Christopher then. "I'm sorry. I didn't like it when he yelled and carried on, and I overreacted."

He didn't acknowledge her apology, but he quit scowling at her.

Lucy turned to Peyton again. "Leonard's is very profitable."

"And yet you fired the chef."

"You have to talk to him," she said. "You speak his language. You know . . . chef talk."

"You better hurry," Christopher said. "When I left, he was packing his knives."

"The restaurant opens at five thirty, and it's booked solid."

"Lucy, will you agree that your job, your only job, is decor?" Peyton asked. "I'll handle the restaurants, and for now everything else — and I do mean everything else — is Christopher's responsibility. When Ivy gets here, we'll reevaluate. But that's the way it is for now. Agreed?"

"Yes, okay."

"That was quick. Do you mean it?"

"I do mean it. I'm turning into a maniac." She frowned at Christopher when he nodded agreement. "I'm really very sweet." He snorted, and she decided to ignore him. "Do you want me to go with you to talk to Damien?"

"It's Chef Damien, and, no, you stay away," Peyton said. "Finn, could you give me a ride?"

She was walking to the door when Finn grabbed her. "Hold on. Leonard's restaurant is part of Bishop's Cove? Strangers coming and going inside the gates to dine?"

"No, the restaurant is outside the gates. Uncle Len bought it seven or eight years ago and remodeled it. We talked him into giving the restaurant his name."

"Any other surprises I need to know about?" he asked as he followed her down to his car and opened the door for her. He put his hand on top of her head when she bent to get inside, and she almost laughed. Force of habit, she guessed. He hadn't realized what he'd done, and she didn't mention it.

The restaurant was just outside the gates on the main road and around a curve. They parked in the rear and as they entered through the back door, they could hear pots and pans banging against metal.

"Oh, it's bad," she whispered.

Standing five feet three inches tall, Chef Damien was a powerhouse. He had a booming voice and seemed to know every curse word in just about every language. At the sound of the door closing, he swung around waving a knife in Peyton's direction. Finn's hand went to his weapon.

"Put the knife down," Finn ordered, his voice hard, tense.

"He's not going to stab me," she whispered. "That's his santoku knife. He wouldn't dare mistreat it."

"Knife down now," Finn shouted. Each word was clipped.

Chef Damien gently placed the knife on the counter. It took only one quick look around the kitchen to know that Chef Damien had no intention of quitting tonight. His sous-chef was busy working on a sauce while his assistants chopped and sautéed. The kitchen was in full swing, getting ready for the dinner crowd's arrival.

Protocol had to be followed before things could return to normal. Chef Damien had to rant for a good long while, and Peyton had to grovel. It was expected, and she didn't disappoint him. She had to make several promises, too, and all of them involved Lucy.

Finally appeased, the chef kissed her on both cheeks, giving her absolution. She turned to leave and suddenly remembered there was a distributor waiting to talk to her.

"Almost finished," she told Finn.

She threaded her way through the kitchen, greeting each employee by name. Turning the corner, she stepped into the dining room and came face-to-face with Drew Albertson.

Sixteen

He was smiling at her, no doubt pleased with the shock he saw on her face. She was so stunned to see him, she took a step back, instinctively trying to protect herself by putting more space between them.

Her arm brushed against Finn's as he moved forward to partially block her. His touch calmed her; her panic eased, and she was once again in control. Her courage came back and so did her fury. She didn't want to back away now; she wanted to borrow Finn's gun and shoot the man.

"You're even more beautiful than the last time I saw you," Drew said, his voice like silk. "I've missed you."

Missed her? What kind of twisted game was he playing? Or was he out of his mind?

"What are you doing here?" she demanded.

The way Albertson was staring at Peyton made Finn want to put his fist through his face. The bastard wasn't trying to hide his lust. Finn wouldn't have been surprised if he'd started rubbing his hands together over the morsel standing before him. Oh yeah, he really wanted to punch him.

"Finn, this is Drew Albertson," Peyton announced.

"I know who he is." He gave Drew a steely look and said, "You're a person of interest in an investigation."

Drew noticed Finn's gun and holster. "Who are you?"

"FBI."

"He's Special Agent Finn MacBain," Peyton supplied.

Drew's eyes widened. Peyton thought that was a nice beginning. She hoped Finn would make him nervous, and from Drew's expression she knew she was getting her wish.

"Who's here with you?" Finn took a step forward, forcing Drew to back up. "Answer the question," he snapped like a drill sergeant.

"No one's here with me. I came alone to talk to Peyton."

"Show me what's in your pockets."

"Why . . ."

Finn took another step as he repeated the order. Drew placed the blue folder he was holding on the table. He tried to look around Finn to see Peyton, but he was blocked. He removed his wallet and his car keys from his pocket and dropped them on top of the folder.

"Sit," Finn ordered. He all but shoved Drew into a chair.

The dining room was empty, but there were still a few tables that needed to be dressed before the dinner guests arrived. Peyton saw two waiters peeking around the corner from the kitchen watching Finn and Drew.

"Where is Rick Parsons?" Finn asked.

Drew blustered with indignation. "What the hell is this? An interrogation?"

"Yes, that's exactly what this is."

"Do I need an attorney?"

"That's up to you. Answer the question. Parsons. Where is he?"

Towering over Drew, Finn's intimidation tactics were impressive. He was even making Peyton nervous. He certainly knew what he was doing because Drew looked panicked now.

"I don't know where he is. In Dalton, I guess. I haven't seen or talked to him in days. What's this all about?" he demanded. "Why am I a person of interest?"

"Someone's been taking shots at Peyton."

Drew was a bad actor. He tried to feign surprise but failed miserably. "Shooting at her?" He shook his head and said, "That's terrible. Who would do such a thing?"

Finn pulled out a chair and sat facing Drew. Peyton took a seat across from him at the round table. Trying to stay composed, she folded her hands in her lap and said, "You sent Parsons after me when I left Dalton. He shot at me several times."

"I most certainly did not send Parsons after you, and I don't believe for one minute that he shot at you." He added with a nervous glance at Finn, "He doesn't even own a gun."

Finn folded his arms and leaned back. "Is that right? So when you boys go hunting, what exactly do you carry?"

"We don't go hunting. We go ice fishing." Turning his attention to Peyton, Drew said, "I would never do anything to hurt you. Never," he fervently vowed.

She wasn't buying that bridge.

Finn continued to question Drew, backtracking on the issue of guns again and again, trying to trip him up on some of his lies, but Drew held firm. The two waiters poked their heads around the corner again. Peyton checked her watch and motioned for them to come in and finish preparing the tables for dinner.

As soon as Finn stopped questioning Drew, it was her turn. "Why did you come here?"

"I wanted to talk to you." He nervously glanced at Finn before adding, "Alone."

"That's not gonna happen."

Drew rushed on. "You left Dalton so quickly, we didn't get a chance to talk. I'm afraid there's been a terrible misunderstanding. I thought we had a connection, that you cared as much as I did. All the signals you were sending said as much." His eyes drooped and he sounded so pathetic when he added, "I would have left my wife for you."

Incredulous, Peyton listened to his pitiful speech. His lies were piling up, one on top of the other, and she couldn't believe he could say them with a straight face.

Drew continued, "After all we've shared, it's come to this."

What was he talking about? "After we shared what?" she asked.

"You know . . . all our nights together."

That was the final straw. She could barely control her anger when she said, "Our nights? We didn't have any nights together. Sexual harassment and threats — that's what you call a connection?"

Drew finally must have realized it was pointless for him to argue. He didn't stand a chance of getting his way. Looking resigned, he leaned forward and shifted in his seat to give Finn his back.

He lowered his voice as though he intended only Peyton to hear him. "I don't want you to sue the magazine. It was a simple misunderstanding." He quickly added, "But the magazine shouldn't be dragged through the mud. That's a little vindictive, isn't it?"

"Why do you think I'm going to sue?"

"I —" He stopped suddenly.

"Yes?"

She could almost see his brain spinning as he tried to come up with a plausible lie. He couldn't very well admit he'd read Mimi's text, and Peyton was certain that was what he'd done.

"I just thought you might be considering it. You left in such a hurry you didn't give me a chance to convince you to stay."

"I'm not going to sue." She didn't add, *unless it's the last resort.*

His reaction was comical. As quick as lightning he flipped the folder open and pushed a paper toward her. "Sign this."

"I'm not going to sign anything."

"How do I know you won't change your mind?"

She shrugged. "You don't know. Just assume I'm as truthful as you are."

His eyes narrowed, staring at her as though he was trying to decide whether she was being sincere or mocking him.

"I was going to sue," she said then, "but Mimi talked me out of it, so you can thank her."

"Then sign this paper," he said as he pushed the document even closer.

She pushed it back. "No."

"What if you change your mind?"

"If I have to keep dodging bullets, I just might."

"I had nothing to do with that. I can't promise it will stop because I don't know who's behind it."

She moved to stand.

"Wait, please," he begged.

"Yes?"

"I just want to be assured . . . if you should change your mind, will you promise me you'll think about your decision for at least two weeks before you file suit? Give yourself time so that you don't do anything rash."

She translated the request to mean that in two weeks he expected to be the new CEO.

"Yes, I'll weigh the decision for two weeks because it makes sense. I don't want to have regrets."

He nodded. "I trust you to keep your word. I don't know what I would do if you broke your promise to me. I just don't know."

"Are you threatening her, Albertson?" Finn was more disgusted than angry.

"No, of course not. I was just telling her I don't know what I would do . . . that's all."

"Are we finished?" Peyton asked, anxious to get away from him.

"Oh, one more thing. I've made some changes at the magazine, and my food critics will now be giving good *and* bad reviews. I've decided to personally review this restaurant. I believe it belongs to you now, doesn't it?" He didn't wait for her answer. "Think of the damage a negative review would do. It would be devastating."

"Yes, it would," she agreed. "But I'm certain it will be a wonderful review. The food here is excellent."

"The review depends on you, and I'm hopeful it won't be negative."

She nodded. "Just as I am hopeful the recording I made in your office won't go viral if I were to put it on the Internet."

Drew stood and with a faint, insincere

smile said, "No one will take that recording seriously. It was a joke between you and me. Remember? We were just having a little fun."

Like Peyton, Finn had had enough. "Two FBI agents will be at your door in twenty-four hours. You damn well better have Rick Parsons there with you to answer some questions."

"I don't fly home until tomorrow afternoon. That doesn't give me much time. What if I can't find him?"

"Then the agents will cuff you and take you in."

"On what charge?" he huffed indignantly.

"Charges . . . plural," Finn corrected. "I've got several in mind."

He motioned for Peyton to stay put and followed Drew out into the parking lot. He made sure he got the license plate number and the make and model of the rental car he was driving, and only after Drew had pulled onto the highway did he go back to get Peyton.

She was helping the waiters with preparations. She carried bud vases with roses and votives and placed them on each table. When she was finished with the task, she lit the candles and straightened the white tablecloths. The most wonderful smells of baking bread and roasting meat floated out of the kitchen, but Finn suspected that Drew had spoiled Peyton's appetite. Her face had lost its color and she looked sick to her stomach.

He waited until she was done, then said, "Are you ready?"

Nodding, she turned to leave. He surprised her by pulling her into his arms and holding her against him. It was a quick but fierce hug.

"Now that you've met him, do you still want to help me get him?"

He smiled. "You always were a pain in the ass . . . and yeah, I'm gonna help you. I want to nail the bastard."

She returned his smile. "You say the sweetest things."

SEVENTEEN

Dinner was a quiet affair. Peyton wasn't in the mood to cook anything fancy, and so she made a simple spinach salad with dried cranberries and toasted slivered almonds tossed in the sweet and tangy vinaigrette she always kept on hand, followed by roasted rosemary chicken, new potatoes with dill, and fresh steamed asparagus with a hint of lemon. Dessert was just as simple — orange and mango slices dipped in chocolate.

She wasn't very hungry, but Finn ate enough for three men.

"Are you feeling okay?" he asked. "You aren't eating much."

She shrugged. "I keep replaying the conversation with Drew, and that's taken my appetite away. I guess you weren't as disgusted as I was," she added with a smile when he reached for the last slices of fruit.

She pushed the small fondue pot toward him.

"I'm used to dealing with the depraved," he said as he dipped the orange into the rich dark chocolate and popped it in his mouth.

"So, no surprises with Drew?"

"No," he answered. "He's a good-looking guy who could probably get most of the women he went after, but that doesn't do it for him. He wants them young and beautiful, and you're both."

Her head came up. "You think I'm beautiful?"

He seemed surprised by the question. "Yeah, I do . . . when you're not being a royal pain."

She didn't understand why, but she was inordinately pleased with the backhanded compliment. Smiling, she was content to watch him finish dinner. She didn't have to ask if he enjoyed the meal because he ate every bit. He needed the fuel. God only knew how many calories he burned in a day. He was a big man and very muscular. She remembered running her fingertips over his broad shoulders, down his rock-hard chest, and over his thighs. She remembered everything about their night together . . . every little detail.

"You still have a swimmer's body," she blurted.

"I still swim," he said as he stood and reached for her plate, stacking it on his and carrying both to the kitchen. He helped her clear the table and load the dishwasher, then picked up his phone. "I've got to make some calls."

"Finn? Do people ever recognize you?" she asked. "You won three gold medals. You could have been a celebrity."

"That happened a long time ago. People see an FBI agent, and that's what I want."

"You could have done commercials," she pressed. She laughed then because he looked so appalled. "Picture it. You in your Speedo holding up a tube of toothpaste, smiling into the camera."

If she wanted to tease, he could, too. "And you could have been a model. Picture it. You wearing high heels walking down the runway in your undies, smiling into the camera."

"Models never smile. It's a rule. No smiling on the runway. And I could never be a lingerie model. I'm not overly . . ." She suddenly realized what she was about to say and stopped.

He saw her blush and wouldn't let it go. "Overly what?"

"Endowed," she finished. "Most of them are overly endowed. And I couldn't be a fashion model, either. Most of them are flat-chested, and I'm not."

His eyes slowly scanned her body, and several heartbeats later he said, "No, you're not."

Every part of her reacted to his sexy voice. How did he do it? He looked at her, and she was ready to tear off her clothes. And his. It really was the craziest thing. One glorious night with Finn had turned her into a shameless nymphomaniac.

The heat that was warming her face was rapidly making its way down her body and settling between her thighs. She hastily folded her dish towel and laid it next to the sink. Stepping around him, she headed toward her bedroom. "Make your calls. I'm going to get into the shower."

As she was closing her door, he called out to her. "Peyton?"

"Yes?" she answered expectantly, hoping he hadn't noticed how flushed she had become.

"Dinner was great. I've never eaten chicken that tasted so good."

She beamed with pleasure. Now, that was a lovely compliment. She was flattered when Finn told her she was beautiful. It was a very nice thing to hear, but she couldn't help the way she looked. She sure as certain could roast a perfectly delicious chicken, though.

She showered, washed her hair, and used a gallon of scented body lotion on her arms and legs. While she dried her hair, she thought about her nightgown choices. Should she wear the short, black silk nightie? Or would that be too obvious? If she walked out into the living room wearing it, he would immediately know she wanted to sleep with him. Not actually sleep, of course. Call it what it was, she told herself. Sex. She wanted him to make love to her again.

As she sorted through the drawer trying to decide, she could feel her heartbeat quicken. She'd never felt or acted this way toward a man in her entire life. It was a totally new sensation, and she took a deep breath to calm herself.

Yes, this was unfamiliar territory for her, but what about Finn? He was behaving normally, in his relaxed and self-assured way. What was he thinking? He certainly hadn't given her any indications that he wanted to go to bed with her again. In fact, he'd been acting rather aloof and business-like since he'd arrived, treating her as though she were just an old friend who needed help. He hadn't even kissed her.

She surveyed her sleepwear choices again. Maybe she shouldn't appear to be so eager. Maybe she should wear her old faded cotton pajamas. But if she chose those, what message would that send? And why hadn't he kissed her? She frowned thinking about that. Maybe sex with her hadn't been all that great, and if so, why not?

By the time she put on her short, pink silk nightgown she was primed for a fight. She was going to storm into the living room and demand to know why he no longer wanted her.

Mimi saved her from making a fool of herself. Peyton had just pulled the down comforter back on her bed and was reaching for her robe when her friend called.

"Want a laugh?" Mimi began.

"Sure. I could use one."

"Bridget told me that now that I'm back in the *Bountiful Table* family — honest, those were her exact words — I'm no longer banned from the celebration of Miriam Swift's life. She personally delivered the invitation."

"She couldn't have. She's dead."

Mimi laughed. "Bridget handed me the invitation. It's such a crock. The celebration is on a Sunday afternoon, and everyone in the company is invited, which would imply they had a choice, right? Not so. It's mandatory."

"When are you going to give your notice?"

"Lars went to HR and handed his in today. They asked him to stay the full two weeks and he agreed. I'll give my notice on his last day and leave then and there," she promised. "We want to drive down to Florida together . . . you know, following each other in our cars. Can you wait that long for us?"

"Yes, but no longer than two weeks and you're out of there. I worry about you. Did Lars tell them where he was going?"

"No," she said. "You know Lars. He can't lie, but he hinted that he was homesick. If they want to believe he's going back to Sweden, that's fine. I'm finished with my news," she added. "What's going on there?"

"You'll never guess who stopped by."

She told Mimi all about her encounter with Drew, and when she was finished, her friend was flabbergasted. "Did he come right out and threaten you in front of an FBI agent?"

"No," she said. "He implied."

"According to his calendar, he's in L.A. checking out a couple of new restaurants.

Guess that's a lie."

"What about Parsons? Have you seen him around the office?"

Mimi thought for a second. "Good old Rick Parsons is usually glued to Eileen's side, but, now that you mention it, I haven't seen him all week. Could be longer. Eileen has been in the cafeteria for lunch every day this week, but Parsons hasn't been with her. I'd remember if he was there. I could ask around."

"No, I don't want you asking questions. In that tight little community everything gets back to Eileen, right?"

"Right," she agreed. "Parsons doesn't come into the main building unless Eileen is here. He's supposed to work in the plant. He's one of the supervisors who doesn't do diddly."

"Drew takes care of his friends, doesn't he? There's no telling what he's put him up to."

"This is all my fault," Mimi said. "Drew must have read that text I sent you before I erased it. That's why he came to threaten you."

"It's okay. I told him you talked me out of suing. You might get another raise."

As soon as the call ended, Peyton went into

272

the living room to tell Finn what Mimi had to say, but he wasn't there. She could hear water running and knew he was in the shower, which meant he was naked. Of course he was naked, she reasoned. He wouldn't shower in his clothes.

"Don't picture it. Don't think about it. Don't . . ." Saying it out loud didn't make any difference. The second she heard the water running she envisioned gloriously naked Finn standing under the spray of water cascading down his muscular shoulders. He was just feet away from her. In her mind she saw the ripple of muscle across his chest, the curly dark hair that tapered just above his navel, and those thighs . . . those gorgeous thighs . . .

"Oh, for the love of . . ." She groaned as she turned around and walked back into her bedroom. "You just had to picture it," she muttered to herself.

This sensation was new to her, and she didn't like it one bit. So this was what sexual frustration felt like. Difficulty swallowing, rapid heartbeat, sweaty palms, and trembling all over. There was heat, too, heat in her belly. Some of these symptoms were signs of a heart attack, weren't they? One way or another, she was probably going to keel over. Hot and bothered. Might as well add those to the list, too. She guessed she knew exactly what they meant now.

She was in trouble, all right. If just thinking about him naked aroused her, there was no hope. Was she doomed to a perpetual state of misery?

For Pete's sake, why hadn't he kissed her?

She sat on her bed and drew her knees up under her chin, wrapping her arms around her legs. She was able to force the foolish thoughts from her mind because the water wasn't running any longer. Finn had clothes on by now. Turning her attention to the resort, she made a mental list of what needed to be done tomorrow. There would be several trades arriving. She would have to coordinate the electricians, plumbers, painters, and movers, but all in all, it wasn't going to be too hectic. She had worked out a schedule for each of them.

Everything was organized and on track, and she was feeling pretty good until the phone started ringing. Four phone calls later she was in a state.

Her uncle Brian was the first to call. He wanted to talk to her about his little girl, Debi. He asked Peyton to let his sweet daughter be part of their exciting venture.

Little girl? She was thirty years old. And sweet? Was he serious? Peyton was surprised he could say "sweet" and "Debi" in the same sentence and not choke. Yes, he was her father and, yes, he loved her, but surely he could see what a shrew she was.

Peyton patiently explained that it wasn't possible to include Debi. A contract had been drawn up and signed by all parties. It was a done deal. When she finally hung up from speaking to her uncle, she knew he wasn't happy, but she thought at least the matter had been settled.

Ten minutes later, her father was on the line. When Uncle Brian didn't get her co-operation, he had immediately called to complain about her. Peyton's father wanted to keep peace in the family, and for that reason, he asked her to give Debi a chance. Peyton once again explained about the contract. She also reminded him that Debi had passed up the chance to run the California resort. According to her father, that was water under the bridge and they shouldn't dwell on it. Despite his protest, she stood her ground, and she ended the conversation thinking, once again, the matter was settled.

Unfortunately, Uncle Brian wasn't through campaigning for his daughter. He called once more and threatened — in loving uncle talk — to tell her uncle Leonard that she was being uncharitable. He would have to wait to speak to his brother because he was in Bali, but as soon as Len returned home, they would have a lengthy conversation about her attitude.

Peyton's father was sick of hearing from his brother and wanted the matter resolved. At least that's what he told Peyton when he called yet again. He pulled out several religious punches. *It's better to give than to receive, isn't it?* No, not always, Peyton silently answered. *She should turn the other cheek with Debi.* Why? she wondered. *Yes, Debi could be difficult,* he agreed, *but in her defense, she was an only child and didn't have sisters to show her the way.* Peyton thought that was a lame argument. She knew plenty of people who were the only children in their families and they weren't dysfunctional or spoiled; however, she didn't say her thoughts aloud. She knew she'd be on the phone an hour if she debated the issue.

She could hear her mother in the background but couldn't make out what she was saying.

"What does Mom want?"

Her father's long, drawn-out sigh came through the phone. "Your mother wonders if you've met anyone down there."

Peyton decided she had two choices. She could either start screaming or she could laugh. She chose humor. "No, I haven't. I've been busy. I've got to go now."

"Hold on," her father insisted. "Do you know where Lucy is? Your uncle Brian has been trying to get ahold of her, but she isn't answering her phone. Do you know why?"

She could tell him the truth, that Lucy was smarter than she was because she had looked at caller ID before answering. Lucy knew why Uncle Brian was phoning and didn't want to argue with him. Her uncle wouldn't give up, though. Lucy knew that, too.

"She probably went to bed. She put in a long day. I'm exhausted, too," she added. "Love you, Dad. Night."

Before the phone had a chance to ring again, she turned it off and plugged it in to the charger. Then she dropped down on the bed on her stomach and closed her eyes.

Finn stood in the doorway listening to Peyton mutter to herself. His gaze went to her long legs and slowly moved up to her sexy backside.

"Peyton? Mind if I come in?"

She rolled onto her side and gave him a disgruntled look. "Sure, come on in."

"What were you doing?" he asked as he

crossed the room and sat on the bed next to her.

"Having a moment."

"Meaning?"

"I was contemplating the merits of being an orphan."

"Ah," he drawled. "I'm guessing Debi's father called."

"How did you know?"

"She promised to get him to call and make you change your mind. In fact, she screamed it as she was leaving. So, did you?"

"Did I what?"

His grin was devilish. "Change your mind."

She was having trouble following the conversation. The man was a distraction. He was wearing a pair of faded navy shorts and nothing else. She wanted to stare at his massive chest, to run her palms down his hard, warm body, to kiss him everywhere, especially those amazing thighs . . .

"No," she blurted. "I didn't change my mind."

Threading her fingers through her hair to give it some semblance of order, she sat up. One of the straps on her nightgown slipped down her arm, exposing a good deal of her breast. She adjusted the strap and waited for him to tell her why he had come into her bedroom.

She vowed she wouldn't bring up the past. Every ounce of her wanted to ask, what is this? To tell him she didn't know the rules and could he please explain them. They did have sex, didn't they? She didn't imagine it. But now he was acting as though they hadn't. Was being blasé about it all the sophisticated way of behaving?

Having sex with her must have been a disappointment for him, she decided, and he didn't want a repeat performance. That much was obvious to her because here she sat in her scanty nightgown, and he hadn't even looked at her. In fact, he was staring at the top of her head, giving the impression he was bored. What were they supposed to be now? she wondered. Pals? Best buddies? Okay, then. If that's what he wanted, that's what he would get.

"Did you say something?" she asked. He nodded but remained silent. She nudged him. "Yes?" she prodded.

"I just got a call. Albertson is at the airport waiting to board the company jet. I've got a man watching him," he explained. "So far, Albertson is the only one there. No Parsons."

"Maybe he's in Dalton, and Drew really did come here alone. When will I get my car back?"

He rubbed the stubble on his jaw. "Tomorrow, probably late afternoon."

She didn't ask if the technicians had found anything that would help them identify the shooter because Finn would have told her.

"How long are you staying?" she asked.

He stretched out on the bed and propped two pillows behind his back. "I don't know yet. Ronan's gonna need some help with a case pretty soon. This is a great mattress."

She watched him stack his hands on his chest and close his eyes. "The mattress in your bedroom is identical. Go try it out."

"I'm kinda comfortable here."

"Listen, pal —"

"Pal?" he repeated, laughing.

He pulled her down beside him and held her close. She struggled to get up until he pushed her head down on his shoulder. "There, comfy now?"

Laughing, she asked, "What are you doing?"

"Relaxing."

She threw one leg over his hips. He blocked her knee before it slammed into his groin. Snuggling up against him, she yawned and asked, "Is the outside door locked?"

"Yeah."

This was crazy, she thought. He should

either kiss her or get out of her bed and go to his own. Yet, it was chilly and his body was wonderfully warm. She couldn't resist the temptation and began to caress his chest with her fingertips. Finn put his hand on top of hers, keeping her still.

"Behave yourself and go to sleep."

Finn had made up his mind that he and Peyton would talk about expectations before they had sex again. No messing around until she understood there couldn't be a long-term relationship. Going forward would be up to her. Until the talk, he was going to be honorable and leave her the hell alone.

Easier said than done. He kept telling himself to get out of her bed and go into his own room, but his body wouldn't move. He liked where he was too much, having her soft body cuddled next to him. Her intoxicating scent enveloped him, and he fell asleep content because she was in his arms.

Five more minutes, Peyton thought. That was all the time she would allow herself to stay with Finn, then she was going to get up and move to his bedroom. She'd never fall asleep with him in her bed. Okay, maybe ten more minutes. She felt so warm and safe next to him, she'd stay ten more minutes and then she'd leave. And that was her last thought before sleep claimed her.

In the middle of the night she awakened in the most peculiar position. Finn was spooning her, and she was rubbing against his arousal. His hands were under her nightgown cupping her breasts, his thumbs slowly rubbing her nipples in the most erotic love play. His mouth was on her neck nuzzling her, and the moans she heard were coming from her. Her bikini panties were around her knees. Had she done that, or had he?

She kicked her panties off and moaned again when he slid his hand down between her thighs to caress her intimately. His finger pushed up inside her as his thumb stroked her, and she could feel herself getting closer and closer to coming undone. She put her hand on top of his and held him there, moaning as she moved against him.

Finn was burning with desire. She was so hot and wet it made him crazed to have her. He left just long enough to seek protection and, when he slipped back into bed, he covered her body with his and gently kissed her lips, then her earlobes, then her neck. He rolled onto his back and lifted her on top of him.

Straddling him, she pulled her nightgown over her head and tried to ease him into her, but they were both so eager, they couldn't go slowly. He thrust deep and gripped her hips.

"Don't let me hurt you," he said, his voice rough with his need.

Cupping the back of her neck with one hand, he pulled her down and kissed her. His mouth covered hers and his tongue delved inside to rub against hers. She tasted so good, so sweet. He showed her how he wanted her to move to enhance her pleasure. His hand slid down between them and he began to stroke the fire inside her.

When Peyton rotated her hips to move seductively against him, she felt a huge burst of raw ecstasy.

Finn knew he was going to climax and wanted her there with him. He was rough when he rolled her onto her back, locked inside her. He increased the pace, his thrusts more uncontrolled, more frantic.

"Let go, Peyton," he demanded.

He felt the first tremors of her release, and that triggered his own. His orgasm lasted longer this time and was more power- ful, more all-consuming. It was blissfully shattering.

It took several moments for him to catch his breath and to slow his racing heartbeat. "Are you okay?" he whispered.

She didn't need to speak. She put her arms around his neck and kissed him passionately.

They fell asleep wrapped in each other's arms. They would deal with the consequences tomorrow.

EIGHTEEN

The day started out to be quite pleasant, but it went downhill faster than a roller coaster. Peyton showered and dressed in white linen pants and a blue cotton sweater, then went into the kitchen. Finn had made breakfast for her. He kissed her good morning and pulled a chair out for her to sit. When he placed the plate in front of her, she wanted to bolt, but since that would hurt his feelings and definitely would be rude, she stayed put. He'd prepared scrambled eggs that looked and tasted like rubber, bacon that was so overcooked it shattered when she took a bite, and limp toast slathered in butter.

"You shouldn't have gone to all the trouble," she said. "I could have eaten cereal."

"I wanted to cook for you. Enjoy."

One small bite of the eggs and bacon was all she could handle. She moved the rest of the food around on the plate waiting for an opportunity to dump it down the garbage disposal, but Finn was watching her as he attached his gun and holster to his belt.

"I checked the weather," she said. "It's already seventy-four degrees. Would you like to go swimming?"

"Where?"

"We have several pools on the property, and there's a lap pool on the roof of the hotel."

"It's a real lap pool?"

"Yes," she said. "It's under a dome. You'll be impressed," she promised.

She could tell he was excited to go. According to Finn's mother, who told Peyton's mother, who told . . . well, just about everyone . . . swimming was therapeutic for Finn. One day she wanted to ask him what he thought about in the water. He had once said his mind got rid of all his worries. What did that feel like?

"You'll have to go with me," he said. "I'm not going to let you run around the resort alone."

"I'll go with you."

"What about work?"

"My first appointment isn't until ten."

"Want to swim with me?"

She shook her head. She held a forkful of

eggs so he could see she was eating.

"I'll get my suit on," he said. He crossed the living room and called her name when he reached the hallway.

"Yes?" she answered.

"Wait until I go into the bedroom to dump the food."

She thought she'd been clever pretending to enjoy the breakfast, but he wasn't fooled. Can't trick an FBI agent, she surmised, laughing.

Finn had left a mess in the kitchen. She cleaned up while she waited for him. Still hungry, she opened a blueberry yogurt and stood at the island eating it. Finn hadn't returned yet, so she checked to see that her laptop was in her backpack, added her cell phone, went to the linen closet to grab a towel for him, and continued to wait. He was saying good-bye to someone on his cell when he finally joined her.

The back of the hotel was directly across the parking lot from her condo. Peyton didn't want to cut through the rear entrance because the corridor connected to the business office, and she thought she'd get waylaid, so they walked around to the front entrance and took the guest elevator up to the roof. Several employees were using the treadmills and ellipticals in the fitness center. She waved to them as she led the way to the pool.

Finn laid his gun, badge, and cell phone on a table next to a padded chair he'd moved for her. She placed her phone next to his, pulled out her laptop and a bottled water and was ready to go to work.

"You need anything?" he asked.

"I'm good," she answered. "Now go swim."

He pulled his T-shirt over his head and slipped out of his jeans. As he walked to the edge of the pool she noticed how faded his navy-blue swim trunks were. She didn't know if the water had been heated, but Finn didn't complain as he knelt down and splashed water onto his shoulders. He checked the depth, then he stood, made a slick shallow dive, and disappeared. The water barely rippled.

Peyton checked the time. It was 7:10. She looked at her watch again when he emerged from the water and was shocked at how much time had passed. He'd been swimming for over an hour and didn't look the least bit winded or fatigued. His stamina was impressive.

During that time Danielle had called Finn twice. Peyton knew because she'd turned his phone around to face her and looked.

Why was she calling him? He had told Peyton that three years ago he'd almost proposed to her but changed his mind and broke it off. So, why three years later was she calling him?

Handing him a towel, she put the issue of Danielle aside. "Aren't you tired? You were in the water a long time."

"It's invigorating."

"If you want, we could come back tonight, and you could swim again."

"Yeah, if there's time, let's do that," he said enthusiastically. "And tonight you can swim with me." He picked up the towel and wiped water from his face.

Dripping wet he was an Adonis. Beads of water on his shoulders and upper arms made his skin glisten. She didn't dare look at his chest or his thighs. She'd be lost. Memories of what they had done during the night rushed into her mind. She blocked them as best she could and said, "We should get going."

An hour later they were walking over to the hotel lobby again. This time Finn's demeanor was different. He had transformed back into an FBI agent. He was casually dressed in khaki pants and a white long-sleeve shirt with cuffs rolled back and the collar open, but the gun and badge at his waist made him look intimidating.

"Do you have to wear your gun?" she asked. "You're not on duty here."

"Until we nab whoever has been shooting holes in your car, I'm wearing it," he said emphatically. There was no room for discussion. "I may have to leave for a while this morning, and I'll need to know who you'll be with. What's on your schedule?"

"The electricians should be hard at work by now. Lucy and Christopher were going to meet them at seven and give them instructions. The older bungalows need new wiring to keep up with all the latest gadgets," she told him. "I'll check on them, and then Lucy and I have a meeting."

"Who are you meeting?"

"A developer named Scott Cassady. His signs are all over the island."

He nodded. "Yeah, I saw a couple of them on my way here."

"He's gobbled up most of the island, and Uncle Len told us he wants Bishop's Cove. When Cassady requested a meeting, Lucy thought it would be a good idea to hear what he had to say. Better to know what we're up against, right?"

"Where are you going to have this meeting?"

"In the lobby. I want it very informal. I don't want to give the idea that it's a business meeting. Just one neighbor visiting another," she said.

Finn opened the door and followed her inside. She stopped short and whispered, "Uh-oh," when she saw Lucy's worried expression. Christopher was behind the counter on the phone.

"No electricians," Lucy announced. "Someone called West Beach Electrical and canceled the order. Christopher's trying to sort it all out now."

"Who canceled it? And when?"

"The woman who does the scheduling said I called and canceled a week ago. I didn't, of course. It's a big mix-up." Frustration brimming in her voice, she added, "And a huge setback on time. The electricians are all out on another job and won't be done for three or four weeks."

Finn's phone rang. When he saw that it was the technician who was examining the bullet holes in Peyton's car, he excused himself and crossed the lobby before he answered. Standing at the front windows, he spotted Debi getting out of her car in the circle drive. Her husband wasn't with her. She waved to a man who was just pulling into the parking lot, and it was obvious they knew each other.

After a brief word with the technician, Finn slipped the phone back in his pocket and returned to Peyton. "Your car is ready. I'm going to leave for an hour. Stay put until I get back," he ordered.

She nodded toward Lucy and Christopher, who were beginning to argue about the solution to their latest fiasco. "I don't think I'll be going anywhere for a while," she said, sighing.

Peyton watched Finn leave and had just turned back to the ensuing fight when she heard the sound of spike heels clomping across the marble floor. Oh no, now she was going to have to deal with her brash cousin. She clenched her jaw.

If Debi weren't such a nuisance, Peyton would have laughed at the sight of her. She looked as though she'd shopped in the preteen department. Her paisley print skirt was too short to be considered decent, and her yellow T-shirt was at least two sizes too small. Debi's breasts, which looked like two overly inflated volleyballs, strained the thin material to its limit. It was apparent her cousin was mighty proud of her latest acquisitions.

Peyton's greeting wasn't polite. "What are you doing here?"

"Didn't my father call you?"

"Yes, he did. We had a lovely conversation, and I told him you were not going to be part of this undertaking."

"I'm not leaving," she snapped. "Lucy, did you talk to my father? He's been calling you." Her voice sweetened when she addressed the older sister.

"I spoke to him this morning, and I also told him no. You really should give it up and leave."

Jutting her hip out and settling her hand on it, she bit her lower lip while she contemplated her next move.

"Okay, look," she began, her tone conciliatory. "I admit I made a mistake taking the money, but that's in the past, and I want another chance. I can be a big help . . . or a hindrance," she threatened. "It's up to you."

"Where's Sean?" Lucy asked.

"My husband flew home to go back to work. We aren't millionaires, you know."

At that moment, the front door opened and Scott Cassady entered. Peyton didn't want Debi there and asked her once again to leave.

"I'm staying," her cousin muttered.

.Peyton walked around her to greet Cassady. It didn't take any time at all to size up the successful developer. There was such a pretentious air about him. Everything seemed staged, from the sandy blond hair that was perfectly gelled — this guy didn't sit in a barber's chair, he had a stylist, she bet — to the meticulous choice in his clothing. He worked really hard to make his appearance look effortless. He wore pressed Levi's and a pale polo shirt, the collar raised ever so slightly, and his polished leather boots looked brand-new, with nary a scuff mark. The only item missing was a cashmere sweater tied around his shoulders.

"Please, call me Scott," he insisted, extending his hand and smiling warmly.

Peyton was about to introduce him to Lucy, but Debi blocked her by thrusting her hand out to the developer. "I'm the cousin, Debi Payne," she said. "And it's a pleasure to meet you. I'm one of the owners of Bishop's Cove."

If she thought she could bluff her way in, she was mistaken. "No, she isn't," Peyton countered. "In fact, she was just leaving."

"I believe I'll stay a little longer," Debi said with a defiant glare at Peyton.

Peyton ignored her. Turning away from her rude cousin, she introduced her sister and suggested they sit, gesturing toward the two new sofas that had been placed in front of the waterfall. They faced one another with a large square coffee table in between. Lucy and Peyton sat on one sofa, and Cassady took a seat across from them. Once everyone was settled, Debi dropped down next to him.

While Cassady was doing his best to charm the women with small talk, Peyton's mind went elsewhere, coming up with ways to get rid of Debi. She could think of a couple of swamps where they could dump her but decided that would be cruel punishment for the alligators.

Peyton heard Cassady say her name and realized she hadn't caught a word he'd said.

"I'm sorry, you were saying?"

Lucy nudged her. "Scott knows all about the deal Uncle Len made with us." She impatiently brushed her bangs out of her eyes before continuing. "How did you hear about it, Scott?"

Cassady seemed to ponder his answer before replying, "I think it was one of your groundskeepers who told my secretary."

"How would the groundskeepers know the details?" Lucy asked. "We haven't shared that information with anyone on the staff except Christopher."

"Then maybe that's who told her," Cassady rushed to answer.

Peyton called out to Christopher who had

just hung up the phone. "Christopher, did you tell anyone about our arrangement with our uncle?"

Christopher looked appalled. "Of course not," he answered. "Lucy asked me not to."

Peyton turned back to Cassady. "Christopher is a very trustworthy person, and I believe him." She sat forward and crossed her arms. "Now, would you like to tell us how you really found out about it?"

Cassady shrugged and, with a chuckle, said, "What does it matter? I'm here to talk to you about the future of the resort — your future."

Peyton was growing more impatient every second. "It matters a great deal. If you want to talk business with us, you'll tell us where you got your information."

Debi bolted to her feet. "Oh, for Pete's sake. Enough already. I told him."

Lucy looked as though she was about to leap over the table and go for Debi's throat. The red splotches on her cheeks meant she was furious, all right, but then so was Peyton. She just wasn't as blindsided by their conniving cousin's behavior as her sister was. Where Debi was concerned, Peyton had learned to expect the worst, and she had never been disappointed.

"I called Scott last week and had dinner

with him," Debi announced. There was no apology in her confession. She turned to Cassady and ordered, "Go ahead, Scott. Tell them what we discussed."

"You two have taken on quite a challenge," he began, addressing Lucy and Peyton.

"Three of us," Debi corrected, including herself.

Lucy had had enough of her cousin's interference. "My sisters, Peyton and Ivy, and I have taken on this challenge. Christopher, would you mind showing Debi to her car?"

"Gladly," Christopher answered enthusiastically.

Debi must have known she'd pushed the envelope as far as she could. She got up and stiffly walked across the lobby. "I can see myself out," she muttered. Christopher rushed forward to open the door for her, but she pushed his hand away. "I'll be back," she threatened. "I'm not finished here."

Christopher sighed. "I know."

Cassady got down to business outlining his offer. "You have taken on a mammoth project. I can help with that," he said. "And I can promise you'll show more than a twenty percent profit at the end of the year.

In fact, I'll guarantee it."

"How can you guarantee —" Lucy began.

"I've been at this a long time," he said. "I've got my own crews and I've worked out all the problem areas. Look around the island. All those beautiful high-rises are mine." He didn't sound as though he was boasting, just stating fact. "I've got a smooth operation, and I know how to make a profit. Bishop's Cove has the most beautiful beach on the island. Eventually I'd like to develop the area, make it what it could be."

"We like it just the way it is," Peyton said.

Lucy nodded. "Perhaps in the future we'll want to build a few more bungalows, but we aren't interested in high-rises. We want to protect this little piece of heaven."

"It's outdated," Cassady countered. "Don't you realize how much money you could make putting up just one high-rise instead of five little bungalows? Who's your target customer? The superrich? Those people are fickle," he rushed on. "Bishop's Cove could be in one year and out the next. I build for the average man who saves all year for a memorable vacation, and I build for retirees who want to live out their lives on a beach. Second homes are still popular. I make them affordable. Well, not affordable for everyone," he admitted with a wry grin.

Christopher sat down next to Lucy. He leaned forward and asked, "What do you want in return?"

"All of it," he answered bluntly. "I'll guarantee you'll make a thirty percent profit, and at the end of the year when you take ownership, you sell it to me. We'll sign contracts now so there won't be any change of heart on either of our parts."

Peyton was finding it difficult to sit still. She wanted to send Cassady on his way. "Are you so certain my sisters and I are destined to fail?"

"To be completely honest, I'd have to say I'd give you a ten percent chance of turning this place around. It would be a long shot."

"If you're so certain —" Peyton began.

Smiling, Cassady interrupted. "Ninety percent certain."

"Why not just wait until the year is over and then buy the resort from our uncle? You don't think he'll sell it to you, do you?"

Scott shrugged. "There isn't any bad blood between us," he insisted. "But we have had our disagreements about the development of the island. I have blueprints for you to look over so that you'll see I'm not going to bastardize the Cove. I'm going to enhance it."

He certainly was confident. Blueprints no less.

"If you don't take my offer, you run the risk of failing and losing it all. I'm a sure thing. If you commit to selling me the resort, I can promise you that you will not fail." The sisters didn't respond and he took their silence as a sign that they were considering his proposal. He pushed on. "You've already seen how difficult it is to manage one of these properties. Is that what you really want? To be tied to a place that needs constant attention? I'm prepared to offer you a great deal of money, more than you'd make in years of running this resort."

"You've given us quite a lot to think about," Lucy said.

"Would you like to discuss money now?"

Both Peyton and Lucy shook their heads. "Not at this point," Peyton said. "We will have to discuss our options with Ivy. All three of us have to make the decision."

"Is there a time limit on this offer?" Lucy asked.

"No. Take all the time you need, but the sooner we get started, the better."

Cassady left a few minutes later. Lucy walked out with him and shook his hand. As soon as she walked back into the lobby, she said, "Holy crap."

Peyton nodded. "I know," she agreed. "Holy crap."

Shaking his head, Christopher started toward his office. Peyton stopped him with a question. "Cassady strikes me as the kind of man who's used to getting what he wants. When we tell him we aren't interested, do you think he'll make trouble?"

"He's already making trouble," he replied. "The electricians we hired are now on a job at one of Cassady's high-rises."

"I thought he had his own crews."

"He does."

"What are we going to do?" Lucy asked.

"We're going to bring in electricians from out of town, and we're going to keep quiet about it. And for God's sake, keep your cousin away from here."

Christopher disappeared around the corner, and Lucy sprawled on the sofa. "What do you think Debi is getting out of this? Cassady must have promised her something, but what?"

"Money, of course. Won't do any good to ask how much. We won't get a straight answer from either one of them."

"Where did Finn go?" she asked.

"To get my car back. Technicians went over it again."

"Oh yes, the bullet holes from Dalton."

There was a hint of hysteria in her laughter. "Did you just hear what I said so casually? The bullet holes."

"I found another bullet hole in the roof."

Lucy straightened. "What are you saying?"

"Someone took another shot at me. That's what I'm saying."

Lucy looked sick. "When?"

"In front of Van's." She didn't give her sister time to react but told her about Drew showing up and what had been said. By the time she was finished, Lucy had tears in her eyes.

"He's behind it, isn't he?"

"Yes, I'm almost certain."

"Did you convince him you wouldn't make trouble?"

Peyton shrugged. "I think so."

"And you won't make trouble, right?"

Peyton didn't answer. Lucy became irate. "You listen to me. Get rid of that recording, and let it go. Once he's named CEO, he'll leave you alone. Isn't that what you said? You just have to be careful until then, and if you don't make waves . . ." She paused to take a breath. "I'm calling Ivy," she said as if it were a threat.

"No, you are not calling Ivy," Peyton countered. "There is nothing she can do, and there's no use worrying her."

"Maybe she can talk some sense into you."

"Calm down," she said. "You're shouting at me."

"Someone's trying to kill you, and you want me to calm down?" She took a breath and said, "You have a choice. Move forward and hopefully live a long productive life, or stay on this crusade to bring Albertson down and risk getting killed. You choose."

NINETEEN

Late that afternoon Mimi called and snatched away any hope of moving forward. She didn't do it on purpose. She simply caught Peyton up on the latest development.

She eased into her news. "For some unexplainable reason Bridget has decided that I'm her new confidante. She's been stopping by my desk more often to chat. She knows I have absolutely nothing to do but keep Drew's calendar and fetch his coffee. When he's out of the office I read. The other day she told me she's madly in love with Drew. Like you and I didn't already know that," she scoffed. "And that's why she stays so skinny. She thinks Drew only likes skinny women . . . and FYI, everyone else in the company thinks you quit because the job was over your head and you couldn't handle it, but not Bridget. She knows the real reason you didn't last is because you weren't skinny enough for Drew."

"She's a sad woman," Peyton said.

"Sad isn't the word for it," Mimi said. "Her worship of him borders on downright creepy. Everything she does is meant to impress him. She moved into his neighborhood, and she even drives the exact same car as his. I don't think Drew notices her most of the time, so I sort of feel sorry for her."

"What else is going on?"

"Glad you asked. HR has two employees out sick, and Bridget asked if I'd help them get caught up. The first task she gave me was to proof an employment ad."

"For a new food critic?" Peyton couldn't hide her disgust at the thought of Albertson looking for his next victim.

"Not this time. Drew isn't even pretending he wants someone who will learn the ropes and become a critic. He's advertising for a personal assistant."

"I thought that's what you were."

"Bridget told me I'm going to be transferred to production in the other building. I'd work under Parsons."

"Hand in your resignation today and get out of there."

"No, Lars and I have a plan, and I'm sticking to it. I acted thrilled about the transfer," she added. "And Bridget bought it. I want to tell you about the ad," she insisted. "No college degree necessary, no experience needed. He'll only look at the female applicants, of course. Bridget says he'd prefer someone younger, maybe a girl right out of high school so he can train her. He must think a young naive girl is more likely to keep quiet. It turns my stomach."

"Okay, that clinches it," Peyton said. "No more waiting. I have to let Randolph Swift know what's going on at his magazine. Drew has to be stopped."

"Getting to Randolph is impossible. He's surrounded now by Eileen's people, and he's caught up in this memorial for his wife. As far as the business is concerned, he's already checked out. Your best hope is Erik. Send him the recording."

"There would be no way to tell what his reaction is. If he didn't respond, I wouldn't know if he heard it, if he ignored it, or if he thought it was just a funny prank."

"What about calling him? That way you could talk to him."

"I can't just call him and play the recording over the phone. He doesn't know me from Adam. I really think I need to meet him face-to-face."

"He's coming home for the memorial. Let

me tell him. Send me the recording again, and I'll try to get to him."

"No, I have to do this. I want to look him in the eye, and I want him to tell me what he's going to do. If I have to threaten him, I will. I want him to know, if he doesn't get rid of Drew, I'm going to sue, and I'm going to make it very public."

They argued about who should do what for a couple of minutes. Then Mimi conceded defeat. "Okay, you have to do it. I get it. But you can't come back to Minnesota. It's too dangerous."

"How else can I see him?"

Mimi suddenly sounded optimistic. "I can help you."

"How?"

"Erik will be flying home for the memorial. He doesn't ever take the company jet. He believes it should be used only for company business. He flies commercial, and HR makes his reservations. He connects through Chicago. I could change that, and no one will ever be the wiser," she boasted. "Flights get canceled all the time. How about I send him home through Atlanta and give him a nice three- or four-hour layover? I know it's a bit extreme, but if you really need to talk to him in person, that's the only thing I can think of."

"I'll do it," Peyton replied. "I'll meet him in Atlanta. It will be a quick trip, and there are plenty of nonstop flights. I could go and be back in the same day."

"I wish I could be there when Erik finds out what his dear old brother-in-law has been up to," Mimi said.

"Don't worry," Peyton assured her. "I'll tell you all about it. Let's just hope that Erik has the guts to do the right thing."

The FBI technician handed the written report to Finn along with Peyton's car keys.

"I found a bullet from a two-seventy. It was in pretty good shape considering. That's a hunting rifle, used for bigger game like deer and elk. Sorry I can't give you more information, but if you find the weapon I can match it to the bullet."

Finn shook his hand. "I'll find it."

The technician had a ride back to the lab, and as soon as he left, Finn drove into Port James to talk to the chief of police. He wanted the chief to be aware of Peyton's situation. Finn knew he would be called away from Bishop's Cove soon, and he wasn't about to leave Peyton in harm's way without protection, though he was hopeful that, by the time he left, the threat would be over.

Port James was a small coastal town and Finn had no trouble finding the police station, a one-story stucco building that sat next to a strip mall. He asked the woman behind the counter if the chief was available.

"No, he isn't," she answered with a friendly smile. "Tom and four other officers are in Jacksonville, attending a funeral," she explained. "Officer Trace Isles is here. Would you like to talk to him?" She made the choice for him and shouted for Trace. The officer opened a door behind her and rushed into the tiny reception area. He was young. He looked as though he could pass for a high school kid, but Finn guessed he was around twenty-three.

Finn introduced himself as a federal agent and shook his hand.

"Chief will be back tomorrow," Trace said when the receptionist told him of Finn's request.

A call came in then, cutting off the conversation. The receptionist went back to her desk and picked up her headset to answer the call. A few seconds later, she turned back to Trace. "There's a man on the roof of the Port James branch of the First Avenue Bank."

"What's he doing on the roof?" Trace asked.

"He's got a rifle." She shook her head. "This couldn't happen at a worse time, what with most of the officers up in Jacksonville. I'll call out to neighboring towns."

Finn could tell that Trace was both excited and nervous as he rushed toward the door. "The bank is only four blocks away. I'll head over."

"Do you want some help?" Finn asked.

Trace stopped. "I . . . uh . . ."

"Sure you do," Finn said. "Where are the vests?"

Trace frowned, looking flustered and not understanding what Finn was asking.

"Bulletproof vests," Finn snapped. "Grab two," he ordered. "And you'll want to bring a rifle with a scope and some ammo," he added.

The receptionist obviously approved. She nodded each time Finn gave an order.

Finn stood by the door while Trace rushed back to gather what they would need. When he returned, he handed Finn a vest and tossed his own into the backseat of the police cruiser, then slid into the passenger seat. Perhaps it was an automatic response, Finn thought. If Trace wanted him to drive, that was fine, but they weren't going anywhere until the kid put on the vest.

"We're wasting time," Trace responded. "I'll slip it on when we get there."

"No, you put it on now." Finn backed the car out of the slot and threw it into drive.

"Three blocks straight ahead, then left." Trace gave instructions as he dove over the seat to get the vest from the floor. He had it on before Finn reached the corner.

"Make sure the rifle's loaded," Finn told him.

"It is," Trace assured him, even as he double-checked to make certain. "Yes, it is."

The dispatcher came over the radio. "The bank manager reported that the suspect on the roof is Roy Jones. His wife, Kathy, is inside the bank. She says her estranged husband is waiting for her to come out so he can shoot her. He told her he was going to kill her. She said he's been threatening her for over a week."

"I know all about Roy," Trace said. "He's a mean mother, and Kathy's a real sweet woman. I knew there'd be trouble when she finally got up the nerve to leave him."

"Did she report threats?"

"No. He isn't bluffing," he blurted. "If he says he's going to kill her, then that's what he's going to do."

"We're not going to let that happen. I'm assuming Kathy is smart enough to stay inside the bank."

Finn turned the corner and discovered that the bank building was actually eight blocks away, not four. There were three cars in the customer parking lot. One was an old Honda Civic that obviously belonged to Kathy Jones because it was now riddled with bullet holes. All four tires were slashed; the windshield was shattered; and the hood was nearly destroyed.

The roof of the three-story building was flat, and Roy Jones was hunkered down on his belly, the tip of his rifle visible. Finn planned to park at the entrance to the lot so that no other cars could enter, but he hadn't even put the car in park before Trace jumped out. A bullet hit him square in the chest and he was thrown back. Had he not been wearing his vest, the shot would have killed him. Finn dove across the seat, grabbed the officer by his arm, and pulled him into the car.

"I'm okay," Trace gasped.

"You stay here," Finn ordered. "You'll get your head blown off. Shots fired. Call it in." He backed the cruiser up a slope next to a cluster of trees. None were tall enough for Finn to climb to get a clear shot, but the branches hung low and obstructed the shooter's view.

"What are you going to do?" Trace grimaced as he asked the question.

Finn reached for the rifle and extra ammo. "I'm going to shoot the bastard."

He ran to the cover of the trees. Pressing his back to the tree trunk, he swung the rifle up and took aim. Then he patiently waited.

Roy was shouting his wife's name, taunting her. "I've got enough ammo to kill half the town, Kathy, and I'll do it while I'm waiting for you to come out." Several seconds of silence followed and then he shouted again, even more enraged. "You think you can walk out on me?" Still no answer. "I'll shoot until you come out, Kathy. I already shot a cop." Now he sounded as though he was boasting. "Here comes a jogger. I'm gonna kill him next."

Out of the corner of his eye, Finn could see a young man in the distance running along the sidewalk toward the bank. His attention immediately went back to the roof of the building. The rifle tilted in the direction of the runner, then gradually a baseball cap appeared, then an arm and a shoulder. That was all Finn needed. One shot and Roy was down.

It was a hell of a day.

■ ■ ■ ■

While Lucy and Christopher walked through each bungalow making lists of what needed to be replaced, Peyton was stuck in the business office with mounds of paperwork. Sifting through all the invoices, contracts, change orders, requisition forms, and inventories, she was nearly overwhelmed by the enormity of what they had taken on. Every discrepancy required a phone call, and it seemed no one was available. Automated recordings of very pleasant voices offered to place her on hold while they tended to other callers, and she thought if she had to listen to the mind-numbing, synthesized, wait-your-turn music for one more second, she would go stark raving mad.

Finn walked in just as she was repeatedly slamming the office phone down. On edge and thoroughly frustrated, she saw him and wanted to throw herself into his arms and make crazy love to him. If he kissed her, nothing else would matter. Just Finn. His eyes narrowed and his expression became intense. He knew what she was thinking, she decided. He was staring at her mouth. Oh yes, he knew. For the first time in her life she was going to give in to her fantasy. She wouldn't tear her clothes off until they were in her bedroom, but that was the only concession she would make.

Her eyes locked on his, and she started to get up. Then Lucy stormed in, stomping all over her fantasy.

"It's going to take at least a year to get this place in shape."

"That's positive thinking," Peyton said.

"She's been full of cheer all afternoon," Christopher remarked dryly as he walked past her and dropped his notepad on an empty desk.

Lucy poked him in the back. "What's that supposed to mean?"

Christopher slowly turned around. "I have to explain it to you?"

"Yes, you do." She was primed for a fight.

"You've done nothing but complain. Either get with the program or get out."

He didn't wait for her to respond. He picked up a phone and punched in the number to get his messages.

Peyton was feeling claustrophobic. She had been sitting at the desk for hours and getting next to nothing done. She stood, arched her back to work out the stiffness, then walked over to Finn who was leaning against the desk with his arms folded across his chest. To a casual observer he looked relaxed. He wasn't, though. She could feel the tension in him. He looked like he was ready to pounce.

"Are you all right?" She whispered the question.

"Yes, I'm fine." He snapped the answer.

No, he wasn't fine. Something was wrong, but if he didn't want to talk about it, she wasn't going to probe.

A couple of minutes passed as they watched the verbal tennis match going on between Lucy and Christopher. The second Christopher had hung up the phone, Lucy commenced with the argument. Lucy made some valid points regarding the upgrades she wanted, but Christopher also made a good argument against her choices.

Peyton was trying to think of something to say to stop the dispute when Finn said, "Christopher's having fun."

She didn't believe him until Christopher turned toward his office and she saw the glint in his eyes. Finn was right. He was enjoying himself sparring with Lucy.

"Lucy doesn't look like she's having much fun."

"She's frustrated," Finn said, keeping his voice as low as Peyton's so they wouldn't be overheard.

"This isn't about sex," she whispered.

He grinned. "Did I say it was?"

"You said she was frustrated."

He laughed, drawing a frown from Lucy before she turned back to Christopher to make yet another point.

"Frustrated because she isn't winning this round," Finn explained.

"Oh. I misunderstood."

Finn glanced over at Peyton. Her face was pink with embarrassment. "I'm just messing with you," he admitted. "She wants him as much as he wants her."

"Aha!" Peyton felt vindicated. She nudged him. "Unless you're a mind reader you can't know what either one of them wants."

"I read people for a living, you know."

She snorted.

"Oh, that's nice," he said.

Peyton could almost see the tension easing from his shoulders. His smile was boyish again. "Do you want to swim tonight?" she asked.

No hesitation there. "Yes," he answered. "And you promised to swim with me."

"I promised? I don't know about that. On second thought, maybe we should put it off until tomorrow. You look tired to me."

"Nice try, Lockhart. You're swimming, and I'm not at all tired." Nodding toward

Lucy he added, "But your sister looks wiped out."

Peyton had to agree. Lucy's face was pale, and there were dark circles under her eyes. She had been working long hours and needed a break. They all did.

Christopher had reached the door to his office when Peyton called his name. "Want to get a beer with Finn and me?" she asked.

He didn't have to think about it. "Yeah, let's do that. I could use a beer." With a meaningful glance at Lucy, he added, "It's been a long day."

"What about me?" Lucy asked.

"You need something stronger," Peyton told her. "You need nachos and beer."

"I do," Lucy said. She perked up the second she heard the word *nachos*. It was her forbidden indulgence. "I really, really do. I'll just get my purse."

Finn put his arm around Peyton's waist and pulled her closer. He lowered his voice so the other two couldn't hear. "You have more bad news to give, don't you?"

"How did you know?"

He pictured her pounding the desk with the office phone. "Just a hunch."

He pulled keys from his pocket and announced, "I'll drive. Where are we going?"

Peyton and Lucy answered at the same

time. "Reds."

"You haven't been banned from that place yet, have you?" Christopher asked Lucy.

She trailed him into the hallway. "That's not funny."

"I wasn't trying to be funny," he countered. "I was asking a serious question."

Peyton slipped her hand under Finn's arm and followed them. "They're a lovely couple, aren't they?"

The bar and grill was just a mile away from Bishop's Cove. On the way out of the resort's gates, Finn stopped to talk to two guards on duty and noticed the photocopy of a picture of Debi taped to the glass. "Absolutely no entry" was written underneath. That's not gonna keep the woman out, he thought. She'd walk ten miles of beach to get what she wanted.

Reds was a local hangout. At first glance, it looked like a dive. The walls, painted a dark red, were cracked and the old wooden floor sagged, but the place was clean. There were several flat-screen televisions on the walls, each showing a different sport. The place was packed and every seat was taken, leaving the area around the bar crowded with standing patrons.

The bartender was pouring brews from

319

the tap when they walked in. He turned at the door opening, and his eyes immediately zoned in on the gun at Finn's side. Setting the full mug on a tray for the waitress, he started toward them with a hand up, signaling them to halt. Finn held up his badge, and the bartender nodded and went back to his job. No one else in the bar noticed the weapon, or if they did, they didn't care.

A booth at the back of the bar was being cleared, and Lucy elbowed her way through the drinking crowd to get to it before anyone else could. Christopher sat next to her.

Finn was stopped by an older couple. "I know you," the man said. "You were on television. You did a heck of a thing. That was you, wasn't it?"

His wife smiled with adoration. "I saw you, too. You were so courageous."

The man insisted on shaking Finn's hand before he would allow him to leave.

Peyton whispered, "I told you someone would recognize you."

"What?"

"You can't take home three gold medals and expect that no one will remember. I don't care how long it's been. What's so funny?"

He wouldn't tell her, but he couldn't stop

laughing as they slid into the booth across from Lucy and Christopher. He faced the bar and the crowd with his back to the wall, a perfect spot to see what was coming. He didn't expect trouble, but he was always ready for it.

As they feasted on nachos and fish tacos, everyone's mood lightened. Peyton was glad to see Lucy having a good time. She even told a joke. It was a lame one, but they still laughed — even Christopher. The laugh lines appeared around his eyes again, and the frown lines that had been furrowing his brow were erased. When he told a funny story about one of the guests of the resort who tried to smuggle a lamp from her room, Lucy laughed so hard she grabbed hold of his arm and leaned into him. Maybe there was something going on between the two of them after all, Peyton thought.

Inevitably, the conversation turned to the work at the resort.

"We'll be back on track tomorrow," Lucy told Finn.

"No, we won't," Peyton interjected.

"Didn't you look at the schedule?" Lucy asked. "The plumbers —" She stopped when Peyton shook her head. "What?"

"No plumbers," Peyton announced.

Christopher didn't seem fazed by the

news. Lucy, on the other hand, went ballistic.

"If you tell me —"

"I am telling you," Peyton said. "According to the scheduler, you called and canceled the order a week ago. Just like the electricians. Now they're on another job and won't be available for at least a month."

"Cassady is doing this," Lucy said between clenched teeth. "I'll bet the plumbers are working on one of his high-rises."

Peyton turned to Finn to explain. "Cassady is trying to sabotage us so that he can step in and get control of Bishop's Cove."

"I can bring in new plumbers, just like I'm doing with the electricians," Christopher offered, "but we'll have to keep quiet about them, too." His calm and pragmatic attitude was reassuring as he went on to lay out his plan. He would go beyond the nearest town of Port James and hire tradesmen. It might cost a little more, he told them, but they wouldn't have to deal with Cassady's interference.

Finn was listening to the conversation, but he was watching the bar. Two men in their late thirties were arguing with the bartender.

Peyton drummed her fingertips on the table. "I think it's time we started playing hardball. Christopher, who is Cassady's biggest competitor?"

Finn smiled. "I like the way your mind works."

"Miller," Christopher answered. "Dan Miller and Scott Cassady have been fighting each other over every project in Port James. Miller is way ahead of Cassady there, but Cassady prides himself on the fact that he squeezed Miller out here on the island."

"You're saying Miller doesn't have a single building here?" Lucy asked.

"That's what I'm saying."

Peyton and Lucy looked at each other and began to laugh. Then Peyton said, "I think it's time to invite Mr. Miller to tour our little cove."

"How soon do you think word will get back to Cassady?" Lucy asked.

Christopher grinned. "Before Miller gets out of his car."

Finn interrupted their discussion by jumping to his feet. "Stay here," he ordered as he unsnapped his gun and headed to the bar. The panicked young bartender was trying to separate the two men who were now going at each other in a shoving match. Each man outweighed the bartender by at least a hundred pounds. One had a large beer gut, and the other had a pronounced double chin. Both were so out of shape, they were panting and sweating profusely. Finn suspected that, if they got into a fistfight, the exercise would kill them. Double Chin was accusing Beer Gut of stealing money from him. It was always money or women, Finn thought.

Everyone in the bar fell silent and scattered to watch the brawl from a safe distance. The argument was getting out of hand, and Finn got there just in time. Beer Gut was reaching behind his back and pulling a handgun from under his shirt when Finn slammed his head down on the bar. "Hands where I can see them," he ordered.

Beer Gut struggled to lift his head. "Who are you to tell me —"

Finn took his gun. "I'm FBI. Now put your hands on the bar."

He turned to Double Chin whose hand had disappeared behind him. "You too," Finn barked. "Turn around and hands on the bar."

"What are you gonna do? Shoot me?" The smirk on his face disappeared and he froze when Finn pressed the barrel of a gun against his forehead.

"Yes, that's exactly what I'm gonna do," Finn said.

Double Chin turned slowly. Finn snatched his gun and pushed him toward the bar.

"What were you planning?" Finn asked the two culprits. "To shoot each other in a bar full of people?"

"He owes me money," Beer Gut whined.

"Oh, then that's all right." Finn wanted to coldcock both of them but he resisted the urge. He patted them down and removed a switchblade from Beer Gut's pocket, then dragged both men to the back of the bar and made them sit on the floor to wait for the police. As he was making the call, he walked back to his table where Lucy and Christopher were watching the action with mouths open and eyes wide.

"It will be a few minutes before we can leave," he told them.

He was worried Peyton would be freaked out, but she wasn't. Smiling, she said, "Then I'll have dessert."

Ten minutes and one scoop of vanilla ice cream later, Officers Trace Isles and Cody Pepperson arrived. Finn was waiting for them, standing next to the two men sitting on the floor.

"Twice in one day," Trace said. "We're sure glad you're here. You cut our crime wave down to zero."

"How are your ribs?" Finn asked.

"Sore, but intact. No cracks from that bullet. You know, it could have been a bloodbath out there."

Finn nodded. "It could have."

"Sorry you had to spend so long at the station with reports."

Grinning, Finn said, "I spent more time on the phone with my boss."

"I didn't think those reporters who showed up were going to let you get out of there," Trace said.

"I just let them know that the Port James Police Department would be handling any statements." He changed the subject and nodded toward the two brawlers on the floor. "About these two . . ." He told what had happened and gave Trace the weapons.

Across the room, Peyton was watching with interest and trying to figure out what was going on. It appeared that Finn was familiar with one of the police officers, and she couldn't understand how they would know each other. When at last the police hauled the two men to their feet to take them away, Finn returned to their table.

"We can leave now," he announced.

"Did you know that police officer?" she asked.

"We've met," he answered.

Still curious, she asked, "Where?"

"I'll tell you later," he answered as he took her hand and led the way toward the door

326

with Lucy and Christopher close behind.

They were halfway across the bar when Peyton noticed that everyone was staring at them and then glancing up at the television overhead. She pulled her hand away from Finn's and stopped. On the screen was an image of a man being carried on a gurney to an ambulance. The picture that followed was Finn's face. Microphones were being shoved at him as he was getting into his car. Across the bottom of the screen scrolled the story of a shooter at a bank and the brave FBI agent who saved the city from carnage.

Peyton looked at the screen and then at Finn in total shock. "You saved a whole city?"

"Come on. Let's get out of here." He put his arm around her shoulder.

She started laughing.

"Of course you did," she said as she let him steer her toward the door.

They made their exit just as the cheering and the clapping erupted. All of it for Finn. The hotshot.

TWENTY

Peyton's idea of swimming was to sit on the side of the pool and dangle her feet in the water. If she were at the beach, she would sit in the sand and let the surf gently wash over her toes. For her, swimming was a leisurely, relaxing activity that didn't involve work.

She knew Finn wasn't going to let her be a bystander tonight. When he said they were going to swim, he really meant swim.

Maybe she could distract him, or at the very least torment him a little. She knew he liked her body — he'd told her so several times now — and if he was going to force her to do laps, she was going to wear one of her old and definitely obscene bikinis. She wanted to make it difficult for him to concentrate, and the suit just might do it. The top of the bikini, two triangles of fabric that plunged to a deep V, revealed the fullness of her breasts, and the bottom — what little there was — was fabric held together by a string tied into a bow at the top of each hip. This wasn't the first time she'd worn the killer suit. She'd put it on several times in the past couple of years, but she had never had the nerve to actually wear it out of her bedroom. Tonight was different. She wanted to drive the man who had just saved a frickin' city out of his ever-loving mind.

She pulled on a University of Texas T-shirt and a pair of white tennis shorts. Just in case the air turned chilly she carried a thick white terry-cloth robe she'd borrowed from linens at the hotel. It would keep her warm on the walk back. She tucked her phone and a few other necessary items in the robe's deep pockets, and she was all set.

Finn was waiting for her by the door. He took her key to lock the deadbolt on their way out and slipped the key in the pocket of his jeans. As usual, his gun was attached to his belt. He noticed her staring at it. "We've been over this. While I'm here, I'm keeping the gun close."

"It came in handy at the bar."

He took hold of her hand. "You're dragging your feet. Let's get moving."

Reluctantly she picked up her pace, her flip-flops slapping against the concrete with each step. "It's a good thing the man you threatened to shoot didn't know you were bluffing."

"I was bluffing?"

That devastating smile was back. He could get anything he wanted with that smile, she thought. She was ready to throw herself at him now, and she imagined every other woman he met felt the same way. Hmm . . . she didn't know how she felt about that. Picturing him with any other woman didn't sit well. That unpleasant thought led to another. Danielle. What was the story with her?

"Why are you glaring at me?" he asked as they made their way across the back lot and headed to a side door of the hotel.

She shook her head. "What did the technician have to say?"

Finn explained what the findings were and ended with, "When I find the rifle that was used, the bullet will match it."

Peyton handed Finn the key to get inside the hotel. What little staff there was had gone home hours ago. It was eerily quiet inside. The soft lighting above the baseboards of the hallway led to the lobby and the elevators. Another key unlocked the door to the pool. The smell of chlorine was faint but noticeable. Finn flipped the lock so that no one else could enter, then turned on the underwater lights, and a shimmering iridescent glow filled the dome.

Peyton watched him strip down to his swim trunks, the muscles across his shoulders rippling as he stretched his arms over his head, his skin dappled gold by the lights. He sat on the side of the pool and waited for her to join him, but she wasn't in any hurry. She turned away from him and removed her shorts, carefully folding them and placing them on the chair next to her robe. Slowly she lifted her T-shirt over her head and tossed her hair back over her shoulder, hoping the action was provocative.

Trying to be sexy took concentration, she decided. Unfortunately, it was a wasted effort because, when she turned around, Finn was in the water already swimming laps. Maybe she would get to sit on the side and dangle her feet after all. The thought cheered her. She dug through the pockets of the robe, found her hair tie, and pulled her hair up into a ponytail. She checked her phone messages next. By the time she was finished with that task, she was sure Finn would have done several laps.

Finn pulled himself up and out of the pool and stood with his legs braced apart waiting for Peyton to turn around. He couldn't take his eyes off her gorgeous backside. He wondered how she'd feel if he told her it aroused the hell out of him. When she finally turned to face him his knees nearly buckled. Her breasts were full and round, and her hips gently flared above her perfect thighs and long amazing legs. She was slender and fit, and yet she was soft everywhere. Damn, he wanted her.

Peyton slipped her phone into the pocket of the robe and looked over her shoulder to find Finn standing on the pool deck watching her. The intensity in his expression and the dark look in his eyes told her the bikini had done its job. She slowly walked over to him, stopped long enough to run her fingertips across his chest, and then continued on. He came up behind her, lifted her into his arms, and jumped into the water. When they came up, her arms were wrapped around his neck, holding tight, and her body was pressed against his.

"Show me what you can do." His order was gruff and sexy as hell.

She kissed the side of his neck, then tugged on his earlobe with her teeth. Her tongue brushed against his skin.

Finn tensed in reaction and instinctively increased his hold on her. "What the hell, Peyton?"

"I'm showing you what I can do," she whispered.

"I meant swimming," he said as he pulled on her ponytail to bring her face up so that his mouth could cover hers. His hands moved down her back to her hips and he lifted her up to wrap her legs around him. Her pelvis rubbed against his groin as he made love to her with his mouth. For that moment in time she belonged to him.

Panting for breath, he finally lifted his head. "What else have you got?"

The challenge was there in his eyes. "Plenty," she whispered.

Her hands moved down his chest, her fingers first circling his nipples, then gliding lower, stroking and caressing. He inhaled sharply when her fingers slid under the waistband of his trunks.

Suddenly she pushed away from him. "But we're here to swim." Laughing, she took off across the pool.

Finn stood there watching her. Long, even strokes, the right amount of kick, her head turning just enough to take in air. Her technique was every bit as good as it used to be. She'd come a long way since the summer all those years ago when he'd gotten stuck teaching her.

He remembered the hell she'd put her

333

parents through. They were desperate for their girls to learn how to swim — to this day, her mother cried whenever she talked about the near drowning. Lucy and Ivy were quick learners. Peyton, on the other hand, screamed bloody murder whenever she got close to the water. Her parents tried everything. Group lessons at the Y, individual lessons at the country club — Peyton, stubborn to the core and terrified of the water, was having none of it. She liked wearing her swimsuit. She just wasn't going to get it wet.

The two fathers — his and Peyton's — came up with the brilliant idea that Finn should teach her. His reaction at the time was not positive. Just what a fourteen-year-old teenager wanted, a girl — what was she then? Five? Six? — screaming nonstop to keep from going into the pool. He had tried to get out of giving the lessons, but her father used Finn's own words to get him to agree, reminding him that he had insisted that Peyton learn how to swim for her own safety. Reluctantly, Finn had acquiesced.

Having been warned about her fear of the pool, Finn showed up for her first lesson prepared for battle, and the strangest thing happened. She didn't scream at all. She put her arms around his neck and willingly let him take her into the water. She was too young to have such absolute trust, but she did, and it took only three or four weeks before he had her swimming like a fish.

As he now stood beside the hotel pool watching her glide through the water, he was pleased to see that she hadn't forgotten what he had taught her. She swam toward him, and when she flipped to begin another lap, he dove in and swam alongside her.

Peyton didn't have as much stamina as Finn. She wore out in ten minutes and got out of the pool, content to sit on the side while he continued.

Her thoughts were scattered. There was so much to worry about she didn't know where to start. Since she had arrived at Bishop's Cove she'd done nothing but put out fires. She hadn't had time to think about the restaurant she wanted to remodel. The building was inside the Cove but had been closed for over a year now. With the right chef, a killer menu, and beautiful decor, it could become the place to go. As soon as the other renovations were running smoothly, she could focus on it.

The new bullet hole in her car was another worry. According to Finn, the shooter couldn't be identified . . . at least, not yet. If Drew Albertson was behind it, she hoped he was now convinced she wasn't a threat to him and had gone home prepared to forget about her.

And that brought her to her biggest worry of all, the recording and getting it into the right hands. She needed to talk to Finn about Atlanta. As soon as Mimi texted Erik's itinerary, Peyton would make her own flight reservation. Hopefully, it would be a one-day trip. The recording was a weight on her shoulders, and the sooner she gave it to Erik, the better.

Apprehension was gnawing at her. What if Erik didn't do anything about Drew? What if he blew it off? Then what? After her experience in Dalton, it was nearly impossible to stay optimistic, but she was determined to try. She wanted to believe that Erik would do the right thing.

Reaching up, she pulled the rubber band from her ponytail, ran her fingers through the tangled mess, and dried it with a towel. Would Finn want to go with her to Atlanta? There wouldn't be any reason for him to, she thought. If Drew believed she wasn't going to make trouble for him, she wouldn't be in any danger.

Finn was suddenly standing in front of her. He rose out of the water like a mythical god, the soft light from the pool casting an ethereal glow around him. She could barely hold a thought when he was this close to her.

He pushed her thighs apart, put his arms around her waist, and lifted her into the water. She wrapped her legs around his hips and put her hands on his shoulders.

"What are you smiling about?" he asked.

She began to massage the back of his neck. "When you came up out of the water, you reminded me of Poseidon. Without the pitchfork, of course."

"Poseidon carried a trident, not a pitchfork," he corrected.

Their smiles faded as they stared at each other, and the air was suddenly heavy with the tension that crackled between them.

He stared at her mouth. "I don't have any control when I'm around you." He didn't sound happy about the admission.

"And that's bad?"

"Yeah," he growled. His open mouth covered hers, his tongue sliding in and out, pushing against hers. There was nothing gentle about his kiss. It was searing and demanding. When at last he lifted his head, both of them had trouble catching their breath.

"Your lips are so soft," he whispered. His thumb gently outlined her mouth. "I love the way you taste."

She shivered in his arms, warmth rippling through her body with his sweet words. He lowered his head and kissed her again, a long, intense kiss that held nothing back. She melted against him. Had he wanted to, he could have taken her then and there. She would have given him anything for another kiss.

Instead, he pulled her out of the pool and put the robe around her shoulders.

Finn didn't say a word to her on the walk back to the condo. He seemed lost in thought.

As soon as the door closed behind them, she headed to her bathroom. "I'm taking a shower to get the chlorine out of my hair."

She slipped out of her swimsuit and had just turned on the water and adjusted it to the perfect warmth when he knocked on the door. Holding the towel in front of her, she called out, "It's not locked. What do you want? Towels are in the linen closet, and soap . . ." She opened the door just wide enough to peer around it. "Did you want something?"

He pushed the door aside and walked toward her. "I want you."

He didn't seem to need her agreement. His hands moved to the back of her neck and he jerked her to him, his mouth covering hers, sealing any protest.

She didn't remember dropping the towel or Finn removing his trunks as he backed her into the shower. The water flowed over their bodies and they melded into one. He reached for the soap and turned her around, lathering her back, then her derriere, and all the way down her calves to her ankles. Turning to face him, he then proceeded to wash every inch of her front. He spent an inordinate amount of time on her breasts, and as soon as the soap was rinsed off, his mouth replaced his hands. He kissed each breast until the nipple was taut, straining. He took one into his mouth and began to suck while he stroked the other. His day's growth of whiskers against her sensitive skin made her cry out, the pleasure was so intense.

He knelt before her, and her legs began to tremble with anticipation. His mouth was hot against her skin as he kissed her stomach, teasing her navel with his tongue. His hands gripped her thighs, and he pushed them apart so he could have better access to her heat. And then his mouth was there between her thighs, kissing her and driving her wild. He teased the sensitive nub with his tongue until she was begging for release, and then his fingers slid inside, pushing her over the edge, forcing her orgasm. Gripping his shoulders, she came apart against him. Her legs buckled, but he wouldn't let her fall.

Finn wrapped her in his arms and stood holding her tight against him while he fought the urge to slam into her. She was so hot, wet, tight. If he didn't have her soon, he thought he would explode.

It took Peyton long minutes to recover. She buried her face in his neck, sighing with pleasure.

"Did you like that?" he asked, rubbing against her.

"You couldn't tell?" she whispered shyly.

His voice was raspy when he answered. "Yeah, I could tell. I love the way you respond to me. It's so honest and raw."

She picked up the soap. "Now it's my turn," she said.

And she washed every inch of his beautiful body. She spent an inordinate amount of time on his thighs, and as soon as he was rinsed off, she knelt before him and drove him out of his mind.

It was the longest shower either of them had ever had. And the most satisfying.

An hour later Peyton was sitting in the middle of the bed with her laptop, looking for flights to Atlanta. Finn was in the living room talking to Ronan on the phone. At one point she heard Finn raise his voice, and she thought the conversation had become heated, but then she heard him laughing.

A few minutes later Finn ended his phone call and went to Peyton's bedroom to talk to her. He stopped in the doorway and stood there staring at her. She wore a cotton nightgown that buttoned in the front. Her hair had dried and hung past her shoulders. When she moved, the strands swayed like a veil across her face. He wanted to run his fingers through her silky hair, to pull her to him and make love to her. He wanted to be inside her again, to feel her surrounding him, squeezing him. He needed her heat.

"What are you doing?" he asked.

She glanced up from the screen. "Looking at flights to Atlanta Saturday. Want to hear the plan?"

Barefoot and wearing nothing but boxers that rode low on his hips, he stretched out on her bed next to her. He punched a pillow behind his head and said, "Sure. Tell me the plan."

"Comfy?" Peyton asked.

"Getting there," he replied.

After she repeated everything Mimi had

told her over the phone, she said, "Erik has been routed through Atlanta, and he has a three-hour layover. I'll talk to him there and make him listen to the recording. Then it's up to him. I'll understand if you can't go with me," she added.

"You're not going without me."

She was surprised by the jolt of relief she felt. "Yes, okay, but you don't expect any trouble, do you? No one in Dalton, except Mimi, knows I'm going to talk to Erik."

"I also want to talk to him. I want to hear what he plans to do. I'm going to nail Parsons," he added, his tone hard. "I don't care how long it takes. Maybe Erik can help with that."

"How?"

"Help find the weapons Parsons is using. And, Peyton, the danger comes after they kick Drew and his wife to the curb. They won't go away quietly."

"*If* they kick them out."

"Have you told Lucy your plan?"

She shook her head. "I will tomorrow." She powered off her laptop and put it on the table next to her. "She's not going to like it." Suddenly feeling overwhelmed, she rested against the headboard and closed her eyes. "I wish I didn't have to do this," she whispered. Turning her head to look at him, she asked, "Want to try to talk me out of it?"

"No."

"Tell me about Danielle."

The question jarred him. "Why are you asking?"

"I'm changing the subject. Tell me about Danielle."

"What about her?"

"You were going to ask her to marry you three years ago, then you walked away. So why, after all this time, is she calling you?"

"About a year ago we ran into each other at a party, and she asked me to go to dinner with her. I thought, sure, why not?"

"So you went out."

"Yes."

Geez, like pulling molars, getting information out of him. "And?"

"She wanted to get back together. I didn't."

"What made you walk away three years ago?"

"She had sex with another man. I couldn't get past it, didn't want to," he admitted. "The trust was gone."

"More than once?"

He gave her a look. "Does that matter?"

"No."

"She had sex with him many times while I

was out of town."

"Once was too much."

Finn remembered how much her betrayal had hurt. He'd be damned if he'd ever go down that road again. "Are we finished talking about this?"

"Yes. I do want to ask you something else . . . but not about Danielle," she rushed to add when he frowned so intently.

"Okay, go ahead."

"If I hadn't called you about the bullet in the roof of my car, would you have called me?"

"I didn't know about the bullet until you called me."

"You know what I'm asking. Would I have ever heard from you again?"

He didn't want to hurt her, but he wasn't going to lie. His answer was abrupt. "No."

TWENTY-ONE

Okay, then. Now she knew.

Peyton was crushed by his answer but vowed he wouldn't know it. He had been so emphatic, and that was enough for her. She didn't want or need to hear his reasons why. She didn't say a word, just nodded to let him know she'd heard him, then got out of bed, picked up her laptop, and left the room.

"Where are you going?" he asked.

"To plug in my laptop. Battery's low." Peyton was pleased her voice didn't sound strained. Determined to be an adult about this, she kept her temper under control. If he didn't want to see her again, that was fine with her. Except it wasn't. They had just gotten squeaky clean together in the shower, for Pete's sake. Her emotions were going crazy. She was angry, frustrated, and feeling horribly vulnerable. She had screwed up again. She never should have kissed him, never should have gone to bed with him, and never should have called him. She sighed. Lesson learned.

"Is that your phone ringing or mine?" he asked as he followed her into the kitchen.

Peyton picked up his phone from the island and handed it to him. She didn't look to see who was calling. Ignoring him, she plugged in her laptop and began searching for her own phone. After she'd gone through pillows and bedding and moved canisters around in the kitchen — she even looked in the refrigerator because she'd left it there more than once in Brentwood — she remembered she'd slipped it into the pocket of the robe she'd carried to the pool.

It was there, all right, but the battery was low. She was about to plug it into the charger when she saw a text from her uncle Len. He wanted to see her and her sister tomorrow to discuss a problem. He would be arriving early in the afternoon. There was also a text from Lucy asking her to call, but she would have to wait until morning. It was late, and Peyton wasn't up for a long conversation with anyone.

Finn was still on the phone when she went to bed. She closed her door, a silent message that he was to leave her alone. It didn't work. In the middle of the night she woke up in his arms. The truth was, she was draped all over him. She went back to sleep thinking she should move.

Peyton was dressed and fixing breakfast before Finn got out of bed. She heard the shower running, and, resisting the erotic thoughts that kept bombarding her, she tried to focus on the task at hand. She was going to be the sweetest hostess there ever was — if it killed her.

She prepared a frittata with Gruyère cheese, red peppers, squash, spinach, and bacon. Then she set a place for him at the island, poured a glass of freshly squeezed orange juice, and scooped fruit into a small bowl.

Finn was adjusting his holster as he walked into the kitchen. "Something smells good."

Smiling, she said, "Your breakfast is ready."

"Where's your breakfast?"

"I've already eaten." Dry toast and orange juice — it was all she could get down. With all the worries hammering away at her stomach, it was amazing she didn't have an ulcer.

Finn ate every bit of the frittata. "You do know how to cook," he praised.

"Thank you. We should get going. I've got a lot to do this morning."

He grabbed her hand. "Peyton, don't you think we should talk about —"

"No," she interrupted in a near shout. "We aren't going to talk about it at all."

"Don't you want to know why I —"

She jerked her hand away. "No, I do not want to know."

Peyton was getting all riled up, so Finn didn't pursue the matter. She looked damned sexy today in tight jeans and a thin camisole under a gossamer-thin blouse. It was decent but still provocative. He wanted to tell her to go back into her bedroom and change into something less arousing, but then he also wanted to take her clothes off and make love to her. Since her indifferent attitude told him there was no chance of that happening, he turned his thoughts to his plans for the day.

He didn't tell her what he intended to do until they reached the hotel. He led her into Christopher's office and asked her to take a seat, then he called for Lucy to join them.

"What are you doing?" Peyton asked.

"We're going to talk about what's going on." And with that he proceeded to explain why he was there. Unbeknownst to Peyton, Finn had already talked to Christopher about the situation. He knew more than Lucy did.

"We've got the bullet from the roof, and we need to find the gun. We're working on that."

Christopher asked, "How can we help?"

"There's nothing to be done," Lucy said. "Peyton has decided to let it go. That horrible man came here to threaten her, didn't he? And she told him she wasn't going to make trouble." She gave Peyton a stern scowl as she spoke, but she wasn't angry; she was scared for her sister.

Peyton looked at Finn before responding to her. "I'm going to Atlanta Saturday to talk to Erik Swift and give him the recording. Then I'll move on."

Tears came into Lucy's eyes. She didn't say a word for a long minute while Peyton outlined her agenda, then she exploded. "No. Absolutely not. Are you out of your mind? You have to leave it alone. You're asking him to come after you. Can't you let it go?"

"Could you?" she challenged. "Knowing what that man is capable of, could you keep quiet?"

Lucy started to answer and then changed her mind. Christopher decided to answer for her. "No, she couldn't keep quiet. She'd try to stop him."

Peyton didn't want to argue any longer.

"Sorry, Lucy," she whispered as she walked past.

Finn followed her to her desk. "I've got to drive into Port James to meet with the chief of police and a couple of other people. Security people," he qualified when she looked puzzled. "You're okay here. Promise you'll stay put."

There really wasn't any reason for him to worry. She had enough work to keep her in the office until midnight. He pulled her into his arms and kissed her before he left. Lucy stood in the doorway to Christopher's office watching, but, other than raising an eyebrow, she didn't comment on the show of affection.

The morning flew by. Peyton found the original architectural plans for the Cove and spread them out on a large table in the conference room adjacent to Christopher's office. There were two pools close to each other that needed extensive work. The longer she studied the plans, the more convinced she became that they should be torn out and replaced with one large pool. Maybe a regulation Olympic-size pool. That thought led to another. Could this place become a training facility a couple of weeks a year? Her mind raced with all the possibilities.

Peyton checked her watch. Her uncle's arrival was getting closer, and she was becoming more and more anxious about the reason for his visit.

Lucy was just as worked up. She was certain the problem was Debi. She opened the door to the conference room and stuck her head inside to offer her speculation. "Our cousin has gotten to Len. He's coming here to talk about her." Fifteen minutes later she came back and plopped down on a chair with another thought. "What if Len is secretly bankrupt?"

Peyton shook her head. She had her own ideas. She was worried that Len had changed his mind because he'd discovered how inept she and Lucy and Ivy were. He was coming to tell them he'd made a mistake by letting them run Bishop's Cove.

Realizing that their guesses were only making them more anxious, the sisters finally agreed to curb their imaginations until their uncle arrived. Neither one of them could predict the reason for his visit. They would find out soon enough.

Finn returned at one, and at one thirty a security guard at the front entrance called. Lucy answered the phone, and after listening for a couple of seconds, she put the caller on speaker.

"This is Dane at the front gate. We've got a situation here," the voice said.

"What is it?" Finn asked.

"There's a crazy lady here throwing a tantrum. She's screaming profanities at Roger and me because we won't open the gate for her. She's the woman in the photo they gave us, and she's not supposed to come inside, right?"

"Yes, that's right. Do not open the gate for her," Lucy demanded.

"Yes, ma'am. But how do we get rid of her? She's causing a commotion. Hear that? She keeps laying her hand on the car horn."

Everyone looked at Finn for the answer. He was trying hard not to laugh. "What?"

"You're an FBI agent," Peyton reminded. "Go shoot her."

He did laugh then. Lucy sided with her sister, which made Christopher laugh.

"Uh . . . Agent MacBain? She's threatening to ram the gate," Dane said.

"Give her one last chance to leave," Finn instructed. "Tell her you're going to call the police. Then do it."

"Yes, sir. Thank you, sir."

As soon as the call ended, Lucy asked, "How long is it going to take for her to give up and go home?"

Peyton shrugged. "She's used to getting

352

her way."

"Maybe if you called her husband, he would come and get her," Lucy suggested.

"Are you kidding? He won't talk to me. He doesn't like me. You call him."

"He doesn't like me, either. If only Ivy were here. He'd talk to her. She's the sweet one."

"There's a sweet one in the family?" Finn asked.

"That's hard to believe," Christopher interjected.

"Hey, we're sweet," Lucy insisted.

Christopher thought her statement was hilarious and continued laughing all the way back to his desk. Finn drew his attention by asking if he could have a moment in private to go over a couple of things.

"What things?" Peyton asked him.

Finn didn't answer. He followed Christopher into his office and shut the door behind him.

"Have you noticed how rude Finn can be?" Peyton asked.

"Have you noticed how obnoxious Christopher can be?" Lucy countered. "With me anyway. He's nice to you."

"Only because I haven't argued with him. He's awfully efficient, isn't he? And smart. It's like he's run a resort before."

Lucy nodded. "I'll never admit it to him, but we need him here. He knows what he's doing."

Peyton agreed, then said, "I've got an idea for the pools. Tell me what you think."

She outlined her vision, bouncing a couple of different approaches off her sister, and was in the middle of explaining what she thought was a brilliant idea when Uncle Len walked in. Both sisters jumped to their feet and hugged him. With the silver hair at his temples and his sparkling eyes, Peyton thought he looked even more handsome and distinguished than ever.

After the greetings were over, Len looked around the office and asked, "Where is everyone?"

"All over the resort," Lucy answered.

"How's Christopher working out?"

Since he was looking at Lucy, she answered. "Good. He's good."

"Where is he?"

"In his office with Finn," Peyton told him.

"Finn's here?" he asked, smiling. "I haven't seen him in years. What's he been up to?"

"Oh, you know, the usual: winning awards, getting promotions, saving a city. Same old, same old."

"He's extraordinary, isn't he?"

"Yes, he is."

"I hope he won't mind if I interrupt. Let's find out." He knocked on Christopher's door and looked in. "May I have some of your time?" He walked inside and shook Finn's hand. "It's good to see you again. Still swimming?"

"Still swimming, sir. Not as fast, though."

Turning to Christopher, Len said, "I've got a little problem I'm hoping you and my girls can help me with."

"Of course," Christopher answered.

Len motioned for Lucy and Peyton to come in and take a seat on the leather sofa as he pulled up a chair to face the desk. Finn leaned against the window and didn't seem inclined to move. Peyton gave him a look she hoped he'd interpret to mean she didn't want him to tell Len his reason for being there, and Finn winked at her. Did that mean he understood her silent message? Or that he planned to spill everything?

Len drew her attention. "A man can take only so much."

Puzzled, Christopher said, "Sir?"

Finn was watching Peyton and Lucy. Their expressions indicated they knew what Len was talking about. They looked horrified.

"I cannot tell you the number of phone calls I've received from my brother Brian.

He's my niece Debi's father," he explained for Finn's benefit. "And of course Debi called, too," he said wearily. "About ten or twelve times a day. I actually thought about changing my phone number."

Peyton had a sinking feeling in her stomach. Lucy elbowed her and mouthed the words *Oh God.* Peyton made the sign of the cross to ward off what she knew was coming, and she swore if she had some holy water she'd douse herself in it. One needed to pull out all the stops when one was confronted by devil girl.

"I know she can be difficult," Len went on. "But she's family, and she's in a bind. Sean filed for divorce. Turns out he's been seeing another woman."

Another marriage gone wrong, Peyton thought. Couldn't anyone be faithful these days?

"Most of the money I gave them went for back taxes they owed," Len explained. "The divorce attorney will take the rest I imagine. Now here's what I propose." He glanced over at his nieces and could almost see their hair rising, and so he quickly said, "Don't worry. I'm not going to let her join you in your venture. Bishop's Cove belongs to you."

Lucy and Peyton sank back against the

sofa in relief. It was short-lived.

"I've talked to Debi, and I've told her I'll buy her a house, a beach house if she'd like, but she has to work here for six months and prove to Christopher that she's worth it. When I say work, I mean work. I don't want her pampered."

"Why here? You have other properties." Peyton sounded like she was being strangled.

"Because Christopher knows how to handle difficult people."

At that point, Christopher looked at Lucy and grinned.

"All right, it's settled," Len said, and Christopher nodded.

"Where will she be staying?" Lucy asked.

"Off-site. I've paid rent on a condo for her for six months. She may not last that long. We'll see. She'll be starting Monday."

Finn glanced at Peyton and then at Lucy. The sisters had identical expressions on their faces. They looked as though a whole lot of bad was about to rain down on them.

TWENTY-TWO

Peyton and Finn arrived in Atlanta an hour before Erik's flight landed, which gave them plenty of time to get to his gate and wait to intercept him.

Mimi had taken a photo on her cell phone of a photo of Erik and had sent it to Peyton, but the photo of a photo wasn't great. The glare blurred the image. Still, Peyton was sure she'd recognize him because everyone said he looked like his father.

"Have you met Randolph Swift?" Finn asked.

"No."

"Have you ever seen him? Maybe walking down a hall, in the elevator or the cafeteria?"

"No, but there's a huge oil painting of him in the lobby of his building. I'm not worried. I'll recognize Erik. Mimi said he resembles Randolph."

"But you've never . . ." He stopped. "Okay, you know what you're doing."

"Yes, I do."

An hour later she had to reevaluate. The first man she approached was a dead ringer for her mental image of Erik: blond hair, tall, skinny, and preppy. He even carried a backpack like a graduate student would.

"Hide your gun," she whispered as they approached the man. "I don't want you to spook him."

"Where do you suggest I hide it?"

"Under your jacket."

Finn stood back and watched as Peyton pulled the stranger aside, introduced herself, and asked if he was Erik Swift. The man gave Peyton the once-over, smiled, then looked her up and down again. Finn wanted to punch him. When he heard the answer, Finn walked forward, ready to get in his face.

"I'll be whoever you want me to be," the man replied. "Want to go somewhere and get friendly?"

Peyton looked over her shoulder at Finn. "Who says that?"

Mr. Flirty sobered when he saw Finn's badge. "Hey, she came on to me."

"I did not come on to you," Peyton said indignantly, her face turning red.

Finn made the man show him his identification, then sent him on his way.

"I don't think I've ever been so embarrassed," she whispered.

"Sure you have," Finn replied with a smile.

They turned back to watch the people emerging from the Jetway. A group of men were following an elderly couple who weren't going to be rushed as they made their way up the ramp.

Finn waited until the men had gotten around the couple, then yelled, "Hey, Erik."

"Yes?" A man separated from the other passengers and turned in Finn's direction.

"There you go," he said to Peyton.

"He doesn't look like his father," she said, sounding suspicious. "I'm nervous," she whispered as she watched Erik come closer.

He was tall and thin just as Mimi described, yet Peyton saw no resemblance to the portrait of Randolph. She knew Erik was in his late twenties, but this man looked much younger, like someone who was about to start college. Dressed in a long-sleeve striped T-shirt and jeans, he had headphones wrapped around his neck, the thin cord tucked in his pocket. He carried his puff jacket and a backpack.

"Erik Swift?" Peyton asked.

"Yes," he answered. He smiled politely yet appeared puzzled, as though she were someone he should recognize but couldn't place.

Peyton extended her hand and, after introducing herself and Finn, she rushed to explain, "We've never met. I worked for your family's magazine for a short while."

Erik then turned his attention to Finn and frowned at the sight of the gun. "What's this all about?" he asked.

"Could we go somewhere quiet to talk?" Peyton said. "There's something I think you should hear."

Reticent but curious, Erik followed them to the airline's lounge, which was a few gates away. Finn's badge was the only identification they needed to get them into the exclusive inner club. Peyton was pleased to find out that Erik wasn't a member because it made him seem more normal and less like Drew and Eileen. Finn pointed to an alcove near the back wall that was far enough away from the other sitting areas to give them some privacy, and Peyton and Erik headed in that direction while Finn stopped at the bar to get them bottles of water.

Erik and Peyton took chairs facing each other, and Finn joined them, setting the bottles of water on the low table in the middle before taking his seat on an adjacent black leather sofa. Erik's body language was telling. He was tense, as if he knew something bad was coming.

"As I said," Peyton began, "I worked for your magazine."

Finn watched Erik closely, waiting for his reaction.

"Your brother-in-law was my boss," she continued.

"I could have guessed that," he said, leaning forward.

"How could you have guessed —"

"You're beautiful," he blurted. "Drew would find a way to get you in his department and under his thumb."

"Do you like your brother-in-law?" Finn asked the question.

"No, I do not. He's an ass."

"What about your sister? Do you get along with Eileen?"

Erik looked a little put off by the question at first. He paused for a moment and then said, "She and I went our separate ways years ago. She was pretty awful to our mother." He shook his head. "I'll never forgive her for that . . . even though my father has," he added as an afterthought. Straightening in the chair, he sounded authoritative. "Tell me what this is all about."

"Where do I start?" she asked Finn.

"How about your first day on the job."

"Yes, okay," she said, and began to describe her nightmare.

Erik blanched several times and muttered profanities; however, he didn't seem to have trouble believing her.

By the time Peyton finished telling about her encounters with Drew, she was trembling. She stood up and reached for her bottle of water. Opening it, she took a sip and would have gone back to her chair if Finn hadn't grabbed her hand and forced her to sit beside him. He seemed to know she needed to borrow some of his strength right now.

"Parsons followed her when she left Dalton," Finn said and told Erik about the bullet holes.

Erik opened his mouth to argue and stopped when he realized their claim was plausible. "I wouldn't put anything past Parsons. He's a bully and a parasite."

"Twice now someone's taken shots at Peyton. Twice," Finn repeated angrily. "And I've got four strong suspects."

Four? Peyton thought. Where did he come up with that number? She turned to ask him, but he put his hand on hers and gently squeezed, and she knew that meant "Ask me later."

"Why don't you listen to the recording now," Finn suggested.

"Since you have headphones, I won't have to put it on speaker and listen to it again," Peyton told him, silently adding, *Thank God.* Hearing Drew's voice made her nerves screech.

She pulled up the recording on her cell phone and handed it to him. Erik plugged the cord in, adjusted his headphones over his ears, and pressed play.

The color slowly drained from Erik's face. A few minutes later, his cheeks flushed, and Peyton surmised that he was hearing the terrible things Drew had said about his mother. By the time the recording ended, Erik looked as though he'd aged ten years. His brow wrinkled into deep furrows and his lips disappeared into a razor-thin line. He gave the phone back to Peyton and removed his headphones.

"Has my father heard this?" he asked.

"No."

"Why not?"

"Your sister guards him like a rottweiler. No one can get near him. He's been shut off from hearing anything negative."

Erik rubbed his forehead. "The trip to Europe to visit all the places my mother loved . . . that was all a sham, wasn't it? To get back in Dad's good graces."

Peyton didn't say anything, and for the next ten minutes, Erik railed.

"What are you going to do about all this?" Finn asked.

His answer was immediate. "Kick him out. Eileen, too. My father's wanted me to take a more active role in the company, and now that I'm almost finished with grad school, I can do that," he said with resolve. "I'll talk to him. We drive to the cemetery together whenever I come home. It helps him, I think." His voice was tinged with sadness when he added, "He misses her, and so do I."

He tapped his finger on Peyton's phone and said, "Will you send that recording to me?" He gave her his number, and seconds later the recording was delivered.

"I'll make Dad listen to this while we're at the cemetery. That's about the only time we're alone. Eileen never wants to go with us."

"Drew thinks he's going to be named CEO by your father at the memorial for your mother."

Erik shook his head. "No, that's changed. Dad called me yesterday and told me he's making the announcement on Friday. He said Drew talked him into moving it up. He didn't want company business to take away from the tribute to my mother."

"That's less than a week away," she said. "How are you going to kick him out once he's put in charge? You better figure out a way to do it before then."

"His appointment is temporary," he explained. "Dad wants me to get in a couple of years learning how all the departments are run before I take over. He doesn't want a son-in-law to reign over the family business."

"Drew will never give it up to you," she said. "Why wasn't Eileen offered the job?"

"She didn't want it," he answered. "She wanted Drew to run the company. She'd be a disaster anyway. The way she treats everyone . . . At times she's insufferable," he said, and then with a weary sigh, he added, "But she loves her husband."

"It's a twisted love," she snapped. "You just heard the recording, for God's sake. You know Drew is a sexual deviant."

"I heard the rumors," he said. "I just didn't . . ."

"Find out if they were true? Are you really that dense?" Peyton asked. She didn't want to sound so unsympathetic, but she was determined to make him understand the consequences of leaving Drew at the helm.

"Not dense," Finn corrected. "You just didn't want to know, did you, Erik?"

He didn't make excuses. "No, I guess I didn't. I knew he was a womanizer, and I knew Eileen didn't care how many other women he had." Without missing a beat, he asked Peyton, "Are you going to sue? You've got a hell of a case if you do."

She'd been sitting on the edge of the sofa. She fell back against Finn and said, "That depends on you and your father. Get Drew out of the company and put the reason why he was fired in his file. I want his past to follow him. And one more thing, Erik . . . I'm putting you on notice. You've been told; you have the recording; and if you don't do anything about Drew, eventually one of his victims will report him for assault, and I'll make sure everyone knows you were aware of his perversion. You let him go unchecked, he'll destroy your company. You better do the right thing."

"You've given me a lot to think about," he said as he stood and reached for his backpack.

Up until then, Finn had appeared to be very laid-back, but in a heartbeat that changed.

"Sit down. We aren't finished here."

367

His voice was like acid to Erik. He visibly flinched before quickly dropping into the chair.

Finn leaned forward with his arms braced on his knees and stared at Erik. He wanted to make him squirm, and he accomplished his goal.

"How often do Drew and his friends go hunting?" he asked.

The question surprised Erik. "I don't know. They used to go a couple of times a year, I guess."

Peyton wondered what Finn was up to. Drew said he didn't go hunting; he went fishing. Wasn't that what he had told them?

"Where do they keep their rifles?"

"Why do you want to know?"

"Where do they keep their rifles?" he repeated.

"They always borrowed my dad's guns. When Dad was younger he liked to go hunting. He took me once. I hated the cold and never went again. He has a pretty big collection of rifles. Some of them are really valuable. That's why he always insisted Drew bring them back the minute he returned."

Erik looked stunned, suddenly realizing where Finn was leading. "Do you think Drew used . . ." The magnitude of the situation was finally sinking in. He turned to Peyton. "He was going to kill you," he whispered. "He was willing to go that far for a what? A stupid job?"

"The money and the power," Finn said. "I want those weapons. Are you going to help me get them?"

Erik nodded. "Tell me what to do."

TWENTY-THREE

"You scared the bejesus out of him," Peyton told Finn. "Poor Erik was shaking when he left us."

"Good. He needs to be scared. If he messes up, if he says anything to anyone before his father can act, what do you think will happen?"

Finn was pulling Peyton along to the gate for their flight back to Florida.

"He'll try to stop him from making trouble."

"That's a pleasant way of saying he'll kill him."

"You can't know —"

"Ah, come on. You made a recording, and he sent someone to kill you. Of course he'll silence Erik. Probably make it look like an accident. Do you have any idea how much money is at stake here? Hell yes, he'll kill him."

"You sound so blasé about it."

He flashed a smile. "How do you want me to sound?"

"I don't know. Maybe concerned." At the very least, she thought. His attitude was a little too cynical for her.

He suddenly stopped and put his hands on her shoulders. Looking deeply into her eyes, he became very serious. "You're my priority. Agents Hutton and Lane will be back in Dalton before Erik gets home. He'll be their priority. Don't worry."

"Back in Dalton? They've been there before?"

"Yes, they interviewed Parsons and several others."

"When did they do that?"

"After I saw the bullet holes near your gas tank, I called them."

The boarding announcement for their flight interrupted their talk. She was weary now; the anxiety and stress of meeting with Erik and worry about his reaction had exhausted her. She just wanted to close her eyes and try to decompress.

Fat chance of that happening. She kept telling herself that she had done what she could, and now it was up to Randolph and his son. If Erik did what he promised, she could finally move forward.

She wouldn't be moving forward with

Finn, though. He had made it perfectly clear he had never wanted nor intended to reconnect with her, and she was pretty sure his feelings hadn't changed. It wasn't until they were in the car and on their way across the bridge to Bishop's Cove that she got up the nerve to broach the subject.

"When this is over, if I want to see you again, do I have to buy a gun and shoot my car?"

He glanced over at her and, frowning, said, "You know if you're ever in trouble, I'll come help you. All you have to do is call."

Oh no, that was never going to happen, she vowed. She wasn't ever going to call him again, no matter what the reason. If he didn't want her in his life, she wouldn't try to change his mind.

Neither of them said another word until they were parked in front of her condominium. Just as she reached for the door handle, he put his hand on her arm to stop her and said, "I really screwed up with you. I never should have touched you. This can't go anywhere, and I know that . . . and you were a virgin, which I just didn't figure. I should have left you alone . . . If I were to continue this, before you know it, you'd get your heart broken. I don't want to hurt you."

"How would I get my heart broken?"

"Let's go inside."

She was desperately trying to hold on to her temper. Had Finn not looked and sounded so tormented, she would have let him have it. She would have shouted, "*Now* you say something? After how many times you made love to me? *Now* you decide it shouldn't have happened?"

"Answer my question," she insisted.

"You might fall in love with me."

It was at that moment that she realized just how clueless Finn MacBain was.

"Okay, now I understand."

"I know that sounded arrogant. It's just that —"

"I understand," she repeated.

She got out of the car before he could come around and open the door for her. She didn't run inside but waited and walked with him so that he wouldn't know how upset she was.

"You and I want different things. I'm eight years older than you, and I don't ever want to get married. That's not going to change," he stressed. "But you're young, and you probably want it all. A husband and kids."

Curious, she asked, "How do you know

what I want?"

"You have a loving heart."

Was that code for *naive*? she wondered. "And you don't?"

"You're not pessimistic like I am."

She handed him the key and let him unlock the door. "You're saying that I still believe in love and happily-ever-after, and you've figured out that it's all nonsense. See? I get it."

He didn't argue with her. It was after midnight, and she was exhausted. "I'm going to take a shower and go to bed. Good night."

A few minutes later she was standing under the shower letting the hot water ease some of the knots in her muscles. She wondered how long it was going to take for her to get rid of her anger and frustration and feel the hurt of his rejection. She wasn't a child; she knew what she was doing when she went to bed with him, and she wasn't sorry it had happened.

She wished he didn't have regrets. It is what it is. That was what her father always said to her when he couldn't come up with a logical explanation as to why something bad had happened.

Her mind wouldn't calm. After she turned off the lights and got into bed, she replayed their conversation. He told her he never should have touched her. Just what every girl wants to hear. And marriage wasn't for him. She laid that decision at Danielle's feet. He had wanted to marry her until she cheated on him. He must have been devastated by her betrayal. It was all about trust, Peyton concluded. Finn had obviously decided that the only way to protect his heart was not to trust any woman. Did he still love Danielle? The possibility made her feel sick.

The week ahead was going to be difficult, and she didn't have time to feel sorry for herself. A single tear slipped down her cheek. It was all she would allow.

Over breakfast Sunday morning Finn told Peyton he would be leaving early Monday.

"Ronan and I have to be in Seattle for a meeting before we go back to D.C., but you'll be all right. Christopher has hired two men from one of the best security firms in the country. I've checked them out, and they're excellent at what they do. They'll keep you safe."

"There shouldn't be any trouble until Drew finds out Erik has the recording."

"Always expect trouble. Be ready for it."

She nodded. She suddenly remembered

something she wanted to ask him. "At the airport you told Erik you had four strong suspects. I count Drew, Parsons, and Eileen. Who's the fourth?"

"Erik."

"But he —"

"I've said this before. Don't believe anything until it's proven. Erik says he and his sister don't have anything to do with each other. That might not be true. For all we know, he could have called her from the airport to warn her."

Peyton thought about what Finn had told her as she poured him another cup of coffee. "Wouldn't it be something if it wasn't any of them, that someone else having nothing to do with Dalton wants me dead. Now that would be a real kick in the pants, wouldn't it?"

He couldn't believe he actually laughed. "Hell, Peyton, a kick in the pants?"

"I'm just saying —"

He cut her off. "Having done a background on Drew and after meeting him, I'm convinced he's behind the attempts. We know he has a shady character working for him in Parsons. Still, there could be an unknown, and that worries me. He could have hired a shooter, someone outside his circle, someone we don't know about."

"If he hired a professional to kill me, he's not getting his money's worth. The shooter is a lousy shot."

Finn moved fast, pinning her against the island. "Don't make light of this. If anything ever happened to you . . ." Staring into her beautiful eyes, he was fighting a battle he knew he was going to lose. "Ah, hell," he whispered a scant second before his mouth sealed hers.

Her arms curled around his neck, and her fingers slid up into his hair. Passion burned between them, and she was holding on to him like she never wanted him to stop.

He came to his senses and abruptly pulled back. He tried to catch his breath as he said, "I'm sorry. I shouldn't have done that. I don't know what's the matter with me. When I'm around you, I can't seem to control myself. It's the damnedest thing."

Indeed, Peyton thought. "Then it's a good thing you're leaving." She put her head on his shoulder and closed her eyes. She wanted to remember his wonderful scent, so fresh and clean and male.

Realizing how foolish she was behaving, she moved away from him. All good things come to an end, don't they?

"We should go over to the hotel now. Christopher is waiting for us," Finn said.

"Why is he waiting for us?" she asked.

"To talk about the security guards and their schedule."

"What if I don't like them?" she asked.

"Then you don't like them."

"I can't trade them in for new ones?"

"No, you can't." He grabbed her hand. "This is serious business."

Christopher was in the lobby with Lucy, arguing about something she obviously thought was important. Christopher looked resigned; Lucy looked irritated.

"Not getting along?" Peyton asked. "What a surprise."

"We're getting along," Lucy insisted. "He's just not being reasonable."

"When will security arrive?" Finn asked Christopher.

"Meeting is at ten, and they'll be on time."

"You personally know these guys?"

Christopher nodded. "I've worked with them in Special Ops."

Lucy took a step closer to the bane of her existence. "Who *are* you?"

"I'm the man who tells you what you can and cannot order, sweetheart, and twelve-thousand-dollar sofas are off the table. You're not getting them. I've assured your uncle that all expenditures on improvements would be reasonable."

Peyton thought about Christopher's statement and it suddenly clicked. Uncle Len had put him in charge so that she and Lucy and Ivy wouldn't mess up. Len didn't want them to fail, and Christopher was there to make sure they didn't. It was odd, but she felt some of the burden lift away. Christopher obviously knew what he was doing.

"All right, then," she said.

Lucy turned to her. "What do you mean, 'All right, then'?"

Peyton held up her hand. "We'll talk about this later. You can vent then."

Lucy nodded. "I'll bring the wine." She picked up a folder on the counter and, straightening her shoulders, marched past Christopher. "I'll be in the office if you need me."

Christopher didn't look the least bit annoyed by her attitude. In fact, the slight curl of his lips as he watched Lucy walk away indicated the opposite.

"You like giving her trouble, don't you?" Peyton asked.

"Yes, I do," he admitted.

Finn was right. He'd told Peyton that Christopher had the hots for Lucy. Peyton preferred to think he was interested in her sister because he enjoyed sparring with her. Her interpretation didn't sound as animalistic. There wasn't any doubt that sparks flew whenever the two were together, and everyone knew that sparks could ignite a flame. Maybe their arguments were simply a way for them to hide their true feelings. A relationship between two people who would be working together for a full year might not be a good idea. Then again, they were both adults. If Lucy wanted to be with Christopher, and Christopher wanted to be with her, it wasn't any of Peyton's business. Except, she didn't want her sister to get hurt. She only hoped that Lucy knew how to protect her heart.

Finn drew her attention. "Security's here."

The front doors opened, and two extremely fit men walked inside. They were quite attractive in a rugged, outdoorsy way. Both had dark hair and deep tans. They were about Finn's age, Peyton judged, and built like him, all muscle, but as far as sex appeal, Finn won, hands down.

It was apparent from their greetings that they were good friends of Christopher's. Laughing, they exchanged several colorful insults before crossing the lobby to meet Finn and her.

The taller of the two stepped forward to shake her hand. "You can call me Drake."

The second man couldn't seem to take

his eyes off her. "Braxton," he said.

They turned to Finn next. After they were introduced, Drake said, "Hey, I know you."

"Yeah, I do, too," Braxton agreed.

Peyton wanted to gloat. Finally, she could say, See? I told you people recognize you from the Olympics.

"You brought in Hayes and got him to confess," Drake said.

"My partner, Agent Ronan Conrad, did most of the work," Finn said. Uncomfortable with the praise, he added before they could say anything more, "Let's go into the conference room, and I'll run through Peyton's situation."

Peyton showed the men through the offices into the conference room, and the guards listened closely as Finn explained what would be expected of them. She didn't think it would take all that long to fill them in, but she was wrong. An hour passed, and they were still going strong with questions.

"Agents Hutton and Lane are in Dalton. They're running the investigation now, and they'll keep you informed," Finn told them.

"They've got eyes on all the players?" Drake asked.

Finn nodded. "This could be over soon. Last night Erik Swift let the agents take all the guns from his father's house. They're in the lab now."

Drake and Braxton were thorough. They insisted on going over every detail again before they were satisfied they could handle the case. When Finn offered to walk around the resort with them to give them the lay of the land, Peyton went to her desk. Since she was already in the office, she figured she might as well work on the designs for the new pool. If they were going to open the resort to the public soon, they had to get things done quickly.

Finn and the two guards were just heading out the door when she heard Drake ask, "When do you want us to start?"

"I've got her until tomorrow morning. Then she's all yours," Finn replied.

What a lovely way to say good-bye, she thought.

Peyton wasn't much of a drinker, but by five that afternoon she thought she might like to guzzle a bottle of wine. Maybe two bottles. No time to rest, even on a Sunday. Christopher was an expert at cracking the whip. He had appeared shortly after noon with a stack of proposals from produce suppliers and asked her to look through them for the resort restaurants. She had just compared her last arugula price lists and had sorted everything into file folders when she noticed the time. Finn hadn't returned yet.

"I want to go for a swim in the ocean," she announced to an empty office. As if on cue, a loud crack of thunder sounded. "Guess that's out." She got up from her desk and stretched. Lucy had gone into Christopher's office for a meeting a few minutes earlier and closed the door. Probably didn't want her to hear them yelling, Peyton thought. She decided to go back to her condo and wait for Finn there, so she headed to Christopher's office to ask him to give Finn the message. She swung the door open and, too late, she realized she should have knocked before walking in. Lucy was wrapped in Christopher's arms, and they were kissing each other quite passionately. Neither one of them noticed her.

She quietly closed the door and was preparing to leave when Finn returned. "What's funny?" he asked when he saw the big grin on her face.

She was sure he would gloat if she told him, so she simply said, "Nothing. Nothing at all." She rubbed the back of her neck. "I'm tired. I'd like to go home now. Are Braxton and Drake still here?"

"No," he answered. "They've gone over

the entire resort, and they know all the weak entry spots. They'll take turns, but one of them will be with you after I leave. You'll be okay."

Was he trying to convince her . . . or himself?

TWENTY-FOUR

Dinner was strained. Lucy had begged off eating with them, and Peyton thought she had probably gone out with Christopher. She could have used her sister's help in easing the tension between Finn and her. He had suggested they maintain a platonic relationship, and she believed he was sincere about remaining friends. She wasn't at all sincere when she agreed, but she didn't want him to know it.

When he left tomorrow, that was it. She never wanted to see him again. If he could walk away from her after all they had shared, then he didn't deserve her. She deserved to be with someone who loved her, really loved her. Unconditionally. Someone who could never walk away.

Was there such a thing as true love? She wanted to believe there was. Until Finn brought it up, she never really thought much about getting married. She just assumed that someday she would, and eventually she'd have children. Did that make her archaic, to want happily-ever-after with the man of her dreams?

Early Monday morning Finn pulled her into his arms, hugged her, and said yet again, "You'll be okay."

"Yes, I will," she answered with conviction.

"If you need me, you call me," he reminded.

A quick kiss, and he was gone. As the door closed behind him, Peyton felt a catch in her heart, but she wouldn't allow herself to dwell on the hurt. She forced herself to think about the days ahead and what she wanted to accomplish. It wasn't easy keeping her emotions under control, but she managed.

Braxton was at her side throughout the day as she made the rounds to all the renovation projects on the resort. Everything was in full swing, and barring any unforeseen problems, they would be able to open the hotel and accept reservations within the next three weeks. Most of the former staff had been given a leave of absence and would be ready to return by then, and Peyton was beginning to receive applications to fill new positions. There were still large projects, such as the makeover of the bungalows and the new swimming pool, to complete, but they wouldn't interfere with the operation of the rest of the resort.

Peyton returned to the office in time to meet Dan Miller, who had arrived for his appointment with Christopher. The developer and contractor was the opposite in temperament and appearance from his competitor, Scott Cassady. Miller was in his mid-fifties, wore work clothes, and drove an old pickup truck that was weighed down by just about every tool known to man. He was calm and self-assured, and wasn't out to impress anyone. Peyton really liked him. She felt the calluses on his palm and his fingers when she shook his hand. Cassady had been smooth and artificial, whereas Miller was blunt and to the point. He didn't seem the sort to tell customers what they wanted to hear just to win them over. He appeared to be a straight shooter, and she was anxious to get his opinion on her plans. What would he have to say about tearing out two small, worn-out pools and building one gorgeous Olympic-size pool? Christopher hadn't vetoed the idea and was willing to listen, so he went with her, Braxton, and

Miller to look at the area and study the possibility.

"What do you think, Mr. Miller?" Peyton asked as they stood overlooking the land she had marked for the pool. "Could it be done?"

"I'm not formal," he said. "Call me Dan, and, yes, of course it can be done. Why don't I work the numbers and get an estimate to you."

Christopher took Dan on a tour to discuss other innovations he had in mind while she and Braxton returned to the hotel. Later that afternoon Christopher called Peyton and Lucy into his office.

"You have to decide what you want this place to be," he told them. "All the bungalows are located on the west side of the Cove, and, Lucy, didn't you tell me you wanted to build more of them closer to the hotel?"

She nodded. "Yes."

"The hotel is on the east side," he continued. "And Peyton wants to put in an Olympic-size pool close to it."

"Two of the smaller pools need major work, and I'd like to replace them with one big one," Peyton explained. "With a fun water feature and the ocean right there in front of it, families will come. We could offer meal plans, make it inclusive," she added enthusiastically. "And eventually I'd like to build another hotel, though no bigger than this one. I've looked at the space, and we could do it without changing the character of the resort. I think Uncle Len would approve. I want the Cove to remain charming."

Lucy didn't agree with Peyton's vision. "When they're remodeled, the bungalows will draw customers who appreciate luxury and are willing to pay for it."

"Can't we have both?" Peyton asked.

A commotion coming from the outer office interrupted the discussion. Lucy and Peyton recognized the high-pitched screech. Debi had arrived. Since Braxton was the only other person out there, Peyton assumed he was getting the brunt of her anger.

"Guess who's here?" Peyton said dryly.

"Wasn't she supposed to start work this morning?" Lucy asked. "Peyton, why are you smiling?"

"Because she isn't our problem. Christopher is her boss."

Lucy smiled sweetly and, keeping her gaze on Christopher, said to Peyton, "Don't worry. He's used to working with difficult people."

"If you'll excuse me," Peyton said, "I'm

going to go save Braxton from Satan's little helper."

The second Debi spotted Peyton, she started in. Pointing at Braxton, she yelled, "This rude man won't let me get past to go into Christopher's office. I told him I work here, but he won't budge. Who does he think he is?"

"Shall we go?" Peyton asked Braxton as she walked past Debi without a response. She could hear her cousin sputtering with indignation as they exited the building, and she smiled with childish satisfaction. Braxton obviously approved. He winked at her.

As Braxton escorted her home, he told her about the conversations he had been having with the agents in Dalton. "They're reporting that everyone is calm, and all the people they're watching are going about their normal routines. Erik Swift is cooperating with them fully and giving them daily updates. There had been some concern that Randolph Swift might be a hindrance, but after he heard the recording you gave Erik he realized how serious the situation is."

"So Randolph is going to take action?"

"Yes," he replied. "One of the agents said that Erik and his father went to an attorney in Minneapolis and changed Randolph's trust. He said they sat there until it was done, signed it with witnesses, and filed it. Come Friday, Drew and his wife are in for a major surprise."

"Friday is the day Randolph was going to announce Drew's promotion," she said.

"Evidently he's so irate about Albertson's behavior, he wants to fire him in front of the whole company. Randolph wants no misunderstanding that he's out, and so is his wife."

"I wish I could be there," she admitted.

"I bet Finn would like to be there, too."

"About Finn," she began, then hesitated while she thought about the right way to say what she wanted.

"Yes?"

"He's a family friend, and I've asked a lot from him. He took time off his job to help, and I really appreciated it, but he's back at work and I don't want anyone to ask for his help again. He's done enough," she stressed. "And we're set, aren't we? If there's trouble, you and Drake will handle it, and if anything should happen, I don't want him notified. I've used up enough of his time."

Braxton didn't seem to have a problem with her request. "Okay," he said. Switching subjects he asked, "Are you in for the night, or do you want to go somewhere?"

"I'm staying in." She checked her phone

to make sure she had his number pro-
grammed, Drake's number, too. "Are you
leaving for the night?"

He smiled. "We'll be around."

Peyton had done an adequate job of
blocking thoughts of Finn during the day,
but as soon as she got into bed, she couldn't
seem to stop thinking about him. Where was
he? Still in Seattle? On his way to D.C.?
What was he going to do there? Probably
stop by the White House to pick up another
award for doing something extraordinary,
she imagined, and that thought made her
smile. With Finn anything was possible.

Or maybe he was reconnecting with Danielle, the woman who had ruined him. Closing her eyes in frustration, Peyton told
herself she didn't care. The man had walked
away from her, and she would never forgive
him for that.

Sleep eluded her. Throwing off the covers
she reached for her notebook and began to
write down more lessons she had learned
that would go into her cookies someday.
Lessons such as: Never waste the expensive
cheese in a frittata for a man who is just going to dump you — or — Never bring out
your most seductive swimsuit for a man who
is just going to dump you — or — Always
lock the door before you shower so you

won't give in to temptation and have sex with a man who is just going to dump you. Okay, maybe her axioms were getting a little long and wordy, and maybe ending every one with "a man who is just going to dump you" was a little repetitive, but that didn't make them any less true. She knew she wouldn't actually insert any of these proverbial warnings in her baking, but writing them down and getting them off her chest made her feel better.

Whenever she thought about Finn, she bounced back and forth between overwhelming sadness and ridiculous anger. By the time she finally fell asleep, she was wrung out.

The rest of the work week was a god-awful mess . . . all because of Debi. On Tuesday the technology-challenged cousin accidentally deleted more than sixty files from the computer, and it took Peyton until midnight to retrieve them all. Wednesday, after printing one hundred too many copies of a file — again, by accident, Debi insisted — she broke the main printer while trying to jam a paper tray into the wrong slot. Thursday morning, Lucy gave Debi a list of tradesmen to call and schedule to work. By nine o'clock, she had alienated every one of them. One tradesman threatened to sue for defamation of character after he talked to Debi. At ten, Christopher gave her a list of errands. Simple errands. She was to drop off a set of plans to a landscaper, pick up paint decks from Dan Miller's office, pick up two packages from the Port James post office, and bring back lunch from a local diner. It should have taken her no more than two hours to get the errands done. Three hours tops. Debi left at ten in the morning and strolled back into the office at four in the afternoon. She was sipping a Big Gulp drink and didn't have any packages with her; however, there were several notice-able changes in her appearance. She was wearing new purple nail polish. Peyton spot-ted it immediately because it was such a horribly neon-bright shade. Debi's blond hair was much lighter and not quite as brassy, and it had been cut and styled. Her clothes were different, too. She'd left the of-fice in black slacks and a fuchsia blouse and returned wearing a floral skirt and a tight purple tank top. Her matching sandals were also new.

Aside from giving each other an oh-my-God-can-you-believe-it look, Lucy and Peyton didn't say a word. They both won-dered if Christopher would notice when he came back. He and Braxton had been outside discussing security for the resort for more than an hour.

Peyton was leaving a Post-it note on his desk when he walked in. He didn't mention Debi or her tardiness but went straight to work, handing Peyton the notes he'd made on his security checklist. Peyton gave him an update on a couple of calls she'd taken and then leaned against the credenza while she went through his notes. The room was quiet as they each attended to the matters at hand. When Peyton finished reading the recommendations, she turned to Christopher to give her approval, but he stopped her. Raising his index finger, he said, "Could that wait just one second?" He then looked through the open door into the outer office and called, "Debi, could you step in here please?"

The newly decked-out employee took her time responding. She finished reapplying her Pepto-pink lipstick, then put it and her compact mirror back in her handbag before sashaying into his office and taking a seat.

Christopher wasted no time. "You're fired," he announced.

Debi looked thunderstruck. "Why?" she asked.

Peyton couldn't believe she had to ask.

Debi looked genuinely astonished. Didn't she have a clue how incompetent she was? Of course she did, Peyton decided. It was all a game to her. Debi's next statement proved it.

"Okay. Then call Uncle Len and tell him you failed, and to buy me a house. He knows which one I want."

Christopher leaned back in his chair and studied Debi for a long minute without saying a word. She squirmed under his scrutiny.

"Well? Call him," she demanded.

"There's been a misunderstanding," he began. "You agreed to work here for six months and do a good job at whatever task you were given, and then, based on your performance I would decide if you merited a house or not."

"*You* decide?"

"I was your last chance with your uncle Len. He didn't want to waste another minute dealing with you and your issues. He's had enough, and so he asked me to take charge."

"Do I get my house or not?"

"No, you do not."

She bolted to her feet, then sat again. She looked panicked. Peyton thought she was beginning to realize Christopher was serious and she couldn't manipulate him.

"Oh no, that's not right. I know what the deal was. I promised Len I would work here for six months and then I'd get my house. I'm doing my part. I'm willing to stay six months. You're the one breaking the agreement."

"You're doing your part?"

"Yes," she stammered. "I've been working. I've done everything you've asked."

Christopher was remarkably calm when he asked, "Did you deliver the plans to the landscaper?"

"Yes, I did," she answered. "It was muddy, so I left them by the mailbox."

"What about the paint decks from Dan Miller?"

"His secretary said he was out."

"You didn't ask her for them?"

"I wasn't exactly there," she admitted. "I called on the phone while I was . . . busy."

"Busy doing what?" Peyton asked. "Getting your hair or your nails done?"

Debi didn't answer.

"And the packages from the post office?" Christopher asked.

"There was a line, and I didn't think you'd want me to spend company time standing in a long line," she said indignantly.

"But it was okay to spend company time at a spa?" Peyton wondered.

Debi's chin came up a notch, but again she refused to answer.

Christopher shook his head. "I don't suppose you remembered lunch, either."

"They weren't serving lunch yet."

"So, you didn't order anything," Christopher concluded.

"I had a scone and a latte," she said.

Christopher didn't lose his patience, which Peyton thought was admirable. He remained composed as he said, "I'm sorry, but this just isn't working out. I'll let Len know. You may leave now."

Debi burst into tears. "You can't fire me. You didn't give me a chance. This is your fault, not mine. No one showed me how to do anything. I don't know computers. That's Peyton's fault. She set me up to fail."

Peyton couldn't keep quiet. "You said you knew how to use all the programs. Why didn't you tell us the truth?"

Tears were pouring down her face now. "I didn't want you to make fun of me."

Peyton rolled her eyes. "We're not in junior high," she said.

"Please, Christopher, give me another chance," Debi begged. "I'll really try this time. Just don't give me stuff to do on a computer until Lucy teaches me how to use it."

"Why Lucy?" Christopher asked, curious.

"Because she's patient. She's not a bitch," she added, pausing to shoot a glare at Peyton. "Lucy can train me."

Christopher was swayed, but not by Debi. Lucy was standing in the doorway behind Debi frantically shaking her head at him. He simply couldn't resist. He got an ornery look in his eyes. "Okay, you get one more chance, and Lucy will train you, but you still answer to me. One more screwup and you're out."

Debi rushed to leave before Christopher changed his mind. She was happy and a bit smug, Peyton thought. Lucy, on the other hand, looked as though she wanted to do bodily harm. Peyton slipped out of the office as her sister stormed past her.

"Christopher? A word," Lucy said.

The door slammed behind her.

TWENTY-FIVE

Special Agent John Caulfield was back in Finn's nightmare. He was helping interview the suspect who had set the fire. Caulfield's hands were charred, his face was all but gone, but his voice was the same, strong and decisive.

The nightmare flashed to the scene of the crime, the two-story house. Caulfield was standing on the top step, one hand resting on the doorknob. He was talking to Finn on the phone, telling him he would wait for backup, that he was going to do this by the book, and to hurry and get to the scene so he could observe the arrest. He was certain the suspect was hiding inside.

He was still talking to Finn when he slowly turned and opened the door. Flames instantly engulfed him, incinerating him, yet he continued to hold his cell phone to his ear and give Finn instructions.

Until recently the nightmare had begun

and ended in the interrogation room. Now, there was a different ending. Peyton was there. She stood just outside Finn's door waiting for him, and right before he woke up, a sense of calm washed over him.

Ronan and Finn were early for the lecture. They sat at a table in one of the larger ballrooms of the Adams Hotel on the outskirts of Seattle waiting for the first speaker. The seminar was mandatory, and neither one of them wanted to be there. From the looks on the faces of the other agents filing in, they didn't want to be there, either.

"What's this first lecture about?" Ronan asked, yawning as he emptied a packet of sugar into his coffee cup.

"New regulations," Finn replied. "That's what I heard anyway."

"I don't get it," Ronan said. "Why did we have to come all the way to Seattle for this? Aren't they running the same seminars on the East Coast?"

"Probably," Finn said. "But we're not just here for the seminar. We're being interviewed for hostage rescue."

"Did you put in for that?"

"No. Did you?"

"No."

"Then what the . . . ," Finn muttered.

"It's gotta be for something else. Maybe I'll call Grayson," Ronan added, referring to his old partner. "Now that he's taken the promotion, he's got some real clout. He could find out what's going on."

"Yeah, call him," Finn agreed.

"If we're here until Thursday, we could catch a game. I know a guy who could get us tickets to anything."

Finn laughed. "You always know a guy."

Ronan and Finn had been partners for only a short time, but they had already learned each other's quirks. Ronan had been raised in Boston's inner city in one of the toughest neighborhoods in the country. He had a rough edge to him and had been on the wrong side of the law more often than he wanted to admit. A full college scholarship had changed his life. That and the Marines. He and Finn made a good team, which was why they had been assigned to work together on several cases. Finn trusted his judgment and knew he'd have his back if things got dicey.

"Any news from Dalton?" Ronan asked.

Finn had told him all about the investigation. "I'm waiting to hear the ballistics report on the guns they took to the lab. I'm betting Albertson's henchman, Parsons, used one of those rifles to take a shot at

Peyton."

"Why Parsons and not Albertson?"

"Albertson's at the top of the list, too, but Peyton is sure that it was Parsons who shot at her car in Minnesota. He's got a record a mile long, and he wouldn't hesitate to try again. I'd really like to get him in an inter-rogation room —"

"You can't do that. You're too close to this."

Finn disagreed. "I could get him to talk."

"He shot at the woman you love," Ronan said. He was very matter-of-fact about it. "You'd go in there and punch his lights out."

"Peyton's a friend."

"Yeah, right. A friend." Ronan laughed. "Just when I think you've got it all figured out, you say something dumb. Your brain must be waterlogged from all that swim-ming you do."

"So, now you're an expert on my love life? Since when did you turn into a girl?"

Ronan wasn't the least insulted. "You're easy to read. You've been different ever since you connected with her. You're —"

"What?" Finn was impatient and ready to argue.

"Happier."

"The hell I am." Only after the words were out of his mouth did he realize how crazy and defensive he sounded. "Let's talk about *your* love life. See how you like it."

"There's nothing to talk about. Collins doesn't want a relationship. She told me it was for the best if we didn't see each other again. We're going down different roads, and it couldn't possibly work out."

It wasn't what he said but how he said it that told Finn there was more to the story. "You don't seem too broken up about it. You sound kind of cheerful."

"I want her to be happy. If she wants to go it alone, that's fine with me."

"What about you? What are you going to do?"

"Marry her," Ronan said. When he saw the skepticism on his friend's face, he reiterated, "Honest to God, I am gonna marry her."

Finn had a good laugh. "You sound sure of yourself."

"She loves me," Ronan said with a shrug. "She's just scared. She'll come around."

"Marriage is a big commitment."

"Sure is," he agreed. "But when you're ready, you're ready. I think you're scared, too, but you'll come around."

Finn shook his head. "Marriage isn't for everyone."

In the blink of an eye, Ronan switched

back to the investigation in Dalton. He asked several questions about Albertson's trip to see Peyton.

The more Finn talked about Albertson, the angrier he became. "I wish I could be there to see that bastard's face when he gets the hammer."

"Why can't you be there? The seminar's over Wednesday evening. You could catch a flight to Minneapolis Thursday, spend the night, and rent a car Friday morning to drive to Dalton. When is the announcement supposed to happen?"

"Hutton said it's scheduled for one in the afternoon. He could get me in without Albertson seeing me. I wouldn't want to ruin his surprise or make him suspicious." He mulled over the idea for a second and said, "I don't know. Maybe I will go. I'll think about it."

Finn couldn't stay away; he had to go. He knew Peyton was worried about the announcement, but he was more concerned about what Albertson would do after he was thrown out of the company. Finn had talked to him and looked him in the eye when he'd shown up in Bishop's Cove and made his veiled threats. He already knew what Albertson was capable of. There were hints of a violent temper in his background. Finn expected him to be enraged and want revenge. The question was, how long would he hold on to his desire to get even before moving on? Randolph Swift was about to snatch millions of dollars out of his grasp and humiliate him in the process. Randolph was probably going to disown his daughter as well. Oh yes, Albertson would want to get even. Agents Hutton and Lane believed he would go after Randolph and perhaps even Erik, but Finn was convinced his primary target would be Peyton. She had been the one to start the stone rolling down the mountain.

It wasn't difficult to make the arrangements. Since Finn's superior was also attending the seminar, it was easy to get his approval without e-mails and paperwork. Finn scheduled his flights in and out of Minneapolis and arranged to pick up a car at the airport.

He thought of everything but the weather. It was sleeting when he drove out of the rental lot. His lightweight raincoat wasn't much protection from the cold. He hated bulky clothes. He wore a suit, but once the heater kicked on, he was able to take off the jacket, loosen his tie, and get comfortable. As he drove north, Peyton kept popping into his thoughts. He pictured her making the drive from Dalton in a blizzard. A couple of months had passed and spring had officially arrived, but there was still snow on the ground and more on the way.

Hutton called him just as he was taking the Dalton exit. He gave him directions to Swift's main office and said, "You can't miss it. It's a giant phallic symbol."

Finn thought he was joking until he spotted the building. Damn, it was ugly. Whoever designed it should get some serious help, Finn thought. He parked in the visitors' lot and met Hutton at a side door. Although he'd talked to him many times on the phone, Finn had never actually met him in person.

Agent Hutton was in his early forties. He had a firm handshake and a wry sense of humor. After he shook Finn's hand, he said, "Was I right about the building? It looks like a phallic symbol, doesn't it?"

"Yeah, it does."

"Come on inside. We'll go up the back way to the auditorium. There's an empty office by the elevators. Erik Swift said we could wait in there. Lane is keeping his eyes on Albertson."

"Where is Albertson?"

"In his office preparing his speech." He smiled as he added, "Is he gonna be pissed."

"There's an auditorium here?"

"Yes, with a big stage. It's outfitted with kitchen appliances and a big island in front. They film a couple of cooking shows for a cable network. Everyone will come in and sit. Oh, and you're gonna love this — Albertson is insisting on filming the announcement. He personally made sure the cameras were ready to roll."

"Yeah, I do love it," he admitted. "Albertson's personal assistant — her name is Mimi. He'll know she's been helping Peyton. You need to get her out of here."

"Already done. Albertson thinks she's taking a late lunch. She won't be back. She and a man named Lars left together."

As they continued up the stairs, Finn asked, "How are you and Lane explaining your presence here?"

"We were here a few weeks ago asking questions about anyone who might have followed Peyton Lockhart when she left Dalton. We didn't get anywhere with that, of course. Albertson and Parsons both had alibis. Ever since you reported the second incident in Florida, we've been keeping pretty close tabs on them. As you know, we haven't been able to make a connection with him or Parsons to the shooting . . . yet," he said. He opened the door to a small office and flipped on the lights. "Albertson thinks we stopped by today to finish up our report, and Erik Swift is backing us up. Albertson's so caught up in his excitement at becoming the head honcho around here, he's oblivious. Hell, J. Edgar Hoover himself could come back from the dead and shake his hand today and he wouldn't notice."

A couple of minutes later, he led Finn into the auditorium. It was built like a theater with a long, wide stage and upholstered chairs that were arranged in a half circle and tiered so that those seated at the top had just as clear a view as those sitting in the front. It was a slick setup, he thought. The stage sparkled with stainless steel and marble. An employee was busy placing folding chairs on either side of the podium, which stood in the center. Another employee was running a microphone and testing the sound. Showtime was in twenty minutes.

"Albertson and the others will go up to the stage from the side entrances," Hutton said. "I've found a good spot for you to watch." He pointed to the back corner. "Over there by the pillars. The lighting will be focused on the stage. If you stand on the other side of the pillar, no one will see you."

Finn took his place in the shadows, and

the auditorium started to fill up with people. Some walking in by themselves, others entering in small groups. In less than ten minutes, the room was full and buzzing with chatter over the upcoming announcement. Finn could hear a conversation between two women seated in the back row. The topic was the change they had noticed in Randolph Swift.

"He's got a bounce in his step lately. Haven't you noticed? We didn't see him for so long, and now he's coming back in the office again."

"Do you think he's met someone? He seems more alive these days."

"He looked like death after sweet Miriam died. She really was a dear woman, wasn't she?"

"Oh, she was. Do you know she never forgot any employee's name? She even remembered my Sarah's name."

"I thought Randolph wanted to get in the grave with her, he was so devastated. But now it appears he's back with us."

"I'm glad of it. I wish he weren't going to retire. It's going to be awful with Drew Albertson in charge. You've seen how he treats women."

"Especially young women," her friend added.

"He and Eileen try to stop the rumors, but I think they're true. With him as boss, I don't know how much longer I'll be able to work here."

The lights framing the stage suddenly brightened, and the employees immediately stopped talking and sat up straighter in anticipation. The side doors opened, and Erik, his expression solemn, took a seat on the right side of the podium. At the same time Drew and his wife, Eileen, stepped out into the lights. They stood together smiling at the audience before making their way to the stage. Drew, acting like a politician up for reelection, waved to the crowd while Eileen smiled and nodded to several people in the front row. They took seats to the left of the podium.

A cheer went up and everyone stood when Randolph Swift came onstage. He was tall and very thin. He had wide shoulders like his daughter and a firm jaw like his son. The lines in his face told the story of a life that had experienced a great deal, but there was a vitality in his step, just as the two women had said. He seemed touched by the ovation and raised his hand to acknowledge the affection. When the cheering and applause did not die down, he raised both hands and motioned for them to take their seats. Finally the noise subsided enough for him to be heard.

He thanked everyone for the kind reception, and then said, "I have several announcements today." He pulled note cards from the inside pocket of his suit and placed them on the podium. "I'd like to begin by saying that it was wrong of me to demand that you attend Miriam's memorial. She'd have a fit if she knew I was doing that. She didn't want me to mourn, either," he said. "I'm still going to have the memorial, but you don't have to attend. If you have other plans, that's all right. She and I both know you loved her."

Another round of applause erupted, and he waited to speak again. "The memorial isn't going to have speeches. It will be a party with food and drink and balloons for the kids. We're going to celebrate her life."

Once again the crowd showed its approval by clapping. Randolph straightened to his full height, then glanced at Drew and Eileen. They were both smiling at the audience as though the adulation was for them.

"And now on to the other changes I'd like to share with you. After much deliberation, I've decided to step down as head of this company. I know this doesn't come as a surprise to most of you." He added with a nod, "It's time. And I'm confident I'm leaving you in good hands. Let me tell you about your new CEO. You're getting a powerhouse. I believe he's much smarter than I am, much more creative, and much more innovative. He won't be afraid to try new ideas, so I have no concern that the company will become stale. He has wonderful plans for expansion and, most important, he truly understands how valuable all of you are to the company. His moral compass is straight and true, and it will guide him in making good decisions."

He paused to glance over his shoulder at Albertson, who was posing with the most sincere look of humility he could muster. Randolph turned back to the upturned faces in the auditorium and continued. "I would now like to introduce to you the new CEO of Swift Publications . . . Erik Swift."

The room vibrated as the crowd jumped to their feet in unison and began to cheer wildly.

Finn watched Drew. He didn't move a muscle, and Finn thought he didn't quite grasp what had just happened.

Eileen understood. Her face twisted in rage, and she nearly overturned her chair as she sprang forward and shouted, "That's not right. You've got it wrong. Drew is the new CEO."

Her panic was explosive. Randolph ignored her, and that only fueled her anger. Turning to the audience, she screamed, "Stop it. Stop cheering. Shut up and sit down." She roared the last demand, then turned to her father and said, "Is this a joke? Drew's the CEO. You're having fun, aren't you?"

Drew grabbed Eileen's arm and jerked her back to her seat. His expression was stony now, but even from the distance separating them, Finn could see the fire in his eyes.

Eileen's horrific reaction to the news had quieted everyone. The air was thick with tension as they waited to see what would happen next.

Randolph tapped the microphone to get their attention. "There's more to share with you. Eileen and Drew Albertson will be leaving the company today." He said the last with steel in his voice.

Drew stood slowly and, with his hands fisted at his sides, asked, "Why are you doing this to me?"

Scanning the audience, Randolph replied, "I could explain why, but I think it would be better if everyone just listened."

He raised a hand to signal the control booth, and Peyton Lockhart's voice, as clear as a bell, came over the speaker.

"Do you mind if I record our conversation . . ."

Twenty-Six

When Finn heard Peyton's voice coming through the speakers, he felt as though his heart had just stopped.

"Son of a bitch," he whispered. As Randolph played the entire recording, Finn's attention locked on the Albertsons. Eileen was tugging on Drew's arm, trying to get him to look at her, but he stared straight ahead and ignored her. His face was cold and impassive. It must have taken every last ounce of his self-control to hold on to his emotionless expression. Finn knew he was boiling inside.

Two security guards headed to the steps to escort Drew and Eileen out of the building. Drew saw them coming. He stood, carefully adjusted his tie, and rigidly left the stage. Eileen rushed after him.

"I can take care of this, Drew. Let me take care of this for you," she pleaded. "He's a senile old man. He isn't responsible. We could go to court . . ." The door closed behind her, muffling her voice.

No one in the auditorium moved or made a sound. Mesmerized by what they were hearing, the employees hung on every word, stunned into frozen silence.

Randolph and Erik had already left the stage. They slipped out the second Drew's voice filled the room with his vile insults toward Miriam.

Finn reached for his phone and called Braxton as he headed out of the auditorium and into the office next door.

"Where's Peyton?" There was an urgency in his voice he couldn't control.

"She's in the conference room working," Braxton answered.

Finn quickly filled him in on what had just happened and said, "Don't let her out of your sight."

"This Randolph guy threw Peyton under the bus playing that recording, didn't he? He could have exposed what kind of pervert Albertson was without pointing the finger at Peyton."

"Albertson would have figured it out. You should have seen the look in his eyes."

"We've got Peyton covered," he assured him. "I'll let Drake know . . . and Christopher. He might want to add one or two more men to our security team."

"Good idea," he said.

"Do you want to talk to Peyton?"

"No, I'll call her later. Just tell her I'm in Dalton."

As soon as the call ended, the door opened and Agent Hutton walked in and blurted out his bad news. "I just got the ballistics report. That bullet doesn't match any of the weapons we took from Swift's house."

"Damn, I had hoped . . ."

"Yeah, me too," he said. "Lane is really taking the news hard. He took an instant dislike to Parsons and was looking forward to locking him up. Now we don't have one thing to hold him on. Zero," he stressed, frowning. "But we aren't going to give up. Before we took the guns out of Swift's house, we followed procedure. We itemized each gun and got Erik's signature. He hadn't told his father he'd given us the guns to test until this morning. He showed him the list and promised he'd have them back in his cabinet soon. Anyway, his father went over the inventory and is insisting that a handgun and two rifles are missing. Both the rifles had scopes," he added. "He thought we messed up and forgot to put them on the list, but Erik convinced him the count was accurate. He then told him about Peyton and how Parsons went after her. He said his father was shocked and angry because he didn't realize until that moment how far Drew and Eileen would go to get what they wanted. Erik said he got a real peculiar look in his eyes, and he thinks that's when Randolph decided to use the recording to publicly humiliate him."

"Did you know they were going to play it?" Finn asked.

Hutton shook his head. "Neither Randolph nor Erik mentioned that was the plan. Albertson looked crazed when he left the building. I think he's gonna go postal on us. We'll keep an eye on him, and Parsons, as well."

"Where is Parsons?"

"He chased after the Albertsons shouting Eileen's name until she stopped and waited for him to catch up."

"You've got to keep surveillance on them."

"I hear you. They're probably going to go somewhere and brainstorm how to fix this. All that money? They won't give up."

"This isn't fixable. Albertson knows that, and in his twisted mind it's all Peyton's fault."

Finn spent the afternoon helping Hutton and Lane interview employees. There were several who were loyal to Drew and Eileen, though God only knew why. One of the employees was a woman named Bridget. She was so distraught she could barely keep it together during the interview.

"That recording we listened to was all a lie," she insisted. "Drew's innocent. That horrible Peyton Lockhart set him up. She trapped him," she said in a near shout. "She made it all up and put it on a recording."

Finn held his patience. "And how did she accomplish that?" he asked calmly.

"She had her ways. Ask Eileen. She'll tell you all about Peyton Lockhart. She figured her out right away."

"And what did she figure out?"

Bridget wiped the tears away from her face with the backs of her hands before answering. "That Peyton was a slut. A bitch and a slut," she added with a nod. "And now Drew's gone and it's all her fault." She began to sob and was barely coherent.

Finn decided to let Lane deal with her while he and Hutton went through Drew's and Eileen's offices. They had already posted security guards in front of their office doors after obtaining permission from Erik and his father to search the premises. They didn't find anything incriminating in Drew's office, but they confiscated Drew's computer to search his encrypted files.

"I'll bet the only thing we're going to find is porn," Hutton wagered.

Finn thought he was probably right. "I wish I could stay here and find the evidence to take these guys down, but I have to get to D.C."

"We can't stay in Dalton, either," Hutton said, "but we've got the local law cooperating with us now. They'll do what they can to help."

Lane poked his head in the doorway. "Just heard from surveillance. A courier delivered a copy of Randolph Swift's new will to Drew and Eileen a couple of minutes ago. That ought to top their day."

And give Drew yet another reason to go after Peyton, Finn thought. He needed to talk to her, to hear her voice, to know she was okay. He waited to make the call until he was out of Dalton and on his way to Minneapolis. As soon as she said hello, his entire body relaxed and the tightness in his chest eased. He felt as though he could take a deep breath again.

"How are you doing?"

Peyton didn't want to waste time on pleasantries. "Braxton told me you were in Dalton. I couldn't believe it. Did you get there in time to hear Randolph's speech?"

"Yes, I did. It was something else," he

admitted, and then he told her exactly what had happened. When he finally finished, she grilled him with questions. Her reaction wasn't what he expected. He described how enraged Drew became and how lethal he looked when the recording began, and she laughed.

"Oh, I so wish I had been there," she said.

"For God's sake, this isn't funny."

"No, of course it isn't. I keep picturing Drew waving to the audience and then getting sacked." She laughed again. "Sorry," she said. "I'll try to control myself. It's over now, isn't it, Finn? Drew's been ousted, and his record will follow him. I can let it go now."

"I don't think Drew's going to let it go," he warned. "You have to be careful."

Reacting to the worry in his voice, she said, "I'll be careful. And if he comes after me, I'll be ready." She didn't have the faintest idea how she would accomplish that feat, but she wanted to put his fears to rest. "Please don't worry about me. That isn't your job now. Braxton and Drake will be on guard until Drew calms down, and so will I."

"I don't want anything to happen to you."

"I know," she said. "I'm going to be all right. Besides, my safety isn't your problem any longer. You've done so much for me, and I really appreciate it, but now you need to get on with your life." *Without me,* she silently added. *You made that perfectly clear.*

"Peyton . . ."

Her voice was whisper soft. "Good-bye, Finn."

TWENTY-SEVEN

Peyton held the phone against her heart and bowed her head. She would not cry. If only she could garner some anger now. She did better being furious at him than feeling as though she was going to break down and weep every other minute.

He did not deserve her tears. He did not deserve her. Lately, those words had become her mantra. It was time for her to get on with her life, too.

She had a long list of things she wanted to get done before Mimi and Lars arrived. They needed temporary housing until they were settled, so she called maintenance and asked them to empty one of the two-bedroom condominiums behind hers that they'd been using for storage. She scheduled painters to go in on Monday, and as soon as they finished, she planned to have the floors polished. The unit was already furnished, and she would make sure there were fresh linens on their beds and food in the refrigerator. She wanted to make them feel welcome.

Mimi was staying in Minneapolis with one of her brothers while she waited for Lars to finish packing. She promised to call Peyton as soon as they were on the road, but she didn't plan on that happening for several days. In the meantime, she was enjoying being with family and told Peyton she'd forgotten how much she enjoyed her sister-in-law's company.

Peyton had taken over the conference room. She liked being able to spread out all her papers. She had a whole stack of notes for menus she wanted to talk to Lars about once he got settled. She didn't have any idea if he could cook, a fact she didn't mention to her sister. Lars had told her he wanted to become a chef, but that didn't mean he knew how to put a recipe together. She discussed the matter with Christopher, and they both decided it would be a good idea to start Lars at the smallest of the hotel's restaurants, Oceans, under Chef Geller's supervision. Aside from being extremely talented, Geller also had a rare trait — rare for a head chef, anyway — of being patient. Once Lars had gained some experience at Oceans, they would consider moving him to

Leonard's, their fine-dining restaurant, where he could work under one of the finest — albeit one of the most temperamental — chefs in Florida. Peyton was excited to be able to give Lars this opportunity and hoped it would be the start of great things for him.

As the days passed, Peyton began to enjoy her work at the resort more and more, and she could actually see the light at the end of the tunnel when the staff began to return to put the finishing touches on the hotel. For the most part, she stayed within the confines of the resort, but either Braxton or Drake was always somewhere nearby, never letting her out of sight. When she suggested that they may no longer be needed, they insisted that their duties would end when Christopher and Finn dismissed them, and no sooner. Since the matter was taken out of her hands, she decided to acquiesce and make the best of the situation by accepting the fact that the bodyguards were going to be part of her daily activity. Drake, it turned out, had a refined palate when it came to food. He could sample new dishes and tell which herbs and spices were needed and which had to go. Braxton had hidden talents, as well. One day, while she was poring over the proposed plans for the new pool, she asked his opinion on the layout and was pleasantly surprised to learn that he had several really good ideas, one of which included the building of a cabana in an otherwise unused corner of the space. Having them around became routine, and after a while she actually enjoyed their company and considered them friends.

Most of the time they tried to remain out of sight, but on the days that she had to leave the resort, they drove her car and stayed near her the entire time. Whether she was in an office or a shop, one of them was just outside the door, waiting.

She had just come back from one of those afternoons in Port James and returned to her work in the conference room when Lucy stopped in to say good night.

"Scott Cassady called today," she told her.

"Still wanting to make a deal?" Peyton asked.

"Yes. I think he found out we're working with Dan Miller and he's afraid he's losing his leverage. He was very cordial and complimentary."

"It won't do him much good."

Lucy started to leave but stopped. "I forgot to ask. How was the doctor's appointment?"

Peyton was sitting with her back to the

door. She faced a row of windows. She didn't bother to turn around when she answered. "She put me on birth control pills and said that they would help me have normal cycles, and that will be a first for me. She also gave me a shot and told me I wouldn't be able to get pregnant for six months. By then the pills will also protect me from pregnancy." She couldn't resist adding, "And as a bonus, because of the shot I can become sexually active right away."

"And whom do you plan to be sexually active with, if you don't mind my asking?"

"Christopher. I've had the hots for him for a long time now," Peyton said, keeping her head down so her sister couldn't see her mischievous grin.

Lucy's reaction was instantaneous. "You can't have him." She was emphatic.

Peyton swung around in her swivel chair to see the effect her remark had on her sister. Lucy's face had turned red in a heartbeat. Peyton thought her little joke was hilarious and was having a good laugh, until Christopher stepped into the doorway. She could tell from his expression that he'd heard every word.

Lucy didn't know he was there. "That's not funny."

"It kinda is," Christopher said.

Lucy jumped. She closed her eyes, took a deep breath, then, trying to be dignified, she straightened her shoulders, turned around, and said, "If you'll excuse me . . ."

He wouldn't let her get past him. She tried again. Pushing against his chest with the palm of her hand, she repeated, "If you'll excuse me . . ."

"I don't want to excuse you," he said. He put his arm around her waist and tucked her into his side. "Braxton's waiting for you when you're ready to leave. He's out front," he told Peyton as he pulled Lucy into his office. Peyton heard him ask, "How come she can't have me?" and then he laughed, a big booming sound that made Peyton smile. His office door closed before Lucy answered.

Peyton imagined they were going to canoodle, as her mother would say. Oh no, was she turning into her mother? She put the disturbing thought aside. Lucy and Christopher didn't know she had seen them kissing, and Peyton didn't plan to tell them. When Lucy was ready, she would talk about the relationship. Until then, Peyton would keep quiet and not prod. It really wasn't a secret, though. Anyone who spent five minutes with them knew they were involved.

The way they looked at each other said it all.

She remembered what it felt like to kiss Finn. She ached with a yearning deep inside. No, she mustn't think about him. It was over, and no good could come from replaying the past. She never wanted to see him again, she reminded herself, and at that moment she embraced the lie with all her heart.

The key to moving forward was to keep crazy busy, she decided. She was going to work like a maniac so she wouldn't have any time to think about him.

Debi helped her with her goal by keeping them all hopping. It seemed to Lucy that their cousin was really trying to do a good job this time; she just happened to be completely inept at everything she touched. Peyton wasn't buying it. No one could be that incompetent.

"You're becoming cynical," Lucy told her.

"Yes," Peyton agreed. "When it comes to our cousin, I am cynical. Tell me this. How come she can get on a computer, check all her e-mails, order clothes online, and check her Facebook page, but she can't learn how to push a button to print? She's playing you, Lucy."

"Office work just isn't her thing," Lucy argued.

Christopher agreed with Lucy's assessment, and so he had Debi running back and forth to the bungalows, checking on the progress of the tradesmen. As it turned out, Debi did have a skill. She liked to flirt. It seemed to be the only thing she was good at. The men refinishing the floors and the painters prepping the walls and ceilings appreciated her talent and took the time to flirt back. By Friday, Debi had three dates lined up with three different men. Evidently Sean was just a distant memory.

The following Tuesday afternoon the weather turned foul. A big storm was moving in. Christopher sent Debi to check each of the twelve bungalows to make sure all the windows were closed. Several had been kept open to let the paint fumes out. Two of the bungalows had brand-new floors, and unfortunately those were the two units Debi thought she had checked but hadn't. All of the windows remained open during the torrential downpour, and the floors were ruined. Too late, they realized they would have to double-check everything Debi did, but they had yet to figure out where to put her that she wouldn't do damage.

Two days later, they feared that Debi's

incompetence was spreading. One of the housekeepers reported that someone had left an open gallon of paint on a brand-new quartz counter. The can was lying on its side, and paint had poured all over the counter and dripped down onto the floor. It was a disaster.

It seemed that every time they took a step forward, something would happen to put them five steps back. It was difficult to stay optimistic about their target opening date for the bungalows. The hotel wasn't a problem, though. Everything was up and ready, including the spectacular waterfall . . . until it flooded the lobby. The return water valve had gotten completely clogged with pieces of clay. Repairing the damage would put the opening date back another two weeks.

In the midst of all the turmoil, Mimi and Lars arrived. It was after six at night when they pulled into the parking lot. Neither one of them had a trailer with them because they had sold what little furniture they owned and were ready to start over. Peyton wasn't worried they would feel they'd made a mistake by pulling up roots and moving across the country. She was certain they would love Bishop's Cove as much as she did. They would fit right in, too.

They loved their accommodations, and while they unloaded their suitcases, Peyton prepared dinner for them. She made a pasta dish with lots of fresh vegetables and a seared snapper with a roasted grape butter sauce. She offered them wine, but neither one of them wanted it. They'd been driving all day and thought the wine would put them to sleep.

They kept their dinner conversation focused on the future, and Peyton could sense their excitement building as she described all the improvements under way at the resort. Once the meal was over, however, Mimi changed the subject. "I've got to catch you up on what's going on in Dalton," she said. "I'm hearing from just about everyone now, including Bridget. Holy smokes, she's still crying over Drew leaving."

Lars nodded. "Tell her about Eileen," he urged.

"You'd think both Eileen and Drew would be hiding inside the house or moving after the humiliation, but the opposite is happening. Eileen's doing what I'd call damage control. She's been all over town telling anyone who will listen that you orchestrated the entire conversation. You led him on and twisted his words, then got him on record so you could sue for sexual harassment."

"That's not all," Lars said. "Drew's out and about, especially at night, right after people get off work. He goes into the bar the employees frequent and tries to buy rounds for everyone. He's become a good old boy, and he has his own story he's telling about you. In his version you seduced him, and some of the things you wanted him to do in bed were pretty gross."

"What does he hope to gain?" Peyton asked.

"If you want my guess, I'd say he's trying to get back into the company," Lars said. "His tactics aren't working, though. People are turning their backs on him. They won't even let him buy them a drink. And in Dalton that's unheard of."

"He and Eileen had a big blowout party last Saturday. No one showed up," Mimi said. "Drew acts like he's on a sabbatical. He's on another one of his fishing trips now, somewhere in Canada. He's probably plotting his next move. Since his smooth-talking didn't work, he's got to be in a panic. Any hope of getting back in good graces is gone."

"What do you think he'll do?" Peyton asked.

"I don't know, and I don't care," Mimi decided. "I'm so happy to be away from there. Now, when do Lars and I start work?"

"You'll meet Christopher and Lucy to-morrow, but we'll give you both a couple of days to figure out where everything is. Lars, I know you probably want your own place, but staying with Mimi is okay for now, isn't it?"

"Of course," he answered. "I've got to get some sleep," he said, yawning.

Mimi followed him to the door. "I'm ready for bed, too." As the door was closing behind her friends, Peyton promised, "You're going to be happy here."

Peyton was excited for Lucy and Christopher to meet her friends, and she was anxious to show off the Cove. She told them to meet at her condo at noon. That would give them time to catch up on their sleep and do a little unpacking. In the meantime, she thought she could get some work done. The phone was ringing when she let herself into the office. Debi, who was always late, was actually early today. She grabbed the phone before Peyton could get to it.

"Bishop's Cove," she answered. "How may I direct your call?" She listened for a minute, then said, "Sure, I'll send someone over. Thanks for calling." She turned to Peyton. "That was a guy at the post office in town. He said he has three big boxes there for the hotel. I'll bet Chef Geller ordered some stuff. The guy said they've been there a while, so come get them."

"I'll send one of the maintenance —"

"No, you have to sign for the boxes. That's what he said."

"Okay. Braxton and I will go get them. It shouldn't take us long."

"Why is that guy always hanging around? And that other one. What's his name?"

"Drake," she answered.

As she was pulling the door open, Debi asked, "Are you like in a threesome or something?"

Peyton rolled her eyes. "Or something."

Braxton was standing just outside the office. When she announced that she needed to make a quick run to the post office, he opened his hand and she gave him her car keys. It had become routine for him to drive whenever she left the resort. On the way to town, she told him what Mimi had reported about Drew and Eileen.

"Yes," he said. "I heard all about the socialites. That's what Agent Hutton calls them. Actually, he put another word in front of 'socialites' but I'm not going to repeat it."

"They threw a big party and no one came," she said. "That would be humiliating for Drew. Did Agent Hutton mention Parsons? Does he know where he is?"

"Oh yes. Parsons has been hanging tight with the Albertsons. He was at their party, and he's one of the chosen who went on the fishing trip with Drew."

"One of the chosen? Who else went?"

"Drew and Parsons and a guy named Cosgrove."

"Don Cosgrove," she said. "He's Mimi's ex-husband. From what I've heard, he'll fit right in with those creeps."

"They're all having a high old time, aren't they? Finn says it's all an act, and I agree. He thinks they're getting ready to do something we aren't gonna like."

"Finn?" Her heart picked up a beat. "When did you talk to him?"

"I didn't. Hutton told me. He talked to Finn yesterday."

The post office was on a quiet dead-end street near the highway, but they had to cut around another Cassady construction site in order to get into the parking lot. There were only three parking slots in front of the small, square building. It looked as though it had been slapped up overnight without much thought to design. It had a flat tarred roof and aluminum siding. Two apartment buildings in various stages of completion

437

towered over the post office. There were two giant Cassady Construction signs in front of each building and a trailer with his name slathered all over it.

There wasn't a soul around. Braxton got out of the car and said, "It's a couple of minutes before eight. Wait here. I'll see if they're open yet."

Her impatience saved her life. Had she stayed in the car, she would have been in the center of the blast. She didn't wait for Braxton to give her a signal. She opened the car door and was walking around the back of the car when she felt what she thought was a hornet's sting. She brushed her hand over her thigh to swat whatever it was and looked down. Blood covered her hand. At the same time, she heard the sound of a whistle, then another and another, and it suddenly all clicked. Screaming to Braxton, she started running.

Braxton shouted for her to get down as he raced to intercept her and get her out of harm's way. She almost made it to the side of the building when the gas tank ignited. The blast lifted her up and threw her into his arms. Something hard struck the back of her head and she screamed again.

She had no memory of being placed inside an ambulance. The doors were open and she had a clear view of her car . . . or rather, what used to be her car. It had been blown to smithereens, and firefighters were working to put out the flames. Braxton climbed into the ambulance to ride to the hospital with her.

"Are you all right?" she asked.

"I'm okay," he said. "You took the hit, not me. Your body protected me. I'm so sorry. I should have seen it coming."

"Tell me what happened."

"You don't remember?"

"It's confusing." She closed her eyes. "I've got a mean headache, but that's all. I don't need to go to the hospital."

"You've got a concussion."

The possibility made her mad. "I do not."

She was trying to block her fear. Whoever was out to get her wasn't giving up.

She fell asleep again and woke up in a hospital bed to a doctor leaning over her, checking a bandage on her thigh. He saw her watching and said, "Just a bad cut. Doesn't even need stitches."

"May I go home now?" she said, trying to sit up. A horrific pain sliced through her skull.

The doctor gently pushed her shoulders back on the bed. "I'm keeping you overnight. You have a concussion."

As much as she wanted to argue with his diagnosis, she thanked him instead.

An hour later she was settled in a hospital room with Braxton and Drake standing guard at the door. The hallway, she was told, was crowded with worried friends. The doctor let each of them look in and then insisted they let Peyton rest.

She felt so awful she wanted to cry, but she didn't dare because she knew it would make her head hurt even more. She closed her eyes and pretended to sleep so everyone would leave her alone. She wished her mom was there to tell her everything was going to be all right. Funny, she thought, when things were bleak, her mom always knew what to say. All the rest of the time she drove her crazy. The bump on the back of her head made her more emotional, she decided, and that was why she was having such nostalgic thoughts about family. Finn kept popping into her thoughts, too.

She woke up in the middle of the night. Her door was open just an inch or so letting light spill in from the hallway. Disoriented, it took her a minute to realize where she was.

She heard a rustling sound, faint but close. Someone was in the room with her. She slowly turned, and then she saw him.

Finn was sprawled out in a chair sound asleep. He shifted positions and there was the sound again. He had no business being here, and tomorrow she would light into him. Not tonight, though. She was content now. And safe. Finn wouldn't let anyone hurt her.

For tonight he was her hotshot again.

TWENTY-EIGHT

On the morning that Peyton's car blew up, Ronan got to see another side of Finn, and it shocked the hell out of him. Finn was interrogating a punk-ass kid they knew had committed a double murder, all because of a dare. Finn had been called in to question the suspect because it was determined the kid would respond well to his methods. Finn had been so successful with his strategy, five new agents stood with Ronan on the other side of the observation glass. They were there to watch the master at work, to learn from Finn who, their superiors and Ronan believed, could get anyone to talk. It was only a matter of time and patience.

Finn didn't have a dark side, and he never lost his temper . . . until that day. Only the suspect, a twenty-year-old who insisted on being called Tic, and Finn were in the room. A small metal table with a legal pad and a ball-point pen on top separated them.

Tic was butt ugly, Ronan thought. Big ears, big teeth, thin lips, and an odd-shaped head. As was the trend with the morons in his gang, he had shaved his head and wore a tattoo of a skull and crossbones on the back of his neck and a smaller one on his forehead. Now, how original was that? After listening to him boast for several minutes, Ronan thought it might be nice to put a bag over his tattooed head so they wouldn't have to look at his gloating smirk.

Tic was big, close to six feet two inches, and weighed around 225 pounds. He wasn't handcuffed, and he was known to have a short fuse. Ronan stationed himself close to the door in the event he became aggressive. He knew Finn could handle the punk, but he wanted to be ready to help.

Even though he had been talking to the suspect for hours, Finn couldn't have looked any more relaxed. He slouched in his chair with his long legs stretched out and one ankle crossed over the other, and it appeared that he was actually enjoying their conversation. Finn had perfected the hint of a smile, just enough to make the suspect comfortable. Tic was trying his best to impress Finn with stories about friends who had gotten away with big-time crimes because they were so much smarter than the cops. He laughed while he told one particularly gruesome story. It was evident Tic loved to brag, and Ronan was convinced Tic would soon brag his way into thirty years to life. If Finn played him just right, Tic would get cocky and want to prove how smart he was, too, and he'd boast about his own accomplishments.

Things were progressing nicely until Finn received a text. His phone was on vibrate. He should have given it to Ronan when he'd handed him his gun before he entered the interrogation room, but it was in his pocket, and he'd forgotten about it. He pulled the phone out and was about to turn it off when he glanced down and saw he had a text from Braxton. He wasn't concerned to see the name. Against Peyton's wishes, Finn had ordered Braxton and Drake to give him regular updates.

Tic was off in his own world, staring at the wall while he fondly reminisced about another crime he thought had been cleverly executed. Then he moved on to the recent double murder. It was obvious he wanted to tantalize Finn, to let him know he'd pulled the trigger four times without actually saying it. Tic became so caught up in the memory and thrill of it all, going on and on as he bragged, he didn't realize he was taking credit for the crimes.

Finn glanced at the window to let Ronan know the confession was on record, and then, while Tic continued to talk, Finn opened the text. He expected to read that everything was okay and that there hadn't been any problems. Instead, he read, Sniper blew up car. On way to hospital with Peyton.

He lunged to his feet. His heart felt as though it had just been ripped out of his chest. Gripping the phone in his left hand, he read the message again. She was hurt, but how bad was it? Didn't Braxton know? He should have protected her. Finn felt a desperate need to get to her.

"I don't have any time left," he said, his voice harsh. "We're going to wrap this up. Pick up that pen and start writing. I want names and I want your confession to be concise. Got that?"

Tic laughed, but the sound was forced. "I'm not going to tell you how I . . . You're not getting a confession."

"You already confessed. Start writing."

Ignoring Tic's protests, Finn read the message for the third time, thinking maybe he had read it wrong.

Outside the room Ronan was explaining to the young agents that, in this case, Finn had quickly realized how important it was to the suspect that Finn thought he was smart, and he took his time and played on the suspect's ego to get him talking. It was a good thing Ronan was looking through the window. Otherwise, he would have missed what happened next. Tic must have realized he had said too much, and believing Finn had made a fool of him, he flew across the table, his fists swinging. All 225 pounds of rage attacked. One second he was in the air, and the next he was up against the wall, his feet off the floor. Finn had his hand around his neck cutting off his air supply. He whispered something into Tic's ear, and while he continued to pin him with one hand, he texted with the other.

Ronan and the other agents rushed into the room. They all stood together as they watched and admired Finn's amazing show of strength.

"Are we clear on my expectations?" Finn asked Tic.

It was impossible for the suspect to answer. His face was bloodred and rapidly turning purple. Finn decided to assume he'd agreed. "Okay, then," he said and let go.

Tic fell to the floor in a heap.

"Crawl over to the table, sit down, and start writing," Finn ordered.

One of the agents rushed forward to cuff Tic to the table so that he couldn't attack again while another agent sat down across from him and shoved the notepad toward him.

"I've got this, sir," he said.

Ronan followed Finn out of the room. "That was impressive," he said. "Texting with your left hand like that. I couldn't do it."

Finn let Ronan read the text from Braxton while he slipped his weapon back in his holster. Ronan cursed. "Albertson's behind this, isn't he? Is Peyton going to be okay?"

"I don't know. I'm gonna call the hospital in Port James, and I should be hearing back from Braxton."

"Then what?" Ronan asked.

"I'm going to Peyton, and when I find the bastard, know what I'm gonna do?"

Ronan answered with a nod. "Oh yeah. I know."

Twenty-Nine

Finn was still there in the morning. It hadn't been a dream after all. Peyton saw him as soon as she opened her eyes. He was standing in the hallway talking to Braxton and Drake and a police officer she remembered seeing in Reds, the bar and grill where they'd eaten nachos and fish tacos. The conversation looked intense, and from their body language she could tell everyone but Finn was angry. Braxton was visibly upset. He kept shaking his head and clenching his fists. Finn was the contradiction. His arms were folded across his chest and he would nod every now and then. He seemed calm yet very serious.

Braxton was the first to notice she was awake. He nudged Finn and then rushed into her room. Stopping at the foot of the bed, he asked, "How are you feeling? That was a close call."

"I'm okay," she assured him. That wasn't

exactly true, but it wasn't a lie, either. Her head didn't hurt nearly as much as it had last night, and she wasn't quite as stiff. "I'll be better as soon as I get out of here."

Finn walked over to the side of her bed and gently brushed her hair away from her forehead. "You might need to stay another night."

"No, I won't stay. People die in hospitals. They check in just fine, and — wham — they get some horrible disease and die."

Finn was trying not to smile. "If they're just fine, why would they check into a hospital?"

He was being logical, and she was having none of it. She wanted to go home. "It happens," she insisted.

He put his hand on top of hers. She tried to pull away, but he wouldn't let her.

"Peyton, I'm so sorry," Braxton said. "I didn't protect you. I should have seen it coming. I looked up at those roofs, and I didn't see anyone. I got too comfortable."

He looked devastated and she wanted to console him. "There wasn't a single car around . . . no workers had arrived yet . . . he was up in one of those buildings, wasn't he?"

Finn answered. "Yes, he was."

"I told her to stay in the car while I

449

checked to see if the door was unlocked." Braxton's voice shook. "If she had, she would have been in the middle of the blast."

Peyton was about to offer a bit of sympathy and tell him to stop blaming himself, but Finn spoke before she could.

"Yes, you screwed up," he said. "And it almost cost both of you your lives. It can't happen again," he added, his tone hard. "So learn from this."

"Yes, sir," Braxton said, all business now.

Drake appeared in the doorway. "I need to talk to both of you," he said.

"I'll be there in a minute," Finn answered. "I want a word in private with Peyton. Shut the door behind you."

Peyton wanted to protest but didn't because Finn had that look in his eyes, that don't-mess-with-me look she was getting real tired of. His clenched jaw was another indicator he was going to be stubborn and tell her something she didn't want to hear. Agent Know-It-All could be a real pain. God, she'd missed him.

"Why are you here?" she asked quietly. "I didn't call you. You won't find any bullet holes in my car. You probably won't find my car, either. It was pretty much incinerated."

"I'm here because you need me." It was an outrageously arrogant thing to say, and he knew it was going to rile her, but he didn't care how upset she became. She did need him.

"I do not need you. I'm a capable adult, and I can take care of myself."

"Where's your car?"

"You know it blew up. I just told you."

"And where are you now?"

"In the hospital, but —"

"So, taking care of yourself . . . How's that working out for you?"

"Normally I'm quite capable of taking care of myself, but this isn't a normal situation. People are trying to kill me, for Pete's sake."

"Precisely," he answered. "Which is one of the reasons you need me."

"I have a security team."

"Peyton, I'm here to stay."

"Wait a minute. What's the other reason I need you?" she asked, suspicious.

The physician interrupted the discussion, and she was glad of it. She had to be at her best to spar with Finn. She was discharged with the stipulation that she rest and take it easy for a week or so. Right. Rest. It took all she had not to laugh when she gave her promise.

Braxton drove them back to Bishop's Cove. Finn got into the backseat with her, and Drake rode shotgun. Peyton tried to keep her distance from him and hugged the door, but it was a challenge not to touch him because he was such a big man and took up most of the space. It was impossible to relax; however, once they'd driven over the bridge and she could see the gates to Bishop's Cove she began to breathe easy.

"It was all a setup, wasn't it? That call Debi took wasn't from the post office."

"No, the call came from a disposable cell phone. A burner," Braxton told her. "No way to trace it."

She thought about it a minute and said, "You know, it really was an ideal place for an ambush. Two tall buildings with a little post office squeezed in between. It was a well-thought-out plan."

Exasperated, Finn said, "Peyton, when have you ever received a call from the post office? Any post office? Let me answer that for you. Never. They don't call when a package arrives. If it's too big to deliver, they send out a notice. And if you don't pick it up, they send out a second notice. And if you still don't pick it up, they send it back. What they don't do is call."

"It was such a small post office in a resort town. I just assumed . . ." She felt like an idiot. She hadn't questioned the call at all.

Hadn't given it a thought. "I told Braxton we needed to go to the post office. I didn't mention getting a call."

Finn took hold of her hand, and this time she didn't try to pull away. "Whoever it is has been here a while scoping out Port James."

"I disagree," Drake said. "It wouldn't take any time at all to find a couple of places to ambush. Port James is a very small town."

"Is Agent Hutton back in Dalton?" Braxton asked Finn.

"Yes. He paid a visit to Eileen Albertson. She told him she didn't expect the boys home from fishing for another week. They changed their minds and didn't go to Canada, but she didn't know exactly where they were. She just kept saying way up north. She asked Hutton if that Peyton bitch was trying to make more trouble."

"Then she didn't send me her love?" Peyton asked.

A few minutes later she was back in her condominium. She immediately changed out of yesterday's clothes and took a shower. The wallop of a bump on the back of her head throbbed each time she touched it, so she was careful not to scrub her scalp when she washed her hair. The water revived her and she felt so much better. After toweling off, she reached for her jeans, but they rubbed the gouge in her thigh, so she put on a pair of old shorts and a silk camisole. Barefoot, she padded into the living room and came to a quick stop. Lucy, Mimi, Lars, and Christopher were all there waiting for her. Lucy had tears in her eyes.

"What happened?" Peyton asked, bracing herself.

Mimi laughed. "We're here to welcome you home, not give you bad news."

Finn came up behind her and slipped his arms around her waist. The show of affection wasn't lost on their audience. They wanted to let her know how much they cared about her, and she thought that was terribly sweet, but she wasn't comfortable being coddled for long.

Christopher was the first to take off. The concrete trucks had arrived and were going to pour the walkways today. It was an expensive undertaking, and he wanted to be there to make certain there weren't any screwups.

"Who's minding the store?" Peyton asked.

"Debi," Lucy answered.

"Oh God."

She'd sounded so appalled, they all laughed. Only then did Lucy seem to realize the damage Debi could do and rushed

454

back to the office.

"How about I cook dinner for you tonight?" Lars suggested.

"No thanks," Finn said. "I've got it covered."

"Are you sure?" Lars asked. "I could do a real smorgasbord for you. I have some pickled herring and —"

"No, that's okay," Finn answered abruptly.

Lars went back to the hotel kitchen. Mimi lingered. Shaking her head, she said, "You didn't warn me about your cousin. She's a manipulator, isn't she?"

"Yes, she is," Peyton agreed.

"If you aren't too tired, we can chat tonight," Mimi said. She patted Peyton's hand and headed toward the door. Finn flipped the deadbolt after she was gone.

"I think I'll go over to the business office, too," Peyton said. "Where are my flats? I could get a little work done, couldn't I?"

Smiling, he said, "Sure you could." Before she realized what he was going to do, he scooped her up in his arms and carried her to her bedroom. While he was still holding her, he kicked off his shoes and dropped down on the bed.

"What are you doing?"

Finn wrapped her in his arms and closed

his eyes. Damn, but he loved the way she felt.

"I didn't get much sleep in that chair last night, and you need to rest." He rolled onto his back and pulled her up against him. Her head rested on his shoulder.

"Finn, you have to leave tomorrow."

Yawning, he said, "No."

She couldn't believe she was actually sleepy. She'd done nothing but sleep since yesterday morning. Settling into his embrace, she had to admit she was happy he was with her. Whenever he was around, she felt protected.

Lifting her head, she saw his eyelids were getting heavy. She put her head back on his shoulder and closed her eyes. A minute passed and she could feel his breathing become slower as he drifted off.

"Finn?" she whispered.

"Hmm?" he answered without opening his eyes.

"When *are* you going to leave?"

He tightened his hold. His answer was faint but unmistakable. "Never."

THIRTY

Peyton slept hard for over four hours, and her headache was nearly gone when she opened her eyes. As soon as the fog cleared, she remembered what Finn had said. She'd asked him when he was going to leave, and she was certain he'd answered, "Never." He'd sounded as though he'd meant it, too. What kind of game was he playing? He did love to tease her. Maybe that was what he was doing. Of course he was going to leave. It's what he did.

While she was brushing her teeth, she thought about how she should proceed and decided she would continue to treat him like a friend. It wasn't possible for her to forget that they had been intimate — every time she looked at him, images of his gorgeous naked body intruded into her thoughts — but she could pretend that they had always just been friends. And if she pulled that off, she should get an Oscar.

Finn was in the kitchen. "Are you hungry? I'll make you something to eat."

"I'm not an invalid. I can make lunch."

Even as she protested, she sat at the island and let him see to the task. As soon as he pulled out a jar of peanut butter, she knew it wasn't going to be a gourmet meal, and that was fine with her. She didn't think her stomach could handle much more.

She couldn't stop staring at him. His T-shirt was snug across his broad shoulders and upper arms, almost as if it were molded to him, and his jeans rode low on his hips. He couldn't look sexier if he tried. She closed her eyes for a few seconds while she reminded herself that he had been demoted from lover to friend.

He placed her sandwich in front of her. The only garnish was the grape jam that oozed onto the plate. He wasn't much on presentation, but the sandwich tasted great.

"Aren't you going to eat?" she asked.

He leaned over the island and kissed her. It happened so fast she didn't have time to stop him.

"I already had a couple of sandwiches," he said. Then he kissed her again.

"We're friends."

"Yes," he agreed.

"But not friends with benefits."

"That's right."

"So you agree."

"Sure do."

And then he kissed her again. His hands cupped the sides of her face, holding her still while his mouth ravaged hers. His tongue sensually rubbed hers, coaxing her to respond. It was impossible to resist him, and within seconds she was as wild as he was. When he pulled back, he looked arrogantly pleased. Her lips were swollen and she could feel her cheeks flush. She could barely catch her breath, and he made her burn for more. She wanted to grab his T-shirt and pull him back for another kiss. Wait, this wasn't going according to her plan.

Finn took her plate to the sink, breaking the spell.

"Friends don't kiss each other with their tongues," she said.

He laughed. "No, they don't."

"And we're friends."

He laughed again.

"You're in a mood, aren't you?" she mumbled. "I'm trying to explain . . ."

"That we're friends?"

"Exactly."

"Okay, I get it. Can this go in the dishwasher?" he asked, holding up a plastic bowl.

She nodded. "I could clean up since you made lunch."

He closed the dishwasher and came around the island. "Do you want dessert?"

She swore his eyes twinkled. "I don't know. What do you have?"

Pulling her into his arms, he asked, "What do you want?"

"This could go on all afternoon," she said, and then she laughed.

"You need to go to bed."

"I just got up," she protested. Lifting her into his arms, he headed down the hallway. "Finn, I took a long nap. I'm not going to sleep."

He smiled. "I sure hope not."

What had come over him? They were going to be friends, damn it. And friends did not have sex. At least normal friends didn't. A knock on the door interrupted his plans to seduce her. Muttering an expletive, he put her down and went to see who was there.

Christopher and Mimi had stopped by on their way back to the office after a trip to Port James to meet the accounting firm who handled the resort's business. Despite Finn's look of disapproval, Peyton invited them in. She was anxious to get Mimi's impression of the resort now that she had had time to look around. And, just as she had hoped, Mimi loved the place. Her face lit up with excitement as she talked about the beauty of the resort and the tremendous possibilities all the renovations would bring. Peyton glanced over at Christopher and could tell he was pleased to have Mimi on the team. They were comfortable working together, and it was evident she knew what she was doing.

"My office will be here in the Cove," Mimi said. "I'll take over payroll and taxes, but I'll also do projections. It'll be fun."

Her enthusiasm made Peyton smile. "Only *you* would think adding numbers is fun."

Christopher had plans he'd drawn up for the Olympic-size pool and asked Finn if he wouldn't mind taking a look.

"Before I make this official, I'd like to know what you think of the design. It's going to be a huge pool, and Peyton's convinced me we could use it for relays and maybe training camps."

"Sure, I'll help," he said.

Christopher spread the plan out on the island, and the two men discussed possible changes.

"There will be a dome over the pool that

461

will retract into the ground with the push of a button," Christopher explained.

"This is going to cost a fortune," Finn said.

"Len's all for it. Once he heard about it, he wanted the Cove to have it. He doesn't want it near the hotel, though. He thinks it should be in the back and away from the beach. It's going to end up being an entire swimming center." He smiled as he added, "He's got grand plans for it, thanks to Peyton."

Peyton wanted to look at the drawings, but Mimi was nudging her to the sofa. "You need to sit down, sweetie. How's your head feeling? You look better, not so pale."

"I'm fine now," Peyton insisted. "Fully recovered. How are you getting along? It's a big change for you, isn't it?"

"Yes, and you were right. This is a paradise. It will be an adjustment not wearing five layers and a heavy coat most of the year. A lovely adjustment," she added with a chuckle. "And I love the work. I feel useful and needed again." She took hold of Peyton's hand and whispered, "Thank you."

Before Peyton could respond, Mimi plunged ahead. "Erik Swift called me. He's a decent man, like his father. It's difficult to imagine Eileen came from the same parents."

"Why did he call?"

"He's talking to all the employees who worked under Drew. He had a couple of names and he wondered if I knew anything about them."

"Did you?"

"I recognized two of them. They were young women who worked in the plant."

"What's Erik looking for?"

"He told me he's helping his father. Randolph wants to find all the young women Drew preyed on."

"And when he finds them? Then what?"

"I don't know. Nothing can change what Drew put them through, but I think Randolph wants to let them have vindication and compensation. Maybe an apology from the company. I think he may be taking legal action, but I'm just guessing. We'll have to wait to find out." Mimi shook her head, a look of regret falling across her face. "I knew that Drew was a sleazy character, but I didn't think he was violent until he tried to break into your motel room. I should have seen it coming . . . done something."

Peyton took her hand. "You can't blame yourself for anything. You couldn't have known. Drew was a master at keeping people quiet and hiding what he was doing."

Christopher interrupted them. "Peyton, do you want to look at this preliminary plan?" he asked.

She had to admit to herself that she was curious to see it, but her enthusiasm for the project had waned because she realized she wanted to build the pool for the most foolish of reasons. If they had such an attraction, Finn might want to come back to swim. How crazy was that? To lure him with an Olympic-size pool? She felt pathetic, now that she realized what her real motive was.

"Do we really need such a big pool?" she asked as she crossed the room to stand between the two men.

Her question surprised Christopher. "You're having a change of heart? You said you wanted a regulation —"

"Yes, I did," she interrupted. "But I've reevaluated. You heard Finn. It will cost a fortune."

"And it will make a fortune," he argued. "It was a great idea you had, and we're going forward."

She didn't argue. She knew Finn was watching her, and so she kept her attention on the plans. "It looks good," she said, and the longer she studied the layout, the more excited she became. It really was going to be a great addition. Did it matter that the only reason she'd come up with the idea was because of Finn?

Her enthusiasm was back in her voice when she told Christopher, "It will be great."

"I've got to get back to work," Mimi said. "Finn, there's a package for you in the office. Would you like me to fetch it for you?"

"No, I'll get it," he said, nodding his appreciation.

"He's a keeper," she whispered to Peyton.

From Finn's quick smile, Peyton knew he'd heard Mimi.

"No, he's in need of a keeper," she said.

Finn waited until he and Peyton were alone before he pulled her back into his arms. "I'm in need of a keeper? Are you up for the job?"

She put her hands on his chest to push away from him and desperately tried not to be swayed by his adorable smile and the sexy look in his eyes.

"You left." She hadn't known she was going to say that until the words were out of her mouth.

He wasn't smiling now. His expression became intense as he tightened his hold on her. "I came back."

She shook her head. "I don't want you here. We've said all we need to say. You should leave."

He nudged her chin up and lowered his mouth to hers. His lips brushed across hers before he deepened the kiss. He wasn't in any hurry, and she sighed when his tongue leisurely explored her mouth. Breathless, she became the aggressor. Her hands moved up to the back of his neck, her fingers splayed upward into his hair. When he tried to pull away, she tugged at his lower lip with her teeth until he gave her what she wanted, and then her tongue rubbed over his. His taste, his scent, his touch aroused her, and at that moment she would have given him anything he wanted. One kiss and he made her ache for him.

"Tonight," he promised as he gently pulled away from her.

Frustrated, she muttered her way to the bedroom.

"Did you say something?" Finn called.

"No, I'm just giving myself a stern talking-to," she said. Her door shut, effectively stopping any other questions.

She stayed in her room making calls and working on her laptop. She kept telling herself she wasn't hiding from Finn; she just needed some space. It wasn't the truth, though. Her emotions were bouncing all over the place, and it was all his fault. He shouldn't have come back, but now that he was here, she was going to tell him to leave her alone. No more hugging or kissing or anything else physical.

Since when did he ever listen to her? He was going to do whatever he wanted to do, and knowing how weak she was around him, she would probably go along. She suddenly remembered opening her eyes in the hospital room and seeing him, and she remembered exactly how she had felt in that moment. Safe and protected, yes . . . and something more.

Finn knocked on her door twice, then opened it. "It's almost five. Do you want to go to the business office with me?"

"Sure." She didn't move; she just sat there staring at him.

He tilted his head. "What's that look about?"

Impossible to explain, she decided. "It's my concussion recovery expression. I'll just get my tennis shoes."

Tucking her phone in her pocket, she walked out the door ahead of him. Braxton waved to them as they crossed the parking lot.

"Oh, just so you know," she began. "As

far as Debi is concerned, I'm in a three-way with Drake and Braxton."

To his credit, he didn't miss a beat. "Okay, three-way."

Debi greeted them at the door. "Just tell me this. Why can't I have a key? Some nights I want to stay late, and I see no reason why I can't be treated like an adult. I could lock up."

Alarm bells went off in Peyton's head. "You want to stay late? Why?" she asked suspiciously.

"To get work done."

"What work?"

"You know . . . the work."

Christopher and Lucy were heading out, but Christopher stopped. "No key. Go home now, Debi."

Debi slung her thirty-pound purse over her shoulder, nearly knocking Peyton down had she not ducked, and marched out in a huff.

Lucy was the only one who felt a little guilty. "I think she's really trying now. She's coming in earlier and staying later."

"And exactly what does she do when she comes in early and stays late? Does anyone know?" Peyton asked. "It scares me to think she's in here alone. The damage she could do . . ."

"She's not getting a key," Christopher repeated. "How are you feeling?" he asked.

"I'm fine," she answered. "I'll be full force tomorrow. We just stopped in to pick up a package for Finn."

"It's in the conference room."

While Finn went to collect the package, Peyton asked her sister if she'd talked to Ivy lately.

"I talked to her last night. I don't want her to feel that we're excluding her from making decisions, so I run things by her, but she's so swamped right now, she doesn't have time to worry about Bishop's Cove. I didn't tell her your car blew up. She'd just worry, and it's all over now."

It's all over? What world was Lucy living in? Until Drew and his sidekick were locked up, nothing was over.

"How come you're all dressed up?" Peyton asked, for she'd finally noticed the new wrap dress Lucy was wearing. It was several shades of blue that made her eyes all the more brilliant. She looked lovely. Then Peyton noticed Lucy was holding Christopher's hand.

"Christopher and I are going into Port James for dinner," Lucy said with a slight blush. "He needed a night away from here, and so do I."

"Has Mimi gone home?"

"She had to drive back to the accounting firm to get some kind of software," Lucy explained.

Finn was back with the package in hand, so they all walked out together. Peyton waited until they were back home to ask him what he was going to cook for their dinner. His track record was abysmal. If history was an indicator, she had a feeling she'd be going to bed hungry.

"I know you told Lars you were taking care of dinner, but I could cook tonight. Something light," she offered.

"No, I've got it covered," he insisted.

"What are we having?"

"It's a surprise."

At seven o'clock there was a knock on the door, and Peyton opened it to find a waiter from Leonard's standing there with a large tray. Finn took it from him, set it on the table, and lifted the silver domes off the plates. Underneath were fabulous steak dinners. Peyton didn't know how hungry she was until she took her first bite. The steaks were grilled to perfection and after eating every last morsel, she complimented Finn on his extraordinary culinary skills and thanked him for the delicious surprise.

"That's not the only surprise," he said. "I

have some after-dinner entertainment for you."

"What is it?" she asked.

He went to the island and opened the package he'd picked up at the office. "It's a DVD of Randolph's announcement in Dalton. Hutton burned a couple of discs, thinking you might want to keep one to remind yourself what a good thing you did. Would you like to see it?"

"I'd love to watch it."

Finn took her hand and led her to the sofa. After slipping the disc into the player, he settled down next to her.

The murmur of the crowd as the employees filed into the auditorium sounded like bees buzzing. One camera focused on the stage. Another camera scanned the audience. Peyton saw Bridget push her way to the front row. She was wearing ridiculously high heels. The side door opened, and Drew and Eileen stepped into the spotlight. The sight of him made Peyton's skin crawl. She gripped her hands together as she watched him.

Finn must have felt the tension in her body because he put his arm around her shoulder and pulled her closer to him.

"Look how he's trying to work the crowd," Finn said.

Peyton leaned back against him and didn't say another word until Randolph made his announcement. She watched Drew's face. It was frozen in the most benign mask, and she could only imagine what was underneath. His eyes widened a fraction the second he heard her voice over the speakers, but as fast as a blink, he was looking bored again.

"He sees the security guards coming," Finn said.

They both watched Drew shrug off his wife's clutching hand and stand. He made a show of adjusting his tie, then turned and strode off the stage.

"Did you see that?" Finn asked.

"See what?"

He reached for the remote and backed up the video. "Watch closely and tell me what you see when Drew gets up and walks off the stage."

"I don't see anything," Peyton said.

"Watch his head," Finn told her as he went back a few seconds.

Peyton looked more closely. "He's looking at someone and nodding."

Finn played it one more time. "He's not just nodding, he's giving a signal."

"You're right," Peyton said, moving closer to the screen. "It's Bridget."

As the video continued to play, they could see the crowd become still, listening to the rest of the recording. Some people looked at those sitting on either side of them and shook their heads in disbelief, but no one noticed Bridget slipping out the side door.

"I'll bet she chased after Drew," Peyton said.

"No, she went to his office. Erik had posted a security guard at the door so that Drew couldn't take anything. The guard told us a woman came to him crying, and when he wouldn't let her in the office, she got really upset. He said he couldn't imagine any woman caring that much about the bastard."

"The woman was Bridget," Peyton concluded.

"Yes," Finn said.

"What was the signal Drew was giving her? What do you think she wanted from his office?"

"Hutton watched them pack up every single item and cart it off. If it wasn't nailed to the floor, it went into boxes and out the door. They've got a list of everything they boxed up. I looked it over before I left Dalton, and I don't remember seeing anything out of the ordinary. Maybe I'll have Hutton e-mail it to me and take another

473

look. There might be something there."

"Like a rifle?" she teased.

"Yeah, like a rifle."

"Can't Drew demand his things back?"

"He has demanded them back. He's not getting them, though, not for a while. Randolph Swift is holding on to them."

Peyton watched Finn as he became very quiet, mulling over what he had just discovered. His brow creased in lines of concentration. Even as he was lost in thought, he didn't stop touching her. At first he had his arm around her shoulder rubbing her arm, and then his other hand began to slowly move up and down her thigh. He didn't realize what he was doing until he looked over at her. He kissed the sensitive spot just below her ear and his warm breath tickled her skin giving her goose bumps. She closed her eyes and with a soft moan she leaned into him and turned her face to his.

Finn wasn't tentative. He kissed her with such raw passion, letting her know that she belonged to him, only him. It was only after he'd ended the kiss that she came to her senses. "No, we aren't doing this again."

Standing, she wagged her finger at him. "We want different things, remember? You don't ever want to get married or have children," she reminded. "I do. So, please,

474

leave me alone."

Time to give herself another talking-to, she told herself, and she rushed to her bedroom and closed the door. She knew she kept giving Finn mixed signals. One minute she was telling him not to touch her, and the next she was throwing herself into his arms. No wonder he was confused. He was confused, wasn't he? She supposed she'd have to ask him before apologizing. Once she explained, there wouldn't be any more mixed signals.

Finn called to her. "Peyton, get your suit on. We're going swimming. I need to think."

Even though her bedroom door was closed Finn could hear her groan. Grinning, he went into his bedroom to find his swim trunks.

Peyton was in a quandary. Should she go with him or not? Seeing him nearly naked again was definitely not a good idea. But then, what harm could there be in a little exercise? Wearing the string bikini was out of the question. She wanted to discourage him, not encourage him, so, after weighing her choices for several minutes, she put on her old, reliable but boring, pink two-piece suit, grabbed her robe, and met him at the door.

He pointedly glanced at his watch, impatient.

"Oh, don't give me that look. I didn't take all that long," she said.

"Twenty minutes to put on a damn suit?"

She heard about the importance of being punctual all the way over to the hotel. By the time he unlocked the door to the pool, he had wound down. She hadn't said a word, just nodded every once in a while to encourage him to continue, and she realized once again how much she was like her mother. Her father liked to occasionally go on a rant about something or other inconsequential, and her mother would seem to be concentrating on his every word, but she really wasn't. She was usually thinking about something she needed to get done.

Content to sit on the side of the pool while Finn did laps, Peyton thought about her parents and came to the conclusion that they had a good marriage. Odd, but she'd never really given it much thought until now.

She watched as Finn glided back and forth, back and forth. She knew he found peace when he was in the water. His mind cleared and he could work out problems as soon as he fell into the rhythm of his strokes. Whatever was bothering him tonight must be very complicated, she thought, because he had done countless laps without a break.

She didn't know how long she'd been sitting there with her legs dangling in the pool, thinking about life in general and Finn in particular, when he suddenly rose out of the water in front of her. Neither one of them said a word as he stared into her eyes.

"I love you, Peyton."

He put his hands on the lip of the pool, lifted up, and kissed her, then dropped under the water and went back for another lap.

Peyton couldn't move. She tried to open her mouth to speak but nothing came out. What had just happened? Did he say what she thought he said? No, her ears were playing tricks on her. She was mistaken.

The next time he surfaced in front of her, he said it again. "I love you."

She slipped into the water and had every intention of letting him wait for her while she did a lap, but she didn't get far. He came up underneath her and, before she realized what he was doing, he turned on his back and she was stretched out on top of him. How were they staying afloat? She decided she would let him worry about keeping them above water. Stacking her hands, she rested her chin on his chest. The warmth in his eyes sent shivers along her spine, and she whispered, "I love you, too. I've loved you for a very long time."

He wrapped his arms around her and they sank beneath the water. He kissed her under water and again when they surfaced.

"Marry me." It wasn't a question but a demand.

"Why?" she asked. Pulling away from him she climbed out of the pool and reached for her robe.

Finn didn't push for an immediate answer. He knew his proposal had shocked her and he owed her an explanation, but he decided he would wait until they were in bed before telling her what was in his heart. Maybe by then he would find the right words to convince her.

Their walk back to the condominium was silent until she glanced up at him and said, "You know what they say. Once burned, twice shy."

"No one says that," he replied.

Peyton knew he didn't understand how scared she was. Finn didn't believe in marriage, so why was he asking her to marry him? What changed his mind? She was determined to find out before she gave him her answer.

After a shower, she put on her nightgown

and got into bed. Then she patiently waited for Finn. The room was dark except for a dim light from down the hall. She had left the door wide open, and she could hear him on the phone. He was still talking as he walked in and sat down beside her. She could tell the phone call frustrated him, but she didn't ask him who was on the line or what the conversation was about.

Finn turned to her with every intention of explaining, but she looked so provocative, he changed his mind. He had her flat on her back in a second and was settled between her thighs. Now that she was where he wanted her, he calmed down. He kissed the pulse beating wildly at the base of her neck, then moved up and tugged on her earlobe. Her soft moan told him she liked that.

"I want you," he whispered. "I always want you."

He showed her how much he loved her as he worked his way down her body. Frantic to have her, he didn't remember removing his clothes or hers. The feel of her naked body pressed against his was exquisite, and she was every bit as aggressive as he was. Their lovemaking was uninhibited. He brought her to a climax twice before he allowed his own, and it was glorious.

Resting her head on his shoulder, Peyton

barely had the energy to move. The scent of their lovemaking surrounded them, and she was blissfully content.

"Peyton?" Finn said softly.

"Hmm?" she purred.

He gently stroked her hair with his fingertips. "There are things about my life you should understand."

She raised up on her elbow so she could look at him.

"I've seen some pretty awful things," he continued. "There's real evil in the world, and when you come face-to-face with it, it sticks in your head. You can't get away from it. Even when you're asleep."

In the shadows she could see him staring at the ceiling as though envisioning some horrific scene, and she wondered what horrible things were lodged in his memory.

"As hard as some of those situations have been, I've only been scared . . . really scared . . . twice in my life," he said. "I've been in knife fights, gunfights, brawls. I was never scared then. The adrenaline would be there, but I was doing my job. The first time was when I was fourteen and looked out my window and saw you go under the water. I almost froze, I was so scared. To this day I haven't forgotten that feeling."

He rubbed his hand down her back as he

continued. "The second time was when Braxton sent me that text that your car blew up and you were on the way to the hospital. I didn't know how bad it was, didn't know if you were going to live or die. That same god-awful feeling of real terror was there inside me. I love you, and I don't want to live without you. I'm better with you. It's as simple as that . . . and as liberating. Marry me."

There were tears in her eyes when she answered him. "I have to stay here a full year —"

"We'll work it out. Marry me."

"I want children."

"I do, too . . . with you. Marry me."

Her smile widened. "Yes, I'll marry you."

THIRTY-ONE

Peyton wanted to wait until Uncle Len returned to Bishop's Cove to make the announcement. He had sent a text saying he expected to see them in two weeks. Peyton wasn't sure she could keep silent that long, but she was determined to try.

The following morning she and Finn walked into a firestorm. Christopher furiously paced around the office, and Lucy was fit to be tied. The only calm person was Debi. She sat at her desk with a notepad and pen, waiting to be given an assignment. Mimi stood in the doorway of her office, arms folded, frowning.

"What happened?" Finn asked.

"The sidewalks," Lucy said. "Half of them are ruined. One of the workers stomped through the wet concrete wearing boots, and now it's hardened and will have to be jackhammered. The expense will be huge."

"Would you like to have a look at the damage?" Christopher asked Finn.

Peyton went with them, hoping it wasn't as bad as Lucy described, but it turned out to be worse.

"This is awful. Didn't he look behind him to see what he was doing? It must have been dark," she reasoned, "and he couldn't see where he was going."

"It wasn't an accident," Christopher said. "Am I right, Finn? It was deliberate."

Finn agreed. "The path curves around into a figure eight, and the footprints not only go out one direction, they come back. Yes, it was deliberate."

"Who would do such a thing?" Peyton wanted to know.

"The question is, who has the most to gain? Only one name comes to mind," Christopher said. "Scott Cassady. He's itching to get his hands on this place. Maybe he thinks he'll wear you down with all these mishaps and you'll make a deal."

"You have to set a trap," Peyton told them.

Both men looked at her, and Finn asked, "What do you have in mind?"

"I don't know. That's your area of expertise. I'm a chef. If you catch him, I'll make you a soufflé."

"I sure would love to trap Cassady," Christopher admitted.

As it turned out, it was remarkably easy, thanks to Mimi. That afternoon, Debi complained to her that the printer was broken and then left for lunch. Not trusting her assessment of the problem, Mimi took a look at the printer and noticed the paper had jammed, and when she removed it, she was surprised to see it was part of a confidential financial report on Bishop's Cove. She hadn't printed out any new reports and figured that Debi had been prying, so she decided to have a bit of fun. She made an extra file of the financials, then changed all the projected numbers, laughing the whole time she was working. Once Debi was back at her desk, Mimi reported that the printer was repaired and should work just fine. She left the door to her office open a crack so that she would have a view of the printer, and an hour later she watched as Debi worked at her computer, then casually strolled over to pick up some pages as they were printing. Glancing over her shoulder to make sure no one was watching, she stuffed them into her purse, looking as pleased and satisfied as a Cheshire cat.

Mimi waited a minute before printing out another copy of the altered report to take to Christopher, who was meeting with Finn and Peyton in his office. She shut the door and said, "I'd like you to look at this financial summary. You're on track to make a billion dollars this year."

She explained what had happened, and when she was finished, Christopher was ready to explode.

"That's it. She's gone," he snapped. "Bring her in with her purse. I want to hear what excuse she'll give for taking confidential reports —"

"No, wait," Peyton said. "Let her leave, and Finn and I will follow her. Aren't you curious to know what she's doing with the papers? Let's find out."

Mimi thought that was a great idea. "All the numbers are bogus. She's not taking any confidential information out of the office."

Christopher relented. "All right. I'll wait until tomorrow to fire her." He stood. "I've got to meet Lucy, and I'm already late."

Mimi started to leave, but Finn asked her to stay. "I want to talk to you about your ex-husband."

She stiffened. "What would you like to know?"

"He's part of Albertson's circle now, isn't he?" he asked.

"Yes, he is."

"Would he lie for him?"

"In a heartbeat. Why?"

He didn't explain. "One more question. Do you think he would be more afraid of Albertson or going to prison?"

She thought about it a long minute before deciding. "Prison. He could run from Drew, but being locked up would frighten him."

"That's all. Thanks, Mimi."

Peyton waited until her friend had left, then asked, "What was that about?"

"They're all back in Dalton. Albertson and Parsons were the first home. They were stopped by the police just outside of town, and they let them search their SUV. No weapons. And funny thing, no fish."

"What about Mimi's ex, Cosgrove?"

"He drove in about an hour later. He also let the police search his car. They didn't find anything."

"No fish? A week-long fishing trip and not a single fish? They're really bad fishermen, aren't they?"

"They're going to use one another for their alibis. The weak link is Cosgrove. I'm gonna want to talk to him."

"I'm leaving now," Debi called from the outer office, and she was out the door before anyone could stop her.

Finn looked at his watch.

"She keeps banker's hours," Peyton said dryly.

Finn left to get the car, and when he pulled up to the office door, he noticed black clouds rolling in. Rain was coming and the humidity was oppressive. Peyton came out wearing sunglasses that were so dark he was surprised she could find her way to the car. After she put on her seat belt, she scrunched down in her seat.

"What are you doing?" he asked.

"I don't want her to spot us."

He laughed. "You're really getting into this, aren't you?"

"Where do you think she's going? I'm guessing she'll go home and pore over those papers." Sitting up straight, she removed her sunglasses. "I don't see her car. Maybe you should speed up and —"

"I know what I'm doing."

Debi was well ahead of them, and Peyton was certain they'd lost her until they reached the arched bridge and she spotted the blue sedan about eight cars ahead of them. Debi drove past the exit to her building and continued on. Near the post office she made a turn into a parking lot behind an office building and stopped in front of a Dumpster. Finn pulled over so they could observe her from across the street.

Peyton watched as Debi got out and opened the trunk. "What is she doing?"

Debi lifted a green plastic trash bag and, struggling with the weight, held it at arm's length as she hurried to the Dumpster and dropped it in.

"What is she throwing away?" Peyton asked. "From the way she was holding the bag, I'm guessing it's garbage."

"Only one way to find out," Finn told her.

They waited until Debi had gone into the building before getting out of their car. They cut across the pavement, zigzagged around some dried-up shrubs, and came up behind the Dumpster from the opposite side. The lid was open and the bag was on top of the trash. Finn lifted it out and dropped it on the ground next to him. Debi had sealed it closed with a twist tie, but it didn't hold. The top opened when the bag hit the ground, and the plastic spread wide revealing a pair of brown boots covered in cement.

Peyton opened her mouth to say something, then closed it. She was so shocked, she didn't know what to think. Why would Debi do such a thing? What did she have to gain? And with Debi it was always about what she could get. She never thought about anyone else.

"Your cousin committed a felony, and here's the proof, should Christopher want to take this any further." He picked up the bag and took it to their car.

"Okay," he said when he returned. "Now that the evidence is secured, let's go find out who Debi is taking those papers to. You've got a pretty good guess by now, don't you?"

She nodded. "Cassady. She's working with Cassady. He must be paying her." She shook with anger. How could Debi do this? They had given her every chance, and she'd done nothing but betray them. "Shall we go say hello?" she suggested, her voice tight.

Cassady Construction was located on the top floor. They stepped out of the elevator into a palatial reception area. It was all shiny marble and granite. A pretty, young woman behind the counter was eager to help them.

"How may I assist you?"

"We have an appointment with Scott Cassady," Peyton lied. "He's going to build a business complex for us."

Peyton thought the woman was frowning, but with all the Botox in her face it was impossible to tell.

"He's with a client," she began hesitantly. "I don't see an appointment. If you'll give me your name, I'll just check with him."

"The client he's with is part of our team,"

Peyton explained smoothly. "We'll just go on in."

The receptionist wasn't sure what to do. She started to nod, then changed her mind. "I'll be happy to announce you."

"No need," Peyton said as she strode past the counter. Finn opened the door to Cassady's office for her. "He'll be thrilled to see us."

"You're a little too good at this," he whispered.

She smiled. "Thank you."

She took it in all at once. Cassady was sitting at his desk, and Debi faced him. Her back was to the door, and she was handing him the papers she'd printed.

"It wasn't easy getting these," she boasted. "I expect a little more than we agreed on for all my trouble. The Cove will be out of business in three more months tops."

Cassady looked up and saw Finn and Peyton. He jumped to his feet and tried to stash the papers under a folder.

Debi turned and gasped. "What are you doing here?"

Peyton ignored her. "Have you looked over that confidential financial information for Bishop's Cove?"

"I don't know what you're talking about," Cassady blustered.

"The papers Debi just handed you."

"I didn't hand him anything," she protested. "You do have an imagination."

"When you get to page six, you'll note that in one month the Cove took in a billion dollars. Or was it three billion?" she asked Finn. "Mimi had such fun making up all those numbers."

Cassady shook his head. "This is all a misunderstanding. Debi is acting as a liaison between me and . . ."

He stopped when Finn pulled his phone out and said, "As much as I'd like to listen to your explanation, I think I'll just call the police. They'll want to hear what you have to say before they arrest both of you."

"I haven't done anything wrong," Cassady protested.

"Why don't we start with vandalism," Finn said.

"That isn't such a big deal," Debi told him. Her arms were folded just above her waist, which pushed her breasts out another inch or two.

"Thousands of dollars in damage is a felony. You're going to be spending some time in prison," Peyton said, wanting to scare Debi. It didn't seem to work.

"That's ridiculous. I haven't done anything wrong. I honestly don't know what you're going on and on about. I was merely trying to smooth relations between Bishop's Cove and Cassady Development because I personally feel that Scott Cassady is a much better builder than that redneck Miller. He dresses like a common laborer."

"You're right, Finn," Peyton said. "We should let the Port James police handle this. Give them the evidence, and let them arrest these two."

"What evidence?" Cassady asked. And on the heels of that question, he reached for his phone. "I'm calling my attorney."

"Good idea," Finn said. He looked at Debi. "We got the boots out of the Dumpster."

"What boots?" she asked innocently, fluttering her eyelids.

"Give it up," Peyton snapped.

"You can't prove those boots are mine."

"Yes, we can. We'll run your fingerprints."

"I'm not sure what you're talking about. I don't know anything about any boots," Cassady said.

"They're talking gibberish," Debi said. "Peyton's just trying to make trouble. She's always been jealous of me."

"Why don't we sit down and have a drink and talk about this," Cassady suggested, his voice smooth as molasses now. "This kind of misunderstanding can ruin a business. I merely wanted to have a look at the projections so that I could make an informed bid. That's all. And this pretty lady was helping me."

Debi was a pretty lady? Cassady needed to wear glasses, Peyton thought.

"Let's not call the police just yet, Finn. We'll let Christopher handle this," she said. Finn nodded and was opening the door for them to leave when she suddenly stopped. "Wait, I forgot something." She turned to Debi, who was glaring at her, and said, "Has anyone ever told you what a horrible person you are? And toxic? As far as I'm concerned we are no longer related. I never want to see you or hear from you again. Oh, and you're fired."

"I'm calling my father," she shouted.

The door had closed behind them, but Debi's shrill voice came through loud and clear. Peyton nearly tripped when she heard her tell Cassady, "Don't worry, hon. I can fix this. I always do."

THIRTY-TWO

Peyton fumed all the way home over Debi's treachery. "Did you hear her? She can fix this? It's what she does? Oh my God, I wanted to scream. She really believes that, doesn't she?"

Her rants didn't require Finn's participation. He tried not to smile because he knew that would really set her off, but her outrage was a little amusing. She kept sputtering, so furious now her words tripped over one another.

"I could tell you stories about some of the terrible things she did to Ivy and me when we were kids. She really is toxic. You heard me tell her so. Lucy's going to be so upset when she finds out Debi did all that damage with those boots. Now, maybe she'll stop making excuses for her. Enough already. Right? Finn, are you listening?"

"Yes."

He didn't say another word until they

were back in her condo. Peyton had calmed down by then, but when she noticed all the messages on her phone, she groaned. "I've got eight messages," she told Finn. She followed him into the kitchen and stood next to him while he searched through the refrigerator. "How many do you think are from Debi's father?"

"So soon?"

"Oh yes, she would call him right away. God only knows what story she'd conjure up. Whatever it is, she's the victim. Debi's all about getting others to do her damage control. What are you looking for?"

He was moving food around on the shelves. "I don't know . . . something." He pulled out some leftover chicken. "Maybe a sandwich."

"I'll make dinner. How about spaghetti?"

"Sounds good."

There was a container of her homemade sauce and meatballs in the freezer. She pulled it out and put it in the microwave. In the meantime, Finn made himself a huge sandwich to tide him over. He ate enough for three men and didn't have an ounce of fat.

Leaning against the counter, she said, "Let's not tell Christopher what happened with Debi until tomorrow. Let him have a nice evening with Lucy."

Finn pinned her to the counter, nudged her chin up, and kissed her. "I don't want a nice evening. I want a sex-filled evening, and I'm pretty sure that's what Christopher wants, too."

She put her arms around his neck. "You men. It's always about sex, isn't it?"

"Yeah, it is," he agreed. Then he kissed her again. He wouldn't let the kiss end as he backed her into her bedroom. His appetite for her was ravenous, and while they made love, he told her over and over again how much he loved her.

Thoroughly satisfied, she lay on top of him nuzzling his neck and tickling his ear with her tongue. He tightened his hold around her and said, "You women. It's always about sex, isn't it?"

"Oh yes," she said on a sigh.

He lightly smacked her backside. "I'm hungry."

Reluctantly, she got out of bed, slipped into a short robe, and followed him to the kitchen. Finn wore checked boxers and nothing else. How could anyone look that good all the time? She passed a mirror and cringed. Her hair was a snarly mess. She made a detour into the bathroom to clean up, and ten minutes later she looked human again.

They feasted on spaghetti and meatballs, a salad, and crusty rolls she'd warmed in the oven. It wasn't gourmet by anyone's standards, but Finn loved it. After the dishes were done, they curled up on the sofa, and each of them listened to their phone messages.

Peyton's first was from Jenson, the owner of Harlow's, the restaurant in Brentwood. She'd worked as a sous-chef for him. He had an interesting proposal. He was hoping she would send him her chocolate cookies to sell in his restaurant.

"Customers are begging for them," he explained. "They loved the taste, and they loved the sayings you put on the bottom. You could send them frozen, and we could bake them here. Name your price, darling. The demand is such, I think the customers will pay just about anything."

It was an interesting possibility, and as busy as she was going to be, she still thought it was doable. She was smiling as she went on to the second message, but the smile quickly faded. Randolph Swift's voice was soft and hesitant.

"We have a situation here I'd like to discuss with you. It has come to our atten-

497

tion that Drew Albertson plans to sue the company for wrongful termination, breach of good faith, defamation, and any number of offenses he can come up with. His campaign to win people over isn't working and he's become desperate. Evidently he wants to claim we had an oral contract. According to my sources, you are going to be named in the suit, as well. You'll need an attorney, of course, which I will be most happy to pay for. If you don't have one, I could recommend several."

He paused as though letting all this information settle before getting to the point of his call. "The company attorneys — and there are quite a few of them — would like to talk to you about the lawsuit. We may have to counter. I think it's very important that you meet with them, and so I'm asking that you come to Dalton as soon as possible. They also believe that Drew may be subject to criminal charges, and your testimony would be essential. I know it's an imposition, but I'll make it as easy for you as I can. I'll send the company jet to get you and pay all your expenses." He sounded as though he was about to hang up but happened to think of something else. "Oh, and while you're here, I hope you will talk to two young women who, like you, were harassed by Drew. They are very hesitant to come forward, and I think you could help them, Peyton. Please call me."

Peyton listened to it one more time, trying not to panic. She had never been sued before, and the thought scared her. She saved the message, knowing Finn would want to listen. He was going to give her trouble about going back to Dalton, but she had to do it, and she was certain he would be with her. It was a no-brainer that he wouldn't let her go without him. Unsure how to tell him, she decided to wait until later. Never do now what you can put off. That was her new motto.

She quickly scrolled through the rest of her messages, and she was right. Debi's father had called twice wanting to talk to her about a simple misunderstanding he wanted to correct.

After returning his calls, Finn yawned and pulled her to her feet. "Let's go to bed."

"Will you listen to something first?" she asked. She handed him her phone and waited.

He looked sleepy when the message began, but he was wide-awake a minute later. "What the hell? That bastard thinks he can sue you? You are not going to Dalton." He added, "What you're going to do is call your attorney. Mark will handle this."

"Finn —"

"Don't start with me," he said.

She didn't try to reason with him. She let him air his frustration while she went into the bathroom and brushed her teeth and put on body lotion. It took him a while to calm down, longer than it ever took her to get past an upset, but by the time she got into bed, he seemed calm enough.

She rolled into his arms. "When do you have to go back to work?"

"I'm on vacation. I've got another week. Two if I want."

She took a breath before broaching the subject, and then said, "I'm going to Dalton."

And he was off on a tirade again. This time she interrupted. "You'll go with me, won't you?"

"Hell, yes," he said, letting out a frustrated sigh.

"Thank you."

He looked at her suspiciously. "You knew that I would, didn't you?"

She didn't answer. She just kissed him on the cheek and smiled.

The following morning Finn carried the plastic bag with the boots into Christopher's office and shut the door. After Finn related what had happened and told him it was his call whether or not to inform the police, Christopher put the bag in a cabinet and locked it. Then he picked up the phone to notify Len. In the meantime Peyton was filling Mimi and Lucy in on Debi's little plot.

Lucy threw her hands up. "No more second or third or fourth chances. She's done."

"Will you call Ivy? She's definitely going to want to hear this, but I've had my fill of talking about Debi. I'm sick of the drama."

"Okay, I'll call her tonight."

"I'm taking a few days," she said then. "Need to get a couple of things done."

Lucy nodded. Her mind was on Debi, and she didn't even ask what things Peyton needed to do. "I'm going to talk to Christopher," she said, and rushed to catch him as he was leaving.

Mimi was more astute. "Where are you going that you don't want her to know about?"

In answer, Peyton handed her her cell phone. "Listen to the message Randolph Swift left for me."

Mimi nearly dropped the phone. "Sue? That jerk thinks he can sue?"

Peyton hurried to shut the door so no one

would overhear, especially Lucy. Her poor sister had enough on her mind. She didn't need to worry about a lawsuit.

"Oral contract? Who is he kidding? When are you going to leave?" Mimi asked.

"I don't know. Finn's making the airline reservations."

"He's not going to use the company jet that was offered?"

"I asked him that question, and his response was, 'Hell no.' "

"You be careful, and if you need anything, you call me, even if it's in the middle of the night. Watch your back," she added. "And, Peyton?"

She was walking away but stopped. "Yes?"

"He'll know you're coming."

THIRTY-THREE

Lars was extremely upset about the trip. He followed Finn to the car with their luggage and helped load the bags into the trunk, all the while explaining how dangerous Drew was. "He'll know about you coming there. Everyone knows everything in that town. Oh, he'll be waiting, and I don't think he'll care about consequences. He might just shoot Peyton the second he sees her. Or maybe he'll ambush her. Have you thought of that possibility?"

"Yes, I've considered that possibility and about a hundred others," Finn replied. "I'm not going to let anyone get to her."

"Make her rethink this. It's crazy to go back there. I can't help but . . . you know . . . worry."

"Yeah, I know."

Braxton joined the men. "I don't think she should be going," he said. "But Drake and I will be happy to go with you and help out."

"Aren't you setting up security for the Cove?"

"Yes, but Peyton comes first. I damn near lost her in that explosion. I want to make up for it."

"I'm not going there with a lynch mob," she said.

They turned to see her standing just a few feet behind them with her hands on her hips. Braxton opened the passenger door for her.

As she walked past Lars, she said, "Thank you for worrying about me."

She made notes on the way to the airport, questions she wanted to ask the attorneys. Finn had questions as well. The flight was late, and they didn't arrive in Minneapolis until after nine that evening. They stayed in a hotel near the airport and headed out to Dalton early the next morning. Spring had arrived in Minnesota, and the drive north was beautiful. The blizzard conditions of her last trip were gone, and in their place were soft warm breezes and green rolling hills. If the circumstances of her return were different, she would have enjoyed the road trip, but she couldn't help but worry about what awaited her in Dalton. She kept telling herself she wasn't nervous, but it was a lie. She was jittery with nerves.

Agent Hutton was sitting in his car in the visitors' parking lot waiting to walk inside with them.

"Are the boxes here?" Finn asked.

They went through the revolving door before Hutton answered. "Just like you asked. Lane's got them back in Albertson's office. What are you looking for?"

Finn shrugged. "Don't know . . . something."

Peyton waited until they were in the elevator to ask, "What boxes are you talking about?"

"Randolph had everything in Albertson's office packed up in boxes and carted off to storage," Hutton explained. "Albertson has tried to get them, but Randolph isn't inclined to accommodate. Finn wants to go through them, and Randolph told Lane it was okay to bring them out."

"What time is the meeting with the attorneys?" Finn asked.

"One o'clock."

"We've got some time then. Might as well go through the boxes now."

"Where would you like me to wait?" Peyton asked.

Finn squeezed her hand and gave her his

don't-mess-with-me look. "You stay with me."

Smiling, she replied, "And I couldn't be happier about it."

The elevator doors opened on the executive level, and Peyton felt a chill roll down her spine the second she stepped out. There wasn't a receptionist on duty, so she led the way into the office area. All the desks were there, hers and Lars's and Mimi's, but no employees. Why would there be? The old boss was gone, and the new boss hadn't started yet.

Agent Lane was leaning against the doorway and straightened when he saw them.

Peyton sat in a chair against the wall of Drew's office and watched the men sort through the contents of each desk drawer, which had been boxed separately. One at a time, the boxes were emptied onto the desk and studied. Most of them contained files or random office supplies. The last box held what had been in the middle drawer: a roll of mints, paper clips, two pens, an extra set of car keys, a Bluetooth headset, and three condoms.

"Anyone want to grab a bite?" Lane asked as he scooped up the items, dropped them in their container, and put the lid on.

Peyton couldn't get past what she had just

seen. "He kept condoms in his drawer? There goes my appetite."

"Not mine. We still have some time before your meeting with Randolph. Let's go down to the cafeteria," Hutton said. "The food is outstanding. Did you know they have two chefs here?"

"Didn't know; don't care," Lane said. "Let me get the security guard back here, and I'll meet you downstairs."

"Can't you just lock the door?" Peyton asked.

"I will," he assured her. "But I'm a paranoid kind of guy. I want a guard to stand in front of this door just in case someone wants to go in and take a couple of souvenirs."

"Maybe we should go somewhere else for lunch," she whispered to Finn.

"Why's that?"

"The first time I walked into the cafeteria, about a hundred people glared at me. I'm afraid it might happen again."

"Glared?" He laughed. "You can handle glares, sweetheart."

"I'm telling you it was weird. They stopped eating, stared at me, and, well . . . they glared. The entire cafeteria was silent. It was mortifying. If it hadn't been for Mimi, I would have bolted."

"If they throw food, I'll shoot them," Hutton promised.

"You can hide behind me," Finn suggested, knowing full well she'd get her back up. Peyton wasn't the type to hide from anyone or anything.

He was right. Peyton stiffened her spine and said, "That's not necessary. I'll walk in first, and you can follow me."

By the time she reached the entrance to the cafeteria, most of her bluster had evaporated, but she took a deep breath, braced herself, and head held high, walked in. As expected, the room grew silent, and every head turned in her direction. Out of the corner of her eye she saw a woman stand. Peyton was afraid she was going to start walking toward her, but the woman stayed where she was and, putting her hands together, began to clap. She was joined by another woman and then another, and before long, every employee in the room was clapping and cheering. What in God's name was wrong with them? She turned to Finn, hoping he had the answer, but he just winked at her.

Hutton explained. "They're clapping for you."

Tears came into her eyes, and she knew she was blushing. She still didn't understand why they were cheering for her. Only later, after the clapping and the cheering had died away and she was sitting at a table, did it all make sense. A woman she hadn't met before stopped by and patted her shoulder. "Thank you," she said. "You got rid of them for us."

"From glares to cheers," Hutton said. "You have to feel good about that. Everyone loves you now."

She spotted Bridget across the room. "Not everyone," she said. "Especially not Bridget."

"Bridget?"

"The woman who wouldn't stop crying when we tried to talk to her," Finn explained.

"Oh yeah, the one who wanted to get into Albertson's office."

"I'm telling you, there's something in one of those boxes she wanted to get for Albertson."

"Because of the signal he gave her?" Peyton asked.

"If it was a signal," Finn said. He knew he was second-guessing himself. "Ronan always says to go with your gut, and my gut is telling me there's something here Albertson doesn't want us to see."

"It would be nice if Bridget would tell us," Hutton said, and then laughed. "But that's not going to happen."

"She adores Drew," Peyton said. "She's kind of obsessive about him. Mimi told me she moved into his neighborhood to be close to him, and she even bought the same car. When he gets a new one, so does she."

Peyton could eat only half of her turkey and cranberry sandwich. Hutton ate the other half. He grabbed it before Finn could get to it.

Finn was distracted. "The shelves . . . we even removed the photos from the frames . . . nothing there. What am I missing?"

"We have time," Peyton said. "Let's go back up and start over again."

Lane joined them with a tray. "I ran into Bridget in the hall, and since she wasn't crying a river, I decided to talk to her. She wouldn't answer any questions, though, unless 'I don't know' qualifies as a response. She's a very unpleasant woman."

"Peyton and I are going back up to Albertson's office. We'll meet you there."

They rode up in the elevator alone. Finn pulled her into his arms and kissed her. "I love you," he whispered.

She got a mischievous look in her eyes. "Have you ever . . . you know . . . in an elevator?"

"There are cameras," he said. "So, no, I haven't. Why? Are you up for it?" he asked, laughing. "You're blushing."

The lighthearted moment ended when the elevator doors opened. Finn was all business from then on. She once again took a chair and patiently watched him go through all the boxes. He was quick and methodical. Until he picked up the car keys. He held them in his hand and looked at Peyton. A slow grin appeared. "Didn't you tell me Bridget buys the exact same car? When he trades in, so does she?"

"Yes, that's what Mimi told me."

"I might have found what she wanted. How much do you want to bet these are her keys, not his."

She stood. "Why wouldn't she say so? Security would have given her the keys if they belonged to her. Why be so secretive?"

"Yeah, why? Let's go find out."

The security guard was playing a game on his phone. Finn locked the door behind him and told the guard not to let anyone in. Hutton and Lane were just getting off the elevator, and after Finn told them his theory, they followed him to the garage.

"Should we start on the top level?" Finn asked.

"No, she parks inside," Peyton remembered. "You could just ask her where her car is."

"No, I'd rather not."

"We're looking for a brand-new Ford Expedition. There are a lot of SUVs here," Lane said.

Finn walked along, and every few seconds he'd press the alarm button on the remote. He was almost to the end of a long row when an SUV's lights started flashing. He hit the remote again to stop the noise.

"That's one big-ass SUV," Lane said. "And it's not Albertson's."

"Now, why would Drew have Bridget's car keys in his desk?" Hutton drawled.

The windows were tinted. Finn looked inside but couldn't see anything.

"Think he drives it sometimes?" Lane asked.

"Maybe," Finn mused. "Or maybe he just needs to get in it sometimes to get something. What would be in that car that he needs to have access to?"

"You're thinking rifles?" Hutton asked.

Finn looked through the back window again. "This has a big cargo area. Great place to stash something out of sight. Might even be something in there right now."

The more he thought about it, the more plausible his theory became. "Albertson and

Parsons need to have the guns when they want them, but since they're in danger of being searched again, they can't carry them. So, they get someone to transport the guns for them."

Hutton was beginning to follow the logic. "I'll bet when they came back from their last fishing trip . . . you know, the one where they stopped in Florida to blow up Peyton's car —"

Finn finished. "On their way back home, Bridget met them somewhere, and they put the rifles back in her car. Yeah, that works. No wonder they didn't mind getting searched."

"Walk me through this," Lane said. "Peyton leaves Dalton, and Parsons goes after her. He uses a handgun to try to stop her. He supposedly doesn't own a gun because he's an ex-con, but there's one missing from Randolph Swift's collection, as well as two hunting rifles."

"That's right," Finn said.

"Okay," Lane continued. "So then when Albertson thinks Peyton is going to sue him, he or Parsons takes another shot at her. This time with a hunting rifle, and the bullet goes through the roof of her car."

"Yes," Finn agreed. "Then he just happened to stop by and threaten her."

"Are you thinking Bridget has been keeping those weapons in her car for them all this time?" Hutton asked.

"Probably not," Finn said. "But she could keep them in her house, and when Albertson wants them, she puts them in her car. No one would think to search her."

"This is all a guess," Hutton warned.

"True," Finn said. "But these keys were in Albertson's drawer. I think it might be worth our while to get Bridget down here to talk to us."

"Finn, she won't talk to you," Peyton said.

"Yes, she will." His voice was hard. "I want to search her car and her house and her garage."

Lane was on his cell phone. "I'm getting the warrant."

"In the meantime, Hutton, go get Bridget and bring her here. She'll give us permission to look inside."

"How do you know that?" Peyton asked.

"I can be very persuasive."

She moved closer to him and said, "I don't understand why Drew and Parsons wouldn't just hide the guns somewhere. Why use Bridget?"

"If I had to guess, I'd say easy access," he began. "And the worry that they were being watched. They didn't want to get caught with the guns in their car. Let Bridget take the fall."

"Even if you find the guns, they'll say they aren't theirs. They belong to Randolph."

"It won't matter," he assured her.

She loved his confidence and couldn't wait to see how he would get Bridget to agree to anything. She worshipped Drew. She'd made him her idol. But idols had a way of crumbling.

"What do you want me to do about the meeting with the attorneys?" she asked.

"Push it back. They can either wait or reschedule for tomorrow."

They heard Bridget before they saw her. She was shouting at Hutton, threatening to call the police because he was harassing her.

Peyton was anxious to watch Finn with Bridget. She expected he would use finesse to get her to cooperate, but he used another technique instead. He scared the hell out of her. And it was impressive.

Bridget was full of indignation and talking a mile a minute to cover her nervousness. Hutton had hold of her arm and let go when they reached Finn. She spotted Peyton, and her eyes narrowed. "You —"

"Don't say a word," Finn snapped. "Just listen. I want your permission to search your car."

"No."

"Okay, then we'll wait for the warrant, and you're going to stand here until we get it."

Hands fisted at her sides, she said, "You don't scare me."

"Yeah? I'm going to."

"What?"

"I know you've been helping your buddies, Albertson and Parsons. If I find those guns in your car or your house or anywhere near you, do you know how many years you'll get? You're transporting weapons —"

"I'm not. No, I'm not."

"We will find them, and when we do, you'll take the fall." His voice had gotten meaner, and he was getting closer to her. "I'm going to search your car. Do you want me to do it now or wait until the warrant arrives? I don't really care how long it takes. I've got all day and all night and you're not going anywhere."

"I don't have my keys with me," she stammered.

"How about this set?" he asked and held up the keys from Albertson's desk.

Bridget's face turned chalky white. "Those aren't my keys."

Finn pushed the alarm button, and Bridget flinched. He pushed it again to stop it. "You wanted in his office to get these keys."

"I left them there."

"If you don't start cooperating, I promise you won't be going home tonight. Do you hear me? The longer I have to wait, the less likely I'm going to be lenient. In fact, maybe I should just cart you off to a holding cell right now."

"Wait, please," Bridget begged. "I want to cooperate. You can search my car, but please understand I was just helping out some friends."

Finn unlocked the SUV and opened the cargo space, and there they were, both rifles with scopes. He didn't touch either one. "Where's the handgun?"

Bridget tried to back away from his anger. "I don't know —"

"Yes, you do. Where is it?" He didn't raise his voice, but the venom in his tone frightened her.

"Some friends have it. I promised to keep quiet," she said.

"Let me tell you what your so-called friends have done to you. You're the one with stolen weapons in your vehicle, weapons that were used in an attempted murder. It's all on you, Bridget. You're the one going down for this. Do you think your friends will step up? Maybe they'll come see you in prison, though I doubt it."

"I was only . . ."

Finn took a step back. "Agent Hutton, read her her rights and cuff her."

As impossible as it was for Peyton to accept, she was actually beginning to feel sorry for Bridget. The woman had started crying and was trying to understand why this was happening to her. "I didn't think I had done anything wrong," she wailed.

"Yes, you knew what you were doing, and you knew it was wrong. Cut the b-s. The only way you might get out of a thirty-year sentence," he said, coming up with a number of years to freak her out even more, "is to give up Albertson and Parsons. You tell us everything you know, and it will go a lot easier for you."

"It was all Rick Parsons's and Eileen's idea. Drew is innocent," she blurted.

"Stop lying for him."

"He would never hurt anyone."

"Not even you?"

"Of course not. He loves me."

"Will he love you when you're in prison?" Finn asked. "No, he'll get on with his life, and you'll be an old lady when you get out."

"But he told me he loves me. He wants to marry me just as soon as he owns the company." Her crying turned into sobs. "I can't go to prison. Please . . . ," she begged. "I can't."

"Then tell us the truth."

"You would talk to the judge?" she asked with desperation in her voice.

"Sure," he said.

"Could I get immunity?"

He shrugged. "I don't know."

Peyton was surprised Bridget hadn't asked for an attorney. She thought she would after she'd been given her rights, but she was too rattled by Finn's threats to think straight.

Bridget sniffled. "I can help you."

Before Finn could ask her if she would be willing to testify against her friends, she said, "I'm supposed to meet them tonight at nine."

"Meet who?"

"Drew and Parsons. They're going to take the rifles and hide them."

"What made them decide to do that now?" Hutton asked.

"The keys in the desk. Drew thought you would figure out they weren't his, and then you'd wonder why he had keys to my car. He was being cautious."

"Where are you meeting them?" Finn asked.

"At Benton State Park, the second shelter.

The park's closed at night, but Drew knows a back way to get in."

"You knew they were going after Peyton." It wasn't a question.

Bridget glanced at Peyton before answering. "Yes, I heard them talking, but I was afraid to let them know I heard. Drew has a temper," she added.

"You could have gone to the police," he said. "The fact that you didn't makes it worse for you."

"I'll testify against them, but I want a deal," she stammered. "And I want a lawyer, a good one."

Did she think he should get her one?

Finn had gotten enough information from her to know he would be able to nail the bastards. Now he wanted to have a talk with Cosgrove, and once he was finished with him, he was certain he'd testify against his friends, too. That would be another nail in the coffin.

Lane announced they were getting their warrant to search Bridget's house. He was extremely happy to see the rifles, and after carefully removing them, he put them in the trunk of his car to transport to the lab. Finn and Hutton had already taken copious photos with their phones.

"You're going to meet Parsons and Albertson tonight, aren't you?" Peyton asked.

Finn nodded. "We'll be there waiting for them." He wrapped his arm around her shoulders. "Having fun?" he asked. "I am."

"What are we going to do now?"

"We'll keep Bridget out of sight, take her down to Minneapolis. In a small town like this, news travels fast, and we don't want Albertson tipped off. Hutton will keep his eye on Cosgrove. After we have Albertson and Parsons, we'll pick him up. I'll get him to talk."

"You're awfully sure of yourself, Agent MacBain."

"Damn right."

"You're going to be busy the rest of the day. What would you like me to do? I want to help."

"I want you to go to Minneapolis with Lane and wait there. As soon as this is over, you can come back to Dalton. Okay?"

"No, I want —"

"That actually wasn't a question, sweetheart. I'm telling you what I want you to do. I have to know you're safe."

"I could be safe here, out of sight."

"No," he said.

She didn't want him thinking about anything but the job at hand. "Okay. Just promise me you'll be careful."

THIRTY-FOUR

Finn and Hutton drove to the park early in the afternoon to find the best places to hide and wait for Albertson. Hopefully Parsons would be with him. Bridget had told them she was to pull up to shelter number two at nine o'clock and wait for Drew, no matter how long it took. She admitted that, if he told her to wait until morning, she would.

The first shelter they drove past was placed in the middle of a patch of ground big enough to hold a baseball field. The area was flat and barren without a tree or shrub in sight. Shelter number two was more secluded. One side was open to the road, and there was a grassy space for campers, but on the other three sides of the shelter were thick trees and shrubs. There were plenty of spots where they could hunker down and wait, but also where Albertson and Parsons could hide.

After they had walked the area and had

returned to their car, Hutton said, "We could park over behind that bluff," pointing to an incline several hundred yards away. "They won't see the car unless they do some recon. What do you think, Finn? Will they be cautious or cocky? I think they'll drive right up to Bridget's vehicle. I don't think they'll sneak around. They're pretty sure of themselves."

Finn agreed. "We'll be prepared for anything. Albertson won't like being cornered."

"Parsons knows he'll go back to prison. I'm betting he'll put up a fight unless we can pin him down before he has time to react."

"This is a tight community and word spreads fast. If Albertson knows Peyton is here, he may want those weapons to go after her again."

"Do you think he knows the meeting with the attorneys was canceled?"

"Not canceled, rescheduled. Peyton told Erik she had an attorney coming and he can't get here until tomorrow. A last-minute flight cancellation."

"I've got two more agents driving up. They'll come directly here. One of them can drive Bridget's SUV in."

"We can use the help."

"Want to walk the grounds again?"

"Yeah, let's do that."

The rest of the day was spent coordinating the operation, and Finn and Hutton were back in the park by seven. They met the two new agents and went over the plan with them.

It was cold and damp. Finn hunkered down on the south side of the shelter, well hidden from the road by the thick underbrush. He didn't move or make a sound while he waited. Time dragged. He thought about Peyton and how she had changed his life. She had such a beautiful heart. And her body was also damned perfect, he thought, smiling. He loved her sense of humor and her determination to do the right thing. He loved everything about her, even when she was aggravating him and making him want to tear his hair out. Yeah, he loved her then, too. Man, he had it bad.

Logistics needed to be figured out. He was going to be doing a lot of traveling for the Bureau with Ronan. Dallas was off the table for his home base, and he would probably be assigned to the D.C. office for a while, but his home could be with Peyton in Bishop's Cove, at least for a year, hopefully longer. It was an easy in and out at the airport. Thinking about her kept him warm and relaxed.

The park had been closed since sundown, but Finn had found the back road without a gate. It was close to nine when Bridget's SUV drove in. Because of the tinted windows and the late hour the driver wasn't visible, but he knew the agent was slumped down in the seat with his gun at the ready. He parked the SUV and kept the motor and the lights on. All of the agents had earpieces so they could talk to one another. Hutton was the first to spot the car careening into the park.

"Showtime," he whispered.

Finn flexed his fingers and got ready. The SUV rounded the corner and came into view. Same make, same color as Bridget's. There wasn't room to pull up next to Bridget's car because of the way the agent had deliberately parked it. They could either cut over to the side, which would put them closer to Hutton, or park behind.

Albertson was at the wheel. He left the motor running, honked once, and then got out. The agent in Bridget's car figured that was a signal and pushed the button to open the tailgate.

Christmas came early, Finn thought, because not only was Parsons with him but Eileen had also ridden along. All of them got out of the vehicle, and Eileen yelled to the person she thought was Bridget as she walked toward the driver's side.

"Is it true, Bridget? Is that bitch Peyton Lockhart going to sue Drew and me? I heard that this morning, and I couldn't believe it." She stopped at the tailgate.

Drew opened the cargo lid. "Where the hell are my rifles? Did you move . . ."

Parsons saw Hutton coming and ran. Instantly realizing what was happening, he reached for the gun in the waistband of his jeans, but Hutton tackled him before he could shoot.

The Albertsons were immediately surrounded. Eileen was screaming profanities while she was being handcuffed, and Drew stood perfectly still. He was enraged, but he didn't try to run. The second Finn walked up to him to cuff him, he attacked. Finn couldn't have been happier because he finally got to punch the son of a bitch. It felt good, too. He wanted to hit him again and then go after Parsons, but instead he read them their rights.

"Went off without a wrinkle," Hutton said.

"That gun isn't mine," Parsons blustered when he saw Hutton pick it up off the ground. "I'm innocent."

Incredulous, Finn asked, "It just happened to drop into your pants?"

Hutton shook his head as he pushed Parsons toward the car.

The blow from Finn's fist left Drew bent over and gasping for air. "You can't get away with this. I know my rights," he panted. "I haven't done anything wrong."

"Oh yeah?" Finn said. "Tell that to the women you molested. Better yet, tell it to the new buddies you're gonna make in prison. They'll get a kick out of it while they're showing you what it feels like to be helpless and trapped."

Eileen was crying now. "This is all because of her, that Peyton woman. She ruined everything. It's all her fault. You should have killed her, Drew."

Yes, Peyton had ruined their lives.

Yet another reason to be proud of her, Finn thought.

The following morning Peyton and Finn walked into Randolph Swift's office. He stood when they entered and rushed around his desk to shake their hands. Erik was with him.

"I'm so glad to finally meet you," Randolph told Peyton. "It's been quite a week. We heard all about the arrests. I don't think we need worry about Drew filing a lawsuit anytime soon."

The door opened, and two young women came in. They were smiling but hesitant. Randolph motioned them forward. "These are two new employees," he began. "Actually, they worked here a short time under Drew's supervision and left, but now they're back."

Peyton knew what that meant.

"It was a terrible time for them," he continued. "I'm going to try to make it up to them if that's possible, and they're going to help write new guidelines for the company. April will be working in HR, replacing an employee who had been taking orders from my daughter, and Maria will be a coordinator in production."

"This is going to be a good company again," Erik promised. "I'll begin working here in June."

"Graduate school?" Finn asked.

"One more paper and I'm finished."

Peyton was humbled and a bit embarrassed when the two women thanked her for all she had done for them.

"I didn't really do all that much," she protested.

"Oh, but you did," April said. "You exposed Drew Albertson for what he was. If you hadn't done that, we wouldn't be here now."

Erik stepped forward. "If you'll excuse us, I'd like to show these two young ladies their offices."

After they were gone, Randolph asked Finn and Peyton to take a seat.

"If you don't mind, I'd like to talk to you about my daughter and her husband." A look of profound sadness came into his eyes as he continued. "I can't begin to tell you how sorry I am for the misery they've caused. And I know I have to accept some of the blame." He saw that Peyton was about to protest, and he raised his hand to stop her. "No, no, it's true. If I weren't so distracted after the death of my dear Miriam, I could have seen what was going on. I knew that Eileen could be selfish, but I had no idea her ambition or her obsession with Drew Albertson would take her to such extremes." He turned to Finn. "What will become of them?"

"I'm certain Drew is going to be doing some prison time, and so is Parsons. The lab has found their fingerprints on the weapons and it's just a matter of time before the ballistics report shows at least one of them was used in an attempted murder. We're already getting cooperation from

Bridget Dawson and Don Cosgrove. Their testimony will help get a conviction."

"Cosgrove?" Randolph asked. "What did he have to do with this?"

"He was Drew's and Parsons's alibi. When the three of them were supposed to be on a fishing trip, he went alone and left a trail to prove that they were with him when, in fact, they had secretly made their way to Florida."

"And what will happen to my daughter?" he asked with a hint of worry.

"I can't say," Finn answered. "She might serve time for her part in all of it, or the court might go easy on her if she agrees to cooperate."

"I'm afraid Eileen has never been a very agreeable person," he admitted. "Maybe this will make her change."

The image of Eileen in the park, screaming that Drew should have killed Peyton, flashed through Finn's mind. He knew there was little chance of her becoming the person Randolph wanted her to be, but he couldn't bring himself to dash a father's hopes.

"It could happen," he said.

THIRTY-FIVE

Peyton and Finn were happy to be back in Bishop's Cove. They arrived late at night, fell into bed exhausted, and yet found enough energy to make love.

The next day the Cove was bustling. It seemed wherever Peyton looked there were men working. The walkways had already been jackhammered, and the concrete trucks were expected to start pouring that afternoon. On their way to the business office, she and Finn met an architect and two engineers who were busy with plans for the new swimming complex. When Len wanted something done, he wanted it done right away. Christopher had told Peyton he expected to get the permits and be ready to begin digging in no time at all. Curious, Finn went with them to see exactly where the pool would be.

Lucy was in the conference room surrounded by fabric samples. She had all the furniture ordered for the bungalows and was busy selecting odds and ends. She hoped to have at least three newly wired units ready for guests in two weeks if everything arrived on time. In the history of Lucy ordering anything, nothing ever arrived on time, but she was determined to stay optimistic.

After Peyton filled her in on what had happened in Dalton, Lucy was so stunned she dropped into a chair, unaware that she was landing on a pile of fabric books.

"It's really all over then?" she asked.

"Yes," Peyton assured her.

The next order of business was telling Lars and Mimi. She called Lars into Mimi's office so that both could hear the news. They had a hundred questions, and all of them had to be answered before they were satisfied she hadn't inadvertently left anything out.

Mimi was reeling from the news that her ex-husband was involved. "Stupid men do stupid things," she remarked. "If he knew they were coming here to hurt you, he should go to prison for a long time. I'm so glad to be rid of him."

Lars stood. "I'd better get back to the restaurant. I'm already on Chef Geller's last nerve. He told me if I mention sardines to him one more time, he's going to hit me with a pot." He laughed as he added, "He'll do it, too." He surprised Peyton by kissing her on the cheek. "I love it here."

"I should see if Christopher wants to go over my numbers for the week," Mimi said.

Peyton walked out with her. She said something funny, and Mimi was laughing as she rounded the corner and bumped into Len. He grabbed her by the shoulders to steady her, then stepped back.

"Hello there," he said in a rich southern drawl.

Peyton quickly made the introductions. With his most charming smile, he said, "How do you do?"

One hand on her hip, Mimi looked up at him and responded, "I do just fine."

Len blocked the doorway as he stood there grinning at Mimi. She kept waiting for him to get out of her way, but he didn't seem inclined to move, so she edged around him. As Len turned to watch her walk away, Peyton tapped his arm to get his attention.

"I'm happy to see you," she began. "We didn't expect you for another two weeks."

"My schedule changed." He straightened and said, "And I talked to Christopher about Debi. Come on, Peyton. Let's go chat with Lucy."

As he crossed the office, he whispered, "Is Mimi married?"

"No, she's available," Peyton told him.

"She's a little spitfire."

She agreed. "Yes, she is."

He let Peyton go in the conference room, then he pulled the door closed behind him. Lucy pushed aside some catalogs so they could sit.

"Now then, about Debi," he began.

Lucy and Peyton shared a look. Another chance? Peyton wondered. Was Len going to ask them to take her back again? She honestly didn't think she had the stamina to go another round.

"I spoke with Christopher and I had a long, long talk with Scott Cassady. He admitted he'd made a deal with Debi to pay her a percent if she helped him get Bishop's Cove. But he insisted she came to him with the idea. He also insisted he wasn't aware of any vandalism. I'm not going to pursue legal action, but he's on notice, and I don't think you'll be having any more trouble from him."

"What are you going to do about Debi?" Lucy asked. "If you want her to come back here, I guess we could . . ." She stopped talking when she saw the daggers in Peyton's eyes.

"No, I talked to her father. Brian has used every excuse in the book for his daughter's behavior." He smiled then. "I told him he should let Debi move back home. I said that Bishop's Cove wasn't a good fit for her, and she should stay with him until I find the right project." After a slightly wicked chuckle, he said, "There isn't going to be another project. I just wanted to get my brother off my back. Wonder how he'll do with Debi living with him."

"Did you tell him about the damage she's done here?" Lucy asked.

"No, and I'm not going to. I don't want you girls mentioning it, either."

No more Debi. Peyton was giddy with joy.

"I have one more announcement," he said. "It's about the deal I made with you for this resort. I've changed my mind."

Peyton's heart sank. She looked at Lucy and could tell she was feeling the same. They'd been at the resort only three months, but it was obvious they weren't going to be able to make a twenty percent profit within the year. There had been too many setbacks that delayed the opening. They might as well face the facts and admit their failure.

Len continued. "I've decided the resort is yours."

"I'm really sorry, Uncle Len," Peyton said. "I know you . . . Wait. What did you say?"

"I said the resort is yours at the end of the year, and you don't have to show the twenty percent profit. There have been too many things that have been out of your control. Plus, I'd really like to add the swimming center, and that will take some time. I've looked around at what you've accomplished so far, and I have to say, despite all the obstacles, you've done an amazing job. I think I'll be leaving Bishop's Cove in very capable hands." He looked at Lucy when he added, "Especially if Christopher is around to help you manage things." Clasping his hands together to finalize his offer, he said, "So, what do you say? Are you up for it?"

Peyton and Lucy answered at the same time with an enthusiastic "Yes!"

Peyton waited until evening to tell Finn the news. He was getting ready to leave and would be back next weekend so they could go shopping for an engagement ring.

They called his parents to make their announcement, and then they phoned her parents and spoke to Peyton's father. He was thrilled.

"I'll let Peyton tell her mother," he said and shouted to his wife.

She came on the line a minute later. Her greeting was predictable. "Have you met anyone?"

Wow, Peyton thought. Once she was married, she'd never have to hear that question again. "I'm getting married —"

"Stop teasing me."

"Mom, it's true. Finn MacBain asked me to marry him, and I said yes."

"Finn? Our Finn?"

"Yes, our Finn."

"And you're getting married?"

Peyton put her hand over the phone. "I think she's in shock."

Her mother sounded as though the weight of the world had just been lifted from her shoulders. "Oh, thank God. Finally."

"Mom . . ."

"It *finally* happened." There was that word again.

"Mother . . ."

"I'm just beside myself with happiness. We have to plan a wedding."

"If Finn agrees, I'd like to be married here in Bishop's Cove."

"Finally. I just can't believe it."

"Mom, do you talk this way to Lucy and Ivy?"

"I'm just reeling."

"I'll talk to you soon. Love you."

She disconnected the call, turned to Finn, and said, "She's happy."

And that was the understatement of the year.

Peyton sat on the bed, watching Finn pack. "What do you think about a small wedding in a church in Port James and the reception here at the Cove? We could be married next year."

He shook his head, dropped the shirt he was folding, and sat down next to her. "I'm not waiting a year. Yeah, we can get married here, but not next year. How about next month?"

She scooted onto his lap and put her arms around him. "Six months."

"No, next month."

"This summer then." She kissed the side of his neck to distract him.

He finally agreed. It would be a summer wedding.

"Remember how you were so opposed to marriage?"

He hugged her and said, "Yeah, I remember. But marriage to you . . . I can't wait to make it legal. You're going to be mine then."

Going to be? Didn't he know? She had always been his.

EPILOGUE

ONE YEAR LATER

The grand opening of the Bishop's Cove Aquatic Center turned into one hell of a party. The hotel and every bungalow were filled to capacity with family and friends who had booked months before. Olympic hopefuls were also there, as well as several top coaches. They all knew who Finn was.

By a unanimous vote it was decided that Uncle Len would officially open the center. The chrome-and-white dome hid the beautiful pool. A huge crowd gathered to watch as Len walked forward. Most of the men and women were in swimming attire and were anxiously waiting to jump into the cool water. Len wasn't much on speeches. After welcoming everyone, he pushed a button and the dome came to life. The sides spread wide, then disappeared into thin trenches that closed seamlessly.

There was a good deal of cheering and

laughing. Finn stood watching the festivities.

The terrace adjacent to the pool was adorned with colorful bouquets on tall pedestals, and two lavish buffet tables sat on opposite ends. Beyond, scattered on the manicured lawn that the gardeners had nurtured, round tables with chairs, all covered in white linen, waited for the guests to sit. Most of them were in the pool now.

The newlyweds, Christopher and Lucy, couldn't seem to let go of each other. Finn understood. He and Peyton had been married nine months, and he still wanted to throw his arms around her whenever she was near.

At the buffet table Lars inspected his delectable creations — all with an aquatic theme — and beamed with pride.

Peyton was on the other side of the pool talking to a couple of Beck's Navy SEAL friends.

Finn's brothers, Tristan and Beck, saw him frowning and came to stand beside him. "What's the problem?" Beck asked in a low voice.

Finn nodded toward Peyton and then toward the two men a few feet away from her. "Those guys are ogling my wife."

"Hey, you've got a hot wife. You gotta

expect guys will notice," Beck said.

"Yeah? They ought to notice she's wearing a wedding ring and leave her the hell alone."

Tristan laughed. "I don't think you have to worry. Peyton's pretty stuck on you, though God only knows why." He scanned the crowd. "Has anyone seen my wife?"

"Over by the fountain," Beck said right before he spotted Ivy and took off.

Finn heard a burst of laughter behind him and turned. Len and Mimi were also having fun. Mimi had just said something funny, and Len looked like a besotted schoolboy.

Was it something in the water down here? Finn wondered. He could see the advertisement now: Come to Bishop's Cove and fall in love. He sure as certain had. No, that wasn't exactly true. It was when he was standing in front of the church at Tristan's wedding. She'd walked up to him and looked into his eyes, and he was a goner.

Peyton walked around the pool to join him. She put her arms around his neck and kissed him. "Those Navy SEALs are wild," she remarked.

"They know how to have fun."

A young man named Elliott came toward him, and one of the coaches Finn had met earlier was with him. Then Beck and two SEALs joined the group. Something was going on because Beck had that devil grin on his face.

"How about racing with us?" Beck asked. "Just two laps."

"Who's us?"

"Some of the team is here," Elliott said. "We go to nationals soon."

Finn shook his head. "I don't think so."

Elliott glanced at Beck, who nodded. Then he turned back to Finn. "Don't you have what it takes now that you're an old man?"

"Are you going to let him call you old?" Beck wanted to know.

"You probably haven't been in a pool since you won those medals, have you?" Elliott asked.

Finn looked at Peyton. She smiled and shrugged.

"Okay," he said. "Two laps."

When the swimmers saw the men lining up, they all rushed to get out of the pool and watch the race.

Tristan was designated the starter. He yelled, "Go!" and the men soared out like arrows and sliced into the water. People began to cheer their favorites.

Peyton saw Finn's dive but could barely make him out as the men splashed their way across the pool. The crowd closed in on her and she had to step around a couple standing in front of her in time to see the swimmers making their flip turns. Suddenly a huge roar erupted from the people watching. She turned and saw Finn gliding home to the finish, his competition still halfway across the pool. Barely winded, he raised up out of the water, looked for Peyton in the crowd, and smiled.

She laughed and thought, Still a hotshot.

ABOUT THE AUTHOR

Julie Garwood is among the most critically acclaimed — and popular — romance authors around, with thirty-six million copies of her books in print. The author of numerous bestsellers, she lives near Kansas City, Missouri.